THE KING'S CHAMPION

THE KING'S CHAMPION

BOOK 3 OF THE BOAR KING'S HONOR TRILOGY

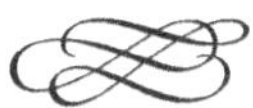

NANCY NORTHCOTT

For my friends across the Pond,
Jules Clark, Gary Hellen, Judy Horwell, Jules Langley, Will Morgan,
Rob Rundle, Anna and Keith Sugden, and Hass Yusuf,
and in memory of Alan Rowley.

This book and the others in the trilogy are better stories because of their contributions.

CHAPTER 1

The Dunkirk Perimeter, France
May 31, 1940

Weary, dirty men in stained, sometimes bloody, brown battledress streamed north along the Dunkirk road. Stone walls abutting the road on both sides kept the mass from spreading out. Lorries, as the British called their trucks, held spots here and there in the ragged procession. No one seemed to notice the sporadic gunfire coming from the Coldstream Guards' line in the woods to the east. The Guards would deal with that, holding off the Germans so these men could escape to the Dunkirk beaches. From there, the Royal Navy would evacuate them to England.

If they made it.

Reporter Kate Shaw also ignored the gunfire as she snapped photos of the bedraggled mass. She was used to it after weeks in the field. Despite being outgunned and outnumbered by the German Wehrmacht, the British Expeditionary Force and the French Army had fought valiantly. But they hadn't been able to stem the Nazi tide.

BOOM!BOOM!B-BOOM!

The sound jolted Kate. She snapped the shutter on reflex before turning toward the stone wall. She could scramble over it, as the soldiers were doing—

"Incoming!"

The shout carried over the thunder of artillery and the staccato cacophony of firing rifles. A man in dirty brown battledress and a battered helmet leaped at her.

He's diving the wrong way.

They collided. She locked her arms around him and wrenched left, out of the inbound shell's path, with all her might. They slammed into the stone wall bordering the road, teetered atop it for a second that seemed eternal, and fell behind it, the soldier on top. The impact knocked her breath out.

Another deafening *BOOM!* rocked the world and showered dirt over Kate, her companion, and his fellow soldiers behind the wall. By some miracle, she still had her camera—and hadn't landed on it. She hunched over it and her pack as the soldier hunched over her. If she died here, maybe someone would take the pack to her bosses in London. Her photos of the British Expeditionary Force's heroic retreat had to make it back.

The shelling and the thundering and the shaking went on. And on. Trying to shatter the guards' line so the Wehrmacht infantry could advance. The infantry wouldn't move, though, until the shelling stopped.

At last, the shelling ended.

Kate's ears rang. The guy on top of her sat up. Staring across the road, he scowled. His lips moved, but she couldn't hear him. He must've known that, for he held up one hand palm out and motioned for her to stay down.

"Thank you," she said, the sound oddly muted in her head.

With a nod, he vaulted the wall, as his comrades did. He scooped up a rifle, likely his, from the roadway. Around it lay groaning, wounded men and bits of men. Kate's stomach did a slow roll, and she blinked back tears at the heart-wrenching carnage.

She took a quick look into her pack. Her other Zeiss Ikon camera and the two spare lenses looked okay, but if they weren't, she couldn't do anything about it now.

At least she could document the sacrifices made and the pain endured by these soldiers trying to stop the Nazi advance. She took several quick photos before closing the camera and shoving it into her pack.

As she did so, gunfire to the east resumed, not desultory now but heavy and steady.

Lew Barnes, her boss back in London, would have a fit if he knew she wasn't taking more photos of the men in the road. The choice between photos and lives, however, was no choice in her book.

Scrambling over the wall, she hurried to the nearest of the men who lay writhing in the road. Blood flowed from a gaping hole in his shoulder, and the outside of his upper arm was in shreds.

Her stomach revolted. Setting her jaw and breathing hard, she dug in her pack and came out with her spare shirt. Hearing loss mercifully muted his cries of pain and those of the others around her.

For a moment, she saw him sitting on a tractor, calling to a young, brunette woman coming across the plowed field with a bag in her hand. Mom had brought Dad his lunch like that so many times. Would this man live to go back to that?

Kate swallowed hard. Her overactive imagination was tormenting her. For all she knew, he was a banker before he joined up.

The end of the bombardment meant the German infantry would advance. She would have to hope the British guardsmen could hold their line.

Using her teeth, she tore through the shirt's sleeve near the shoulder seam. That let her rip it off of the garment. It made a passable tourniquet above the wound. He still had the standard-issue bandage pack in its designated pocket on his trousers. She pulled it out, ripped open the stitching on the brown cloth packet, and pulled out one of the two dressings in it. Taking care to not touch the inside of the folded gauze pad or let the attached bandaging strip fall in the dirt, she unfolded the dressing. The worst damage was to the front of his shoulder, so she applied the dressing there. His back arched, but he gritted his teeth as though stifling a yell. Kate used the gauze strip to bind it in place, securing it with the included safety pin.

A man knelt beside her. "Good job. Now let's see to that shoulder." The red cross on his shallow, rimmed helmet offered a ray of hope. He nudged her aside and pulled a new dressing and a roll of gauze out of his pack. Despite the dirt smearing his face—as it did for all of them, including her—he had an air of competence. Kate steadied his patient and helped the corpsman dress the other wound.

Rifle fire and the distinctive *brr-rrr-rrr* of a Bren lightweight machine gun erupted from her right, toward the front line.

"Right, then, mate. Steady." The corpsman patted the wounded man's leg and moved on.

Stuffing the remnants of her shirt into her pack, Kate followed him. "What can I do?"

"Who are you?" He dropped to his knees by another wounded man and dug in his pack.

"Photographer. Kate Shaw, Consolidated News Union. I'm covering—"

"A Yank, eh? Long as you're not with the Jerrys, the rest doesn't matter." He shoved two rectangular dressing packets into her hand and jerked his head at a man a few feet away. Tiny, bleeding cuts webbed his face, and he bled from a hole in his side. "See that lad over there? Hold one of these dressings against that wound in his side until I can get there. You know not to touch the inside of the folded bandage?"

When she nodded, he said, "Right. Then clean his face. Any water in your canteen?"

Rising, Kate shook it. "Yes."

The man turned back to his patient. Kate darted to the other man. Again, her imagination punched her in the heart with a vision of him bouncing an infant girl on his knee. She shoved the image out of her mind. Best to focus on the reality of his wound.

The gauze pad she held against his side soaked rapidly. "Come on," she muttered. "Stop bleeding." She put as much hope as she could into the words, and her bloody, sticky fingers tingled from holding the dressing in place. Blood seeped through. She dropped the saturated dressing in the road and opened the second one. He also had a bandage in his front pocket if she needed it. Cleaning his face would have to wait.

The medic arrived. Gently, he nudged her aside and lifted the dressing. His brows rose. "Huh. Not as bad as it looked. That's something, anyway."

What had appeared to be a gaping wound was now smaller than her palm.

Weird. That was seriously weird. And unsettling. Like the way she'd just...*known*...the soldier who'd tried to save her had misjudged the shell's path. Not the first time something like that had happened, but—

"Wake up, luv." The medic slapped another dressing into her hand. "Start on the lad over there."

"Uh, sure." Kate hurried to the man he indicated. There were so many, most of them horribly wounded.

Kate avoided looking directly at the severed lower leg she stepped over as she hurried to the young man. He clutched at his stomach and sobbed in pain.

"I'm here to help," she told him, dropping to her knees beside him.

"Y-you? Wh-what can you do?"

Altogether too little, but that wasn't a reassuring reply. Instead, she told him, "Whatever the medic says."

She moved his hand aside and swallowed hard at the big, jagged abdominal wound. She'd never actually seen a human's intestines before.

Trying not to think about that, she ripped open the field dressing and applied it, along with same *stop bleeding* mantra. It probably didn't help, but at least she felt as though she were doing something. Mom had a lot to say about the power of prayer. Gran had said the same applied to good wishes and hope.

An image of him flashed across her sight. He wore a suit and sat at a desk, writing something with pen and paper. The loss of that stabbed into her.

Kate blinked fast and banished the scene. She had no idea what he'd done as a civilian. That was just her imagination taking over, as it had too often lately.

At least there were few refugees on this country lane. The casualties would've been worse if it were as crowded as the main roads had been. People streamed away in all directions from the fighting to the south and east.

On the northern horizon, a distant pillar of smoke marked the location of Dunkirk. One of the officers had said earlier today that the oil storage tanks there were burning. The Royal Navy was sending ships there for as many of the BEF and French forces as could reach the beaches before the Nazis broke through the shrinking perimeter. Once they did, anyone still here was trapped. Awareness of that loomed large in everyone's minds, but if she let herself dwell on the prospect, dread would swell into bone-deep terror.

The medic joined her and checked the wound. "Good job for a photog." He ripped open a roll of bandages. "You ever a nurse?"

"Farm girl."

"Kate Shaw?" a man said at her shoulder. She looked up into the dirty, sweat-streaked face of a young soldier. The grimy hair under his bowl-like, rimmed helmet might have been brown.

"Corporal Thirsk," he called over the din of gunfire. "North Yorkshire Fusiliers. We're your ride to the beach."

The words didn't make sense. Kate blinked at him.

Another young man, his lanky build and narrow, grave face familiar, ran up to her. Corporal Hay of the Coldstream Guards, his rifle in hand.

"You're for the beach now," he announced.

She glanced down at the man she'd tended. "I could help—"

"The army's responsible for you," Hay interrupted. "Captain wants you gone while that's still possible."

His face was implacable, and the last thing she wanted to do was distract the soldiers. She nodded at the medic. "Good luck."

"Same to you." He answered without looking up.

"This way." Thirsk set off at a jog.

Trotting beside him with Hay, Kate poured water on her sticky hands. Fishing the shirt remnants from her pack would get blood all over the outside, so she wiped her hands on her fatigues.

"You're a civilian, remember," Hay shouted over the roar of battle. "Would've sent you out sooner if we could've."

The BEF had tried. Originally with the Sherwood Foresters, she'd been sent toward HQ on the back of a dispatch rider's motorcycle a week ago, only to find the way barred by heavy fighting. Rather than risk her life in the midst of the shooting, the man had diverted to leave her with the Coldstream Guards. She didn't like to think about what that delay of his message could've cost, but arguing with him had achieved nothing.

At least being unable to leave had given her a chance to craft some in-depth stories. She'd been sent to France to write about preparations and training, important stories but nothing that would stand out. Everyone had rested securely in their misplaced faith that they would have plenty of warning of a German invasion and thus time to evacuate her. Unfortunately, the Germans had circumvented France's famed Maginot Line defenses by attacking from Belgium and steamrolling across the country. Kate had found herself sitting in the middle of one of the most important stories of the century.

Documenting it, she'd taken gritty photos and done heart-wrenching interviews with men who might never make it home. If she let herself think about them, about the men she'd helped bandage over these past three weeks, she would sit down in the road and bawl.

Her stories wouldn't matter, though, if she couldn't make it back to England. The vaunted Coldstream Guards had stood fast against dreadful odds. So had the Sherwood Foresters. Part of the territorial army, they'd shipped out for France last year with their training not even complete.

They didn't have the skill or precision of the regular army units, but no one could fault their courage. The BEF and their French allies deserved to have the world know how valiantly they'd struggled to hold a contracting perimeter for everyone else to retreat within. She would do her best to blast that word out.

On the road south of their position stood a line of big, brown-canvas-topped trucks surrounded by resolute-looking infantry. The men made space for her to follow Thirsk.

At the front of the lead truck, Hay stopped. "Miss Shaw." When she turned to him, he continued, "I must return to the front. And you must, truly must return to England. Make sure everyone knows how brave our men have been."

"I will." The words felt inadequate.

Hay nodded and jogged away. Thirsk led Kate down the line of trucks. He stopped at the rear of the next to last. The dirty, weary soldiers seated on the benches down the sides and in the floor regarded her with some curiosity. Each of them sported a bandage on his head or a limb.

"This lady's Miss Shaw, a reporter. Behave yourselves, fellows, or she'll tell the world on you."

"Might be worth it," one man replied with a teasing grin and a wink.

His mates hooted and mocked his chances.

Thirsk said, "That's all talk. They're good blokes and won't bother you, miss. They do, you tell the driver. Up you go, now."

He offered a steadying hand, but Kate had climbed in and out of enough trucks to manage alone, even with her pack. One foot on the bumper, one on the floorboard, and she was in the truck, hunched over under the covering tarp.

The men on the left-hand side squeezed down to make a space. Kate thanked them and sat, her pack on her lap.

Outside, someone shouted a command. The tramp of feet came through the tarp, and the soldiers visible beyond the truck started marching.

With a grinding of gears, the truck lurched into motion.

The man across from Kate caught her eye. "So tell us," he said, raising his voice over the noise around them, "where are you from, Miss Shaw?"

"Missouri. I'm with Consolidated News Union."

"A Yank, eh?" He raised his eyebrows. "What made a Yank crazy enough to cross the ocean and run toward a war?"

"It's a long story."

"Looks like we've time," the man returned.

"Yes, tell us," said an older man with a seamed face and one arm in a sling. "What's the attraction of this charming spot?"

A flippant reply hovered on the tip of her tongue. Kate swallowed it. These men had put their lives on the line every day for three weeks. They deserved an honest answer.

"The truth," she said slowly. "I want to tell the truth, to make everyone back home see the truth about the threat Nazi Germany poses. Before it's too late."

Coming out of her mouth, the words sounded grandiose. Self-important.

The men around her, though, had first-hand knowledge of that threat. They'd lost friends to it, and none of them looked doubtful.

"Pretty big ocean between the Yanks and Hitler," someone down the bench observed.

"There is." Kate shrugged. "If he conquers everyone else, though, he can take his time seeing to us. I don't doubt he eventually will try—unless we stop him first."

The men made general noises of approval.

Kate fished in her pack and pulled out her notebook and pen. "Who wants to tell me his story—where you come from, why you joined up, and what the last weeks have been?"

"I'll have a go," the man across from her offered.

Kate dutifully started writing, thankful as always for the speed of shorthand. During the weeks she'd spent in England awaiting accreditation from the army, she'd grown accustomed to the various British accents, so she didn't have to struggle to catch what he said.

"I joined up with my mate Bill Kelso, rest his soul," the man told her. "He died holding the line at the Yser."

"I'm so sorry." All she could say, though the words felt stunningly inadequate. Especially when the image of two young boys running in a field together flashed across her sight.

Everyone here knew they might not make it to Dunkirk beach. Even if they did, they might not make it back to England. The Germans would be fools to let the evacuation proceed unhindered, and whatever else they might be, they were not fools.

Everyone probably felt the same pervasive dread she did. Stewing about the risks wouldn't help, though. All the retreating units could do was keep moving forward.

And hope.

Meanwhile, in Dover, England...

The jangle of the telephone jolted Sebastian awake. The front legs of his chair *banged* down on the floor. Before lifting the receiver, he took a deep breath to settle his heartbeat and his voice.

"Mainwaring," he said.

"Sgt. Wilton from the coach depot, Major. We had a message from Essex Coach Service. One of their coaches is stalled six miles out of Dover. They can't locate their mechanic."

Well, of course they couldn't. Having a mechanic on hand would break the pattern of at least one thing being arsed up every harrowing night of this desperate evacuation.

"Ring the motor pool. Have them drive a mechanic out to fix the coach. If we don't have anyone who can do it, ring me back."

The sergeant signed off. Sebastian swallowed a curse. Operation Dynamo, removing the BEF from the beaches of France and bringing them back here to England, was only the first step. Once they arrived, the army needed to move each boatload of men off the Dover waterfront quickly so more could disembark.

Sebastian ran a hand over his face. He hadn't meant to fall asleep, but he was so bloody tired. Everyone here at Dover was. Bringing the army back a few boatloads at a time was a huge operation even without the Luftwaffe bombing and strafing and U-boats hunting the convoys. Now the Royal Navy had commandeered every seaworthy civilian craft, large or small, they could find, and crewed them with civilians and naval ratings. Other people with boats had volunteered, simply falling into the groups departing from Channel ports without bothering about naval clearance. That increased the navy's carrying capacity each night but also brought its own headaches.

No one slept except in brief, rare snatches. There was no time. They could sleep when they had as many men as possible back in England.

Sebastian shoved out of his chair, donned the waist-length, brown battledress jacket, and grabbed his helmet, otherwise known as a tin hat. Perhaps some fresh air would help him revive. He snagged his cane from the corner beside the desk and walked out into the narrow, underground corridor.

The tunnels in Dover's chalk cliffs had been created for the Napoleonic Wars but hadn't seen much use in the Great War. *The "War to End All Bloody Damned Wars." Right. Good one, that.* They were coming in handy now, though, with plans to expand them.

He stopped at the office next to his and tapped on the door frame. "I'm going out for a breath of air, Moss. Back in a few." He explained about the coach problem. "If Sgt. Wilton rings, see what you can do with the motor pool. I'll be near the doors if you need me."

"Yes, sir. I just took a call from Dover Marine Station. Trains are coming in on schedule."

"Excellent. Keep me updated."

Sebastian continued on his way. The sergeant should've spoken to Cpl. Moss first but was a believer in going to the person in charge if possible. Since he was extremely efficient, Sebastian put up with it, as had most of Wilton's prior superior officers.

The spiral stairs to the surface level made his knee protest, but he ignored it. Fractured during a little foray into Czechoslovakia after the Nazi invasion, it hadn't healed properly. Still, he'd managed to talk his way into a desk job instead of being mustered out of the army with a war obviously on the way. Detached duty with the War Office was better than a seat on the sidelines.

He pushed open the heavy outer door and walked into the cool evening air. After so many hours underground, the breeze on his face lifted his spirits. He strolled to the edge of the cliff so he could see the harbor far below. A steady stream of ships cruised through the opening in the breakwater to enter the English Channel, as usual. With them tonight, however, went a flotilla of small boats, everything from yachts and Thames excursion boats to tugboats to freight scows to fishing boats.

A vision flashed over his sight. A beach crowded with men in combat gear. Thousands of them sat in masses or snaking lines on the sand. Waves lapped the shore, the water unusually calm. Overhead, Messerschmitts made strafing runs. Men jerked or spasmed and fell to the sand. Some of his fellow soldiers fired back at the attackers with their rifles. The planes were too high, out of range, but he couldn't fault the men for trying. Helplessness and anger must be the order of the day.

The familiar bitterness welled in his throat. He should've been in

France. Had trained for years to do just that sort of thing. For nothing, now.

"Sebastian."

The familiar voice yanked him out of the vision.

At his side stood the ghost of his many-times-great grandfather, Richard Mainwaring, his predecessor as Earl of Hawkstowe from early in the reign of Charles II until late in that of Queen Anne. Though he'd lived into his seventies, he appeared as a man in his early thirties. His dark hair fell to his shoulders, and he wore the knee breeches, doublet, and hose popular in his youth, with lace at his collar and cuffs. His black hair, chiseled features, and blue eyes, all traits of Mainwaring men, might've come from Sebastian's mirror.

No one else would be able to see Richard, but conversation would be awkward if anyone was near. A quick glance reassured Sebastian. Richard looked tired, though, which was unusual. A trick of the light, perhaps? What could weary a ghost?

Sebastian smiled. "Hello, Richard. Why so solemn?"

"There's a wizard headed for the beach at Dunkirk. When she returns to England, you must speak with her."

"I assume there are a few in a force the size of the BEF, so—hang on. 'Her'? Is she a nurse?"

"She's a journalist, approved by whoever manages such things. She's been with several units over the last weeks."

Someone should've sent her back to England straight away when the Germans rolled into France, but it was too late to fix that. "Why are you telling me this?"

"She's a very distant cousin of yours, Kate Shaw. Powerful in her Gifts but untrained."

Sebastian gestured toward the harbor. "I've a bit much on my slate for training a novice, distant cousin or not. I can see if someone at the Merlin Club might help." The covert group of Gifted operated in Britain's defense without being bound by edicts of the British wizards' governing body, the Conclave.

"That won't do. She doesn't even know she's Gifted. Her parents died in an automobile crash when she was a baby. In America. The family who adopted her gave her a good life, but they are practical people and taught her not to believe in magic."

An image flashed into his mind, a woman standing on a beach amid legions of Tommies. The hair tucked under her tin hat might be brown or dark blond when it was clean. Dirt splotches on her face didn't conceal the strong, attractive features or her full mouth. She appeared to be a few years younger than his thirty-three. The determined set to her chin and the grim resolve in her eyes drew him.

He banished the image with a shake of his head.

"Again," Sebastian said, struggling for patience, "I haven't the time for this."

Richard regarded him steadily. "She's a seer."

"You must be mistaken." There had never been more than one in a generation and not always even one. In this generation, Sebastian was it.

"I know how rare that Gift is," Richard told him. "Over the centuries, however, our line has spread far and wide. Each of you carries Miranda's blood and the potential for her Gift."

A potential that rarely manifested. Richard's wife, Miranda, had brought the seer Gift into the family line, but it often skipped generations. To have two at the same time, with war coming, the strategic advantage—

"We've often discussed how ill-prepared Britain is for this war," Richard reminded him. "Kate would be a great help to you, especially if you cannot break the German codes."

"If she cooperates. If she knows what she's about. If she even accepts that she has such a Gift." Yet he didn't need to be a seer to sense the possibilities her coming offered.

"You must convince her. You're a kinsman, however distant, and a seer. You must gain her trust, persuade her to recognize her Gifts, and teach her to use them."

Richard made it all sound so simple.

Sebastian grimaced. "If she's a journalist, her film and her story must go through the censors. This likely means I'll need to take her film and possibly her camera, if there's film in it when she disembarks here. I doubt she will see me as a potential friend."

"Someone else could do that."

"Everyone else will be busy with arriving troops. We weren't expecting any journalists." Besides, whoever had authorized a woman reporter to enter the war zone was a bloody fool. Bad enough that nurses were there.

"You're a persuasive man, grandson." Richard gestured to Sebastian's cane. "As shown by your continued service in the army."

Sebastian stared out at the Channel. The last of the ships had passed out of the harbor. Their wakes made faint trails of white on the water.

Each night, thousands of men came home, but hundreds died on the beaches and in the Channel. The losses pushed him to the edge of despair. On top of that, they'd had to abandon almost all their equipment.

No one knew how long the embattled, shrinking perimeter around Dunkirk could hold. If the Germans broke through, the thousands still on the beach would have no choice but surrender. If Britain had no army, if she couldn't equip her soldiers before the Germans came calling, she would be forced, as Norway and Holland and Belgium had been, to seek terms.

Many of the Gifted stood ready to help, but agreements dating back centuries barred them from direct use of magic for national gain. While the Merlin Club would secretly wiggle around that, most others would not.

The availability of another seer might make a great difference. If she could be persuaded and trained in time.

From where he sat now, that looked like a daunting project.

Sebastian took a deep breath and blew it out. "I'll see what I can do. If she makes it back."

~

Refugees fleeing south clogged the road. Men and women with weary, defeated faces dragged carts or carried bundles. Some bore children on their backs, the little ones' eyes wide and full of dread. A lucky few actually had horse-drawn carts, likely farm wagons, with belongings and family jammed into them. The soldiers and their trucks moved through the mass at a crawl.

At last, as the day waned, the truck ground to a halt, apparently on the outskirts of a town. The ruined buildings lining the road stood between two and four stories tall. Some were narrow, while others had as many as six windows across. None of them had any glass remaining, and chimneys stood like grim sentinels where upper floors and roofs had been blasted away.

"Everybody out," someone called from the front of the truck.

Kate scrambled out with the men around her. They melded into the ranks of the infantry.

"Road's blocked ahead," the stocky man climbing down from the cab announced. "It's faster to go on foot. The Jerrys have destroyed the port.

We're to head for the beaches on its east side." He left the engine running and removed the radiator cap.

Kate had seen soldiers do that before. The engine would eventually seize, making it useless to the Nazis.

She fell in with the men around her. No one had more than a pack and his rifle. Deserted buildings lined the road, their doors and windows gaping, empty holes revealing shadowy piles of rubble within. Here and there, the setting sun hit a west-facing window and illuminated the wreckage inside.

There was still enough light for photos. Kate dug out her camera. Stepping out of the mass, she clambered onto a chunk of broken masonry that looked like part of a brick wall.

Ahead, a giant pillar of smoke filled the horizon. An acrid whiff of something that might've been burning oil rode the breeze.

She opened her camera, focused on the men marching toward her, and clicked the shutter. Then she faced forward to capture the men marching away. The photos might be a little underexposed, but maybe she could fix them in the darkroom.

Closing the camera took only a moment. There might be other opportunities, though, so she held on to it as she joined the men marching past.

When they eyed her curiously, she smiled.

"Kate Shaw. Consolidated News Union." She offered her hand to the man on her right. He shook it carefully, with hardly any pressure.

"What's your unit, and how has it been for you fellows?" she asked. Assuming they were all North Yorkshire Fusiliers might be a mistake. As soldiers raced for the beach, units became jumbled. Or so she'd heard.

Before the men could answer, someone up front shouted, "Take cover!"

Everyone looked up. A trio of planes headed their way, swooping low.

"Messerschmitts!" a man farther forward yelled.

The fighters could strafe, and everyone on the road was exposed. They all dashed for the nearest buildings. Huddled in a wrecked kitchen with two of the men, Kate did what she'd done so many times since the fighting started. Clenching her fists, she closed her eyes and thought, *Don't see us. Don't see us. Don't see us.*

She'd been the Cobbettown, Missouri, hide-and-seek champion, and she'd done this ritual every time. Intention and will, Gran had said, could never hurt. Though everyone inside a structure was probably safe from strafing as long as they avoided the window openings.

The planes made a couple of passes. At last, the engine noise died away.

"They're gone. Move it, you tossers," a man in the street called.

No one needed any more encouragement. Dodging blast craters, rubble, and wrecked autos, the soldiers double-timed it through the ruined streets. Kate set her jaw against fatigue and kept up.

At last, they came to the end of the pavement. Dunes a short distance away flanked the access to the beach. Each dune had a machine gun emplacement atop it covering the approach. The unit rushed past them, and the men in front pulled up short. Only because there was room to the sides did those behind them avoid a collision.

"Sweet Christ," the man beside Kate breathed.

She couldn't blame him—or the ones who had stopped so abruptly.

The beach was covered with men. Thousands of them. Standing, sitting, or lying on the sand or on stretchers, they waited for the promised ships.

Somehow, she hadn't expected there to be so many left. But she did know Britain needed every one of them. Hitler would surely aim there next.

Kate's throat tightened. She opened the camera and snapped several photos of the crowded beach. It would take a miracle to transport all these men away. But Britain would need every one of them in the coming days.

If she went on an early boat, she would take a slot one of them should have.

Thirsk stepped out of the throng streaming toward the beach. "Come with me, Miss Shaw."

Following him, she gazed over the sea of men on the sand. They should go before her. But if the Nazis broke through before she boarded a ship, she and everyone else remaining would become prisoners.

The United States was neutral. Of course, Norway, Holland, and Belgium had been neutral too. Now they were occupied. Yet Germany wanted the U.S. to stay out of the war. At least, the cynical side of her thought, until the Nazis had conquered everyone else. So the Germans had no reason to hurt her and every reason to send her safely home.

Kate swallowed hard. She had to do what was right. "Corporal Thirsk, would you do me a favor?"

He looked baffled, probably wondering how he could do anything for anyone on this crowded beach.

Kate offered him her pack. "If you would see this gets to Lew Banks and Consolidated News Union in London, at number seventeen Manchester Square, suite B, I would appreciate it. The story of this retreat needs to reach CNU, to be published."

"Why can't you take it?"

"You men should go first. I'll take the last boat. Do a few interviews, maybe—"

"Bollocks to that. My orders are to see you make it back." As though to emphasize his resolve, he caught her arm.

It was just her luck to pick someone chivalrous. If she could shake him, though, someone else might listen. In the distance, coming nearer, the silhouettes of ships and smaller boats darkened the sunset-dappled water.

Hurry, she thought. Foolish, as they were undoubtedly coming as fast as they could.

Thirsk led her past a man sprawled on the beach. Stepping around him, Kate realized he was dead. So was the one a few feet away. And there was an arm. A riddled torso. Another body, with the left side of his body gone and the sand beneath him blood-soaked.

They were just lying there? But...of course. Because there was nowhere to put them.

Her stomach revolted. She clenched her teeth.

I will not be sick. I will not be sick.

She'd thought she had learned to bear such sights. Yet the men dying here, with rescue on the way, somehow made seeing their mangled bodies worse.

Seeking somewhere safe to look, she turned her eyes toward the sea. The water looked unusually calm, moving in slight, gentle swells instead of waves. A man stood chest-deep in the water, as though waiting. Beyond him...a floating corpse. Bits of corpses.

Dear God.

Kate swallowed hard and gritted her teeth. This beach might be the road to salvation, but it looked like a slice of hell.

Thirsk marched her up to a man barking orders about staying in line. He wore the same battledress as everyone else but had a Royal Navy patch sewn to the top of his sleeve.

"Join a queue," the man barked, leveling his sidearm.

Kate froze.

Thirsk, unperturbed said, "Happy to, once this lady has seen whoever's in command."

The man jerked his head to his right. "Royal Navy. Foot o' the mole."

"Really," Kate said, "there's no need—"

A great, dread-laden shout from the waiting men drowned the words. As the queues scattered along the water's edge, the drone of aircraft engines and the scream of Stuka divebombers' sirens drowned their shouts. Messerschmitts strafed the waiting men.

"Bloody sodding blighters." Thirsk pulled Kate back from the water. "Get down," he ordered.

She was already diving for the sand, useless though that was with no shelter. Around them, men lay down, pulling corpses over them as though for shields. Others fired back at the planes with their rifles though the attackers were well out of range.

Don't see us, don't see us, don't see us. Hard to believe they wouldn't though. Even in the fading light, everyone's brown battledress must stand out against the sand.

"Stay down," Thirsk shouted, dropping down on top of her.

Wishing her cameras were under her, she complied. But she couldn't help peeking under his arm at the beach to the east.

Far down the sand, something hit the ground. An instant later, it disappeared in a spray of sand. Then came a thundering, concussive roar. Men flew in all directions, and then something hurled Kate. Everything went dark.

When the world came back, Kate's hearing was mostly gone again. Her body felt as though something had slammed into it. Thirsk sat beside her, shaking his head. He retrieved his tin hat and pushed to his feet. Glancing at the sky, he shouted, "Let's go, before the tossers come back."

She barely heard him. Dazed, she let him tug her to her feet and guide her down the beach.

"What happened?" she yelled.

"Concussion bomb. We were lucky to be on the edge of the blast."

They reached a short stairway leading up to a concrete walkway. Beyond the concrete, a long wooden walkway on stilts extended into the harbor. Was this the mole? Soldiers jammed every inch of it, and more lined up at its base on land.

By the steps stood a Royal Navy officer in battledress who was well over six feet tall. "Here now, wait your turn," he barked, pointing at Kate and Thirsk.

"Happy to," Thirsk replied, "but I need your help with this lady."

"It's nothing," Kate shouted, her voice sounding muffled in her ears. "We can wait."

The tall officer held up a hand, palm out, with a warning expression on his face. "Corporal, report."

A cheer went up from the men on the beach and the long walkway. The officer glanced over his shoulder and nodded. Boats approached the shore, a flotilla of small craft. These weren't military. Had civilians risked the Luftwaffe and the U-boats to come for their army?

Kate's throat closed with admiration for their bravery. Farther out, in deeper water, larger boats and ships loomed, growing larger. The light was going, a flash useless at this range, but she would try for a photo as soon as this business about her leaving was settled.

Thirsk explained Kate's situation and what he called her *barmy notion* of waiting for the last boat.

When he finished, the officer frowned at Kate. "Show me your papers."

She fished them out. He glanced over them and handed them back.

"I know I'm a low priority," she said, "and you're going to need all these men. I only want my story to make it to London. I can wait, but the story…it might make a difference back home."

His frown deepened to a scowl. "If the Nazis break through while any of us are still here, it'll be devil take the hindmost. Imagine their joy if the Royal Navy leaves an American woman, a civilian, on this beach. Imagine what hay they might make of that."

She could imagine it. Could actually, for a moment, see the sickening headlines. Her attempt to be selfless might backfire horribly.

The naval officer's expression softened. "You're leaving as soon as we can put you on a ship, miss, and that's all there is to it."

His tone left no room for argument. Besides, he was right.

Reluctantly, Kate nodded. "Yes, sir."

"You see her onto a ship," he ordered Thirsk. Pointing, he added, "Tell that rating."

As Thirsk nodded, the officer turned to a waiting soldier.

Kate dug her camera out and took several photos. The standing, cheering men, the little boats in the twilight, and the larger ships anchoring in deeper water.

Everyone pushed to their feet as naval ratings shouting orders hustled down the beach. Corporal Thirsk stayed close to Kate. When the man the officer had indicated went by them, Thirsk stopped him to explain.

"That one." He pointed to a tugboat with weathered red and blue paint on her hull and wheelhouse. Worn, black lettering on her side proclaimed her to be the *Thames Lady*.

"They'll ferry you out to one of the ships and come back for another load." The young sailor pointed at Kate. "You, miss, stay in the wheelhouse. It'll be better for you on a small craft than jammed in with this lot."

The tired-looking sailor hurried to the nearest line of waiting men.

Thirsk turned to Kate. "Right, then. Let's go. You need help with your pack, sing out."

They joined the mass of Tommies slogging through the incoming tide to the tugboat. As the water grew deeper, Kate hoisted her pack above her head. She'd already discarded everything not necessary for her job except her precious stock of soap and shampoo, one pair of spare underwear, and her dirty, but at least not bloodstained, spare trousers.

The Messerschmitts roared out of the sky, strafing beach and water. Kate hunched her shoulders but kept going. Bombs made a thundering roar on the beach.

By the time they reached the boat, the water was nearly up to her shoulders.

Men swarmed toward the tug, jumping to reach the top of the side. A stocky sailor on the deck in battledress shouted, "Here now, you lot! Form a queue! Two at a time, make a bloody queue, or you'll swamp her!"

The men complied, and Thirsk tugged Kate forward. When their turn came, he raised his voice over the sounds of strafing and explosions and told the naval rating, "If you'll take this lady's pack, I'll boost her."

"No pack. Drop it. We need the space for men."

Of course they did. But...three weeks' work. Her precious, essential, expensive cameras.

Looking past them, he shouted, "You men drop those guns. No room for 'em." He frowned down at Kate. "Come on, luv, let's go."

Soldiers moved past her and Thirsk. Kate turned her most pleading look on the sailor. "I'm a journalist. This is all my work since the invasion." He opened his mouth. Quickly, she added, "I can't afford to replace my cameras. But if there's no space, no locker or something where the pack can be out of the way—"

Thirsk put in, "She has orders to ride in the wheelhouse."

The sailor's face softened. "You can ask the captain, but if he can't stow it, it goes over the side." To Thirsk, he added, "You hear me?"

The corporal nodded. "I'll see to it."

"You won't have to," Kate told him, feeling sick. "If it comes to that, I'll do it."

"Come on, then," the sailor said. He leaned over, grabbed Kate's pack, and dropped it on the deck beside him. The other line of men continued to scramble aboard.

Saying, "Boost her," the sailor reached down. He and Kate gripped each other's wrists.

Crouching, Thirsk stepped behind Kate and set his hands at her hips. "Jump," he said, "Now!"

Kate jumped, Thirsk lifted, and the seaman hauled her up to the side of the boat. He steadied her while she scrambled aboard.

As she thanked the man, Thirsk clambered over the side. He ushered her to the wheelhouse. The sturdy, grizzled man at the wheel, introducing himself as Captain Darrow, labored to hold his boat steady in the surf.

"We'd like this lady, Miss Shaw, to ride back to Dover in here with you," Thirsk explained. "Her work for the last three weeks is in this pack. Can you put it somewhere it won't take up space a man could fill?

"Put it there." The captain pointed to the floor behind a round dial on a pole with a stick at the top. "Too small for anyone to stand there."

"Thank you," Kate said, her lips trembling. The rush of relief that ran through her was premature. They were still under attack.

The captain nodded to the corner by his control console. "Sit there and stay out of the way."

"Right," Kate answered. Her wet clothes dripped onto the deck and clung to her, chilling her, but there was no help for that.

"You're set, then." Thirsk touched the brim of his tin hat. "Good luck to you."

"Same to you, and thank you for everything."

"My pleasure." Stepping out of the wheelhouse, he took station by the door.

Kate pulled her pad and fountain pen out of her pack and sat in the corner. Several men stepped into the wheelhouse but gave the captain, and thus Kate, plenty of space.

"Do me a favor," the captain said over his shoulder. "Keep an eye on the boarding. When she looks full, let me know."

Kate stood to peer out the wheelhouse's back window. Men scrambled aboard on both sides of the craft now. The deck space quickly filled with soldiers. There were a couple of dogs in the mix too.

"Captain, it looks jammed to me."

He half turned and scanned the scene through the windows. Sticking his head out the open door, he bellowed, "That's a load. Stand clear, and we'll be back."

Officers on the deck made the waiting men move away. Despite some understandable grumbling, they complied readily enough. The captain swung his boat into a slow, wide turn.

Kate leaned back in her corner and took notes. Once they headed to England, maybe the captain would give her an interview. He would be a terrific story.

"How long will the trip back take?" she asked.

Darrow shrugged. "At top speed, if we can maintain it, five or six hours. P'raps a bit more. Them as are on the longer routes'll have it slower."

They made several trips between the beach and the destroyers out in deeper water. Tommies swarmed up rope netting hung over the destroyers' sides to board and passed the dogs up one at a time. The tug always emptied even faster than she filled. With other small boats ferrying men to the each of large ones, they reached capacity quickly.

"Why is the water so calm?" Kate asked between loads. "Is it always like this?"

"Not so far as I've heard. According to the navy blokes, it's never so calm. Whatever the reason, though, it's all to the good. Makes wading out to the boats easier."

After the tugboat's fourth run to the beach, Captain Darrow flashed his running lights. "That's it," he announced. "With this lot, we dash for home."

Kate glanced at her watch. Two-ten a.m. There was more than an hour until daylight, and thousands of men still darkened the beach. "I thought we would stay until dawn."

"The Jerrys would love that." Darrow snorted.

"I don't understand."

"They have guns at Calais. Once it's light enough for them to see us, they can shell us. Besides, we must be through the tricky part of the route back, the minefield and sandbanks, before the sodding Luftwaffe have enough light to improve their targeting."

As she digested that, he added, "And never mind the bloody U-boats cruising for targets."

A bigger ship would've made a bigger target. But it also would've had a better chance to withstand a hit.

"How do they find us in the dark?"

"The engines stir up something that glows, and it makes a bright trail in the wake. Points directly at the vessel causing it."

Kate swallowed hard. "So we need to hope they don't see us."

"Nothing more we can do about it." He shrugged.

The *Thames Lady* passed the mole with its mass of waiting men and entered the English Channel. Darrow cut off his lights.

Kate stood to look ahead. A hulking shadow, probably a larger ship also running without lights, blocked the stars. Sure enough, it left a bright, glowing trail in its wake. She closed her eyes and clenched her fists.

Don't see us. Don't see us. Don't see us.

She needed a distraction. Without one, repeating that mantra all the way back to England would ratchet up her tensions. Fishing in her pack, she sat down again. "I'm a journalist, Captain Darrow. Consolidated News Union. Do you mind answering some questions?"

He shrugged. "Why not?"

"Great. Thanks." She balanced her pad on her knee and uncapped her fountain pen. "How did you come to join this expedition?"

Another shrug. "Royal Navy said they was looking for anything seaworthy. Wanted to take the *Lady* and put a navy crew aboard. I told 'em they could give me a sailor or two, but nobody drives this boat but me."

"So here you are. Is this your first trip, and how does it compare to what you expected?"

"My second. I didn't expect no flood of men, that's for certain."

Kate jotted down his answer in shorthand.

Before she could ask her next question, a faint whine sounded overhead, growing louder, rapidly building into the distinctive shriek of a diving Stuka's Jericho siren.

Kate froze.

Darrow muttered something that might've been *sodding blighter.* To Kate, he said, "Hang on, miss. Let's see if I can evade this bloody Jerry."

Kate clenched her fingers on her pen and pad. *Don't see us, don't see us, don't see us.*

CHAPTER 2

The sun was fully up now, but there was still no sign of the mysterious Kate Shaw. Standing on a box for a better view, Sebastian scanned the crowds of men streaming off the piers. A few groups formed up and marched in good order, but most trudged along the pavement. Some would go to bases in Kent by coach. Others would march to Dover Marine Station on the harbor's west side. The first trains and coaches had already departed, with trains rolling roughly every twenty minutes.

All the arrivals looked weary and bedraggled, and no wonder. Stressful as coordinating the evacuation was, they had been through much worse. Some wore uniforms that were literally shredded due to sand flung out by bombardment. He'd Seen it, and his soul ached for the men who'd been through it.

There wasn't time to give these men a meal and still keep the trains moving. But they did receive tea and sandwiches from the Shorncliffe barracks as they boarded, along with fruit, pork pies, or buns provided by the Women's Voluntary Service. On top of that, people all down the line had rallied to feed the men when trains stopped briefly in their towns.

Stray dogs ran in and out among the clumps of men, so many that he had to wonder whether they'd brought back half the strays in France.

According to Grandmother Miranda's ghost, Kate had left the beach at Dunkirk on a tugboat called the *Thames Lady*. Miranda had then departed to keep watch over Kate. Since she hadn't come to tell him there was a problem, Kate probably would arrive safely.

As though his thought had summoned his many-times-great grand-mother, she appeared at his side. Like her husband, she preferred the attire of the period she'd lived, a full-skirted gown with an off-shoulder neckline and full, elbow-length sleeves. Today's blue gown matched the one in the family portrait hanging in his London house. Lace trimmed the neckline and the edges of the sleeves. She wore her dark brown hair caught up in a knot at the crown of her head with ringlets framing her face.

"Kate is on the boat just now crossing the breakwater," she said, pointing at a weathered blue and red tugboat. "That's the *Thames Lady*."

Sebastian nodded. With soldiers shuffling past and stocky, alert Sergeant Lane at his side, he couldn't answer her. As with Richard, no one else could see or hear her, and he had no desire for his comrades in arms to think he was muttering to himself.

"I've thought about Kate's refusal to believe in magic," Miranda said. "When she was a child, she liked the idea. Fairy tales and such appealed to her. But she refused to believe Richard and I were anything but figments of her dreams. Her parents are practical people. They emphatically discouraged any idea that magic might be real. So we've never appeared to her when she was awake, as we habitually do with you and others of our grandchildren. Since she knows and trusts us, perhaps nudging her toward accepting that we are not dream figments but ghosts might be a good place to start with her."

She paused. When Sebastian nodded acknowledgement, Miranda added, "We'll try to win you an opening. I'll let you know how she responds. Until then, perhaps you should leave this to Richard and me."

Gladly. But he could only nod.

Miranda gave him an insubstantial pat on his shoulder and vanished.

At Admiralty Pier, near the train station, a flat-bottomed Dutch barge called a schuyt finished disembarking its solders and cast off. The tugboat Miranda had indicated cruised toward the pier, the decks jammed with tired, dirty Tommies. Watching the boats coming in from the Channel, Sebastian shook his head. The harbormaster was doing a brilliant job of managing the traffic.

Some of the men's clothes were in tatters. They would be directed to a makeshift clothing depot in the station.

Ambulances waited to transport the seriously wounded to local hospitals. Unfortunately, some of the men on the decks had died in transit. A shore party waited for the living to disembark before heading down the ramps to board the vessels and remove the dead. The port and the town had makeshift morgues waiting for them.

The *Thames Lady* finally pulled alongside the pier and tied up. Weary-looking men in dirty brown battledress spilled off her and headed for the end of the pier, where staff officers directed them to transport. Only bringing them back was the Royal Navy's job. Once they stepped ashore, they were the army's responsibility.

A woman in battledress, her hair mostly hidden under her helmet, stepped onto the now-empty deck around the tugboat's wheelhouse. When she raised her head, he recognized Kate Shaw from his brief vision the night before. His heart gave a surprising little kick.

In one hand, she held a camera. In the other, she carried a small, square box. She consulted it, squinted at the sun, and set the box down by her feet. Frowning, she fiddled with the camera, likely the settings. Then she braced her feet and started taking pictures of the men piling off the ships and the small boats.

That could be a problem. The War Office would decide how many of those photos ever saw the light of day. The government would present the return of these men in the most positive possible light, but nothing could change the fact they were fleeing from a military debacle. Published photos underlining the debacle part of the event would damage morale.

Still, he had to give her credit. She'd had as unnerving a time on the beach as all the men, but she was still doing her job. If she looked a little grim and dirty, she had a great deal of company. Dark, red-brown streaks marked the upper legs of her trousers. Was that blood?

She collapsed her camera, stowed it and the light meter in her pack, and turned away. Passing the wheelhouse door, she paused, said something to the pilot, and grinned. The grin brightened her face and made the dirt suddenly irrelevant. With a wave to the shadowy figure in the wheelhouse, she joined the queue of men moving down the pier.

Sebastian leaned down to Lane. "There's a woman coming off Admiralty Pier any minute. She's not in the army, and I must speak with her. Bring her here, please."

The sergeant's square, seamed face twisted in a scowl. "A civilian woman? Some Frenchie?"

"I believe she's a journalist. Be polite, Sergeant, but firm. She doesn't leave the harbor until she and I have spoken."

"Yes, sir." Threading his way through the mass of incoming soldiers, Lane made his way to the near end of Admiralty Pier.

Sebastian located Kate again. She walked with her shoulders back, despite the pack hanging from the left one, and her chin up. Her eyes scanned the harbor, taking it all in. Although her poise and curiosity could prove troublesome, he couldn't help admiring them. And the friendly warmth when she spoke to the pilot.

A vision flashed over his sight, himself and Kate Shaw arguing in his London flat. Kate looked furious. She made an emphatic, chopping motion with her right hand. Then the vision faded.

Trouble, indeed.

She and Lane made their way through the crowd. Sebastian set his face into the amiable but bland expression that served so well at his mother's many social gatherings.

K ate would've traded everything she had, except her cameras and the film she'd shot, for a hot bath and a meal. There'd been no food on the beach and precious little water. The Royal Navy had delivered some, but it hadn't been nearly enough for the hordes of men awaiting rescue.

Her trousers were stiff with blood and dried seawater, her hair was so dirty and sweaty as to be glued to her head, and she could smell herself. A bath felt even more urgent than food. It would almost be worth renting a hotel room just to have a bath.

A blockish, four-story hotel stood near the train station, but she and her guide were heading away from it. Besides, she had no clean clothes other than her spare trousers, which qualified as clean only in contrast to the ones she now wore.

Ahead of them, out of the traffic flow, a tall, broad-shouldered man in the brown battledress of the British Army stood atop a box. He leaned heavily on a cane. Below the brim of his tin hat, he had strong, almost chiseled features, a generous mouth, now set in a grim line, and deep blue eyes. The single crowns on his epaulets marked him as a major. He cut an impressive figure, especially in contrast to the bedraggled men making their way off the piers.

As well he should. He'd been safe here in Dover while the Luftwaffe attacked the Dunkirk beaches. Not his fault, given the cane, and of course someone had to coordinate on this end. But could he understand how awful that had been?

Their gazes met. He nodded to her, and an image flashed across her mind. He and she stood together beside a table in what appeared to be a hotel ballroom. At tables around them sat a mixture of young women and officers of the army, Royal Navy, and RAF.

She pushed the image resolutely away. Funny, the tricks her mind played when she was bone tired.

Leading with the cane, the major stepped carefully off the box. He seemed oddly familiar, but she was certain they'd never met. He must resemble someone she knew. A reporter met a great many people, after all. She'd had this sensation of familiarity before, but it never amounted to anything.

"Miss Shaw, sir," the sergeant said. "Miss Shaw, Major Mainwaring." Sergeant Lane touched his fingers to the brim of his tin hat and stepped back.

The major extended his right hand. "Welcome to Dover, Miss Shaw."

He had a firm, warm handshake with no overlong clutching, icky stroking, or bone-crushing squeezes. "Thank you. What can I do for you, Major?"

"Do you have your credentials?"

She dug them out of her pack. He scanned them briefly and handed them back.

"You were taking photographs just now. I assume you've done so since joining the BEF."

Kate raised an eyebrow. "That's my job."

"Indeed. I'm sure you're aware the War Office has the right to determine which of your photographs are acceptable for publication and to approve any story before you print it."

"Yes." She kept her voice cool and composed, but this was not going in a good direction.

"Good. I'll need to check all film you've shot, including any now in your cameras, any developed photographs, and any notes you've taken since you deployed."

Oh, great. The longer she waited to write this story, the less immediate it would feel. Only an idiot would snap at him, though. He held all the cards.

"Isn't there someone in London who can do that? I'm anxious to let my boss know I'm back. Besides, if I open the camera out here, the light will ruin the film. I understood that only the material we wanted to publish required review."

"The censors in London, as you note, review all proposed publications, but this is a unique situation. We've decided to err on the side of caution." He bent to retrieve a leather rucksack from behind the box. "If you'll put your film, cameras, and notes in here, we can keep them together."

"My cameras," Kate replied, fighting to keep her voice even, "are my livelihood." The idea of leaving them with strangers gave her a sensation much like panic. Besides, the undeveloped rolls of film held some terrific shots, if she did say so herself. What if the army lost them?

"I understand." Major Mainwaring looked sympathetic, maybe because they both knew she had no choice.

With a sigh, she swung her pack off her shoulder and opened it. The major took a pad from the rucksack, wrote out a detailed list of what he took, signed it, and handed it to her.

"If you'll give me your office address, I'll see the cameras and whatever else is acceptable are returned to you."

Now the tightening in her throat truly was panic. "I won't leave Dover without my cameras. I can't." She nodded at the hotel by the rail station. "I'll book a room. You can reach me there." She could at least take a bath and rinse out some things in a bathroom sink. Maybe there would even be room service. "How long will this take, anyway?"

With thousands of men still waiting on the beaches in France, the major surely wouldn't have time to have her film developed and review her notes soon. The longer he held her materials, the less impact her story would have.

He pursed his lips. "I can't say when I'll have the opportunity to look over your material. As for the hotel, it's full of military personnel. I've a friend here in Dover, Doris Launceston, who could put you up. She offers B&B accommodation to friends of friends. Her house will be quieter than the hotel, and she'll feed you well." With a wry smile, he added, "I expect you could do with a good meal by now."

"I wouldn't mind a bite to eat." Admitting she actually felt starved would be a sign of weakness, though, and her instincts said she needed to keep her backbone intact around this man. His friendly manner had steely resolve under it.

He fished a card case and a fountain pen from his inner chest pocket, extracted a card, and uncapped his pen. "Sorry we can't spare anyone to drive you, but it isn't far. Follow York Street. Durham Road will be on your left. I'll jot down the address."

Newsworthy events would happen at the port, not in some cottage tucked away on a quiet street. "I would rather stay here so you can reach me easily."

"This isn't a time for civilians to be at the harbor. The Luftwaffe may decide to favor us with their attention again, and the hotel is too close to the rail station." He gave her a direct, level look. "I must insist, I'm afraid, that you leave the port."

Arguing would, again, achieve nothing and might spur him to be uncooperative—or, rather, more uncooperative—about her photos. Nothing about him gave her a warning chill, and she felt he wasn't a vindictive sort, but best not to make an enemy of someone who had power over her work. Still, having to wait around here when the censors in London could surely handle the task—and likely would need to pass the story anyway—was an aggravating waste of time.

"As for imposing, you'll be doing her a favor." He wrote on the small rectangle of pasteboard. "She's recently widowed and will welcome the company in the house as well as the board fee. The army will reimburse her since we're the ones holding you up."

"That's very generous." A bit too generous for the army. If the major meant to pay her shot, that was unacceptable. That would not only put her in his debt but would skate the bounds of propriety. Kate would just pay this woman herself.

He handed her the card and beckoned to the sergeant. "Lane, please show Miss Shaw to the road and deposit her belongings in my office."

"Yes, Major. Miss, if you'll come with me?"

Offering his hand again, Mainwaring said, "We'll take good care of your things and return them as soon as we can."

He looked and sounded sincere, even regretful. He was only doing his job, just as she had done, but that didn't make the delay any more palatable.

~

As the major had promised, Durham Road wasn't very far away. The short walk, however, served to remind Kate how little sleep she'd had in the past few days. Without her cameras and film, her pack felt disturbingly light. As though she'd forgotten or lost her gear. The army had better take good care of it. If they lost it, she couldn't afford to replace it.

You're tired. You'll cope better after a few hours' solid sleep.

At least the hill the road climbed wasn't steep. Bluebell Cottage stood about fifty yards below the crest. It was one of half a dozen brick row houses—Victorian, to judge by their tall, narrow windows and the white gingerbread trim on the top-floor gables and over the doors. Each door had two narrow windows in the upper half, and a sign beside each one named the cottage. At Bluebell Cottage, lace curtains hung over the bright blue door's double windows.

Standing on the single step in front of Mrs. Launceston's house, Kate looked down at the major's card. Blockish letters engraved in the center of the pasteboard read, *Major the Earl of Hawkstowe.*

So he was an earl. But the sergeant had called him Major Mainwaring, not Lord Hawkstowe.

He'd squeezed a message onto the back. *Look after our American cousin for me,* it read in black, slanted letters. *She doesn't know our ways.*

Huh. Odd phrasing, too. She tapped the card against the fingers of her other hand. The British and Americans were sort of cousins, but the context didn't seem to fit. And what did he mean about not knowing British ways? After living in England for six months, waiting for the army to decide whether to accredit her, she liked to think she'd learned to fit in.

Well, ultimately, his meaning didn't matter. The only thing that counted was how soon he returned her gear, notes, and photos. She could recreate some of the notes but not all—and none of the photos, of course.

It wasn't quite seven o'clock. Hoping she wasn't too early, Kate knocked on the door.

The petite, sturdy woman who opened it wore a simple green dress and shoes. So Kate at least hadn't awakened her hostess, who appeared to be in her mid-fifties. She also had that eerie feeling of familiarity. *You're exhausted, Kate. That's all it is.*

The woman's friendly smile turned wary. Behind gold-rimmed glasses, her blue eyes widened. "May I help you?"

"Mrs. Launceston? Major Mainwaring sent me." Kate offered the card.

One glance at it, and the older woman's wariness dissolved in a wide smile. "Of course I can look after you, dear. Come in. Are you just returned from France?"

"Yes." Kate introduced herself and stepped into a shadowed hall that ran the length of the narrow house to the kitchen. Beyond the back windows with their lacy, white curtains, bright flowers bloomed in a tiny, walled yard. A handful of photos, probably of the Launceston family, adorned the walls around her. The plank floor gleamed with recent polish, and overstuffed furniture covered in flowered chintz made the room to her left inviting. The place had a homey, welcoming feel.

It was safe.

A shiver of grief ran through her. The memory of the carnage in France washed over her sight. Kate gritted her teeth and banished it. This was not the time to give in to her emotions.

"Are you all right?" Mrs. Launceston asked.

"Yes, thanks, only tired and unfortunately dirty. I haven't had a proper bath in three weeks, and I waded through seawater to reach the boat last night." At least from here, neither a washing machine nor piled laundry were visible. That was a complication, so Kate summoned her most apologetic look. "I can see it isn't laundry day, and I don't want to impose. If I might have a bath, I'll take care of the tub, the water, and all of that. I don't mind if there's an additional fee."

The older woman made a *tsk* sound. "I beg your pardon for saying it, but you look asleep on your feet. I expect you've done enough work in the last few days. I run the tea shop near Dover Priory station, but I can help you set up the bath before I leave. Though I've already used my five inches of hot water for bathing this week, I'm afraid."

"Cold water is fine." Any non-salty water would be an improvement.

The offer of help was unbelievably tempting. Taking even a cold bath meant setting up a metal tub and—if Mrs. Launceston didn't have running water, hauling it in from a central pump—then dumping it all out after. Help from someone who wasn't exhausted would make it all go so much faster. Still, she shouldn't impose.

"I can manage the tub. I don't want to put you to any trouble."

"With two of us to set it up, it's no trouble. Have you clean clothes?"

"Not really." Hesitantly, she gestured at her trousers. "These are blood-stains. They probably won't come out, but I do have a spare pair. I'll be fine."

Washing meant scrubbing everything by hand using a plunger in a round tub. It was an unpleasant job without bloodstains. It was also a great deal of work to set up the washtub, carry and heat the water, and so on.

"I'm happy to help you. Come along, and I'll show you your room."

In the months since Kate had left home, no one had cosseted her. That was fine, as she could manage on her own, but her hostess's kindness made her miss Mom.

Mrs. Launceston ushered Kate up the stairs to a bedroom papered in gray with white petunias. The cheerful yellow coverlet over the soft bed looked far too inviting, but climbing into it filthy would be a mistake.

"The loo is just outside the kitchen door," Mrs. Launceston said. "We bathe in the kitchen alcove. I'll leave a nightgown on a chair there for you in case you want to have a lie-down. If you'll leave your trousers and shirt on the floor, I'll see what I can do."

"I appreciate that very much, but—"

"Oh, now, you don't want to wear dirty clothes again tomorrow, do you? Leave them on the chair, and I'll have a go. If it's too complicated, I'll set them aside."

Kate could almost hear her mother's voice reminding her never to impose, especially not on strangers. Exhaustion, however, screamed a powerful counterpoint.

"That's very kind, thank you. By the way, most of the money I have on me is in francs, but my office can wire some to your bank. How much do you charge per day? And for the bath?"

Mrs. Launceston waved her hand dismissively. "I'll settle up with Sebastian. Major Mainwaring."

Just as Kate suspected. Interesting, though, that this woman of humble station was on a first-name basis with an earl. "No, really, I insist on paying."

"You and he can work that out. Meanwhile, let's settle you in."

Arguing with her hostess would only make staying here tense. After all, Mainwaring—again!—was the real problem.

CHAPTER 3

An image flashed into Kate's mind, the dead who lay where they fell because there was nowhere else to put them. The Stukas screaming as they dived out of the afternoon sun. Bombs blasting men and parts of men across the beach. Messerschmitts strafing. Terrified, angry Tommies firing back with rifles even though they knew it was useless.

But the sun had been setting when she was there.

Imagination, Kate. Don't let it run away with you.

Shuddering, she forced the image away. Better to pay attention to her bath.

The oval metal tub was only about a foot deep and less than three feet long. She had to sit with her knees bent close to her chest. Her hair was mostly clean, though, and the cool water was refreshing in the warmth of the day.

After the trials of the last three weeks, sitting in the water and doing nothing was a relief.

Mrs. Launceston had left for work a little while ago. The privacy was welcome, but Kate was too tired to appreciate the bright, tidy kitchen.

Idly, she swished her hand over the surface. Little ripples rolled outward to lap against the sides of the tub.

Like the unusually calm tide at Dunkirk had lapped the beaches.

And the bodies.

A shudder rolled through her. A sob welled in her throat. She gritted her teeth against it and clenched her suddenly burning eyes shut.

She'd battled her too-active imagination and its visions, though never one nearly as dreadful as this, since childhood. Had learned to banish them in her teens.

This one, though…this one sank claws into her heart and twisted.

The sob broke free. She snatched the towel off the floor, wadded it up against her face and wept into it.

All those men. So many would die.

Most of them would come home. The certainty of that rang in her bones, a feeling that had never steered her wrong. One of her hunches, Gran would say.

It wasn't much consolation, though. Not with so many dead and doomed.

The vision changed. The embattled Coldstream Guards waited for nightfall, then slipped away to their new position. As they did, the perimeter around the beach contracted again. Dug in, they awaited the dawn and whatever the Wehrmacht chose to throw against them.

As though her imagination opened a door she'd barred, the memories of the last weeks roared back. Wounded men. Dismembered limbs. The dead on the line of battle and in the road and on the beach, their open eyes staring at nothing. Blood. So much blood.

Kate tightened her fingers on the soft cotton in fury. She was safe. Safe and having a civilized bath while men across the Channel hoped and feared and fought for their lives. Yet she couldn't stop weeping.

Don't be such a selfish baby.

The admonition did nothing to stop the tears.

At last, the racking flow ebbed. Kate hiccoughed into the towel and wiped her face.

She was as clean as she could be now, so she climbed out of the tub. Drying off, she still couldn't banish the memories. It was as though her ability to block them had faded away.

Maybe that was fitting. Such sacrifice shouldn't be forgotten.

The sad, frustrating truth was that she could do nothing to help the men on the beach or, of course, the ones now beyond help. But she could honor them all. She could write their story.

If Major the Earl of Hawkstowe tried to block that, she would simply have to find a way around him.

~

Sebastian hung his tin hat on a hook by the door and draped his jacket, or blouse, over the back of the tiny, windowless room's one chair. His tie followed. The day's load of evacuees had all gone on their way. Planning for the next wave was in order. At least the latest load of sandwiches from Shorncliffe Barracks in Folkestone, where everyone available was making them round the clock, due at the station late this afternoon.

For the moment, Sebastian had nothing critical to do. He had an hour, perhaps two if he was lucky, to sleep.

Unbuttoning his collar, he dropped onto the low cot against the far wall. He propped his cane against the wall by the bed, but it slid down to the floor. He shrugged. It would do just as well there.

Richard shimmered into view at the foot of the bed. "Greetings, Sebastian."

"Greetings." Sebastian tugged off one shoe. "I've a very short while to sleep, so unless this is urgent, it must wait."

"I'll be brief. Miranda is watching over Kate. She seems to be having distressing visions. While we would all prefer to have spared her the horrors of the last weeks, what she's seen may spur her to embrace her magic as a way to help."

"Let's hope so." Sebastian lay back on the bed and snapped out the light beside it. "Miranda didn't talk to her about it?"

"Kate is exhausted. Miranda judged it not the time." Richard's glowing form remained at the bed's foot. Was that sadness in his eyes? Or was Sebastian imagining it?

"We don't have a great deal of time, Richard. The Germans can launch an invasion anytime after they secure the French coast. Barring a miracle, that won't take them long."

The ghost sighed. "I was born at Hawkstowe in June 1642. I have… existed…for nearly three hundred years. Miranda is only a few years younger. I would hope we've developed some sense about broaching difficult subjects in all that time."

"You're tired," Sebastian realized. Now that he thought about it, Richard looked less…substantial than he had. Fatigue must be blurring Sebastian's senses.

Richard nodded. "Sometimes. Many of us begin to despair of ever finding the evidence needed to lift the curse. To know Edmund's confession still existed in the last century, yet be unable locate it, is discouraging."

The family curse bound him and all the Mainwaring heirs since 1483 to a shadowy, wraith-infested realm between life and death. If no one lifted the curse before Sebastian died, his soul would join those trapped there.

"I haven't given up hope," Sebastian said. Feeble though that sentiment was.

"Nor have I." A wry smile curved Richard's lips. "Miranda will not allow it. With every year that passes, though, the likelihood of finding the confession diminishes, and after so many centuries, there's little hope of finding anything else that can free us. With a war on, you and the others will have even less time to seek such proof."

"There will always be someone looking."

"Of course. Rest well, Grandson." Richard faded from view.

Shifting to take the weight from his damaged knee, Sebastian closed his eyes. In 1483, Edmund Mainwaring, then Earl of Hawkstowe, had magically helped the Duke of Buckingham's agents sneak into and out of the Tower of London. He hadn't realized they meant to kill Edward IV's two sons, who'd since been immortalized as the Princes in the Tower. An unwitting accomplice to murder, Edmund had thrown himself on the mercy of King Richard III, the boys' uncle, who had placed them in the Tower for their safety as plots swirled around the throne. The king had forbidden him to speak until the political situation stabilized. Unfortunately, King Richard had died under his white boar banner at Bosworth Field in 1485, killed by the usurping Henry Tudor, without ever giving Edmund leave to speak.

Telling the truth under the Tudors, who'd made a great show of blaming King Richard for the boys' deaths and anything else they could lay at his feet, would've been fatal. Desperate to make amends somehow, Edmund had written a confession, which had since mysteriously vanished. He had also cursed all the direct heirs of his line to not rest in life or death until they—or someone—proved the truth of the murders.

Sebastian sighed. The confession survived in a hidden location, probably a place belonging to the Earldom of Wyndon. His many-times-great Aunt Amelia, Countess of Aysgarth, had Seen it in a vision she caught from the Lord Wyndon of that day. She had been able to summon visions of it all her life, but no one else could do so. Neither she nor any other

Mainwaring seer had managed to penetrate the wards concealing its location. Until they could, knowing it existed wasn't much help.

Someday...

But someday was a goodly time away. Meanwhile, he had a war to fight.

CHAPTER 4

Day four in Dover, and no word from the army about Kate's gear. Granted, the army had its hands full, but that didn't make the delay less frustrating.

Kate lifted her face to the sunlight. Doris, as Mrs. Launceston insisted on being called, had done a brilliant job of washing Kate's dirty battledress. Kate had found her clean, damp trousers and shirt hanging alone on the line in the back yard when she'd come down to supper last night. They'd been far too filthy to clean by hand, but the laundry equipment didn't look as though it'd been used. How odd.

Still, the garments were clean. Going around and around about how was pointless.

Lew had said she should stay in Dover at least until the army returned her things and, if possible, interview some civilians. Maybe wheedle Major Mainwaring into letting her talk to someone about the evacuation. He hadn't returned her calls—no surprise with the evacuation ongoing—and the people in the shops had been reticent, maybe because she was not only an outsider but an American.

Now, though, she was tired. And missing her cameras. And having a hard time keeping the memories back. Working would help with that, but she'd been stymied there.

Sighing, she rubbed a glass of water over her forehead. What wouldn't she give for a tray of ice right now? But the British hadn't developed their

American cousins' enthusiasm for drinks with ice. At the memory of ordering iced tea her first week in London, she grinned. The poor waiter had been so shocked.

She'd left her socks and boots upstairs. At least the grass felt cool under her bare feet.

A bee flitted from the bright red and purple stock to the fat, yellow roses. A breeze rustled the tree leaves and flicked her loose shirt collar. The little garden was a restful place, if she could only make her mind relax.

"You look much better," Miranda said, appearing at Kate's side. "Major Mainwaring is bringing you lunch shortly."

"I would rather he brought my cameras and—wait! What are you doing here? Did I fall asleep?"

Surely not, with the glass cool against her face and the grass tickling her bare feet. Yet this was no dreamscape, and she could see the rear yard's brick walls through Miranda's translucent form.

"No, you're awake." Although Miranda smiled, wariness lurked in her eyes. "I've come to talk about ways you can help."

"But I'm not asleep!" The uneasiness rolled back, prickling Kate's nape.

"Nor is it necessary that you be. Richard and I come to you in your dreams because that's the only way you've been willing to accept us. It's time for that to change."

"That doesn't make any sense." Kate pinched her own forearm, but the sting did nothing to banish her visitor. "I dreamed you up."

"No." Miranda shook her head. "We're not dream figments, Kate. We're ghosts. We have been since long before you were born."

"That's impossible!"

"Only," Miranda replied, watching her closely, "to those who don't believe in magic."

"You're kidding. This is a joke, right?" Had the recent weeks twisted Kate's sense of what was real?

"No. Richard and I are your great-grandparents many generations back. Your birth mother was our descendant, and her husband, who fathered you, was a son of the royal Scottish Gifted line. You've magic in your blood and bones."

The words rang true. They struck an inner chime of certainty.

Yet magic was only a trick for children. Surely it wasn't real.

Miranda continued, "We always meant to let you be. But now, with the world on the edge of ruin, you must accept your magic—"

"That's crazy. Really, Miranda, be serious." Kate shook her head.

Miranda studied her. "When you were young, did you ever wish for a bird or a butterfly or a mouse to come to you, only to have it do so?"

"Well, sure. Animals like me."

"It's more than that. Did you ever know what was about to happen before it did?"

Kate shrugged. "Intuition." Yet that chime inside her was growing louder. There was that soldier who'd tried to save her. How had she known he was diving the wrong way?

"Think about it," Miranda said. "Think about the soldiers in France whose wounds proved less severe than they seemed at first after you treated them. Your adopted family are good people. Loving people. But their emphasis on the practical sometimes blinds them to possibilities."

"Let's leave my family out of this. You don't know them." But the wounds had seemed smaller. Much smaller. Was it possible…?

"Oh, Kate. I've watched them since the day they adopted you. Of course I know them."

"Uh-huh, sure. Look, Miranda, I've had a lot of strange dreams since I went to France." And since she'd come back. This was just more of the same, if less horrible, but she wasn't about to discuss that with a dream figment claiming to be a ghost, one who already had wacky ideas.

What if they're not so wacky? the inner voice asked.

"Think about it," Miranda suggested. "You're dedicated to helping the war effort. Accept your Gifts, and you can."

She disappeared, but a host of questions lingered behind her. A host of unsettling memories.

Kate went back into the house and dropped into a chair at the kitchen table.

She'd imagined the whole thing. Frustration, anger at the Nazis, fear for what would come, they all had led her to put words in her dream friend's mouth. Crazy words.

Then where did they come from?

True, Mom and Dad were practical people. Fairy dust didn't increase the crop yield. Good, old-fashioned fertilizer did. Magic didn't plow the fields. That was Dad or Glenn, Kate's older brother, on the tractor.

Kate stared, unseeing, out the window. The part of her that loved fairy tales yearned for there to be magic and for good people to wield it. But she knew better. Of course she did. She was a sensible, responsible woman.

A tiny, deeply buried part of her, however, wanted it to be true. Had always wanted something like this.

I've had a dreadful few weeks. Of course I want an escape. Want to believe I could do something against this evil.

Wishing doesn't make it so.

As Mom had often said.

Miranda and Richard had always been there, celebrating, comforting. They had never before pushed her. Although…they had once mentioned magic to her when she was about ten or eleven. After Kate had spoken to Mom about it, however, and told them there was no such thing, they'd let the subject drop.

She had long ago forgotten that. But they must've been serious, or Miranda wouldn't have mentioned it today.

I'm thinking about them as though they're real. They're not. I dreamed them up.

A figment of my imagination wouldn't have any thoughts or comments other than those I gave her.

But she might talk to me about subconscious wishes. No matter how desperate I am for a way to help, I can't let imagination lure me into time-wasting foolishness.

If only that blasted major would release her work. Then she could return to London and forget this strange waking dream.

～

Sebastian parked his car by the curb in front of Doris Launceston's house. He would've walked a distance as short as this, bum leg notwithstanding, but he had only a little time to spare.

Miranda's faint outline appeared in the passenger seat and solidified, or appeared to. She was still immaterial, with the paper sack from Doris's tea room and the leather rucksack on the floor visible through her full, yellow skirts.

"I spoke with Kate," she announced. "Thanks to her practical upbringing, she is determined not to believe in magic. Or to believe Richard and I are ghosts." Sighing, Miranda rubbed her forehead. "I did sense a little doubt under her certainty, so perhaps I made some progress."

"She truly has no idea of her abilities?" Such ignorance was hard to imagine, but he'd grown up knowing he was Gifted.

"Richard and I…when it became obvious she had no desire to learn more about magic, we decided not to press the matter. She was happy. Cherished. Why cause discord over something that would make little difference in her life?"

"Why, indeed?" he said softly.

He stared through the windshield without truly seeing the street or the tidy yards lining it. Feeling his way, he said, "If she is a seer, the truth, once heard, will ring in her heart. She cannot deny it."

"She can try." Miranda shook her head. "Kate is honest, both with others and with herself, but she is also strong-willed. Determined. Else she wouldn't have kept pushing until your army agreed to send her to France. Her…boss, I believe is the word…pushed, too, but Kate made a point of meeting those in authority. She did all she could to impress them, and she succeeded. If she truly wishes to deny her Gifts, she will."

Perhaps they should let her.

Except they needed her. Britain now stood alone, with a lethal enemy just across the Channel and no one to fight for her but those within her shores. The Empire was vast, but help from those nations couldn't reach here quickly. A second seer, another Gifted willing to skirt the rules of ancient compacts, could be invaluable.

There must be some way to convince her to cooperate. Even with the soldiers who were coming back, thousands had been lost. Vast stores of equipment were abandoned. If the Germans rolled across the Channel soon, Britain was doomed.

With Richard's guidance, Sebastian had scried her actions in France and in the Channel on the ride back. She'd unwittingly demonstrated healing powers, invisibility glamour, and foresight. Not to mention the magical strength required to change the direction of a grown man's momentum so they landed behind the rock wall instead of in the road. Under all of them had been great courage and, as Miranda said, determination.

He rubbed his hand over his gritty eyes. "I've no time to approach her about this today. From what you've said, perhaps it's better I don't."

"I think so."

"Then it's as well I brought lunch and some of her things. I can be apologetic about the delay and friendly and sympathetic. Make a start at gaining her trust."

Miranda laid her insubstantial hand over his. "Accepting something she has always denied will be difficult for her. Indeed, it is for us all. Be patient with her."

With that, she vanished.

At least he now needn't ask her to move. Reaching through her lap for the lunch sack or the satchel had seemed vaguely lewd.

Sebastian climbed out of the car, grabbed his cane from the floor beside the seat, and walked to the passenger side to retrieve his cargo. He swung the rucksack over one shoulder. When he grabbed the bag from Doris's tea room, bottles clinked. Two ham sandwiches and half a dozen ginger biscuits, which his distant American cousin probably would call cookies, would make a delicious, quick meal. He even had ginger beer to wash everything down.

With meat rationed since March, Doris was lucky her tea room shared the restaurant exemption to rationing. That would surely change, though, if the war dragged on. Sebastian's estates provided his family with meat, so the situation wasn't as sticky for them as for most others.

After he closed the car door again, he took a moment to think. Kate was a practical person, so perhaps logic was the way to convince her. Logic and honesty. It was past time she learned what she was. But first he had to convince her that what they both were was even possible.

Oh, what great fun that would be. But he had no more time to delay.

Sebastian tugged his battledress blouse down and made sure his cap was square on his head. With the rucksack over his shoulder and lunch in one hand, he marched up to the door. In the fourteen months since his injury, he'd become adept at carrying various burdens while using his cane.

Assuming an expression he hoped was mildly friendly, he knocked.

A few moments later, Kate brushed aside the lace curtain over the door windows. She nodded to him and opened the door. Her golden-brown hair hung in soft waves to her shoulders, and the brown shirt and trousers draped enticing curves. Despite the wary expression on her face, she was a very attractive woman.

"Good afternoon, Major." She stepped back to admit him.

Sebastian entered and removed his cap. After hanging it on the coat tree behind the door, he turned to her. "I apologize for not sending word I was coming. I've very little time."

"I understand. What can I do for you?"

"I've brought lunch." He hefted the bag. Was that surprise in her eyes? "Did I say something wrong?"

"No, someone else—but it doesn't matter."

"I also have some of your things to return."

Delight brightened her face, transforming her from merely attractive to gorgeous. She took his breath away.

Steady, lad. Remember the mission.

"I regret that I can't yet give you everything. We're a bit busy at the port, but one of the photographers had time to open your cameras in the darkroom and extract the film. So your cameras and your notebook are in this bag. We did redact a few bits about troop movements, and anything you want to publish must still pass through the censors."

He swung the rucksack off his shoulder and offered it to her. "We should be able to develop your film and check it in the next few days."

She gripped the leather strap. "Thank you. Some of the photos on one roll are underexposed. I planned to correct that in the darkroom."

"I received your message about that and will pass it along, though I don't know that there will be time to correct for that. I apologize for not returning your calls."

One corner of her mouth quirked up in a wry smile. "I've seen how busy you are, you know."

"Indeed you have."

They smiled at each other, and sudden color rose in her face.

"Well," she said. "I'll just run this upstairs and bring you back your bag. If you like, you can have a seat in the parlor."

"I know my way round Doris's kitchen. I'll set out the meal."

"Thanks. I'll be right back."

He resolutely did not watch her leave the room. After setting down the lunch, he removed his blouse and put it on the coat tree as well. He could manage without the cane indoors if he wasn't tired or in pain and didn't have much walking to do, so he leaned it in the corner. If he needed the sword concealed within it, he'd seriously misjudged the day.

Finding plates took only a moment, and he soon had the sandwiches and biscuits set out on Doris's varnished oak table. He'd just poured the ginger beer into glasses when he heard Kate's booted footsteps on the stairs.

He turned to greet her, and an image swept over his sight. Clad only in his maroon robe, Kate walked into the bedroom of his London house with her hair tousled and a tender light in her eyes.

His body hardened.

"Major?"

He blinked, and the vision dissipated.

Standing at his side, Kate regarded him with a quizzical expression. "Something wrong?"

"No, uh, nothing. Make it Sebastian if you would."

"Then I'm Kate. Need any help?"

"Thanks, but it's done." Inwardly, Sebastian groaned. Trivial, inconsequential conversation wasted time, and he had so little just now. Still, if it covered awkwardness, he could accept that.

He held Kate's chair for her, which seemed to surprise her, and sat across from her.

"To beating the Nazis," he said, holding out his glass.

"To the safe return of the BEF." She clinked her glass against his.

They drank the toast and set the glasses down. The dreaded awkward silence descended.

Kate cocked her head. "Can I ask you something?"

"If you like, though I may not be able to answer."

She grinned, causing that same gut punch of admiration as earlier. "It's only an etiquette question. The sergeant introduced you as Major Mainwaring, but your card says you're Major the Earl of Hawkstowe. So if I need to refer to you or introduce you, should I call you Major Mainwaring, Major Lord Hawkstowe, or Lord Hawkstowe?"

"The form is a matter of preference these days. Except on very formal occasions, I prefer Major Mainwaring, but it doesn't much matter to me." He grinned back, and her eyes danced. "Honestly, as long as what you call me is printable, I'll be content."

"I'll bear that in mind. Speaking of your card, how do you know Doris?"

"She's a friend of Mum's." The two women had served on the Council, the governing body of the Wizards' Conclave. Kate might be his very distant blood cousin, but Doris, as a Gifted woman, was his honorary cousin. This was not the time, however, to explain that to Kate.

"Speaking of Doris, she won't let me pay her. I strongly suspect you intend to cover the charge, and don't tell me the army is doing so. That's far too generous for any army in the circumstances."

He shrugged. "Guilty as charged." Giving her the truth as much as possible would, perhaps, if he was very fortunate, cut down on her distrust when he raised the subject of magic. "I'm delaying you. It seems only fair that you not pay for the privilege."

"Then you have to let my office reimburse you. We can't accept favors from anyone we might want to interview or otherwise cover at some point." While her tone was polite, the stubborn set to her jaw warned him not to argue.

Who said I would let you interview or cover me?

Still, he had to admire her ethical stance…and the determination Miranda had mentioned.

"If you insist," he conceded. "It won't be a great deal, as Doris was doing me a favor."

"Thank you."

But Kate still looked troubled.

"Is something the matter? he asked.

"No, but…" She set her sandwich down and looked directly at him. "Did you mention to anyone that you were bringing lunch here today?"

"Only Doris, when I stopped by the tea room for the food. Why?" Had Miranda mentioned it? She or Richard might well have seen him stop for the sandwiches.

"No reason. It's just…someone said something that…"

"Yes?" Would she trust him by mentioning Miranda?

"It doesn't matter." She took a long swallow of ginger beer. "Thanks for bringing the food. Doris left me the fixings, but it's nice to have them done."

Too soon for trusting him, then, perhaps because she didn't trust her own perceptions. But maybe… "Kate, men who've been in combat, who've seen the sorts of things you have, often remember them. As vividly as though they were there again."

Confirmation flashed in her eyes. Toying with a biscuit, she asked, "Does that happen a lot?"

"All too often."

Not looking at him, she took another drink of ginger beer. "Do they… imagine things?"

"Nothing unrelated."

She ran her fingers down the side of her sweating glass. "Can I ask you something crazy?"

"You can always ask." He grinned to cover the hope rising within him.

"Do you believe in ghosts?"

Progress! Casually, he replied, "I'm acquainted with several."

She blinked. "You're serious. Huh. But I suppose, being an earl and having an estate and all, you probably have family ghosts?"

Behind her teasing tone, she was serious.

Sebastian shrugged. "You could say that. Why do you ask?"

"Oh, no reason. Just…something someone said." Yet the doubt in her eyes had to be a good sign.

Her chin rose, and she seemed to shake off the odd mood. "I realize you can't discuss details of military operations, but do you know when you might be able to return my film?"

If he wanted her to trust him, perhaps he should demonstrate trust in her. "Are you asking for your news network? Or as my luncheon companion?"

Although Kate hesitated, her gaze remained steady on his. "Everything you say at this table is between us. Firmly off the record. If I want to follow up on something for the news, I'll ask and then abide by your decision."

"Fair enough." Miranda had better be right about her honesty, but his own Gift told him Kate was telling the truth. "Tonight is the last of the evacuation. The perimeter cannot hold much longer, and we're taking great losses in ships and the men they carry. On top of that, the civilian captains are reaching the limit of their nerve, for which no one blames them. They've performed brilliantly. We couldn't have done this without them."

"The men holding the perimeter…they'll be captured, won't they?"

"I'm afraid so." That was one of the worst parts of this wretched disaster. After holding the line for others to escape, many British and French soldiers would become prisoners. Assuming the SS didn't kill them all out of hand, as they'd done with some units who surrendered.

Kate regarded him gravely, but her gaze held no judgment. "I'm sorry. That must've been a miserable decision for whoever made it."

"Yes. I'm grateful that wasn't on my slate."

They ate for a few minutes in silence. Somewhere in the garden, a bird chirped happily. A breeze wafted the lacy window curtains. He'd always loved summer, but this one promised to be dreadful.

Yet Kate's simple, too-casual question offered hope. Perhaps he could win her over to accepting her gifts. If he could find the right angle. If he could avoid missteps.

One small step at a time. One bit and then the next.

If only Hitler gave him time to go so slowly.

CHAPTER 5

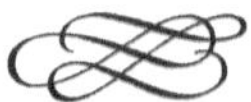

elcome back to London, Sebastian thought. His office in the
War Office building in Whitehall might be more comfortable than the one in the tunnels at Dover, but the work
remained dismal.

He checked his tally again. Alas, the figures hadn't changed, nor would
they. There was no getting round the fact the army had precious little
equipment on hand. Thinking about all the guns, artillery, and transport
abandoned in France with an invasion coming made his gut knot.

Someone tapped on his open office door. When he looked up, Ken
Gerald, an assistant to War Secretary, stood in the doorway. The sturdy,
balding man regarded him with sympathy from behind horn-rimmed
glasses. "That bad, is it?"

Sebastian shrugged. "It's all very well for the prime minister to talk of
fighting to the last inch of ground, but we've precious little gear to use in
that battle." Churchill's ringing speech in the House of Commons the
night before last had steeled the nation's spine, but backbone counted
only for so much.

Grimacing, he added, "Perhaps the cannons on *HMS Victory* are still
operable." Admiral Nelson's flagship from the 1805 Battle of Trafalgar
had been sitting in dry dock at Portsmouth Harbor with her 100-plus
cannons still aboard since sometime in the 1920s.

Ken rewarded the feeble joke with a wry smile. "I imagine the Royal

Artillery Repository has some old field pieces, but I hope we don't come to that. Even if those old guns are operable, we would need to manufacture the shot for them and find someone conversant with details such as how much powder to use when loading. Perhaps the PM can convince the Americans to chip in."

"I'm sure he'll try. They seem to feel very secure with two wide oceans flanking their coasts, though. If they aren't worried about invasion, their isolationists may prevail upon the government to avoid aggravating Herr Hitler." Sebastian leaned back in his chair. "What brings you down here, Ken?"

"The secretary wants to see you."

The summons could've been conveyed by telephone. Ken must've wanted to stretch his legs.

Sebastian donned his uniform blouse and grabbed his cane. Ken walked with him as far as the stairs. When Sebastian started up, Ken headed for the entry doors. "Going out for some air," the secretary's assistant said.

Sebastian made his way up the wide marble stairs slowly. He could've used the lift, but not doing so was a point of pride.

By the time he reached the next floor, his knee, already overstressed by the stairs at Dover, was throbbing. Perhaps he had too much pride.

He pressed his lips together in a line. The bloody thing could throb all it liked. He was still in the army, and that was what mattered most. Sitting on the sidelines while the world exploded would've been unbearable.

Not that any of their choices would matter if the Germans launched an invasion soon. Air Chief Marshall Sir Hugh Dowding, Commander-in-Chief of Fighter Command, had notified the government that he lacked the planes and pilots to hold off an invasion for more than forty-eight hours.

At least there were no signs of boats gathering on the French coast. Invading this island would require transporting a great number of soldiers across the Channel. If the Nazis started massing transport in France, as Napoleon had once done, at least Britain would have warning. Whether she would be able to capitalize on it, of course, would depend entirely on how much military rebuilding she accomplished before that happened.

The war secretary's office, the Haldane Suite, lay above the main entrance. Sebastian walked over bare marble flooring to the entry. The receptionist told him to go on in, so Sebastian tapped on the inner door.

When Secretary Eden responded, Sebastian entered, closing the door behind him.

Anthony Eden, a tall, serious man in his early forties with neatly combed brown hair and a tidy mustache, gestured him to a seat. "This conversation is confidential, Major."

"Of course, sir."

"What do you know of the Earl of Wyndon?"

"Very little. We were at Eton together briefly but didn't move in the same circles, as he's about a decade older. I attended Oxford, and he studied at Cambridge."

Eden regarded him solemnly. "I would like your personal impressions, please."

"As I said, sir, I don't know him well." Nor did he wish to. At a charity dinner Sebastian's mother had dragged him to some years ago, he'd over-heard Wyndon say the main purpose of the church and the army were to give useless younger sons something to do.

Nor had Sebastian ever used his Gift to investigate the man beyond trying to learn whether his family still possessed the confession that could lift the Mainwaring curse. That effort had produced neither confirmation nor denial.

But Eden wouldn't ask unless the answers mattered. Sebastian replied, "He was reputed to be rather arrogant, very much concerned with his own precedence and privileges."

The earl's family, a junior branch of the de Veres, were all known for arrogance and placing their own interests before any others. The current Earl of Wyndon, Gerald de Vere, supposedly ran true to form.

"I see." The older man frowned. "I dislike gossip, but it often holds a germ or two of truth. Lord Wyndon spends rather a great deal of time with the former king's set, many of whom are, if not outright German sympathizers, somewhat inclined to make excuses for them."

"I hadn't noticed that, but I generally avoid large social gatherings." Edward VIII, the king who had abdicated to marry his divorced American lover several years earlier, was known to have Nazi sympathies. Sebastian's family had never cared to ingratiate themselves with that set. "As at Eton, Wyndon and I move in different circles."

"That's to your credit in this instance, but I must ask you to renew your acquaintance with him."

A miserable prospect. "Do you suspect him of disloyalty, sir?"

Eden hesitated. "Suspicion may be too strong a term. Let us say instead that I and other ministers have concerns. If you can arrange to mingle with him and this pro-Teutonic set of his, see whether anything appears untoward, that would help."

"I'll do what I can, of course." Starting with a scrying and any visions he could summon. Unfortunately, that wouldn't spare him from spending much time around the man. Direct, personal impressions mattered.

"Report to me weekly. We've time for you to be subtle about this, or so I hope, but move as quickly as you can." With a slight smile, Eden added, "Your tendency to work long hours is well known, but this is also in aid of the war effort. If it will help for you to make yourself socially available several evenings a week and at the weekend, you should do so."

"Yes, sir." Sebastian's older sister, Rosamund, would love that. She had taken his lack of social activity as her personal project.

"Keep me informed," Eden said, signaling the discussion was over.

Sebastian agreed and made his way back to his own office. The discussion with Eden had an unsettling undercurrent. If the War Office could spare Sebastian so often, was the work he did here truly important?

When he reached his office, he closed the door and dropped into the desk chair. His leg ached from going up and down the stairs, so he stretched it out, massaging the muscles around the injured knee with one hand while he glanced over the papers on his desk.

Knowing exactly what resources had been abandoned in France and how many were now available here was important. But he was merely checking the army's figures, acting as a backstop for the tallies of missing equipment. Anyone could do that.

After honoring his father's wishes by earning his degree from Baliol College, Oxford, he'd attended the Royal Military Academy at Sandhurst. Had burned for his chance to defend his country. According to his superior officers, he'd shown great promise.

Until Czechoslovakia.

Now riding a horse soon caused his knee to throb, and walking for more than a couple of miles, especially on rough terrain, or riding a long distance in a car caused pain that eventually became muscle cramps.

He was in the army, yes, and grateful still to be there. Yet he hadn't fully accepted that he would never lead soldiers in battle, never actively participate in the war engulfing Europe unless—God forbid!—the Jerrys reached London.

At least he was still alive, still able to contribute even in a small way. Those who'd fallen in France would doubtless happily change places.

As Milton had said, they also served who only stood and waited. So it would be for Sebastian. He would do what he could, remain vigilant in case he saw a chance to do more, and serve his country as well as possible.

Sliding into de Vere's social set would offer more of a challenge to his wits and his self-control than tallying lost equipment. He might even discover something useful.

Also, of course, there remained the problem of Kate. If he could bring her aboard, that might matter far more than anything else he could do.

~

Stringing sentences together was difficult when scenes of death and destruction kept sweeping across Kate's sight. She stopped typing and flexed her fingers. The men who had fought in France deserved her best effort, especially those who hadn't come back.

What if Miranda was right? She'd hinted that Kate could do something to help. But surely that was Kate's imagination talking.

Major Mainwaring and his colleagues had actually redacted very little of her material. She'd written up her experiences in France, chosen the necessary photos, and given the story to Lew to edit and then submit to the censors. Now she was working on her interviews with the soldiers.

She had photos of most of them, but looking at them made her ache inside. How many of them had not made it home?

Remembering the cameras made her think of Sebastian. In the end, he'd been kind and probably as accommodating as he could about her photos and notes. That was no reason for the way his blue eyes lit when he smiled to keep popping into her head, but that would surely fade in time.

A scene flashed into her mind's eye. She stood before a crackling fire in an unfamiliar parlor. Frustration scalded her throat. Gesturing to the fire, she said, "I can't do this. It doesn't happen for me the way it does for you."

She wheeled and met Sebastian's steady gaze. He cupped her cheek gently, and warmth flowed through her at his touch. "It doesn't," he replied, his voice calm, "because you don't truly want it to."

Kate shook her head hard. The vision cleared. *Talk about over-active imaginations!*

Yet the scene she'd observed also sent a shiver of uneasiness down her spine. It had first flashed into her mind after she said good-bye to him at

Doris's, when he'd brought lunch. It had happened again on the train coming back from Dover. And now a third time.

Gran had often said ideas that popped up three times should be examined. There couldn't be anything to this one, though, could there? Or to imaginary Miranda saying Sebastian was bringing lunch. That was probably Kate's unacknowledged wish to see him again talking.

Obviously, she was drawn to him. So what? That wasn't going anywhere, nor did she particularly want it to.

Now all this daydreaming had made her lose her train of thought. No wonder, when she was so weary. The persistent nightmare of German planes and tanks rolling through the English countryside kept her from sleeping except in too few, too-brief snatches.

Lifting the top end of the paper in the typewriter, Kate scanned down the sheet.

At least she had the six-desk office the CNU London Bureau reporters shared to herself. Four desks stood by the walls, facing into the room. While she was in France, Lew had added two facing each other like an island in the center. There was just enough room to walk around.

In the outer office, two doors down from where Kate worked in the reporters' bullpen, the phone rang. May, the receptionist, answered it.

A few moments later, her rapid tread, heels clicking on the wood floor, came down the hallway. The petite, slender blonde stopped in the office doorway. "Kate, the phone's for you. A Major Mainwaring. Shall I transfer him?"

The smart move was probably to say no, but letting a little attraction get in the way of developing a possible source was stupid. Kate nodded and thanked May, who bustled away.

Without getting up, Kate pushed her wheeled chair sideways to the phone on its table by the door. It rang a moment later, and she answered it. "Kate Shaw."

"Hello, Kate. It's Sebastian." The sound of his rich, deep voice created warm fizzing in her stomach. Frowning, she pressed her hand to her tummy as he continued, "I hope your return to London went smoothly."

"It did, thanks. What can I do for you?"

"I'd like to talk to you. Off the record. We could walk in Hyde Park if that suits you."

The solemn note in his voice killed the warm fizzing. Unease replaced it. She should say no. But she might learn something useful about the war effort. Perhaps convince him to smooth the way for some interviews at the War Office.

Hyde Park was a popular spot for walkers. It was after five o'clock, but the summer days were long in England in June. She would have plenty of time to make it home without the inconvenience of traveling during the blackout.

"Of course," she answered, proud of her relaxed tone. "Can you meet me at Marble Arch in twenty minutes?"

"See you there."

Kate hung up. Despite her internal pep talk, the unease deepened. He'd never given her any reason to feel unsafe around him, though. Maybe this was a result of finding him appealing when she wanted to develop him as a source, which required being objective.

You're a grownup, Kate. Act like it.

She glanced at her watch. She could wind up this story and still be on time to meet the major.

~

The last part of Kate's walk to the park took her along Oxford Street. The shops that lined it were closing, spilling their workers onto the sidewalks. Several had piles of sandbags in front of their plate glass windows, which also had been taped in X patterns to prevent shattering and the creation of shrapnel if a bomb exploded nearby.

She threaded her way through commuters hurrying into the Marble Arch tube station but had to wait for a red double-decker bus to pass before she crossed Park Lane to the arch. Some forty-five feet high and sixty wide, the pale stone structure actually included three arches, a tall one in the center flanked by shorter ones on each side. It supposedly commemorated the British army and navy of the Napoleonic Wars, but Kate had never spent much time on it.

A man in the brown uniform of the army stood in front of the central arch with his back to her. Her pulse skipped, a silly reaction. He might be anyone, even with the cane in his right hand.

He turned. When his gaze met hers, Mainwaring smiled. Her breath caught. Her mouth curved in a wide, answering smile.

Good grief, Kate.

She took a deliberate breath in and blew it out. Despite her foreboding, she remained irrationally glad to see him. At least she tamed the silly smile to something more composed.

"Good evening, Major."

"Sebastian, remember?" He grinned. "How are you, Kate?"

"Busy, but I like it that way."

"I'm not surprised. Your notes and photos demonstrated your devotion to your job as well as an eye for detail."

He'd paid that much attention? "Thank you."

"Only the truth. Shall we walk?"

They crossed a paved plaza behind the arch, crossed another street, and entered the park. Kate took a deep breath. The wide, beautifully landscaped parks of London, with all their greenery and gardens, were as close as she could get to home. Traveling past the farms of France had involved too much war and death to be a pleasant reminder. The trenches dug in some London parks for makeshift bomb shelters marred the feeling of tranquility, but at least she hadn't yet seen any in this, the largest park in central London.

They walked for a few minutes in silence. Kate cast a sideways glance at her companion. He wore a thoughtful expression, as though unsure what to say. His limp seemed more pronounced than it had in Dover.

At last, she prodded, "What did you want to discuss?"

He glanced at her. "The war effort," he answered, and misgiving rippled down her spine.

"What about it?"

"Before we get to that," he replied slowly, "I have other information to share. I believe honesty is the best groundwork for any dealings, so I shall be honest with you."

Dread bubbled in her stomach. "Am I going to wish we were on the record?" The teasing note she'd tried for fell flat.

A rueful look crossed his face. "I very much doubt it."

Kate frowned. "Sebastian, I dislike dancing around things. Please just say what's on your mind."

He nodded. "Growing up, I wasn't much like most of the children I knew. I had…hunches."

"What kinds of hunches?" She didn't know whether she dreaded his answer or longed for it.

"I often knew what was about to happen. Sometimes, what had already happened. I could see these things in my mind."

Finally, something inside her shouted, *finally, someone like me!*

But that was ridiculous. The things she thought she saw were imaginary. Yet a tiny corner of her mind didn't believe—maybe didn't want to believe—they were.

"That must have been, ah, unsettling," she ventured, her heart pounding in her throat.

"It might've been, but my parents believed that was no bad thing and encouraged me to heed those feelings. And the visions that came with them."

He flicked a sidelong glance at her.

Visions? Kate's mouth felt desert-dry. She swallowed again.

"The Nazis will come for us sooner or later," he continued. "If it's sooner, I can't say I like our chances of beating them back. Still off the record, of course."

"Yes." His candid comment displayed a great deal of trust, but that mattered less in this moment than whatever he was hinting at. "Major— Sebastian—why are you telling me this?"

He took a deep breath and blew it out. Gesturing to a bench ahead of them with his cane, he asked, "Might we sit?"

"Of course."

They settled onto the seat side by side. He stretched his bum leg out and shifted to face her. "I knew you were coming to Dover before you ever embarked at Dunkirk."

That didn't make any sense. "By radio or something? Why would anyone care?" Although there was the business about her being a civilian—

"No." Watching her closely, he answered, "We have mutual acquaintances. Their names are Richard and Miranda." Over her gasp, he added, "Richard and Miranda Mainwaring."

His words slammed into her chest. For long seconds, she could only gape at him. "That's your last name."

"Yes, because I'm descended from them. For that matter, so are you."

Kate scowled at him. "That isn't funny."

"No, but it's true. I've known them since I was a child." Before she could reply, he added, "Let me ask you something. Are you seeing scenes of the war? Ones you didn't actually witness?"

Every instinct said he was trustworthy. Yet he was asking something ludicrous.

"Think what an advantage it would be," he said, leaning forward, "if we knew when the Nazis are coming. If we knew how. And how many of them."

True, but...

"Whether we call them hunches or visions, these premonitions of ours could determine whether my country survives."

Premonitions of ours. The phrase warmed a lonely corner of her heart she had long since stopped acknowledging. But what he was talking about was impossible.

Sebastian glanced at a couple coming down the walk. Only when they had moved out of earshot did he continue. "This forewarning isn't fully controllable or even entirely dependable. I can teach you ways to deal with it. If there were two of us trying to figure out the Nazi plans, the odds would improve drastically."

Try to summon a hunch? "That's crazy."

"It isn't." He hesitated. "It's magic."

"There's no such thing." But the words lacked conviction.

"There is, and deep down inside, you know it."

As though he'd evoked it, that inner chime of certainty rang through her again.

"Give me a chance to prove it. Have tea with me on Saturday at four. Let me explain how magic works. I promise I'll tell you the truth."

Part of her wanted to meet him, to learn more about him and maybe, just maybe, more about herself. That was silly. Yet…

"What can it hurt to listen? If I'm wrong, all you've given up is an afternoon. If I'm not, you could do something that matters. As a show of good faith, I'm working on getting you a story other American journalists won't have."

He looked so earnest. She wanted to deny him, but she'd never lied to herself. What he was saying touched a chord deep within her.

Kate took a deep breath. "I need some time to digest all this, but Saturday will do."

"I understand needing time. This must all sound very strange, and I'll answer any questions you have then." He gave her his address.

If he was right, it would change everything, and not necessarily for the better.

But if she could help against the Nazis, she had a duty to do so.

CHAPTER 6

Saturday was a double-edged opportunity, Sebastian thought. With luck, he could convince Kate, even if he only managed to win a bit more acceptance. If he bungled the thing, however, she might close the door on possibilities.

Taking his time, he limped down the sidewalk to the Grosvenor Gate, crossed Park Lane, and entered Mayfair. At least the walk to his house in Charles Street wouldn't take long. There were few people about, mainly clerks from the shops or staff from the pubs. The bankers and lawyers who were his neighbors were likely still at work.

Not needing to worry about dodging or giving way on his weak leg made the walk easier.

Kate was a seer, and she'd been presented with the truth. She'd also just come through the horrors of the German invasion of France. According to Miranda, emotional shock could sometimes unlock the seer Gift. It had for her, more than 250 years ago, when she saw an old woman who possessed no magical Gifts at all hanged as a witch.

Turning into Charles Street, Sebastian let out a sigh of relief. His Georgian brick house, one of the wider homes on the street, lay about halfway down the block. It had been in the Mainwaring family since 1735. His was only the latest generation to call it home.

It also had only one step between the entry and the street, which was a particular relief tonight. He opened his front door and doffed his cap. As he tucked it under his arm, his butler, Bradshaw, came through the green baize door below the stairs. Despite Sebastian's urging that he and his wife, the cook-housekeeper, work regular hours, they never departed before Sebastian returned home at the day's end.

"Good evening, sir." The thin, fiftyish man smiled behind his gold-rimmed glasses.

"Good evening." The familiar routine offered a bit of comfort after the dismal news that'd filled Sebastian's day. "It's nice to be home."

"When should we serve dinner?"

"In about an hour, I think, but I need a moment with you, please."

The butler's eyebrows rose, but he said nothing.

"You know I've had the cellar reinforced," Sebastian said. "It's possible —indeed, likely—we're in for a rough time sooner or later. If you and Mrs. Bradshaw would like to move into one of the spare bedrooms for the duration, you're welcome to do so."

"That's very good of you," Bradshaw replied. Despite his bland demeanor, surprise flashed in his eyes. "I'll talk to my wife, and we'll see. Thank you, sir."

"The offer remains open, so take your time."

Bradshaw nodded and went back through the baize door.

Sebastian steeled himself and made his painful nightly climb up the stairs.

Changing his uniform for soft trousers, a cotton shirt, and wool slippers took only a few minutes. He poured himself a brandy and sat down before the hearth in his bedchamber. The delicate antique clock on the Robert Adam mantel chimed half six. As always, a fire was laid, but he wouldn't need it unless he decided to scry instead of relying on his ability to summon visions.

No one knew how long the Germans would wait before they launched an invasion. If it was soon, Britain lacked the war material, planes, and pilots to oppose them effectively. With Kate's help, he might be able to learn when they planned to move. How they would do it.

To his left, his father appeared. "Good evening, my boy."

"Hello, Dad." Reginald Mainwaring looked grim but not as worn as Richard and Miranda had lately. "Something on your mind?"

"As a matter of fact, yes. Richard doesn't want you told, as he knows you've a full slate. He may be considered the head of our family, but he's not your father. I'll decide what we should share with you."

"That sounds ominous."

"It is. Some of our older souls are losing hope we'll ever lift the curse. As they do, they…fade. Eventually, they disappear. Eustace, Miles's grandson, vanished yesterday."

Eustace had been born in…1601. "How long as this been going on?"

"A few years. We've lost three, so far as we know. I wasn't well acquainted with Eustace or with the other two, Francis and Geoffrey, but the loss of any one diminishes us all."

"Is this why Richard looks so weary of late?"

"I believe so. No one expects you to do anything about this, Seb, as your duties come first. As long as you remain under Edmund's benighted curse, however, you've a right to know." His father rubbed a hand over his face. "Somehow, we must find the bloody confession. It's our only hope."

~

All through dinner, Sebastian's father's news haunted him. With a war coming, the young men would be called up. The young women would fill their jobs, leaving fewer available to research the problem. Perhaps some of the older scholars he knew could help.

If only he didn't have a war looming on the horizon. He'd tried to summon visions of Nazi Germany's plans, but he'd seen only aerial combat over the Channel. Were their plans too much in flux? Or did he need a more specific focus?

He had even gone into the afterworld, which allowed him to travel into the past, to eavesdrop. Without knowing where to go or when, he hadn't managed to learn much. He could watch any Nazi meetings but couldn't know which ones truly mattered or what they entailed because he didn't speak German. He'd tried scrying, summoning images in the fire. He'd seen buildings but couldn't see inside them. He'd been blocked by magical wards. Even without that, the language barrier would remain.

The fact that German government buildings had magical warding could only mean Nazi wizards were violating the Compact of Prague. Signed by representatives of all groups of European Gifted in the 1400s, it codified the ban on using magic for national or tribal gain that had been accepted since King Alfred's day. That violation more than justified involvement of the Merlin Club, a group of Gifted secretly dedicated to using their abilities in Britain's defense. Sebastian was one of its three directors, but the others didn't know about his ability to enter the afterworld. That secret was too dangerous to divulge.

He settled into the armchair by the hearth in his bedchamber and stretched out his bad leg. At last, he could truly rest it.

Perhaps he would have better luck with Wyndon. Gossip said a hard man lurked beneath Gerald de Vere's apparent boredom and superior attitude. Given the history of the Mainwarings and the de Veres, with a feud dating back to the mid-1470s, that wouldn't be surprising. The antipathy had been less intense since a collateral line inherited the Wyndon title in 1815, but the two families remained estranged.

Sebastian sent a stream of witchlight to the candle on the mantel to light it. He couldn't scry in it or feed a vision into it, but it would help him ignore the world around him. Some seers worked off other prompts, according to Miranda. Things such as objects or portraits. Or none at all. The candle had always worked well for him.

Shifting in his chair, he faced the mantel. The tiny flame flickered slightly in the breeze coming through the window.

Sebastian fixed his eyes on it and slowed his breathing. As his heart rate settled and the street sounds faded, he extended his power toward the candle, reaching into the realm of Sight.

Purple-gray mists rolled over his vision, and the stench of rotten eggs stung his nostrils.

Gerald de Vere, he thought. *Lord Wyndon.* As a seer, he didn't need to scry to see what he sought, though the information he wanted sometimes eluded him. When it did, scrying wouldn't help either.

The fog receded to reveal a well-furnished parlor. A Chesterfield sofa stood against one wall with leather-covered armchairs in burgundy or brown scattered about the room.

De Vere's home, Wyndon House? Or somewhere else? The inner knowing that sometimes came with Sight said this was somewhere else.

De Vere sat with a stocky, square-faced man with iron gray hair, and Sebastian's pulse leaped. That man, Davis Lendall, was a prominent member of The Link, a Berlin-funded propaganda group that had ostensibly shut down last year.

The men's relaxed postures and genial expressions and the brandy snifters in their hands, implied they were friends at least. Scrying didn't carry sound, but visions such as this did.

Yet the men talked of nothing important. Sebastian needed more information to focus the vision on what he needed. With a slow breath, he let it fade. At least he had a link between the two men now.

He also had another tactic available.

One advantage to a family fortune was being able to afford a telephone in his bedchamber. Sebastian pushed himself out of his chair and made his way to the bed. Sitting, he picked up the black Bakelite receiver and dialed the number for his sister, Rosamund, Countess of Borrowdale. He could see her in his mind's eye, a tall, athletic woman with their mother's dark brown hair instead of the black most of the Mainwaring men inherited, her features similar to his but softer.

She had a live-in staff, so the butler, Petersham, answered the phone. Sebastian identified himself and asked for the countess. She came on the line in only a few minutes.

"What's this, Seb? You're calling in the middle of dinner."

"Sorry. I forgot you don't keep society hours." Over her snort, he added, "I need your help, Rosie. It seems I must expand my social connections."

Silence answered him. Rosamund wasn't a seer, but she had strong Gifts and a fair degree of intuition.

At last, she said, "Why do I think you're not looking for a bit of fun for your evenings?"

He grimaced. "Will you help me out?"

"Certainly. I have some lovely friends I want you to meet. You ought to be thinking of the succession, you know."

He rolled his eyes. "I have plenty of time to start a family."

"Um-hmm. Any particular circles you want to join?" she asked.

"I would like to further my acquaintance with the Earl of Wyndon."

Another silence. "I won't ask why," she told him quietly. "I'll see what I can do and let you know."

Relieved, he smiled. She possessed not only good intuition but common sense and a fine awareness of the moment. "Thank you, your ladyship."

"Remember that when I introduce you to my friends."

"Always a price with you," he teased.

"Of course."

She rang off, and he set the receiver in its cradle. Little though the idea of spending time with Wyndon appealed, it was necessary. The sooner he started his assignment, the sooner he would fulfill it and could return to avoiding the blighter.

～

Purple-gray fog that reeked of rotten eggs rolled into Kate's dreams. As the fog thinned, the booming of antiaircraft artillery pummeled her ears. Flak exploded in the sky, but the big, green troop carriers with the Luftwaffe's black bar cross on the sides and under the wings came on. As they passed, paratroopers jumped, chutes blooming like deadly flowers.

Wave after wave of them drifted downward...toward Buckingham Palace. The palace guards fired, hitting some, but not enough. Not nearly enough. A Messerschmitt strafed the roof, and guardsmen fell, dying. She somehow *knew* it.

The parachutists steered around the blimp-shaped barrage balloons surrounding the palace area. Landing on the roof, they disappeared behind the parapet.

Kate jerked awake with her mouth dry and her heart racing.

The room was pitch dark, thanks to the blackout curtains. She needed a moment to orient herself.

In the bed by the windows, Betty Lee, her roommate and a reporter for Reuters, slept. Her deep, even breathing was faintly audible.

It was a nightmare. A bad dream.

Yet it had felt so very real.

Kate climbed out of bed and groped her way to the door. Over the months of the blackout, she'd gotten consistently better at finding it in the dark.

Outside the bedroom, she groped for the flashlight they kept on a small table between the bedrooms, switched it on, and went out to the sitting room. Blackout curtains made it as dark as the bedroom.

Leaving the light on for the comfort it offered, she filled a glass of water from the pitcher they kept on a small table at night. The building had a shared kitchen on the ground floor, too far to go at this hour. Slow sips should help her settle.

What if it wasn't a dream? What if it was what Sebastian said, foreknowledge?

She didn't want it to be. Yet her ability to doubt it had diminished.

Her heart rate finally settled. She set the glass under the table so no one else would use it instead of the clean ones by the pitcher and headed back to her bedroom.

As she set the flashlight on its table by the door, leaving her in blackness, churning clouds of purple-gray that reeked of rotten eggs rolled across her sight.

Staggering, she leaned against the wall, its cool plaster reassuring. The fog cleared and revealed a sunlit beach with Panzer divisions coming ashore from beached barges. German soldiers unloaded equipment from other barges. Tanks speckled the pebble beach with the white cliffs of Dover in the background. Larger ships lay at anchor offshore, and motorboats full of soldiers headed for the beach.

Kate stifled a cry and wrenched her mind back to the present. The beach vanished.

In the dark hallway, her heartbeat thundered in her ears. It was a wonder Betty and the others didn't hear it.

The scene had seemed so real. Maybe…just possibly…it was real? Or would be? If so, didn't she have a responsibility to do something about it?

~

The morning sun slanted between the buildings and cast their shadows into St. James's Square when Sebastian stepped onto a narrow porch in a nearby street. The brick building, wider than its neighbors because it had once been an inn, occupied a secluded corner of this exclusive neighborhood. Its gray-green paint and black door blended with the quiet elegance of its surroundings.

The deceptively dull exterior concealed an interior that was a hive of Gifted activity. The former inn only masqueraded as a traditional gentlemen's club. In reality, it was much more.

On the wall beside the door, a brass plaque engraved with a small falcon called a merlin turning its head and the words *The Merlin Club* proclaimed the building's exclusive nature. Sebastian laid his right palm against the plate and released a small trickle of magic.

The lock clicked, and the door swung open. As usual, the parquet floor beneath the blue, maroon, and gold Persian runner gleamed with polish. The stairs rose along the right-hand wall, just past the entrance to the lounge with its leather armchairs and small side tables, before curving gracefully left across the foyer to rise to the first floor. The heavy treads and ornate banisters proclaimed the staircase's origins in an earlier age. As well they should. Richard Mainwaring and his closest friends had founded the club in the late 1670s.

Stepping inside gave Sebastian as strong a sense of homecoming as his house in Mayfair or the manor at Hawkstowe. Smiling, he shut the door and hung his cap on the coat tree beside it. The scents of tea and warm scones and the rustle of newspapers drifted from the morning room on his left.

"Good morning, Sebastian." Their sturdy, middle-aged porter, Albert Gray, a Gifted veteran of the last big war, hurried forward to greet him. "Genevieve told us you'd be coming in. She's waiting for you in her office. Have you eaten?"

"Yes, thanks, but I could do with some tea."

"She has a pot already, and an extra cup."

Nodding his thanks, Sebastian walked past the stairs. Bradshaw, his very correct butler, would find the informality mortifying, but the Gifted considered magic a leveler. They had a long tradition of addressing each other by their given names and ignoring social rank.

The club's library took up half the first floor, with bedchambers in the remainder of that floor and the next and quarters for staff who wanted them at the top. The library was a popular spot for conferences, but he and Genevieve could fit in her office here on the ground floor. He sometimes wondered whether she chose to meet here to spare his knee, even though the club had squeezed a lift into one corner of the entry hall decades ago.

An archway under the stairs led to the archives and the manager's office on the left. Directly ahead, behind the lounge, lay Genevieve's office. He loved this room, with its bookshelves on the side walls and the large painting of ancient Westminster hung behind her wide mahogany desk. An Axminster carpet in subtle blues and grays cushioned the parquet floor.

Today, she sat at the round walnut table near the door, her favored location for private meetings, with a stack of papers in front of her. Lamp light glinted on the short, iron-gray hair she styled in finger waves. As usual, she wore an impeccable suit, today's a deep russet.

The Director of the Merlin Club was always a descendant of the club's founders or their close relatives. Genevieve qualified for the position by virtue of having Richard's good friend Christopher "Kit" Grayson, Earl of Havelock, as her many-times-great grandfather. The current earl was her cousin. Sebastian and the current Earl of Aysgarth, Sir Roger Winfield, as descendants of the other two founders, were her assistant directors or seconds.

Before he could tap on the door, she looked up. "Good morning, Sebastian."

Smiling, she poured tea and set it in front of the chair beside hers. He sank into the cushioned seat gratefully. His leg already throbbed, and it wasn't yet half seven.

"I suppose you want the news from Germany?" she said.

The Wizards' Conclave, their official assembly, and its governing body, the Council, read the Compact of Prague as barring anything involving the use of magic for national gain but allowed it for defense of self or others. The Merlin Club took a broader view of *defense of self or others*. As it had been founded to do. So its agents had infiltrated Germany before the 1938 Munich conference.

"I do, but I've news and another matter I'd like to set in motion." Sugar was precious, so he contented himself with cream. The club had an ample supply of that because so many members had cows on their estates. Members also supplied the kitchens with meat, poultry, fish, and produce.

"There's a new seer in London," he announced, stirring his tea. As Genevieve's gray eyes widened, he added, "She's untrained in her Gifts and is skeptical of them. I'm working on that, but we're in a war. If something happens to me or I'm posted away, someone else should know." He explained about Kate.

Genevieve's brows rose. "What do you need from us?"

"For now, nothing. If I can convince her to learn her Gifts, I may need help training her. I've never instructed a novice."

"We can assist you, of course." She shook her head. "A second seer… that's almost too wondrous to believe."

"I know." He sipped tea, savoring its warmth. "Keep that news close, please."

"Certainly. You said there was another matter?"

He laid out the situation with Wyndon. "I'm investigating, but I would appreciate it if you share any information the club's agents turn up."

"Of course." Genevieve frowned. "We've enough problems without British Fascists stirring the pot."

"Or the Communists."

"Unfortunately true." She sipped tea and slid her papers aside. "Are you ready for the news from Germany?"

Sebastian shrugged. "Any chance the Führer dropped dead overnight?"

"Sorry, no." Genevieve extracted a paper from her stack and frowned down at it. This would be a compilation of reports from Merlin Club agents inside Germany. Each wrote a letter first thing in the morning, sat with it laid flat on a table for fifteen minutes, and then destroyed it utterly with witchfire. Back in London, someone scried that report, looking into the past if need be, and jotted down the contents.

"It's vague," Genevieve said, "and all the more disturbing because of that. There's some sort of serious dispute among the Luftwaffe, the Kriegsmarine, and the Wehrmacht. Our agent, Algernon Booth, believes they're arguing over something large they're to work on together."

"Something like an invasion," Sebastian said, his voice flat.

"That's a logical possibility and the most disturbing one. Though I suspect the Nazis are too busy driving toward Paris to bother with us just yet."

"It would be comforting to think that drive is the cause of the dispute, but they don't need the Kriegsmarine to take Paris." Sebastian held the warm cup between his hands and inhaled the aroma. The day might be coming when having tea with a friend was a nearly forgotten luxury.

Thinking aloud, he continued, "Photo reconnaissance shows no buildup along the coast thus far." The Merlin Club agent in that unit would've told them if there were. "At least that's one thing we're better at than they are. That and interservice planning. The Jerrys don't know how to work together."

"We should hope that continues." Genevieve set the paper aside. "I don't suppose you've had any premonitions?"

"Not thus far." Sebastian shook his head. "It's a capricious Gift. Doesn't always serve as one wishes." Sometimes the Gift needed a trigger to focus it on the desired events, but the necessary trigger wasn't always obvious. He might not know what it was until he actually had it in hand.

"I had to ask," she said, her voice wry.

"Of course." He didn't need to be a seer to know what she was thinking. Where one seer couldn't learn what was required, could two do better? The question also applied to finding the missing confession.

Somehow, he must bring Kate around.

CHAPTER 7

Kate hadn't slept well since her conversation with Sebastian last week. Dreams of German ships massing on the coast of France, of skies full of dueling planes, or of men in gray uniforms plotting over maps kept her from sleeping well. She didn't speak German, but the men in her dreams kept saying something that sounded like *zeeloovuh*.

As if that weren't enough, she couldn't shake the feeling Sebastian might be right about her hunches.

If only her imagination and worry would allow her just one night of uninterrupted sleep.

"Kate?"

Startled, she jerked her head up. Seated at the desk across from hers, fiftyish, weathered-looking Jed Hanks gave her a quizzical look. "You with me?"

"Sorry." She mustered a rueful smile. "I was trying to decide on a new angle. Since Italy declared war on Great Britain last week, I've been trying to think who I could interview."

Jed frowned. "You hear about the internments? That's nasty business."

"Yes, it's bound to sweep up a number of innocent people." The British government had ordered all Italians who'd been in the country less than twenty years interned. They'd already rounded up the Germans, even those initially thought unlikely to be a threat. "I would love to interview whoever's in charge of the not-so-secret camp for the Italian internees at Ascot." Rumor had it the place was the winter headquarters of a circus.

"Every reporter in London's trying for that." His lips quirked in a wry smile. "You're not the sugar-sweet type, but if you turned on the charm for the right person…" He shrugged.

"Thanks." She'd fought against being considered sweet and girlish ever since she'd left Cobbettown, but she could be friendly. "I'm not above dropping a smile or two in the right direction. If I knew what that was."

"We'd all like to know that." He gestured to his typewriter. "This is a piece on how the ration board works out its per-person allotments. Hell, who cares? There's still fighting going on in France. I'd rather be there."

"So would I."

Their boss, Lew Banks, knocked on the open door. Short, wiry, and in his late forties, he had a seamed face below thinning blond hair. "Need to see you, Kate. My office."

"I'll be right there."

Lew wheeled and disappeared. Kate exchanged a baffled look with Jed, who shrugged. Lew usually sent his summonses via the receptionist, May. Kate pushed up and crossed the corridor to his small, unadorned office. The door was open, and he sat behind the desk.

"Close the door," he said, gesturing to the chairs in front of his desk. "Have a seat."

Kate complied.

He shook his head. "It's the damnedest thing."

"What is?"

"You did beautiful work in France, Kate. Pulitzer-quality work. I want you to know that."

Misgivings skittered down her spine. He'd already told her that. One compliment from him was rare. A second seemed ominous. "Thanks, Lew. So why do I think I won't like what you're going to say?"

"Because you won't, damn it. In your place, I wouldn't either." He blew out a hard breath. "There's no way to cushion this, so I'll just say it. The British Army has pulled your accreditation."

"What? Why?"

Again he shook his head. "You know they were reluctant to send a woman with the BEF in the first place. You being caught up in that disastrous retreat, now that whoever manages such things has had time to think about it, could have been a publicity disaster at a time when the Brits are desperate to pull our country into this war."

"But I made it back safely."

"What if you hadn't? That seems to be the concern there."

"Hell's bells, Lew, thousands of men didn't make it back. They should worry about that, not one civilian reporter who returned safely."

"I'm sure they do worry about it," he said gently, making her ashamed of her outburst. "They can't afford anything that makes them look bad."

"Can I appeal to someone higher?"

"If you had Churchill's ear, maybe. But I don't think it would do you any good."

Yet he still looked grim.

"There's more," she said, her voice flat. "What is it? Am I covering Women's Institutes and ration recipes now?" She'd fought so hard not to be pigeonholed into fluffy, undervalued *womanly* pieces.

Lew sighed. "I'm as sorry as I can be. Kate, CNU wants to send you home."

"What?!" She gaped at him, but his stony expression told her she hadn't misheard. "That's ridiculous. Is CBS pulling Shirer out of Berlin? Or the rest of Murrow's team out of god-knows-where they all are scattered this week?"

He shook his head. "There's a difference between you and them, Kate. A big one."

They were men. Of course.

The old frustration spiked into her chest. Kate took a deep breath and leveled her voice. "Breckinridge is a woman, and she's all over Europe like the other reporters under Murrow."

"Murrow has more clout at CBS than I do in our shop," Lew admitted. "Besides, Breckinridge is older than you. She has a rep while you're just building yours." Leaning forward, he added, "The work you did in France will help you build it. That just takes time."

"I want to stay. The important stories are here, not across the Atlantic at home." What she had to say next grated like ground glass in her mouth, but it might be her only hope. "If that's what it takes, I can cover society teas and charity efforts and women-pigeonhole whatnots."

Those stories mattered, of course, but such events didn't have the wide-ranging effects of the ones on the political and military beats.

"Write up a pitch, and I'll pass it on. I want you to stay, Kate. Right now, though, they don't see a slot for you."

Kate walked slowly back to the bullpen. Her roommates hadn't said anything about being sent home. But maybe the hammer hadn't dropped yet.

What could she do?

~

The next afternoon, Sebastian opened his front door himself. Kate was already nervous, and the formality of a butler might be off-putting to an American.

She stood on the stoop in loose, cuffed blue trousers and a flowing white shirt that draped the curves of her body. The uncertainty in her face, though, countered any physical urge to touch. He mustn't frighten her away. England desperately needed her Gift.

"Come in, Kate." When she stepped across the threshold, he added, "We'll have tea upstairs, in the parlor."

She nodded. "I'm being sent home," she blurted. "My bosses are nervous about having a woman in a war zone—a little late, but now they're adamant—and the army pulled my accreditation. So all this may not matter in the end."

Bloody hell. "Is this definite?"

"I'm hoping to come up with something."

"Perhaps I've an opportunity that will help. My sister, Rose, the Countess of Borrowdale, has an interview lined up for you. A group of her friends run an organization called the Officers' Sunday Club at the Dorchester Hotel. It's meant to give young officers in the city on leave something to do that will, to be honest, keep them out of trouble. If you're free next Sunday, the seventeenth, you can meet the organizers and talk to some of the officers.

"That's...very kind."

"We're happy to help. Just so you know, there are no strings attached."

Silently cursing the slow pace his knee mandated, he led her up to the first floor and turned left for the parlor. Walking beside him, she glanced at the landscapes and portraits in the corridor without apparent curiosity, simply scanning what was there. Suddenly, she stopped.

"What is it?" He turned to her.

Her face had gone pale. A light sprinkling of freckles across the bridge of her nose, invisible every other time he'd seen her, now stood out in stark relief. Her eyes looked huge.

"Kate?"

Her throat worked in a hard swallow, and he tracked her gaze…to the portrait opposite the parlor door, a painting of Richard and Miranda with their three sons and their daughter.

Hellfire. Why didn't I think to move it?

Because he'd become so accustomed that he barely saw it, that was why. Now he had no choice but to deal with the consequences.

"But…I dreamed them up."

"I'm afraid not, as they were entirely real in their day." Gently, he said, "I told you we're both descended from them." *In for a penny, in for a pound, lad.* "That's why they can come visit us. Or our cousins. We're their descendants."

She looked slightly dazed but let him usher her into the parlor.

"If you'll come in and sit down, I'll explain everything." They took seats in low, armless chairs on opposite sides of the hearth.

His grandmother's porcelain tea service, deep pink decorated with small, plump white roses and gold trim, sat on the table in front of the sofa. Beside it sat a plate of biscuits and tiny cakes, Mrs. Bradshaw's forte. Kate didn't seem to notice.

"Would you care for tea?" he asked.

Shaking her head, she replied, "Thanks, no."

Perhaps she would eat something if he could earn her trust. Sharing food was a sign of camaraderie, after all. Or it could be.

"I'll help you any way I can, Kate, regardless of what happens here today."

"That's very kind. I realize I've no claim on your help."

"But you do—as a distant cousin and as a Gifted woman. We wizards help each other."

Her eyes widened, and she shook her head. "Wizards…do you realize how unreal that sounds?"

"I'm beginning to." He smiled. After a moment, she smiled back.

"Ask your questions, Kate.

"Okay. Why do you think magic is real?"

"Because I know it is. I would like the chance to show you that it is."

"Oh, sure." She gave him a *try harder* look. "I've been to magic shows. Everything is a trick."

"Until it isn't." That seemed to bring her up short, so he quickly asked, "Will you tell me why you're so certain magic is always a trick?"

Kate shrugged. "I grew up on a farm. We used science to increase our crop yield—crop rotation, fertilizer, natural pest repellents. The carnival that came through town had a magic show, and my dad always said it was a gimmick, even the sawing-someone-in-half bit. When I was in college, a friend who knew a magician explained how lots of those tricks are done. They look amazing, but they're all fake."

Except when they weren't, of course, but best to wait a bit before proving that.

She cocked her head, her eyes keen despite her casual manner. "So what kinds of magical powers do you think you have?"

"I told you. I'm a seer."

"Then what's in my purse?"

His mouth crooked up in a wry smile. "It doesn't work that way."

"Then how does it work?"

"I think of a person or a place or an event I want to See. If I'm lucky, it appears before me, usually preceded by a purple-gray fog that smells rather nasty. When it catches me unawares, perhaps caused by something on my mind or nearby, there's no fog."

Again, recognition flickered in her eyes. She'd definitely been having visions.

He continued, "That's how the seer Gift works. There are other skills that come from the magic within—casting fire or ice, witchfire, witchlight, or raising wards. One can also scry, which means summoning images of what one wants to see in a fire. Such images, unlike a seer's visions, don't carry sound and cannot penetrate a warded area."

"Warded?"

"Warding is a magical shield that blocks other magic."

"So it's like a wall of magic?"

"Not precisely. A wall keeps things that are inside in and those outside out. Most wards keep magic out. Someone inside a ward can exit through it unless it's designed to stop that. This house is warded but only against magical intrusion. Anyone can open the door and walk in if it isn't locked."

"And witchfire or witchlight? Are they the same?"

She sounded curious, even thoughtful. Perhaps he was making headway. Perhaps a demonstration…

"Not quite," he answered. He held up his right index finger and summoned power. A blue, glowing sphere about the size of a thimble appeared above his finger.

Kate's eyes widened, and her throat worked again. So at least he had her attention.

"That's a trick," she croaked.

"It isn't." He directed the ball to the hearth, where it hovered above the stacked logs. "That's witchlight. I can make it bigger, up to about the size of a small melon. Or several of them. Witchfire is the same but with the element of fire. I can use that to light the fire or the candles if I wish."

"Holy Jehoshaphat." Kate sat with her lips parted, her expression dazed.

Sebastian summoned the light back to his hand. As she watched, he brought it into his palm, fed more power into it, and made it bigger. Then he sent it over to the closed door.

A flick of his hand dissipated it. "Magic," he said. "Breathe, Kate. Slowly."

Pressing her lips together, she took three deep, slow breaths before her chin rose.

"I…I saw it, but…"

"It's a shock. I understand. If there's no such thing as magic, how can I be so well acquainted with your childhood dream friends? How could I have their portrait on my wall? You're welcome to have that authenticated if you like. It was painted in 1684."

Kate waved that away. He couldn't read her face. Had no idea what she was thinking.

"They've been with me at difficult times," he continued. They'd stayed with him in Czechoslovakia when he hadn't been sure his team could elude capture and return to England. Had helped the group evade patrols. "In good times as well. I would miss them if they went away."

If they lifted the curse in his lifetime, he would lose them, perhaps immediately. The thought jabbed his heart.

"Okay," she replied, frowning.

"Have you ever heard of scrying before?" he asked.

She shook her head.

"It's the art of feeding magic into a fire and summoning what one wishes to see. As I said earlier, magical wards can block it. I assume there are no such wards around your home in Missouri."

"Of course not," she said slowly. "Why?"

"Would you like to see your parents?"

Her eyes narrowed. "What kind of question is that?"

"Yes or no?"

"Yes."

He didn't bother with witchlight this time but simply shot a stream of argent power into the logs on the hearth. Kate gasped.

Feeding more power into the flames, he directed them to show her family farm. A few wizards had to know the faces of those they sought. Most did not, and seers definitely didn't.

A two-story, sprawling wooden house appeared in the flames. It had porches across the front and the back. Green shutters contrasted with white paint, and tidy flowerbeds lined the foundation by front porch with what might've been herbs filling the beds in the rear.

"If you can see that," he told her, "it's further confirmation of your Gifts. Only the Gifted can see a scrying."

Kate stared, apparently frozen in place.

A red barn stood some thirty or forty yards from the house. A windmill by the barn turned lazily. Beyond the barn, a garden spread out with rows of low, green plants he didn't recognize extending into the distance.

Wiping his hands on a rag, a fiftyish man in overalls and a faded green shirt emerged from the barn. His graying brown hair flopped over his brow and brushed his collar. He walked toward the house's rear porch. A woman wearing a bright yellow apron over a floral-print dress emerged from the back door. Beneath graying blond hair, her oval face was cheerful, with faint laughter lines at the corners of her brown eyes and her mouth. She said something that made the man grin.

"Stop," Kate choked. "Stop it."

Sebastian banished the image in an instant. "I didn't intend to upset you." Though he'd known that might be the result.

"It's not that. I miss them so much." She scrubbed her hands over her eyes and blew out a hard breath. "Okay. Let's say I accept that some people can do uncanny things we call magic. That you can. It doesn't mean I can."

Yet the yearning in her eyes made him long to turn jubilant handsprings. Perhaps it was time for a full-out effort. "What if I could prove you have magical Gifts?"

K ate had never felt so cold, never experienced the churning mix of emotions inside her. Dread warred with hope and a tinge of excitement, with *yes, of course* battering at her common sense.

"How can you prove that?" she managed.

His steady gaze made her feel faintly, inexplicably ashamed of herself.

"In France, you helped the medics treat wounded soldiers. You shrank their wounds, Kate. While you waited for the medics. I Saw you magically."

So Miranda had said. And Kate had wondered at the time... *That explains a lot. Too much!* But maybe she'd been mistaken about the wounds at first.

Her gaze turned to the hearth. "I want to say that's impossible, but..."

"You did that on the way to Dunkirk and on two other occasions when you assisted with the wounded. In Dunkirk itself and en route to Dover, you created an invisibility glamour."

"I don't even know what that is." Yet her denial wasn't nearly as firm as she wanted it to be. Crazy hope was pushing doubt aside.

"You cloaked yourself in magic so that you and those around you were invisible."

She knew how to pick a hiding place. That was no trick. Yet she'd always been unusually good at hide and seek.

Sebastian leaned forward. "On the return trip, a Stuka bombed the ship behind yours. When I look for yours by scrying, which means summoning magical visions in fire, as I did a moment ago, it winks out of sight as the Stuka dives and doesn't reappear until it's gone."

A tiny little corner of her soul said he was right. Her heart pounded. "But...I didn't try to do anything like that."

"I know. Do you have a mirror in your handbag?"

"Yes. Why?"

"Will you take it out, please, and hold it pointed at your face?"

Kate did as he asked, setting the mirror on her knee. It reflected her face at an upward angle.

"Now, if you will, close your eyes and remember the ride across the Channel. The crowded boat, the noise of the engines. The men on the deck."

His soft voice took her back there. She could see Captain Darrow's silhouette against the starry sky beyond the wheelhouse glass. Could hear the sounds Sebastian evoked.

"Then the roar of an engine above," he said softly. "The scream of a siren…"

It stabbed into her ears, drowning his voice. *Don't see us, don't see us, don't see us.*

"Kate, open your eyes."

She did, staring directly into the mirror. But her face wasn't reflected. The mirror showed the subtly patterned wallpaper and the landscape painting hanging behind her. She wheeled to look, confirming what she'd seen. Her heart kicked hard and slammed into her throat.

Kate gasped. The mirror dropped from her nerveless fingers.

Paralyzed, she watched Sebastian retrieve it. He offered it to her, and now it showed her face.

"That," he told her quietly, "is an invisibility glamour."

"I…I guess it is." Yet the words didn't quite slot into her brain. How could she cope with that? If he was right, what did that make her?

Sebastian laid the mirror gently on her handbag and retreated. "Kate, you went through a dreadful experience in France, and that can spur the seer Gift, the visions. What's more, you used your power more often than you likely ever had. The more we use our Gifts, the easier doing so becomes."

Like all her strange dreams lately.

No. That's nonsense. "They're just nightmares." She turned to him, hoping he would confirm that, but the denial in his face killed that chance.

"An abruptly triggered Gift can cause visions so frequent as to interfere with sleep. With life. If that happens, I can help you. As I said the other day."

She bit her lip. "You know how crazy this sounds, right? All of it? I mean…I grew up on a farm. I'm not a—a witch or whatever you call it."

"A wizard. And it isn't crazy if it's true." The sympathy in his wry smile made her throat burn. "Would you rather be a wizard or a lunatic?"

"When you put it like that…" Kate shook her head. "Where does this seer business come from?"

"Ah, a history lesson then." His warm smile seemed to carry approval. Kate smiled back before she thought about it.

"The seer Gift," he began, "comes of the old blood, the powers native to this land. It often accompanies the summoning Gift. The ability to create glamours, such as your invisibility screen, is a newer Gift. It comes from folk who arrived around the time the Romans left Britannia. The bloodlines have intermingled over the centuries, so it's difficult to say which one any Gifted primarily belongs to."

"Gifted?"

"Magically, I mean. We also call ourselves, as a group, the Gifted."

"Right."

The odd sensation churning through her felt like the time she'd stood on the bluffs above the Missouri River with Dad and stared at the rushing water below. Danger and wonder and a strange hope beckoned.

CHAPTER 8

I don't think she's coming." Standing beside Rosamund, Sebastian stared down Park Lane toward Marble Arch. Men in suits and hats and women in flowing afternoon dresses and bright hats strolled along the sidewalks, but there was no sign of Kate. "Perhaps I pressed too hard. Pushed her, though I didn't mean to. I've scuppered it."

"Perhaps not. It only a bit past three."

Behind them lay the courtyard in front of the Dorchester's curved main entrance. Sebastian wheeled right, pacing past the bar's windows, now covered by sandbags.

Had he pushed her too hard? The German entry into Paris two days ago underscored the need for her help.

Stalking back to Rosie, his cane clicking on the pavement, he paused for two approaching officers. They exchanged quick salutes.

Sebastian checked his wristwatch. Three twenty-one. She wasn't coming.

A flash of white, blue, and lavender down the sidewalk caught his eye. Clad in a white, below-knee dress printed with blue and lavender morning glories, Kate stepped around a strolling gentleman. Relief out of all proportion to the event washed through Sebastian. The wary look on her face reinforced his doubts.

Still, she'd come. Perhaps he worried for nothing.

He stopped beside Rosie, who was looking her over, doubtless wanting to be sure the woman she was taking under her wing wouldn't embarrass her. Kate's dress had a fitted bodice, elbow-length sleeves, and a flared skirt. A blue belt encircled her waist. In the modest vee of the neckline, she wore a gold locket. A round, low nothing of a hat in white straw accented with cloth morning glories perched atop her wavy, shoulder-length hair. White gloves, white shoes with ankle strap, and a white clutch purse completed her ensemble. She ought to blend well, though he would wager no other woman brought a square leather valise that likely contained cameras.

He shouldn't care about anything beyond the task at hand of introducing her, but he couldn't help noticing the gentle curves of her hips and breasts, the soft contours of her mouth, now covered in deep pink lipstick, and her long, smooth stride. His mouth went dry.

He truly was a bloody idiot. The woman had no interest in him beyond what he could teach her.

"She made wise choices," Rosie murmured. "That's a good sign." Rosie wore a similar dress in apple green silk with matching shoes, hat, and purse, and white gloves.

When his gaze met Kate's, she gave him a tiny, hesitant smile. He and Rosie stepped forward to meet her. Sebastian performed introductions, and Kate offered Rosie a firm handshake.

"I understand you're sponsoring me at this event, Lady Borrowdale. I appreciate your time and the opportunity."

Rosie smiled. "I hope you'll call me Rose, and I'm happy to help. Your dress is lovely, by the way."

"Thank you." Kate's shoulders relaxed, and her smile widened.

Perhaps she'd only been nervous about whether she'd dressed properly. Afternoon tea wasn't a common ritual in rural Missouri, after all.

"The receptionist in our office is from Leeds," Kate continued. "She advised me."

"You both did well." Rosie led the way to the hotel entrance.

With a small bow, a doorman in a black top hat and a green frock coat opened the door and held it for them.

Sebastian gestured for Kate and Rose to go first. Kate gave him a nod of thanks as she passed. She would've told him if her bosses had denied her appeal to stay. If he could come up with enough stories other reporters didn't have, perhaps that could make a difference.

He stepped inside and doffed his cap, tucking it under his arm. As he followed the two women down the corridor, he mentally ran through the people he knew in government outside the military. Perhaps someone in the Home Office had a project that could use press coverage.

~

Walking through a long, wide seating area with Sebastian and his sister, Kate surreptitiously ran a hand down her skirt. Mom had made this dress for her last summer, and wearing it was a reminder for Kate to hold on to her common sense around the major.

Near the end of the corridor, a double doorway on the right opened onto a long, low room. Elaborate chandeliers hung from the ceiling, and a recessed area in the center also gave off light. The murmur of voices filled the air. Kate had never seen a room so large. To one side of the entry sat a low table with a vase of flowers and a cashbox on it.

Two young women in bright summer dresses sat behind it. Tables set with white linen filled the long ballroom. By most of them stood a woman who wore a red, white, and blue bow on her dress. The older women's badges had a silver *H* in the middle, while younger women wore smaller bows with badges encompassing the emblems of the Royal Navy, the Army, and the Royal Air Force.

At the far end of the room, a band in RAF uniforms were warming up.

"No wonder they chose this for their gathering place," Kate murmured. "It holds quite a few people."

"Yes," Rosie replied, smiling at the two women behind the table. "It has plenty of space, though there are already signs we may outgrow it. There's dancing, and we often have a cabaret. Tickets are five shillings, but the committee and their guests don't pay."

She led the way down the left side of the room to a table where four middle-aged women waited.

The room was empty, its sea of round tables covered in snowy linen and laid with settings for...two, four, six...ten? They must expect a great many officers.

Smiling, Rose stopped beside the women's table. "Ladies, I believe you know my brother. This is Miss Shaw, the journalist I mentioned to you. She represents Consolidated News Union." Rose concluded by introducing each of the women.

The stout woman in the center, the Dowager Marchioness Townshend of Raynham—and wasn't that a mouthful?—invited Kate to sit. Sebastian held her chair, surprising her. He then seated his sister before he sat down.

As waiters brought teacups, Lady Townshend smiled at Kate. "Tell us a bit about yourself, Miss Shaw."

Despite her amiable facial expression, Kate had the firm impression this was a test. Especially because Lady Borrowdale stiffened slightly in the chair beside Kate.

"I grew up on a farm in Missouri. My uncle ran the local newspaper, a small weekly, and encouraged me to write for him. I started with school events, taking my own photographs, then moved to local politics, such as that was, and social events. I studied English and education at the University of Missouri in Columbia. After graduation, I worked for a small paper in Joplin for two years before joining Consolidated News Union."

The thin woman seated to Lady Townshend's left, a graying brunette wearing a blue ensemble with a pearl necklace and earrings, leaned forward, her brown eyes keen behind the light blue veil of her hat. "Why do you want to interview our men? You must understand we're very protective of them."

"And of the organization you've built for them, of course," Kate noted, and the women across from her relaxed slightly. She continued, "The war effort—any effort, actually—becomes more real if it has a human face. People back home need to see who's standing in Hitler's path."

Sebastian added, "Miss Shaw has just returned from France with the BEF. You can trust her to know what she's about."

His sticking up for her sent a jolt of pleasure through Kate. He hadn't owed her that.

"So Rosamund said," the woman in blue admitted.

"All of Britain," Kate said, "is girding for war. You're all pulling together, even more than you've done since the declaration of war last September. People at home should see that."

The woman on Lady Townshend's other side, a stout, thirtyish blonde clad in a rose floral print with a pale green hat, raised her eyebrows. "So you intend to win Americans to our cause?"

"That isn't for me to do. Persuasion is for the editorial boards of the newspapers who run CNU's pieces. My job is to present the facts of the situation, put a human face on it, and see what happens." No matter how much she might root for a particular outcome. Kate nodded at the valise by her chair. "I brought my cameras and would like to take some photographs."

The fourth woman across the table had a sour expression on her face, and her gaze below her yellow hat was sharp. "I don't know about photographs," she said, her voice unexpectedly soft. She glanced at Lady Townshend.

The group's leader looked thoughtful. "You're welcome to take some general photographs of the room, of course. But no pictures of individuals or small groups, nor anything that could help identify the men."

"That's reasonable," Kate agreed. The story would have less punch without putting faces to quotes, but it was probably wise to be cautious.

Lady Townshend excused herself to greet the arriving officers. A steady stream of soldiers, sailors, and airmen came through the door. They all looked excited and hopeful. A fist clenched Kate's heart. How many of them would survive the summer?

They checked in at the table beside the door, and a young woman led them into the room to seat them.

"Let's allow them time to sort themselves out before you speak to them," the woman in blue said.

Kate nodded. "While we wait, perhaps you could all tell me how you came to start this group and what these gatherings entail."

An hour later, the room had nearly filled. Some couples danced while others sat at tables and chatted. Here and there, a woman in uniform sat in a group, no surprise since Rose had told Kate women officers also were welcome.

Kate had taken her photos and interviewed the committee's representatives, including Rose. She packed up her cameras and asked, "Do you think things have settled enough for me to do some interviews?"

The lady in blue, Mrs. Raynall, nodded. "Rosamund, would you like to take Kate and introduce her to a couple of tables?"

Kate left her gloves on the table but took her notepad and fountain pen.

As she and Rose left the others behind, Rose softly said, "I do beg your pardon for that interrogation. I had no idea they meant to do any such thing."

"That was fairly tame."

Rose looked startled.

Smiling, Kate continued, "Women journalists are not commonplace and are considered, in some quarters, rather odd." If that stung, it was her private problem. "It's understandable that they want to protect what you've all created here. It seems as though this provides a safe place for the men to relax for a while, and of course you don't want anything to disrupt that."

One corner of Rose's mouth quirked up. "We want them to relax a bit, flirt a bit—all in good fun, of course—and have a nice tea."

She led Kate to a table where four young men in army brown sat with four young women who looked to be in their late teens or early twenties. A couple of pots of tea and two serving platters bearing small cakes and pastries, all in fine white china, adorned the table along with teacups and small plates.

When Rose and Kate stopped by the table, the young men shot to their feet.

"As you were, gentlemen," Rose said. Her gaze swept the group, including the young women. Nodding to the woman with the red, white, and blue badge, she said, "Kate, this is Mrs. Harris, the table hostess. Sally, this is Miss Shaw, a journalist from the States. She would like to talk to everyone if they've no objection."

"About what?" one of the young men, wearing the two boxy star pips of a Royal Armoured Corps lieutenant on his epaulet, asked. His brown eyes regarded Kate uneasily.

She offered her warmest smile. "About how you men came to be in the army, what you like best about it, how you ladies became involved with this club, and anything else you want to talk about. I'm under instructions not to pry into military matters, so this will be your personal views."

The soldiers exchanged glances. "Right, then," one young man said.

Kate reached for a chair. The nearest soldier, a fair-haired, stocky man who was no taller than she and looked painfully young, leaped to seat her. She thanked him with a smile.

"I'll leave you to it," Rose said. "When you finish here, give me a nod. I'll find another table you can interview."

Uncapping her pen, Kate directed a friendly look around the table. "I'd like to know a little bit about all of you. Lady Townshend has directed me not to identify any of you, so we'll use only first names if that suits you."

When they agreed, she asked, "Who would like to go first?"

The young soldiers exchanged glances again. "Ah, I will, I s'pose," the one who had seated her said.

"Your first name, please, and what you do in the army?"

"David, and I'm in the Royal Armoured Corps." Pride rang in his voice. "I'm a tank driver. Tanks were invented up in Lincoln, you know, during the Great War."

The one expected to end all wars. If only.

"What do you like about it?'

"We can go over ditches and other obstacles. And I like artillery practice." Indicating his uniformed comrades, he added, "We're all in the armoured corps."

As they talked, Kate took down first names and jotted notes. Her vision wavered, and she blinked. When she looked back at David, the room winked out. She saw him and two of the other men at the table inside a closed space that must be a tank. They wore brown battledress and rounded, brimless helmets. He peered out a window in front.

A steady sound like hail on a tin rooftop rebounded around them. Gunfire. It must be.

"Steady, lads," David said. "Only a bit farther until—"

Something slammed into the vehicle, breaching the cabin. Kate choked back a cry. An explosion obliterated the sight, and a name flashed into her head, El Alamein.

"Miss Shaw?" Something touched her arm.

The dreadful image vanished. The brunette on Kate's right eyed her with concern. "Are you ill?"

"No. Thank you." Kate took a deep breath and blew it out. Forcing a smile, she added, "I was…caught up in the story." Yet she had to clench her hands around the pad to hide their shaking. Was this what Sebastian had meant by visions taking over? "Let's continue, shall we?"

Holding on to her composure by her fingernails, she managed to finish interviewing the table. She looked over at Rose, but the countess was talking to her brother.

"Where are you from?" a slightly older brunette asked.

"Missouri. I grew up on a farm."

Sally, the quiet blonde seated across from Kate, smiled. "We have a women's land army who farm so the men can go and fight. Did you know?"

"I've heard of it, yes." The dreadful image of the burning tank and its dying crew hovered at the edge of her awareness. Somehow, she had to banish it.

"Do you think they'll start anything like it in the States?" Sally asked.

"Unless our country enters the war, I doubt it."

Rose arrived at the table. "Ready to move along, then?"

"Yes." Kate stood and managed a shaky smile. "Thank you all for your time. I wish you the very best."

As they walked away, Rose asked, "How did it go?"

"They were friendly."

"I hope you'll forgive me, but you look a bit pale."

"I'm a little tired, that's all."

Though Rose looked doubtful, she didn't argue.

"Do the officers usually arrive in groups?" Kate asked.

"Often. We seat them together if that's what they want. There're also a couple of tables with no hostesses for couples who arrive together. The hostesses encourage conversation and dancing, especially with different partners. That doesn't generally suit couples."

Rose stopped by another table, this one occupied by two naval officers, three from the RAF, and four young women. Again, the young men rose as if jerked upright. Rose introduced Kate to the hostess, and Kate seated herself in the vacant chair to the left of the two girls.

Turning to the near one, a sweet-faced teenager, she asked, "How did you become involved in this club?"

"I wanted to do something," the girl answered, her expression earnest.

As she explained, Kate jotted notes in shorthand. When she looked up, the girl, Helen, was still talking, but her voice faded away.

The room winked out.

Not again! Damn it, no!

This time, the scene that supplanted the ballroom was of smoke and rubble. A wrecked street with damaged row houses and blown-out windows. Dust filled the air. The men wading through the ruins of a building coughed and choked. They shifted chunks of masonry, and dread speared Kate's heart.

One of the men froze, then straightened. "Found one," he said, grim-faced.

The others hurried to him, moving debris in desperate haste. Then they, too, stopped.

Kate already knew what she would see when they lifted a limp form onto a stretcher. Helen lay unmoving, a gash down the side of her head, her arm at an odd angle, and dirt all over her. When the stretcher-bearers covered her face with the blanket, Kate wanted to scream.

She jerked herself free to find Helen regarding her oddly. "Miss Shaw?"

Again, Kate forced a smile. She could worry about these visions later. At present, she had to hold herself together. "Sorry. My lunch apparently doesn't agree with me. You were saying?"

They picked up where she hoped they'd left off. Pilot Officer Neville, who looked about twenty, with a thin face and kind eyes, offered her a cup of tea. When she accepted it, their gazes met.

The room vanished again. Silently cursing, fighting it, Kate clutched her cup.

Now she was up in the sky with the young pilot in a sunlit cockpit she somehow knew was that of a Hurricane fighter. Far below, the blue waters of the English Channel gleamed in the afternoon light. To the right, partly obscured by haze, lay the green fields of southern England and a town. Folkestone?

"Jerry on your tail, Ray," Neville snapped into his radio. The plane to his distant right, a Spitfire, started zigging and zagging. "I'm coming."

The Spitfire dived, a Messerschmitt behind it, firing. Neville lined the German plane up in his sights and fired. Smoke burst from the Messerschmitt. It spiraled into a dive.

Neville watched it, his eyes now grim rather than kind, until it hit the water and broke apart. "In the drink. No chute," he reported.

"Jack, watch out, three o'clock," a voice on his radio crackled.

As he veered, bullets raked his fuselage. "Bloody buggering hell," he ground out, fighting the controls as smoke bloomed around his starboard engine.

Wrestling the controls, he turned toward the countryside. Would he make it?

The vision faded. Her glance met the concerned one of a young naval officer, and a sunlit ocean obliterated the room. She stood on a gray metal deck in high seas. Although the deck pitched dramatically, she didn't feel sick. She couldn't feel anything but dread of what she might see.

Shells burst in air all around. The young officer called, "Here they come. Steady!"

Stukas dived on the ship, their screams growing louder.

"Fire at will," the young officer shouted as the ship veered hard to port.

"Kate."

The low, firm voice banished the vision. Kate looked up into Sebastian's face. The room flickered. He lay in a narrow iron bed, his face pale and his eyes closed. Lines of pain marked his face. The mound under the covers where his legs should've been was far too short on the right side.

No, oh, no—

He touched her arm, and the ballroom blanked out the disturbing vision. Only then did she realize she was standing.

Though his expression was calm, worry shadowed his blue eyes.

If what she had seen was real, he would lose his leg—but maybe it wasn't real. Maybe it was imagination spurred by these dreadful visions.

"Is something the matter, miss?" Neville asked. The officers were all sitting much straighter, probably because Sebastian outranked them.

"No. Thank you, I…I'm sorry to be so distracted."

"Are you ready to go?" Sebastian asked her.

No. No, she was not. She'd done a sloppy job so far, and this story had to be excellent.

She glanced past him, and a thirtyish man in RAF blue smiled at her. The room flickered. *Not again!*

Sebastian caught her arm, and the flickering stopped. She still stood with him in the crowded ballroom. When she turned a surprised look on him, he released her immediately.

She tensed, fearing another vision, but the room remained steady. Yet the familiarity of the scene resonated with her. She'd seen this place before.

"My apologies," he said. "You looked a bit unsteady for a moment."

"Her stomach's troubling her," Helen volunteered with an apologetic look at Kate.

"Yes," Kate said. "Thank you, Major Mainwaring." Glancing around the table, she added, "You're kind to let me interrupt your afternoon, but I've taken enough of your time."

They said their farewells, and she walked out with Sebastian.

"You don't look well," he said. "You look as though—"

A young woman gave Kate a friendly nod, and the room flickered again. An image of a field hospital lay over it like a ghost picture.

Again, Sebastian caught her arm. The room came back into focus.

In a low voice, he said, "You're having—you're Seeing things, are you not?"

"Every time I make I eye contact with anyone. I have to get out of here."

"Rosie can mix a tisane that will help. We'll go to her house."

If these visions came faster or became more dire, she would fall down screaming, and she had no idea how to stop them. Reluctantly, she nodded. "Thank you."

CHAPTER 9

With petrol rationed and so many men joining the military, the number of cabs cruising London's streets had dwindled. The doorman flagged one down. When the black cab pulled up beside them, he opened the rear door.

"I'll put your case up front with the driver," Sebastian said.

The stout, graying cabbie helped him settle the camera case. Rose climbed in the back first, and Kate followed.

Before squeezing in beside her, Sebastian gave the driver an address. "It's in Belgravia," he told Kate. "Not far."

The cab pulled away, heading toward the river.

Kate glanced past Rose to the park, at the greenery that so often soothed her. The landscape rippled like a shaken curtain. When it steadied, bombs fell from the sky, blowing chunks of turf outward. People ran, screaming, toward the underground station at Hyde Park Corner. Kate shuddered and squeezed her eyes closed.

Warm and sturdy, Sebastian's hand closed over her gloved one. The horrible scene vanished, leaving the usual greenery in its wake. She let out a long, shaky breath.

Letting go of his hand, not being clingy, would boost her pride, but she needed its bracing effect a few moments more. "Why does everything clear when you touch me?" she asked in a low voice.

"Not far now," he murmured. "Then I'll explain all."

They drove past Hyde Park and along the rear of the Buckingham Palace gardens before the cab turned right. Beautiful, terraced houses, which Kate's American brain still labeled row houses, lined the streets. She didn't have to see inside these grand homes to know they would be beautifully and expensively decorated.

Well, what else should you expect from people with titles and the lands to go with them?

The cab halted in front of a four-story, corner house with a narrow portico a few steps up from the street. A balcony above the ground floor ran across the entire front and held small trees and shrubs. Behind them, ornate columns against the wall rose the height of the next two stories to a long pediment that ran across the front. Iron railings lined the sidewalk.

They climbed out, Sebastian a bit stiffly because he maintained his grip on her hand.

"I can manage," Kate told him.

Irritation sizzled in the look he gave her. "There's no need, thank you."

His reply stung, and then she realized, with some sort of weird intuition, that he thought she'd been referring to his injured leg. She had no idea how she knew that, but she had no doubt of it at all.

The taxi driver also climbed out. He extracted Kate's case from the space beside his seat and set it on the pavement.

Still holding on to Kate, Sebastian fumbled for his wallet.

"Petersham will see to it," Rose said.

As if on cue, the front door opened. A sturdy man of medium height with thinning, brown hair came down the steps quickly but without the appearance of haste. Nice trick. He wore a white shirt with a black suit and waistcoat. Again, she had the feeling she'd seen him somewhere before.

"I'll see to this, madam," he said in cool, confident tones.

"Thank you, Petersham. This is our guest for the afternoon, Miss Shaw."

Petersham inclined his head, a polite smile on his square face.

"Nice to meet you," Kate told him. What did a person say when introduced to a butler? She'd never seen a butler. Still, any polite response should do.

Rose and her brother swung toward the house, but Kate balked. "My cameras," she said.

"Never fear, madam," Petersham said. "I'll keep your case safe belowstairs."

"He'll take good care of them," Sebastian assured her.

When he drew her hand through his arm and covered it with his own, she let him lead her into the house. His arm brushed hers as they walked. Awareness of him rippled through her, but he gave no sign of noticing.

Once she'd had this tisane—was that a drink?—perhaps she could let go of him at last.

"Kate, if you'll go with Sebastian to the upstairs parlor, I'll fetch my herbs and mix your drink."

Drink. One guess correct. "What's in it?"

"Nothing alcoholic. Chamomile, lavender, and valerian root mixed with a bit of magic."

Magic. Okay. Weird, but Kate would take whatever worked.

She thanked Rose and let Sebastian escort her up to the first—second to her American brain—floor. They entered a sunlit parlor with upholstered furniture decorated in gray, rose, and green chintz. French doors led onto the front balcony. Two loveseats back to back occupied the center of the room, one facing the hearth with the other facing toward the side wall. Armchairs flanked them both, with a low table in front of each loveseat. In the corner stood a bookcase with a radio atop it. A desk sat beside the glass doors, and a gray carpet lay over the shining wooden floor.

Sebastian steered Kate to the rose-and-gray-striped loveseat near the door. He dropped onto it beside her with a slight, pained wince and a stiff face.

"You said you would explain," Kate said. "Why are you holding my hand? Surely you could let go now that we're at your sister's house."

"I can't, I'm afraid. Does your hand feel warm?"

"A bit, but maybe that's from my gloves."

He shook his head. "I'm feeding magic into you via your hand to help control the visions you're having."

That sensation of standing above the rushing, churning river rocked her again. She searched his face, trying to absorb that.

Quietly, he said, "Traumatic experiences can trigger a seer's Gift, as I said earlier. You've just returned from France, where you saw death, violence, and grave injuries. Many of the men involved were ones you'd come to know at least a little. An experience like that can unlock the Gift, as appears to have happened for you."

"Okay, but how do I stop it?"

"It's a contrary Gift. All the things I told you we Gifted can do, we can control. No one with proper training creates witchlight by accident. The exception, the only ability its wielder cannot control, is the seer Gift. It sometimes shows a seer something he doesn't want to See, refuses to show what he's trying to summon, or, when danger threatens, manifests unexpectedly and with alarming intensity and clarity."

Again he paused.

Turning over what he'd said, she asked, "Does danger include war?"

"It has in the past." He took a deep breath and blew it out. "Ours is a rare Gift, so no one knows as much about it as we do about other, commonplace skills."

His hand around hers was warm and somehow reassuring, and that was dangerous. She couldn't let go, though. Not until these hallucinations ebbed.

"There is a theory," he said, "propounded by Julian Winfield, the Gifted Earl of Aysgarth and a scholar of the history of magic in the last century. He was married to a Mainwaring seer."

"A relative of yours?"

"Of ours," he corrected quietly. "The seer Gift warns of what might happen, and if the seer ignores the warning when action is needed, the visions come faster and more strongly. Ignoring them leads to matters becoming worse."

"Well, mine certainly have been." She gave herself a gold star for pulling off that dry, calm tone when her insides were doing the Lindy Hop.

"The more dire the situation, according to Julian, the more intrusive and insistent the Gift becomes. Ignoring the visions only aggravates the problem. If you were trapped in a scrying, I could break you free magically in an instant. Interfering with a seer's vision is more difficult."

Rose joined them with a teacup and saucer in her hand. She set them down in front of Kate. "This will be bitter, I'm afraid, as sugar interferes with the effect. Best to drink it fast."

Kate looked down at the dark liquid. A wisp of steam rose from the cup. "This is herbs, you said? And magic?" That still sounded weird to her.

Rose nodded. "It will make you a bit drowsy."

Kate tugged off her gloves, laying them on her purse on the low table, and picked up the cup.

"Best drink it quickly, as I said."

Kate sniffed it. The scent was mild but with bit of a bite. When she took a swallow, the bitterness of it rolled across her tongue. She drained the liquid as quickly as she could.

"Hold onto my hand," Sebastian said, wrapping his fingers around hers again, "until you feel yourself relax."

"Talk to me," Kate urged. Sitting here waiting for a feeling she didn't entirely understand would make her tense all by itself.

"Have you a large family?" Rose asked.

"My parents and two brothers, one older than me and one younger. They all work our family farm. My younger brother, Dwight, is airplane mad, but so far he's content with crop dusting." With a war coming, she feared he might join the air force.

But that was enough about her. "If you don't mind my asking, is it hard to be both an earl, which I assume involves some responsibilities, and an army officer?"

"Sometimes. I've a superb manager for the estate—a steward, he would've been in the old days, and he handles almost everything. Rose and our brother, James, know they can speak for me if he can't reach me. As does Mum."

He hesitated. "I never expected to be the earl. I had an older brother, and I was keen for the army anyway."

His grief seemed to wash over her. "You lost him. I'm sorry."

He nodded his thanks. "His name was Reginald, after Dad. They died in the same boating accident." As though trying to lighten the mood, he pulled a wry smile. "In the space of a day, Captain the Honourable Sebastian Mainwaring became Captain the Earl of Hawkstowe."

"You would rather have them back," she said softly.

Startled, he jerked in his seat.

Kate's cheeks heated. "I'm so sorry. It's presumptuous of me to comment on your feelings."

"Not at all," he assured her. "Very kind of you to offer sympathy. And yes, I would much rather have them than the title."

An awkward silence fell.

Sebastian cleared his throat. "We have a saying. *A seer need not scry to See what is, what was, and what will be.*"

"Nice if it's true, I suppose." And if a person wanted to see those things. "What's this about this talent just acting on its own and causing visions?"

Sebastian and his sister exchanged a glance. She shrugged.

"It's the nature of the Gift," he replied. "This will sound even crazier than what I've already said, but there is a ghostly realm that lies alongside this one. It touches all places and all times."

"You're right," Kate said. "It's kind of crazy." It was entirely insane, but she softened the comment to be polite. And because everything in her affirmed his words.

Maybe she really had lost her mind.

He smiled. "One grows accustomed."

What if *one* didn't want to?

He continued, "Julian's theory, backed by cryptic references in old grimoires, was that a seer's mind taps into that realm. He believed the Gift is drawn to dire situations and impending danger. That its nature is to spur the seer to act." He shrugged. "I'm aware it sounds mad, but his wife, my many-times-great aunt Amelia, had visions of the Battle of Waterloo the day Bonaparte escaped from Elba. Because she warned Julian, he was able to muster the Gifted to gather intelligence as Bonaparte marched toward Paris."

That didn't sound as wild as it should. In fact, by the time he finished talking, the world had gone slightly fuzzy.

"I think I'm relaxed," Kate said. "Thank you so much. I'll get myself out of your way now."

"Do you mean you intend to leave?" Rose asked.

"Well, sure. Of course." Kate tugged her hand out of Sebastian's and peered into his face. The room remained steady. It did seem a bit distant, but that didn't matter. "You've solved my problem, and I do thank you."

Rose leaned forward, "Kate, I told you that tisane would make you drowsy."

"The tisane provides a temporary solution," Sebastian added, frowning. "Only learning to control your Gift will stop this from happening again. Meanwhile, leaving here in your present condition would be a mistake."

He seemed sincere, but her perceptions felt fuzzy now too. "Convenient for you," Kate muttered.

"If only it were," he grumbled.

She blinked again. He and Rose both had wavery edges. "What was in that thing?" she demanded.

A moment later, her eyes rolled up in her head, and the room went dark.

～

Oh, that went well." Rosie frowned at Sebastian. "Did you not warn her the brew would make her sleep?"

He eased Kate down onto the cushions. Lifting her feet onto the seat, he replied, "You said *drowsy*. You're the expert at herbals, not I."

"Fair enough." Rosie sighed. "I hope she won't be cheesed off when she wakes up."

"As do I, but you know it wasn't safe to let her leave."

Rose leaned over and carefully removed Kate's hat. "I would hate for her to roll over and crush it." She set the hat next to Kate's purse and gloves on the low table in front of the sofa. Kate should see it when she awakened.

"Seb, would you turn on that light? She may sleep until dark, and I don't want her to wake up and be confused."

If she slept that long, *cheesed off* was probably a mild term for what she would feel. He turned on the desk lamp.

Thanks to the blackout, taking her home after dark would be something between an adventure and an ordeal. If she lived anywhere near her office, that was much too far to walk in the dark, and driving with the headlights covered except for narrow slits posed a hazard to both motorists and pedestrians. The latter generally carried hand torches similarly masked and were urged to carry a sheet of paper or wear white. Curbing was painted with white stripes to make it more visible.

"Coming in and out while she sleeps seems wrong," he said. Even though there were several hours of daylight remaining, he drew the heavy blackout curtains.

"She'll sleep soundly," Rosie said, "and I'll look in from time to time."

Sebastian followed her out of the room. In the corridor, Richard and Miranda waited.

"How is she?" Miranda asked.

"How much do you know?" Sebastian looked from her to Richard.

"She had a vision cascade, and Rose mixed her a tisane," Miranda replied.

Richard slid his arm around her waist. "Miranda could explain the need to heed these visions, however, unwelcome, from her own experience. If Kate would listen to her."

Miranda hesitated a moment. "You've never had such a problem, Sebastian, have you?"

"No, but I've never balked at using my Gift. I know the two of you met because you had visions that disrupted your life until you obeyed their urging and summoned Richard. You've not said a great deal else about that."

"There's very little to say." Miranda glanced up at her husband. "I, at least, knew I was having visions. Being new to magic, as Kate is, that must seem frightening."

Sebastian glanced back at the closed door. Kate possessed courage and determination, as Miranda had said. If matters were different...but there was no use dwelling on that. Her Gift could make a great difference in the war effort, and that had to come before all else.

Kate awakened slowly on an overwhelming wave of confusion. Opening her eyes, she froze. Where was this? How...Sebastian. The visions. A cascade, he'd called them.

Whatever he called them, they'd happened. There was no denying that.

What would Mom and Dad, who always urged practicality, who believed in what they could see and touch, except for church, think?

Kate's stomach did a slow roll. At least she didn't have to face them right away.

Rubbing her face, she sat up slowly. The blackout curtains were closed. Had she slept that long? How would she make it back to the flat?

Someone tapped on the door.

Steeling herself, she called, "Come in."

Rose stepped inside and smiled. "How are you feeling?"

"Better. Thank you." The room wasn't wavering, and looking at Rose didn't cause anything distressing.

"I'm sorry I didn't warn you the tisane might put you to sleep." Rose sat in the chair by the loveseat. "I made it strong because your visions were so persistent. I may have overdone it."

"It's okay." Rose was clearly sincere, and Kate had other concerns now.

"Would you like something to eat or drink?"

"Maybe some water. I'm not hungry. Thank you." Slowly, she smoothed the skirt of her dress. Mom had taken such pleasure in making it, in thinking of Kate wearing it in the great city of London. Would she be so excited if she knew the path her daughter was taking?

"Forgive me, Kate, but you seem troubled. Can I help?"

"My mom made this dress." She ran her hand over the skirt again.

"It's lovely. And very becoming."

"Thank you. She—" Kate pressed her lips together and took a deep breath through her nose. "If she knew—or Dad—about the magic, I think they would be disappointed in me. Maybe not because of the magic itself so much as because they would think it's silly."

"Sebastian explained to me," Rose said. "I don't know your parents, so forgive me for presuming, but they might surprise you." She walked over to a tapestry strip hanging by the desk and tugged it.

The few minutes that passed while they waited for a response gave Kate a chance to master herself. Her worry wasn't Rose's problem. But she wrote home every week. How could she explain this? Her parents would never believe it, and they would worry. If they did believe it...that might change the way they saw her.

A young, blond woman in a simple dress walked into the room. "Yes, madam?"

"A pitcher of water and two glasses, please, Clara."

The woman nodded and walked out.

Rose turned to Kate. "As I said, I don't know your parents. I am a parent, however, of two young boys. You won't meet them because we've sent them away. They're back at Borrowdale, where bombs are less likely to fall." Despite her light tone, her face looked strained.

"You miss them," Kate said.

"Constantly. But we did what we knew was best. I would do anything for them."

"Of course you would." Mom and Dad were probably missing her. If they knew this, would they still?

"I don't think you take my point, Kate. I understand you're very close to your family. If that's so, perhaps you're not giving them enough credit."

Kate shrugged. If only Rose was right, but there was no way to find out soon. This was not the sort of news that belonged in a letter.

"The thing is, you're on the opposite side of the Atlantic from your parents. You've time to consider how to break this to them. You needn't tell them until you're ready. Indeed, you needn't ever tell them."

The idea made Kate's throat ache. She'd never kept anything that mattered from her parents. This changed who she was. How could she hide that from them?

Footsteps came down the hallway. A moment later, Sebastian limped through the door. He carried a tray with a glass pitcher of water and three low glasses on it. It also held a small plate piled with golden cookies. Biscuits, he would say.

"Feeling better?" he asked, setting the tray down on the table.

"Yes, thanks." Her worry over her parents wasn't his concern either. "What time is it, anyway? I should head back to my flat before dark."

"It's almost ten." Sebastian sat in the armchair across from his sister and poured water into the glasses. "Unless you live nearby, returning home will be a bit of an adventure."

"You're welcome to stay here," Rose said. "I can lend you a nightgown."

"I've imposed enough. Besides, I need to be at work early in the morning to write up my story." Staying here, sleeping under Rose's roof, felt too…intimate.

Rose leaned forward. "You must know how dangerous traveling during the blackout is. Stay the night, and I'll send you home in our car early in the morning. You can go to your office, submit your story, and then perhaps return here for some magical instruction in the evening."

Magical instruction. Despite Kate's misgiving, something inside her perked up at the thought.

"I hate to use your gas—I mean petrol—ration," she began.

Rose shook her head. "We rarely use the car, so it isn't a problem."

"I have more ideas for stories you might cover," Sebastian said. "The Local Defense Volunteers, for one. The Women's Land Army. If you do well with those, as I'm sure you will, they may help open other doors."

"I'm grateful," Kate said. She took a sip of water that did nothing to cool her aching throat.

"We Gifted help one another," Rose told her. "On top of that, you're our cousin, however distantly related."

Sebastian added, "There's also a tradition among the Gifted, a belief that our shared Gifts make us kindred of a sort. When no unGifted are nearby to hear, we call each other *cousin* in honor of that tradition."

Cousin? Where had she heard…? "You wrote that on your card for Doris. About me. I thought you meant it in the sense of British and Americans being cousins. But you meant magic."

"I did, and I trusted Doris with that information because she, too, is Gifted."

The memory of wet, clean fatigue trousers hanging on Doris's clothesline though there'd been no signs nor sounds of the extensive preparation needed for laundry flashed into Kate's mind. "Can magic remove bloodstains?"

"I've never tried it," Rose replied, "but I don't see why not."

Sebastian said, "Magic can be useful in small ways, Kate, and in more important ones. The soldiers you helped in France will never know you magically made their wounds less severe, but I know it. I Saw it. You likely saved several of their lives."

If she had, that was a good thing. A less troubling thing, though the idea of magic still made her tense.

He continued, "You may also have prevented the Stukas in the Channel from bombing your boat."

"So they bombed others." Kate grimaced. The warmth from helping the soldiers turned to ash. How many had she caused to die?

"None of that," Sebastian said. "Don't take their choices on yourself. Once they found that convoy, they would've all been after it in any case."

Maybe. But still…

"Stay the night," Rose urged. "If you absolutely must leave, I'll have Wilson, our chauffeur, drive you—or Sebastian can—but you know that's dangerous."

It was. Pedestrians sometimes walked in front of cars. With the headlights mostly obscured, drivers didn't see them, leading to disastrous results.

"You're right. I'll stay, and thank you," she said, "though I need to phone my roommates so they know I'm okay."

"We can do that," Sebastian replied. "I know this is strange and perhaps a bit intimidating, but Kate, if you can master your Gift, you can make a great difference."

"I hope so." Only that would make the personal turmoil worth it.

CHAPTER 10

Sebastian settled into one of the two upholstered chairs in his nephews' bedroom. A snifter of fine brandy sat on the table between the two chairs, but he hadn't yet touched it. Although he'd changed into the pajamas, robe, and slippers he kept here, he yet had work to do. He planned to have another go at Seeing what the Earl of Wyndon and his fascist friends were about.

A lone beeswax taper in a silver candlestick from the parlor mantel sat on the hearth in front of him. With a trickle of green witchfire, he lit it.

Yet he hesitated. Seeing Kate so vulnerable brought out all his protective instincts, but teaching her required him to rein them in. A teacher sometimes needed the option of bluntness.

He pushed her to the back of his mind for the moment and focused his attention on the candle. His awareness of the house sounds—creaking boards, distant voices, and intermittent water in the pipes—all faded.

He opened his awareness and reached for the Earl of Wyndon.

Purple-gray, stinking fog rolled across his sight, obliterating the room. The fog rolled back, revealing a room lined with dark bookshelves. Leather-upholstered armchairs flanked the hearth, and a similar sofa faced it. Clad in trousers, a brocade smoking jacket, and slippers, the earl sat on the sofa with a book. A crystal snifter with golden-brown liquid sat on the table to his right.

No help there.

Sebastian pushed back into the day, to Wyndon leaving home. Instead of the morning scene he expected, the fog swirled to reveal Wyndon stepping into the darkness outside his flat in the fashionable Albany courtyard off Piccadilly. Carrying a torch with the lens covered so only a narrow beam of light emerged, he turned right out of the courtyard and walked down Piccadilly. Gifted eyes adapted better to darkness than unGifted ones, but he still wouldn't be able to see clearly in the blacked-out streets.

Despite the darkness, the seer Gift let Sebastian See him clearly. Wyndon stayed close to the shops and walked down to Berkeley Street, where he turned right. Heading for the square? Did he have friends who lived near there? Nothing in the vision gave Sebastian a time reference, but full night had fallen sometime after eight, so this occurred between then and now.

Wyndon entered the square by the path in the center of the near end and strolled down to the third bench on the left. Sitting on the bench's far end, he shut off the torch. He drew something Sebastian couldn't see, something small enough for his hand to conceal it, from the inner pocket of his suit jacket. After transferring whatever it was to his left hand, he dangled his left arm over the bench's armrest.

He rose and flicked on the torch, for the little good it did.

He'd left something behind. Sebastian shifted the vision back in time to Wyndon putting whatever it was into his pocket. It was a metal cylinder about the length of his index finger.

But what was in it?

The fog swirled in front of the scene. When it ebbed, Sebastian had a view of Wyndon writing on a small sliver of paper. *Stonehenge, Wiltshire plain*, it read. Wyndon rolled it up and put it in the cylinder. He shrugged into his jacket, tucked the cylinder into the inner breast pocket, and picked up the blacked-out torch.

He was leaving a message. But for whom?

Sebastian focused on the cylinder, but it was still there. If he'd been at home, he might've gone out to investigate. Berkeley Square wasn't far from his house. From here, though, it was a bit of a walk for a man with a bad leg. Especially during the blackout.

In the morning, he would See who picked up the cylinder.

Someone tapped on the door.

"Come in," he called.

His brother-in-law, tall, lanky John Kendal, Earl of Borrowdale, opened the door. He'd missed dinner because of his work at the Home Office. Now he held a brandy snifter with an inch of amber liquid in the bottom. He looked tired, his eyes shadowed behind the lenses of his gold-rimmed glasses, but Sebastian didn't comment. They were all tired, all under strain. Remarking on it wouldn't help.

Leaning on the door frame, John nodded at Sebastian's brandy snifter. "I came to see whether you're set, but it seems you are."

"Yes, thanks. I've been doing some magical snooping." When he could snatch a minute from that, he would go to the afterworld and find out more about this fading business.

John raised one blond eyebrow. "Rose tells me you had an eventful day. Do you think Miss Shaw will master her Gift in time to help?"

"I hope so. The strength of her cascade today could be a sign of a very powerful Gift." Sebastian shifted, stretching his bad knee. "First, though, she has much to learn."

When Kate walked into the office at eight, May greeted her with her usual bright smile. "Morning, Kate. Another Monday, eh?"

Kate pushed her mouth into a smile and agreed. At least looking at the receptionist didn't cause anything odd. Perhaps, as Sebastian had said, paying attention to the visions was enough to mollify the Gift. Though that made an innate ability seem much like a petulant child.

"How was your weekend? Was your dress all right for the tea?"

"It was perfect. I got a good story." Nightmare visions or no, she would make her notes into something worthwhile. She had to. "Thanks again for your help."

"My pleasure." With a grin, May added, "Us girls have to stick up for one another. I doubt I'll be going to the Dorchester anytime soon. Was it nice?"

"Yes, very. Lots of pretty chandeliers, thick carpets, and lovely china. Very…posh, I think is the word. Not much like what I grew up with."

"Me either." May paused and cocked her head. "Is everything all right? You look a bit tired."

"Yes, thanks. I didn't sleep very well. May, I'm going back to start on my story. Let me know if you need me."

May agreed, and Kate hurried back to the shared office. No one else was in yet. She hung her hat on the coat tree, tucked her gloves into her purse, and extracted her notebook. Laying the notebook on the desk by the typewriter, she opened it to yesterday's notes. The last step before she started work was feeding two sheets of paper with one of carbon paper between them into the typewriter on her desk.

She'd taken a tiny sip of Rose's tisane at breakfast and had a vial of it in her purse. She also had instructions from Sebastian. If the world wavered, she was to take a deep breath and think of a place that soothed her. She had supposedly been too caught up in the cascading visions yesterday for that to help. When she wasn't, she should be able to redirect the Gift to something that wasn't distressing. Though that seemed at odds with the instruction to heed the visions' warnings.

He knows more than you do. For now, just trust him. You can ask him to explain tonight.

Braced for disaster, she read the first line of her notes. Then the second. Then the third. Nothing scary happened. This might've been any other story.

The more she read without incident, the more she relaxed. The notes were choppy, yes, but she had enough for a decent story. Once she had it written, she would develop the photos and choose the ones to go with it. Lew would take care of passing it through the censors.

Kate slipped her shoes off under the desk and started typing. The more she thought about it, the more she doubted a feature like this would be enough to save her job. It was all she had, though. Even if keeping her place here weren't an issue, she owed those young men and women her best effort. Especially the ones who weren't going to live through this war.

The visions she'd had in the hotel rolled across her sight. Fighting them, she reached for the orchard on the farm back home, sunlight filtering through the branches and glistening on the stream's shallow, placid water.

At last, the visions subsided. Kate took a deep breath and went back to work.

She wrote a paragraph about the event and the sponsors to start. That ought to make them happy. For once, she didn't have to worry about how to handle a story. The generosity of the Officers' Sunday Club organizers was laudable.

The paragraph about the first table, with the young tank officers, had her throat closing again. The awful vision of their tank on fire sprang into her mind. She pushed it away, though. It was a memory now, not her uncooperative talent flaring up.

Kate took her glass out of the office and down the corridor to the lavatory to fill it with water. Sipping it slowly, she went back to her desk.

As she passed Lew's office, he called out to her. She stopped in the doorway as a hint he should hurry. She needed to get this story written.

"I want you to know I'm trying," he told her. "I cabled New York on Friday about giving you a chance to turn up something unusual. Haven't heard back. You working on something?"

She explained about the Officers' Sunday Club story.

"Interesting," he commented, "but probably not enough. Not really your kind of story anyway, is it?"

"Not exactly, but it could open other doors. And meeting those young people was inspiring." In more ways than he could know.

Sometime during the restless night, she'd realized this unwanted ability might lead her to promising stories. Whether it did or not, though, whether she wanted it or not, she had a talent that could help against the Nazis. She couldn't turn her back on that and still respect herself.

"Well, stay on it," Lew said. "I'll keep an ear out for something more you could do."

"Thanks, Lew."

He meant well, but she couldn't help being glad she had other sources now. Lew had to answer to the bosses in New York, but Sebastian and Rose didn't.

In his office, Sebastian frowned at the reports on his desk. He'd asked for information on British aristocrats with Nazi sympathies of any degree. Very few were considered potential threats, as opposed to dabblers. The Earl of Wyndon was on the list, and rightfully so. This morning, Sebastian had scried the cylinder he'd left in Berkeley Square. The fortyish, blond man who picked it up had taken it directly to a house in Fitzrovia. Magical wards kept Sebastian from scrying the interior, but the vision he'd summoned showed the man reading the message and burning the paper.

Going through the afterworld, though, Sebastian could bypass wards. His dead kin there couldn't, but the rules were different for a living wizard. He'd taken advantage of that ability to search the fellow's house when he was away from home. Sebastian had found a wireless set and a code book in a concealed closet. He had reported both to Secretary Eden and submitted photos he'd taken of the code book.

According to the secretary, the Secret Intelligence Service, MI6, had acknowledged the War Office's reports and said they would handle it. Eden still wanted Sebastian to investigate, though. He would periodically search again and examine the code book to see if it had changed.

Infiltrating Wyndon's social set required knowing who they were. Sebastian had Rosie, with her extensive web of high-ranking friends, on that. He also periodically scried or summoned visions of Wyndon to see whom he met socially.

Much as he disliked the idea of spending much time around Nazi apologists, he couldn't avoid it altogether. Magic had its limitations, after all.

CHAPTER 11

On June 17, France asked Germany for terms of surrender. Anyone who paid attention had seen that coming, but it was still demoralizing. It cast a pall over dinner of breaded haddock, peas, and fig pudding at Rose and John's.

The meal wouldn't have been beyond Kate's mother's skills. The china and fine crystal, though, the silver utensils, and the snowy linen tablecloth felt like a reminder Kate didn't belong with these people. Mom's prized possession was a silver serving spoon that had been in the family since the 1870s. At home, they drank out of plain glassware and ate from crockery given to Mom and Dad as wedding gifts. They used tablecloths Mom had made of fabrics printed with fruit or flowers in bright colors. All that felt much more comfortable than these elegant pieces.

The meal ended with a selection of cheese. As a maid set the platter on the table, Rose smiled at Kate. "We sometimes leave the gentlemen to their port, but since you have lessons tonight, I think they can make do without that."

"You're so generous, Rosie." Despite Sebastian's dry tone, affection for his sister gleamed in his eyes. It made Kate homesick for her brothers. What were Dwight and Glenn doing tonight? Did they miss her at least a little?

Around eight o'clock, Sebastian ushered her into the same parlor as yesterday. Kate frowned at him. "Are we keeping Rose and John from relaxing in here?"

"They've a private parlor. Please sit anywhere you like." Sebastian fetched a long taper in an ornate, silver candlestick from the mantel.

A private parlor. Another sign that this family lived very differently from hers, and that also made her miss the simple, familiar life at the farm.

Kate chose an armchair upholstered in gray chintz with little white flowers sprinkled over it. During dinner, she'd managed not to think about this. Now she felt jumpy with nerves. She wiped her hands on her trousers.

Sebastian sat on the loveseat, thus putting himself at a right angle to her. He placed the candlestick on the low table in front of his seat, beside an ornate silver tray with a cut-crystal pitcher of a soft drink called lemon squash, two cut-crystal glasses, and a plate of cookies. Biscuits to her hostess, Kate supposed. Rose had said they used most of their sugar ration to make biscuits so everyone could have a treat from time to time.

In an open-necked blue shirt and loose trousers of darker blue, he looked less imposing than he did in his uniform. But the new senses Kate was only just beginning to recognize felt the power behind his casual façade.

When he looked at her, another image of him superimposed itself over his face and form. This Sebastian wore a stony expression, his eyes narrow, and power crackled around him. Yet Kate didn't fear him. Instead, she envied his complete ease with his power.

The image vanished, and he flashed her a quizzical look. "Everything all right?"

"I'm just a little nervous."

"That's wise. Anyone who isn't nervous about wielding this sort of power is a git who shouldn't have it."

A git? Oh, British for an idiot.

He continued, "Magic's a bit like a pond. It's shallower and easier to manage near the edges. The deeper one goes, however, the more challenging it becomes. Tapping greater power requires increased control."

"That makes sense."

When he smiled, the wry humor in his face made him suddenly appealing. "Unfortunately," he continued, "the Seer gift, of all the magical abilities, is the deepest part of the pond. It's the most complex, the most powerful, and the most difficult to control."

"So I've been dropped into the center of the pond without a life jacket." Kate blew out a breath.

He gave her hand a quick, firm squeeze. As the sudden contact sparked a flicker of warmth deep inside her, his smile faded.

"You do have a life jacket," he told her, his gaze level and open. "I'm your life jacket. I will not let you drown. I promise you that."

Their gazes held, and awareness flooded her in a rush of otherworldly *knowing*. He was an honorable man, one who had known pain and risen above it, a man who was steadfast and strong inside. A man to trust.

Kate's mouth went dry. Stunned by what she'd seen, she drew a slow breath. He mustn't suspect what she'd seen or its effect on her. "Thank you, Sebastian."

"Of course." He withdrew his hand, leaving hers suddenly cold. "For now, we'll stay near the edge of the pond. We start fledglings with a very simple bit of magic, lighting a candle."

"With witchfire." The nerves surged, but excitement bubbled below them.

"Possibly. We teach beginners to use witchfire. Some of us continue to do so, as I do, because that's comfortable. Familiar. Others move beyond that and can extend their power to light the candle without the power being visible."

She didn't ask how that was possible. There was already so much she needed to learn that the beginner level suited her fine.

"Ready?" Sebastian asked. "Take a deep breath, blow it out slowly, and feel the power inside you."

"I don't know how to do that."

"Right." He thought for a moment before extending his hand, palm up. A faint, silvery aura surrounded it. "Lower your fingers toward my palm until you can feel the magic."

Slowly, forcing herself to do it, Kate complied. "I feel a kind of warm tingle. Like—it's a feeling, but the closest comparison is a sound, the one a bubble bath makes as the bubbles pop."

"That's good. Now continue paying attention to your fingertips but turn the remainder of your perceptions inward. Your magic should respond to mine and help you locate that same feeling within you."

Kate closed her eyes and tried to do as he said. To find anything that felt fizzy or different.

At last, she found a tiny burbling below her heart. Indigestion? No, because this wasn't uncomfortable, only...strange.

"Find it?" Sebastian asked.

"I think so." She kept her eyes closed lest she lose track of that tiny flutter. Pressing her fist below her sternum, she said, "It's here."

She'd felt that bubbly flutter every time she used her *don't see me* chant. Had felt it when she'd helped those soldiers in France. But she'd mistaken it for nerves when she noticed it at all.

"Excellent." He withdrew his hand, leaving her on her own.

But she had it now, didn't she?

He continued, "Imagine a current of that power flowing from where you feel it now into your arm. When you feel it in your arm, prop your elbow on the chair arm with your forearm and your hand pointing up and the fingers spread."

Kate tried. "It isn't coming."

"Don't try to go so quickly. Picture it moving a bit at a time, like a caterpillar, up to your shoulder. When you bring it that far, hold it there and tell me."

He made it sound so easy. For him, it probably was.

She tried again, locating that fizzy flutter and imagining it as a caterpillar moving up her chest. When it was just below her shoulder, she lost it, and the sensation ebbed back into her chest.

"Drat it," she ground out.

"That was a good effort. Try again."

She did. And tried another time and another and another. No matter what she did, she couldn't draw the power as far as her shoulder.

After the sixth time, she wiped beaded sweat off her upper lip. "I don't understand how to do this."

"Let's stop for a bit." Sebastian poured squash into a cut-crystal glass and handed it to her. "Breathe deeply. Feel your breathing settle."

Kate nodded. Her breathing slowed, but frustration clawed at her throat.

As though he knew—and maybe he did, thanks to his Gift—he said, "It's a process of baby steps, Kate. We generally start this with children when their Gifts manifest, around age five or six. At that age, most of us have a vague sense of the weather, of who's near, and of whom to trust or avoid. Some can manipulate small objects nearby or, with seers, summon small animals. Parents make a game of channeling the magic, teaching the young ones to do it before they learn to be self-conscious about it. The ability to do more comes into full bloom around age twelve or thirteen.

By then, a Gifted child has learned enough control to build on it in managing the increased Gifts."

She hadn't had that experience. Would this be easier now if she had?

"You've come into your power by a different path," Sebastian noted. "It's possible that your mistrust of it blocks you from gaining access to it intentionally."

"Yet I see these things. I supposedly healed soldiers and made a boat invisible. If I could do those things, why can't I do this?"

He smiled, and the warm understanding in his eyes eased a little of her frustration. He offered her the plate of biscuits. Spreading a napkin over her knee, she took one. It turned out to be tart lemon with a hint of vanilla. Too bad her nerves wouldn't let her fully enjoy it.

"You weren't consciously trying to do those things," he replied. "The mind deals with unsettling issues in its own way. When you thought you were doing something innocuous, something ordinary, that wasn't unsettling for you. Deliberately using something you've believed didn't exist is another matter altogether."

"That's for sure."

He glanced at the window, where the light had noticeably faded. "We'll try a few more times, and then I should see you home before the blackout begins."

Kate finished her cookie, wiped her hands and mouth with the napkin, and set it on the tray. Taking a deep breath, she braced herself.

"Whenever you're ready," Sebastian prompted.

At least she had no trouble locating the fluttery pool of power inside her. Picturing it moving, she mentally tugged it. The warm feeling crept up her chest. Almost to her collarbone. To her shoulder—"Yes!" Kate cried. Then the power roared down her arm and burst into a dazzling shower of green around her hand and wrist.

She gasped, and the light winked out. The power rushed back into her chest.

"Gosh darn it," she choked. "I had it!"

"Indeed you did." Sebastian smiled, and they shared a glance of pure triumph. He offered her the cookies again. "Let's have a celebratory biscuit."

Munching on his cookie, he regarded her with a thoughtful expression.

"What is it?" she asked.

"I wonder whether it would help you if you actually Saw your actions in France, as I did. If you saw the *Thames Lady* apparently vanish or the wounds—"

"I don't want to." She forced herself to take a slow breath that failed to still her suddenly-churning stomach. "Sorry to be abrupt, but I really, truly do not want to see any of that."

He raised both hands in a token gesture of surrender. Or perhaps of apology?

"You needn't if you would rather not. Doing so when you find the idea unsettling would likely hinder more than help." Glancing at the window again, he noted, "The light is definitely fading. Let's call it a day."

Gladly. "Sure, that's fine."

"Let me tell Rose we're leaving," Sebastian said.

"I should thank her for supper."

Sebastian guided her down the corridor to an open doorway. Beyond it lay a small parlor furnished in greens and pale yellows. John and Rose sat in matching yellow armchairs on either side of a stained-glass lamp floor in pale yellow. They looked relaxed and comfortable.

Sebastian tapped on the open door's frame and ushered Kate in. "We're off, Rosie."

"I didn't realize it was so near dark," Rose said. "I'll have Wilson drive you."

"No need," Sebastian said. "We can take the Tube."

They said their goodnights, and Sebastian accompanied Kate down the stairs. Sure enough, they'd stood in the foyer for only a minute when Petersham pushed through the door under the stairs with Sebastian's cap and cane in hand.

Sebastian and Kate walked out the front door. "Victoria is the closest Tube station," he said.

She gave him a quizzical look. "Isn't that the wrong line for Mayfair?"

"I'm seeing you home."

The gesture pleased her irrationally, but it meant more walking on his painful knee. "That isn't necessary. I can manage."

"Your American is showing," he said in a light voice. As she bristled, he added, "You're a lady. I like to think I'm a gentleman. I'll see you home."

At this point, she couldn't very well stop him. Walking quickly would be not only rude but childish. Reluctantly, she nodded her head in assent.

Strolling down streets lined with beautiful mansions, she slowed her pace to allow him to keep up. His limp seemed a bit worse than usual today.

Sebastian glanced sideways and smiled. "You did well today, Kate. You made definite progress."

"It doesn't feel much like it."

"Someday it will."

They walked the rest of the way in silence.

Oddly, she felt no need to make small talk. Somewhere in all the to-ing and fro-ing of the last days, she'd become comfortable with him. Did that mean she was growing comfortable with the magic?

They waited for the train together in companionable silence. When it arrived, their car was crowded, probably from everyone rushing to reach home before the blackout began. Men in brown army uniforms, the blue ones of the RAF, and civilian clothes mingled with women in summer dresses or lightweight trousers, gloves, and hats.

A young airman gave Kate his seat. Sebastian declined one from an army lieutenant. Instead, he leaned against a pole in front of her seat, bracing himself with his cane. He would probably not thank her for mentioning he'd gone a little white around the mouth. At least he would soon be home and able to rest his injured leg.

They had to change trains for the Northern Line at Charing Cross. After exiting the train at Goodge Street, they showed their tickets to the guard at the barrier. Only when they reached the sidewalk did Kate ask, "What was that crack about Americans?"

Sebastian shook his head. "I didn't mean it as a jibe. Americans, especially American women, tend to be independent." He paused. With a sidelong glance, he added, "Must be that revolutionary spirit coming to the fore."

Kate opened her mouth to retort and saw the glint in his eye. Instead, she laughed.

He grinned. "Didn't think you would mind if I took the mickey out of you."

They walked down Tottenham Court Road and along Chenies Street. Beside the Chenies Street Chambers, they turned left. The brick housing block with nice bay windows had been built at the turn of the century for professional women. Kate had marveled when she heard that, not having realized Britain had professional women in 1900.

Sebastian, however, frowned at the building as they walked past it. "You're not here?"

"Heavens no." Kate chuckled. "Those are far too nice for any of our employers to commit themselves to. I'm farther down, in these row houses converted to flats."

They crossed the street to reach her door, one of ten identical ones in this row. Or terrace, as he would likely call it.

"We have the front on what you would call the second floor." She pulled her key out of her purse. "Well, ah, thank you."

"Shall we do the same tomorrow, dinner and then lessons?"

The prospect both appealed and made her wary. "I hate to impose on your sister again."

"We could use my house," he said, "but I thought Rosie might offer a bit more propriety. Besides, she and John say the house is too empty without the boys."

"I can understand that." The farmhouse had been that way when Dwight and Glenn had gone camping with the Boy Scouts. As for the idea of Sebastian's house, that felt a little too intimate. "If you're sure, I'll come there after work."

"I'll see you then."

Yet he made no move to walk away. Neither did she. Seen this close, his eyes were a very deep blue. Mesmerizing. They warmed and softened. He leaned in, and a whiff of spicy aftershave teased her nose. Her mouth went dry.

"Kate," he breathed.

The building door opened. A man she didn't recognize walked out. Kate moved aside, and he slipped past with an apology.

The irritating heat lingered in her face. Fortunately, Sebastian seemed not to notice. He now stood a step farther away than he'd been a minute ago.

"By the way," he said, "you probably shouldn't practice without me or Rosie nearby. We don't want anyone else wondering."

Anyone like her flatmates, he meant. That was more than okay with her, so she nodded.

"Well. Good night," Sebastian said. "I'll wait until you're inside."

She nodded and let herself in. The man's interruption had been well timed. Kate had no business letting herself get involved with Sebastian. He lived here. Had an earldom tying him here, and a farm girl like her would be nuts to think of herself as countess material. Besides, she was going back to the U.S. when the war ended, if not before.

Avoiding involvement was definitely the smart option.

~

Sebastian changed trains at Leicester Square, his knee protesting every step. At least he found a seat this time. Many Londoners would already be in for the night by now.

As the Piccadilly line train rattled its way west, one thought kept running through his head. He'd nearly kissed Kate. His blood hummed with the too-slowly-waning desire to finish what they'd almost done. She would've kissed him back, too. That soft, almost tender look on her face clearly said so.

Good job, that fellow stepping out when he did. Sebastian needed Kate's trust. Needed to maintain the objectivity of a good teacher.

His admiration for her courage in facing a situation she both disliked and feared and for her innate determination could cloud his thinking if he let them. So could his excitement over finding a second seer when his country needed her most.

Besides, where could anything between them go? Numerous parts of his life tied him here. Her family and her long-term career interests lay an ocean away.

No, best to keep things friendly and stop there.

His body unfortunately disagreed with his common sense, but he'd long since learned to discipline his impulses. Kate was his student. He owed her clear thinking.

The train finally arrived at Green Park. What with all the walking he'd done tonight, his sodding knee was screaming bloody murder.

He massaged it carefully before trying to stand and was the last one off the train. That was as well. His slow pace wouldn't hinder anyone trying to rush home.

The walk through the twilight from the station to Charles Street seemed to take forever, each step jabbing a dagger up into his hip. Sebastian gritted his teeth and mentally repeated, *One step at a time, soldier. One more step. Now another...*

At least there weren't many people about to see his turtle-like progress. *Not much farther now.*

Miranda appeared beside him. "Will it help if I talk to you?"

"Can't hurt," he gritted out. "Have you news?"

"Actually, yes. Miles is bored, and he has devised a scheme to amuse himself that might help us all."

"Does it involve boats?" The spirit of the Elizabethan sea captain liked to hover near the ports. Even talking about naval action made his blue eyes, the same shade as Sebastian's and Richard's, snap with pleasure, and he often ran his hands through his black hair.

"Not this time." Miranda smiled. "Miles has decided that if Edmund's confession is hidden at a Wyndon property, he'll investigate them all until he figures out which one."

"Didn't someone try that back in the 1800s? Besides, how can he do that? The wards will keep him out. He won't learn anything except that they're warded, which we already know."

"Hiding something well enough to block a seer's Sight requires more than mere wards. Miles believes the warding around that document's hiding place must be different from the usual."

"They would have something extra," Sebastian mused. "That's a point. How will he determine that?"

"He believes such wards would have a different feel."

Sebastian stared at her. "The magic in them…it sounds ludicrous, but perhaps."

"A Mainwaring ward feels different to us than any other family's. Perhaps that's because those of us who're dead can pass through wards raised by those of our blood and not through others." Miranda shrugged. "I've never paid attention to how one family's magic feels different when I come into contact with it than another's does. It cannot hurt to have him try, though."

"Indeed."

Slowly, she said, "If naught else, this quest will occupy his mind."

"Are you worried about him?" His father's remarks about fading and lost Mainwarings jabbed his conscience.

"I worry about all of them." With a sigh, she added, "They've been in that dreadful realm for so very long, some for more than four hundred years. Every year that passes eats away at their hope of ending the curse."

"It's eating away yours, isn't it?" For the first time, he noticed how tired she looked, with lines at the corners of her eyes and around her mouth unusually pronounced.

"I've dedicated myself to keeping their hopes alive, so I cannot admit this to any of them, even Richard, but yes, I too am losing faith. We hope

Edmund's confession, which would free you all, still exists. But in the century and more since Amelia discovered the Wyndons had it, we've not located it. Doing so begins to feel like a forlorn hope."

"I'm sorry," he said. "I wish I had more time to search."

"You have a country in danger to protect." She gave his shoulder an insubstantial pat. "Of course that must come first. You can help by making a list of Wyndon's properties—past and present, as there's always a chance the document is in the cellar of a forgotten ruin—and leave it on your desk where Miles can see it. That will tell him where to hunt."

"I'll start on it in the morning. Compiling an exhaustive list going back to 1483 will take time. Perhaps some of my grandfathers could help with that."

"And thus give them something to occupy them." Miranda smiled. "You're a good man, Sebastian." She leaned in to brush her ghostly lips over his cheek. As she vanished, he realized he was home.

He opened the door, and Bradshaw hurried to greet him. The butler's blank expression could only mean Sebastian's face reflected his pain. Thank God, he could trust Bradshaw and his wife not to go on about it.

Bradshaw said only, "Shall I run a bath, sir?"

"Yes. Thank you." Turning an old dressing room into a bath and piping in both hot and cold running water had cost a great deal of money, but every time Sebastian's leg flared up, he was grateful he'd done it. Of course, since then, hot water had become rationed—under an honor system, but for good reason—so he ran cold water and heated it magically. Bradshaw, who was not Gifted, might consider what he assumed were cold baths odd, but he would never question it.

Thinking of the brandy decanter in his bedchamber, Sebastian made his way slowly up the stairs. From down the corridor came the sound of running water. Soon he would be able to soak his blasted knee and perhaps convince it to shut the bloody hell up until tomorrow.

He poured an inch of brandy into a snifter and drained it. That would make a start on pain relief, but he wouldn't repeat the mistakes of so many injured soldiers and drink himself blind.

Changing into his dressing gown took only a moment.

The distant sound of running water shut off. A moment later, the telephone rang. Sebastian hobbled toward it, but it stopped ringing. One of the Bradshaws had gotten it.

He perched on his bed with another inch of brandy in the snifter and waited.

Bradshaw tapped on the open door and stepped inside. "Your bath is ready, sir, and Lady Borrowdale would like to speak to you."

Sebastian thanked him. When his butler had made his quiet way down the hall, Sebastian picked up the phone. "Rosie?"

"Don't say I never did anything for you. I've secured an invitation for you and a companion to attend a house party outside Peterborough the weekend of the twenty-eighth through the thirtieth."

"Wyndon?" he asked, massaging his knee.

"Wyndon. Other guests who may interest you are Mr. and Mrs. Algernon Lemieux, who're reputed to be in favor of an accommodation with Germany. That doesn't make them Nazi sympathizers, of course, but perhaps makes it wise to pay them some attention."

Lemieux's conversation with Wyndon might be revealing. "Why me and a companion?"

"I thought it might help Kate's job situation if she could persuade some of the guests to allow her to interview them," Rose said quietly. "You needn't ask her, or indeed, anyone, if you would rather not, of course."

A weekend with Kate? Tempting—and thus wiser to avoid. But Rose was right. Kate did need help to save her job. And he might be able to work some interesting lessons into the mix.

"You're right, though. I'll ask her."

Rose hesitated before she said, "Your knee's playing up, isn't it? You needn't answer. I hear it in your voice."

"I was about to soak in a bath."

"Go do that. Let me know if I can help."

"You already did. Thank you, Rosie."

He made his way slowly to the bathroom. If the house party weekend went well, both he and Kate might benefit from it.

CHAPTER 12

"Excuse me." Kate smiled at the man emerging from the market in Fitzrovia. "I'm Kate Shaw with Consolidated News Union. Do you mind if I ask you a few questions?"

"What?" He blinked at her.

At least he didn't run away. Good thing she'd had plenty of practice dealing with people who couldn't grasp the idea of a woman reporter.

"I'm a journalist," she said, "from the States. Might I ask your opinion on the French seeking surrender terms from the Germans yesterday?"

The man frowned, and Kate uncapped her pen, holding it ready. She'd removed her gloves before stationing herself out here. Washing ink out of white cotton was nearly impossible. Men and women strolling the sidewalk or going to or from the other shops lining the street stepped around Kate and her companion.

"Well, I'm not surprised, I can tell you that. The Frogs always needed us to save their...that is, er, to pull their chestnuts out of the fire. Our lads went over there to help, and what do the Belgians do? They crumble like a stale biscuit, that's what. With the Frogs doing the same."

French troops heroically holding their part of the Dunkirk perimeter for the evacuation had wound up prisoners of war, but saying that would accomplish nothing.

"We're better off without 'em, I say. Better for us to stand alone than depend on allies who'll fold their tents when the going gets rough."

A woman going into the market paused. "Do you mean the French?" she asked.

"I do indeed," the man replied.

The woman sniffed. "Well, what can you expect, really?" On that note, she sailed into the market.

Kate took the man's name. As he strolled away, she donned her white, wrist-length gloves and tucked her pad and pen into her handbag. She would try the barber shop down the way next. A good man-on-the-street story might help her chances to keep her job. Probably not as much as an interview with a government minister would, should she land one, but every solid story should count.

No matter how she felt about the magic, she couldn't say Sebastian hadn't kept his word. He and Rose were doing what they could to help her.

Calling a countess by her first name still felt presumptuous, but they were kin, however distant.

Through Richard and Miranda. Kate hadn't seen Miranda since Dover. Had her skepticism made Miranda feel unwelcome? Thinking of her as a person still felt strange, but so did so much else these days.

Kate paused in front of the barber shop, tucked her gloves in her purse again, and drew out her pad and pen. A portly gentleman in a worn suit emerged. She flashed him her most polished professional smile. "Excuse me, sir. I'm Kate Shaw, a reporter with Consolidated News Union. May I talk to you for a minute?"

"Sorry?"

She explained again and asked him his opinion of the French request for terms.

"Typical, innit? They're forever making a dog's dinner of things and needing us or the Yanks, begging your pardon, miss, to prop them up." He gave her his name and strolled on.

Kate had to think a minute about *dog's dinner*. Oh, yes, that meant a mess.

The French soldiers she'd seen in France had fought valiantly. Whatever their generals did or didn't do, no one should fault their courage.

A thin, well-dressed man who'd been listening took a step closer. "To be sure, miss, it's a right cockup over in France, but I don't know what some expect them to do. The Germans're forever marching into their country and making trouble."

"Thank you, sir. May I have your name?"

He gave it and strode away, probably proud of being the voice of fairness among all the critics.

Kate glanced over the pages of her pad. She had a dozen quotes, several from women, and a range of opinions. Any more would be too repetitive. She tucked away her pad and pen and donned her gloves.

There was no easy way to take the Underground to the office in Manchester Square from here. At least it was a lovely day for a walk. On the way, she started writing the story in her head.

As on Oxford Street, many of the shops along the way now had sandbags piled in front of their windows, and some of the windows bore X-shaped tape, supposedly to hold them together in a blast so they didn't generate shrapnel.

The people, though, carried on. Women still wore pretty hats and gloves and fixed their makeup just so. Men still dressed in suits. People walking together talked and smiled.

Here and there, though, someone carried a gas mask. Or looked worried, though that could've been for any reason. As Kate passed Cavendish Square with its round greensward and garden in the center, she met a sixtyish woman whose expression was blank. Unreadable.

Well, we all have our own ways of coping.

By the time she reached Manchester Square and entered the office, she had most of the story organized in her head.

May greeted her with a smile. "You've a message, Kate."

She accepted the slip of paper and glanced at it. *Ring Major Mainwaring*, it read.

Sebastian. Her mind flashed back to last night's almost-kiss and the warmth and tenderness in his face.

No. There was no sense indulging that attraction.

Shaking her head, Kate pushed the memory away. She removed her hat, hanging it on the coat tree, tucked her gloves into her bag, and stowed it in her lower desk drawer. Only then did she allow herself to call the war office. She asked for Sebastian and waited.

"Major Mainwaring," his deep voice said, and another irrational little squiggle of happiness ran through her.

Stop that, she chided it. "It's Kate, returning your call."

"Good morning." The warmth in his voice was gratifying, and she gave herself another mental kick. He continued, "I've an invitation for you, a house party where some gentlemen with fascist leanings will be present. I'm invited and can bring a guest. If you come, we'll need to disclose that you're a journalist and promise you'll quote no one without permission. You might well land an interview, though. What do you say?"

"Are you kidding? Of course I'll come, but I may need some advice from Rose about what to wear."

"She loves to advise people," he replied, his voice dry, "so I'm sure she'll happily drop a wagonload of suggestions on you."

"I welcome them."

"Be careful what you say." He paused. "I suppose you've heard the prime minister will address Parliament today. The BBC will broadcast the speech afterward, at nine tonight. Rosie wanted me to invite you to stay over so you can listen with us and needn't go home after dark. If you leave before the speech, that won't give us much time for lessons."

"I hate to impose yet again." Or to risk growing closer to these distant relatives.

"We're kin, however remote the connection. You're always welcome. We can skip lessons tonight, of course. If you prefer."

That was the smart option. She should go back to her flat, have dinner with Marge or Betty or Janet, whoever was home, and listen to it with them. But she also wanted to know what Sebastian thought, and only in part because he was with the war office. His soldier's viewpoint, even if she couldn't print it, might be enlightening.

"Let me ask you something, Sebastian. I've been assuming dinner and lessons would be occasional meetings, but I get the impression you see them occurring more often."

Silence, and then he replied, "I apologize for not making myself clear. I assumed we would have dinner and lessons daily until you mastered your Gifts. The more lessons you have, the faster you'll gain control. Rosie enjoys having company because John often works late and she dislikes dining alone. We both thought a relaxing meal with an immediate segue to practicing your Gift would save time. Of course, you needn't fall in with that scheme if it doesn't suit you."

Unfortunately, what he said made sense. The idea of imposing on his sister, whose kinship was extremely distant, no matter how she and Sebastian chose to treat it, was discomfiting. The idea of spending every evening with him…appealed far too much. Dangerously much. Yet failing to master these new abilities would prevent her from helping the war effort and might even lead to another cascade that was mentally paralyzing.

"Kate?"

"I'm thinking."

Common sense required her to manage her Gifts. Honor required her to use them against the Nazis to the extent she could. If that put her heart at risk—and that voice, that *knowing* deep inside her, warned it surely would—she would simply have to deal with that.

"Thank you, Sebastian, and please thank Rose. I'll bring a bag tonight. As for daily lessons, I see the logic behind that. I'll be there unless I have to work."

"As will I. Duty does occasionally call in the evening. Rose has a couple of leads on other stories you might want to cover. She can discuss them with you over dinner. Any word from your boss?"

"Not so far. I think he's waiting to hear from New York." There was no sense telling Sebastian the Officers' Sunday Club story probably wouldn't be enough. He and his sister were doing what they could to help, supposedly because they were kin. Kate had a hunch, though, that they were also doing it because they were kind people who liked to be helpful.

That would be fine if one of those kind cousins were not also dangerously attractive. Kate sighed. She needed the lessons and the career help, so she would simply have to keep her emotions under control.

～

Because Rose's husband, John, had to work late, only she, Kate, and Sebastian sat at the dining table with its snowy linen and elegant china and beautiful silver and crystal. The linen and silver seemed less intimidating this time, but Kate knew better than to let herself begin thinking this was normal. For people like her, it wasn't.

After a dinner of roasted chicken, fresh bread, peas, and creamy trifle, Rose poured tea for everyone. Seated across from Sebastian, Kate turned to Rose. "This was a wonderful meal. Thank you."

Rose smiled. "We're glad you're able to join us, Kate, tonight and going forward. Seb tells me you don't want to impose, so let me assure you that you aren't. I enjoy knowing I won't be sitting here alone to eat. The house is so dreadfully quiet without the boys. When John works late, I feel a bit like an old pebble rattling around in a boot."

"That's very kind, Rose. With everything rationed, though, I feel guilty eating here so often. I would gladly use some of my ration coupons to bring meat or vegetables."

Rose and her brother exchanged a startled look.

"Let me explain something," Sebastian said. "As soon as the government started the Dig for Victory campaign last year, we put in a large vegetable garden at Hawkstowe. The staff have been canning since the first crops came in. We also financed allotments for all the villages near our properties. We have sheep on our lands at Hawkstowe. In addition, we raise chickens and helped others start doing so. The estate lake is stocked with trout, and the rivers on our properties have various sorts of fish, including salmon at the old hunting box in Scotland. The villagers nearby have permission to hunt and fish on our lands, with limits to ensure the game isn't hunted to extinction. Fish isn't rationed, at least not yet, so it's a good substitute when other meats are scarce."

"That's very generous." They could've kept all that bounty for themselves. Instead, they'd shared with neighbors who had fewer resources.

"It was Seb's idea." Rose leaned forward. "The ration coupons are adequate, but having extra allows us more flexibility and will allow us to donate some if the need arises."

"As it almost certainly will at some point," Sebastian said, his eyes grim.

"How are your sons?" Kate asked.

Rose's face lit. "They're doing very well, thank you. Most of the staff at Borrowdale have known them from infancy, and the boys are used to being with them. Mum's there from Hawkstowe, of course, and our brother, James, stops in from time to time. We've also opened the house to children evacuated from London, so Thomas and Frank have plenty of company."

Quietly, Sebastian added, "I expect James will join up soon. Having the other children there gives Mum something to do besides worry."

Of course she worried. Sebastian remained in the army, though injured, and now his brother was going into uniform.

"Do you know what he wants to do?" Kate asked.

"Royal Navy, I expect," Sebastian replied. "He dislikes flying, so that rules out the RAF. He's always loved the water, so the army wouldn't suit." He took another sip of tea and smiled. "Kate, we've about ninety minutes before Winston's speech. Ready to put that time to use?"

"Yes, of course."

Together they walked upstairs to the same parlor as before. Someone had set out a crystal pitcher of lemon squash, glasses, and a plate of dark biscuits. The candlestick stood on the low table.

As they sat, Sebastian said, "I've an idea that might make this go more smoothly. When you use your strategy that makes you invisible, what do you do?"

"I concentrate on not being seen."

"That's all?" When she nodded, he continued, "Please do that now."

"All right." She closed her eyes and tried to blank out everything in the room. *Don't see me, don't see me, don't see me...*

After a long minute, Sebastian said, "I still see you."

"Drat." Kate opened her eyes. "It's hard because now I'm self-conscious."

"What if I don't watch you?"

"That might help." She wasn't sure, though. How could she be when she'd never done this intentionally before?

Without using his cane, he limped to the window, where soft evening light filtered into the room. He faced out to the street and closed the blackout curtains. "Try it now."

Kate closed her eyes again. *Don't see me, don't see me...*

Time passed, but she wasn't sure how much, before Sebastian spoke. "Now try to keep me from seeing your right index finger. Only that one finger. I'm turning round again now."

Kate shifted her attention to that digit. She could still feel it. If she opened her eyes, she likely would see it. She never lost sight of herself when hiding.

"You had it," he said, "but you lost it. I see all of you now. Try again."

Taking a grip on her patience, she complied.

On the fourth try, he softly said, "Very good. I can see you except for your right forearm. Do you feel the power around your finger?"

"Um..." The sensation in her forearm echoed what she'd felt when she touched his power. "I think so."

"Very good. Now push that power to the tip of your finger... Oh, well done."

Kate tamped down a wave of excitement. Doing it this way, using the magic the way she always had, came naturally.

"Hold it steady and listen. I want you to envision that power swirling above your fingertip... Oh, almost. Try again."

She had to start over with the hiding, but directing the power to her hand and then to her finger was easier this time. When she pushed it up to her fingertip, it flowed smoothly into an eddy above her finger.

"Now think of that swirl of power as fire."

Sparks flickered like fizz over her fingertip, then died.

"I did it a little," she said, opening her eyes, "didn't I?"

"Indeed you did. Your casual use of your power, infusing intention or desire with it, may be the key to your mastering it. Formal exercises may actually hinder you. Try it again."

Kate concentrated on the power around her and on its shift to her right forearm. It was like a fizzy breeze moving under her skin—spooky and yet familiar because she'd been evoking power this way since childhood.

Gradually, she pushed it into her hand and then up her finger. Then into the swirl. She drew on the memory of Sebastian using witchlight. A rush of power along her arm startled her, but she managed not to release the power. Holding fast to the swirl above her hand, Kate opened her eyes.

Above her right index finger hovered a sparkly swirl of green flame. She gasped, delighted and yet afraid to move lest she lose it.

Sebastian grinned at her and seated himself. "Point it at the candle and imagine it moving from your finger to the wick."

Again she called on the memory of what he'd done. Green witchfire flowed around the candle wick, and yellow flame appeared within it.

"Oh, well done indeed," Sebastian said, and Kate released the power. It flowed back to its usual spot below her heart.

She smiled so widely that her cheeks hurt. Sebastian's grin hadn't faded.

"Brilliant, Kate." He squeezed her left hand on her knee. The contact sent awareness of him flashing up her arm and ignited a different kind of bubbly warmth deep in her body. She returned the hand squeeze.

Sebastian's grin and her smile faded. They stared at each other. His eyes softened and warmed, and the bubbling inside her became yearning. If she leaned in—

No. That would be a mistake.

He realized it too, for his expression cooled as she withdrew her hand.

Sebastian topped up their glasses. He was giving them both time to settle.

Kate set a napkin from the tray in front of him and unfolded one on her knee. He took a biscuit from the plate she offered but didn't look at her.

That was fine. She wasn't looking directly at him either. Better not, at least for a moment or two.

As she set the plate down, her gaze fell on the glasses of squash he'd poured. Candlelight flickering on the surface of the liquid and the gleaming facets of the crystal brought her pride and satisfaction rolling back.

She could learn this. It would give her a way to help with the war effort and even, maybe, help save her career.

"It's nearly time for Winston," Sebastian commented. "If you like, we can practice with the candle a few more times afterward."

"That's probably a good idea. Um, do you call him Winston because you know him or…just because?"

"Many people think of him as Winston." Sebastian rose and edged around the table. He wasn't using his cane, but he moved very deliberately. "That's a good trick on his part, convincing everyone from laborers to barristers to think of him, a duke's grandson, as one of their mates."

The radio, a burnished wood case about two feet tall and eighteen inches wide, sat on a bookshelf that gleamed with polish. The radio's case had three rounded peaks on the top, the highest in the center and the other two equal. A speaker, the on/off and volume knobs, and the tuning dial were embedded in the center panel. Sebastian turned it on, and classical music filtered into the room.

They were alone, and the longer they sat without talking, the more aware of him she became. His clean-cut profile in the soft lamplight, the intelligence in his eyes, and his dedication to duty all drew her. His sympathy and his concern for his less-fortunate neighbors also spoke well for him.

Their eyes met. They both looked away quickly, but her cheeks warmed. Tension crackled between them.

Oh, help!

Better to broach a difficult subject than let this whatever-it-was between them deepen. Besides, for all she knew, part of it might be her admiration for his mastery of his magic.

Kate cleared her throat. "I gather Miranda and Richard talk to you."

"Yes, and to many others." If he thought the question odd, it didn't show in his face or voice.

"Are they here now?"

He hesitated. "They may be in the house somewhere. They won't be in this room, nor would they have been in the dining room earlier. Miranda wanted to give you time to adjust to knowing they aren't imaginary."

"I wish I'd handled that better."

"They won't hold that against you. They want you to be happy. If not for the war, they would've let you be about the magic." He looked directly into her eyes. "So would I."

That strange internal knowing confirmed it. He did regret having to push her where she was still a bit reluctant go. But he was a man who did his duty.

"Now, though, your country needs us both."

He nodded. "Thank you, Kate, for understanding that."

"I'm thick-headed, but I do eventually see past my nose." With a sigh, she added, "I suspect my fate was sealed when I went to France. I think you're right that the experience broke down barriers in some way. If that's so, I would be much worse off without your help and Rose's."

"It's my privilege."

Their gazes locked again, with the warmth in his like a caress over her heart.

Sebastian wrenched his eyes to the side.

A moment later, Rose joined them. The difficult moment passed.

"I have a couple of other story possibilities for you," Rose said. "It occurs to me that your farming background makes you would be uniquely well suited to cover the Women's Land Army."

"Food production is vital," Sebastian said, resuming his seat. "We import much of our food, and we'd be fools to count on that continuing undisrupted."

Because of course the Nazis would go after the food supply. At least Britain anticipated that and was taking steps to compensate.

Rose added, "I believe I can also help you gain access to the Local Defense Volunteers."

"I can help there too," Sebastian said.

"That's all very kind. Much more than I expected when you offered me help."

Rose glanced at her brother. "You're our cousin, Kate, however distant. You're also Gifted. That makes you family twice over. So of course we'll help you in any way we can."

Kate smiled her thanks. Maybe the *family* bit was the key to reorienting her view of Sebastian. If she could come to think of him as she did of her cousins back home, there wouldn't be any of these disturbing moments of attraction.

~

The announcer interrupted the regularly scheduled dance music and introduced Churchill. Sebastian watched Kate. She listened with her eyes slightly unfocused, her mind fully on the speech. Surely there was no harm in admiring her determination to master her Gift, the honor she demonstrated by vowing to use it in the Allied cause, or her tenacity in doing her job. As for admiring the fall of her hair onto her shoulders, the way the light glinted on the strands caught back in combs at the side, and the soft blue of her eyes, well...*there be dragons.*

Winston started by recapping the Dunkirk evacuation, the ensuing rearguard actions, and the resulting losses as well as the successful return of many of those who'd fought elsewhere in France. Others still battled there despite the French request for terms of surrender.

Sebastian rubbed a hand over his jaw. Today was the one hundred twenty-fifth anniversary of Waterloo, which the British and Allied commander, Lord Wellington, had described as "a near run thing." So, too, had been the evacuation from Dunkirk. And so would be the battle ahead, especially if the Yanks kept to their resolve to stay out of it.

Winston shifted his focus to the Royal Navy. Of course he took pride in it, having been First Lord of the Admiralty. Thus he dismissed the Italian navy's threat to come out of the Mediterranean and make trouble.

In the armchair to Sebastian's right, Kate fidgeted slightly, frowning.

Keeping an eye on her, he turned his attention back to the speech. The prime minister now assured the nation its navy could defeat any large invasion force coming by sea.

Kate blinked. Her shoulders tensed.

"Kate?" he asked.

Rose's head snapped around.

"I'm all right," Kate answered through gritted teeth. "Really."

Bloody hell if she was, but he would stay back unless she asked for help. Perhaps she was controlling whatever vision had come to her. Examining it.

Now the speech moved to the resources and skills of Fighter Command and Bomber Command. Called the British people to strengthen their resolve.

Throughout, Kate's frown deepened. Her eyes looked less focused, as though her sight were turned inward.

Sebastian kept himself in his seat by force of will. Rose watched Kate with a troubled look on her face.

Sebastian shook his head at his sister. "Wait," he mouthed softly.

Churchill finished. Next would be a speech by General Charles de Gaulle, self-proclaimed leader of the Free French forces.

Kate didn't react to the program change. Lines of strain appeared in her face.

"Sebastian," she croaked, holding out her left hand.

He gripped it. "I'm here."

"I can't...I can't break out of it, but I think maybe I shouldn't. This feels important."

"What do you See?" he asked. He didn't feed magic into their clasped hands. She hadn't asked him to help her out of this.

Rose, doubtless wanting something to do, refilled Kate's glass.

"Boats. Many, many boats along a coastline, facing the sea."

"Describe them."

"They're...like barges. But some are bigger. Ships. Troop carriers. They...there are tanks rolling aboard some of the barges. German tanks."

This was not a present vision. Britain had Germany well and truly beaten in photoreconnaissance. Both the war office and the Merlin Club would've known if the Nazis had boats massing in France.

"I've seen these boats before," she murmured. "Right after my return from France. I dismissed them as a bad dream. I dismissed so much as dreams, and now I wish I'd paid attention. That I'd remembered."

"You're seeing it now. As for earlier visions, you can summon them by thinking of them and willing them to appear."

"Okay. It's...Dear God, there are hundreds of them. Maybe thousands..."

For several seconds, she said nothing.

Sebastian tightened his hold. "Kate?"

Her face turned pale. Her lips trembled.

"Kate!"

No response. He looked to Rose, who nodded.

Sebastian fed magic into her hand. "Come back to me, Kate."

"S-sebastian?" But her gaze remained unfocused, her head turned toward the wireless.

"Yes, my dear." Carefully, he fed her more magic. "Listen to my voice. Imagine you're talking to me in the place you like best."

"The orchard. At home." Her lips trembled. "They won't—I hope they'll understand when they know."

If they turned her away, they were heartless fools. Fools he would make regret it.

Slowly, her eyes regained focus. After a few moments, she closed them. "I see the orchard now. Only the orchard."

"Open your eyes and look at us."

She did, and he smiled at her. "Are you fully with us now?"

Kate nodded. "Thank you."

Her smile trembled slightly at the edges, but she was trying. When she picked up her drink, her hand was steady.

"Have a biscuit," Rose suggested. "Magic burns your body's fuel. You must always eat after any extensive use of it."

"I am a bit hungry," Kate admitted.

Rose stood. "I don't care to listen to General de Gaulle. Do either of you mind if I turn that off?"

They shook their heads, so she shut it off. "I thought Winston did rather well," she said. "It was a rousing call to arms."

Yes, and it was just too bad they still had very little equipment to repel an invasion. Sebastian didn't say so, though. He and Rose discussed the speech while Kate nibbled a second biscuit and sipped squash.

When her color returned to normal, Sebastian cleared his throat. "Kate, do you mind answering some questions?"

"No." She looked doubtful, though. "If doing that pulls me back into it, you'll help me out, right?"

"Of course. It shouldn't, but we can deal with it if that happens." When she nodded, he asked, "Could you tell when this vision occurred?"

"Not fall or winter. Maybe not spring." Frowning, she added, "All the trees were fully leaved, and everything was green."

"So most likely it was summer?" he asked.

"Most likely." Doubt darkened her eyes. "I can't be sure, though."

"Of course. Don't worry about it." Meanwhile, he would worry more than enough for the both of them. If she was seeing this summer, how much time did they have to prepare?

CHAPTER 13

The next morning, Sebastian stopped by the Merlin Club before going to work. Genevieve greeted him with a smile and called for another teacup. Pouring for him, she said, "It's still strange to see you so early. You used to stop in after work, even have a meal now and again."

He shrugged. "Evenings are busy. I'm determined to bring Kate along as quickly as possible."

"Of course." Genevieve sipped her tea. "How is she doing?"

"Fairly well, actually." He filled Genevieve in on Kate's progress. "She is resolved to use her Gift against the Nazis."

"That's wonderful news." Running an elegantly manicured fingertip around the rim of her cup, Genevieve added, "So she has both common sense and a sense of duty."

"Indeed." Hearing someone assess Kate that way made his teeth lock, but he held back any sharp comment. Genevieve meant well, and as Director of the Merlin Club, she needed to know the state of all Gifted assets in the realm.

"I had a letter from Lachlan MacGregor," she said. "He'll be in London next week. His son Kenneth is mad for the navy, and Lachlan talked him into one last family visit to London before he enlists." Grimacing, she added, "I must break this habit of thinking of him as a lad. He's twenty-three."

"That makes me feel old," Sebastian commented.

"Welcome to the club. I suspect the entire family will come along."

"I expect so, and I'll be particularly glad to see Lachlan. Genevieve, Kate's latest vision worries me. This isn't the first time she's had it, but she previously dismissed it as a bad dream. It shows a serious threat in the not-so-distant future. As Mage Laird of the Isles, Lachlan can muster impressive offensive power."

The Mages of the Isles were the Scottish Gifted's secret warriors, a cadre sworn to defend Scotland as the Merlin Club and its members swore to defend Britain. The Scottish wizards, though, could blast magical energy with a force and over a distance very few English ones could match. As the mage laird and thus their chief, Lachlan directed the use of that ability.

Genevieve replied, "Not if many of his young men go to war and his young women take up their jobs."

"We'll deal with that if we must."

Thinking how to put this, Sebastian sipped tea again. "Kate saw a great many boats, and our intelligence says the Germans would need at least a couple of thousand to bring over enough soldiers and tanks to gain an operational foothold."

"Probably true. Considering that, I'm not at all certain even the offensive power of the MacGregors and the other Mages of the Isles will be enough."

"It's too bad the Scots keep that secret so close, but you can't blame them. As we've often said, many of our kind would stop at nothing to gain that power."

"Granted, but we certainly could use it now." Genevieve shook her head. "What are you dealing with today, if I may ask?"

"I leave later this morning for the Channel Islands. We're evacuating them, starting today, and Secretary Eden wants a liaison there."

"I pity the people leaving their homes, but I suppose there's no help for it. Those islands are too close to occupied France. 'Occupied France.' Christ, what a dreadful phrase."

"I can't argue with that. 'Occupied Britain' would be worse, though."

"Indeed it would."

Sebastian glanced at his watch and rose. "I must go. I've matters to attend to before I catch my train."

"Before you go, one thing. Do you think your protégée would make a good agent for us? If so, do you think she would agree to join us?"

Kate join the Merlin Club? If she joined, he wouldn't need to keep the club's doings secret from her. They could share more tasks. He liked the idea.

She might not, though.

"Let's see how things go. If the time seems right, I'll broach the subject."

"Fair enough. Be careful, Sebastian."

"Always." He would be doubly so when it came to anything involving both Kate and the Merlin Club. If he brought her in and she wasn't ready, that would lead to catastrophe. Best to be cautious and see how things went.

No word came about Kate's job. The days passed slowly. She collected impromptu reactions to Churchill's speech and de Gaulle's and wrote an article about travel around the city during the blackout. Lew arranged for her to interview a member of the Commons from Portsmouth, location of a famous navy yard. With Rose's help, she gained an interview with General Sir Edmund Ironsides, commander of the Local Defense Volunteers. She'd submitted that story yesterday.

She filed her stories without expecting them to help save her place here. Changing the executives' minds about a woman in a war zone would take not merely a good story but a spectacular one.

She'd forgotten to ask Sebastian to arrange a meeting with Richard and Miranda. The idea of meeting with a ghost felt like something out of a movie, *Topper* or something like it, maybe, but they were part of the strange new world she'd stepped into. She paid her debts, even when the currency was an apology. But now that had to wait until he returned.

Friday, she had dinner with her flatmates. They pooled their ration coupons for chicken, which they stretched by making it into stew, and for a salad. They shared a pot of tea with the meal.

They did the dishes down in the kitchen together and settled into their little parlor afterward with the tea and lemon biscuits they'd used their sugar ration to make. At least tea wasn't yet rationed, though it would certainly be before much longer.

Marge Henderson, a statuesque brunette in her thirties who worked for United Press International, tucked her legs up under her skirt. "Kate,

I've hardly seen you, and I'm dying to hear about your fabulous titled relatives."

"Who's this?" Janet Cooper demanded, helping herself to a biscuit. "What did I miss?"

The slender, brown-haired woman was the London correspondent for the *Yorkshire Clarion*. This past week, she'd been up in Yorkshire helping to cover the local war effort.

"It's nothing," Kate said. "As I mentioned to Betty a few days ago, I discovered some cousins here in London, Sebastian Mainwaring and his sister, Rose. He's the Earl of Hawkstowe, and she's the Countess of Borrowdale, though neither of them seems to set much store by the titles. They've taken me under their wing, and we've been getting acquainted."

Meanwhile, Kate was sitting on the biggest scoop of the twentieth century, the fact that magic was real. She couldn't print it, of course, and even if she did, people were more likely to think her a lunatic than to believe it.

"You look tired, Kate," Janet said. "Is anything the matter?"

Besides distressing visions of disaster, which she couldn't share? "I'm still worried about my job. Lew hasn't heard from New York, and I just…I have a bad feeling that what I've done won't be enough to convince them to keep me."

She was trying very hard not to attribute that feeling to her seer Gift. If it came from that, as she understood matters, it was accurate and her job was doomed.

Kate sipped tea while the other women waited. They might joke and tease each other, but they were also loyal. Even though they worked for competing news services.

"The good stories are here," she said, "not back in the States." Her spot on the government beat in Baltimore had probably already been reassigned. Then what would she do? Write about teas and charity fundraisers while Europe blew up?

The others all nodded agreement.

"What else do you have planned?" Marge asked.

"I'm to go to Dorset tomorrow and interview members of the Women's Land Army. Lew lined me up an interview with a family installing an Anderson shelter in their yard on Monday." The semicircular metal tubes sunk into the ground about halfway down with dirt on top didn't look like very effective shelters, but everyone seemed to think they were better than nothing.

"Meanwhile, I've filed an interview with General Sir Edmund Ironside about the Local Defense Volunteers."

"Those should impress your New York bosses," Betty said. The curvy blonde poured more tea into her cup.

Marge put in, "Especially that last."

"We'll see." Kate shrugged.

"Any other prospects?" Betty asked.

"Rose arranged for me to attend a house party next weekend. Some people interested in politics are expected to be there, so that might produce something useful."

Janet smiled. "It's good of them to help you."

"I would love to have a countess help me," Marge added.

Betty grinned. "I'd rather have a countess's wardrobe, but I would also like a mansion in Hollywood and a date with Gary Cooper. I'm used to doing without."

They all laughed at that, and the conversation turned to work.

While her friends' talk ebbed and flowed around her, Kate followed it absently. Sebastian would return tomorrow, which meant lessons resuming. There was still no word from New York.

Maybe it was a good sign. Maybe. But she wouldn't have anything solid to follow up the Officers' Sunday Club story until later this week. By then, it might be too late.

The next afternoon, with Janet and Marge visiting friends and Betty out for a walk, Kate had the flat to herself. The quiet was welcome. Her subscription to the London Library gave her access to a wide range of reading matter, but she had little time to read.

Her current book, a volume of Robert Burns's poems, failed to hold her attention. Maybe living on the edge of a war made idyllic poetry feel too distant for an effective distraction.

The distant sound of the phone ringing caught her attention. The six main flats in this building shared a telephone on the first-floor landing. The smaller one at the top had a phone outside its door.

Kate hurried to the door, but the ringing stopped. Standing in the open doorway, she waited to see whether the call was for her.

Sure enough, the voice of the man on the first floor, a shop clerk, called, "Kate Shaw? You there?"

"Coming," she called, and she hurried down to the landing. The phone sat on a table in one corner, the receiver lying next to the handset.

Picking it up, she said, "Kate Shaw."

"Kate, it's Sebastian."

A smile spread over her face. "Welcome back." Did this mean they were having lessons tonight?

"Thanks. How was your week?"

His voice sounded strained. Hearing it, she *knew*, in that weird way she was slowly becoming accustomed to, that his knee was hurting him a great deal. Into her mind flashed an image of him sitting on a four-poster bed in a room with dark, masculine furnishings.

Oh, far too intrusive, that. She banished it quickly and was pleased she could.

"Busy enough," she answered. "I did some impromptu interviews about the speeches and a few other things."

"Do you still want to go to Peterborough this weekend?"

"If it's convenient, yes, but if you need to cancel, that's fine."

"No, we're going." A pause, and then he said, "This has been rather a long week for me. Would you mind if we resume your lessons tomorrow instead of tonight?"

"Of course not. We can wait longer if you're busy." She'd almost said *if you need to rest* but had realized just in time that the suggestion would mortify him.

"Tomorrow will do. Kate, Richard and Miranda were concerned about your vision cascade, and I forgot to ask whether they had checked on you. Have you seen them?"

"No." She had to choose her words carefully out here on the landing. "If you see them, could you ask Miranda to come see me? I would like to mend fences."

"I'm sure that's not necessary."

"It is to me. Will you help me arrange it?"

"Of course. Miranda has been keeping Rose company while I've been gone and John has been working. If she's still there, shall I send her over or ring you back?"

"The phone's on the landing, so you don't need to call back unless she isn't there. Thank you, Sebastian." Although she hadn't let herself admit it, she'd missed the ghostly companions of her childhood.

"It's no trouble," he assured her.

Still, she should shoo him off the phone. The sooner he stopped worrying about her, the sooner he could do whatever he did to relieve the pain in his leg.

An image flashed into her head, Sebastian chest-deep in a bathtub. Heat swamped Kate's cheeks, but not enough to keep her from noticing similar heat low in her body. "Well…you must have things to do after being away. I won't keep you."

"If I don't ring you back, expect Miranda shortly."

Kate thanked him, and they hung up. She went back to the flat. Now, however, the book interested her even less. How did a person apologize to a ghost?

Unable to sit still, she paced.

She marched toward the window and back through the sitting area, pivoted, and headed back toward the window. All the while, she listened for the phone. Surely Sebastian would have called if Miranda wasn't coming.

Kate turned at the window and froze. Miranda stood in front of the door, its outlines visible through her body and her green gown.

The ghost offered a rueful smile. "I apologize for not knocking. That is one thing I can no longer do."

"Of course." Now that Kate's many-times-great grandmother had arrived, what should Kate say? Nothing came to mind.

You're a journalist. Words are your living. Say something. Yet so much had changed between her and Miranda that it left her flummoxed.

"Ah, come in," she finally managed. "Have a seat. That is…if you sit?"

Inwardly, Kate winced. Both Miranda and Richard had sat beside her many times in encounters she'd believed were dreams.

Miranda settled onto the chintz-covered chair by the loveseat and smiled at her. "It's good to see you."

"I've missed you. I didn't mean to drive you way."

"Of course not." Gently, Miranda said, "You were taken by surprise. I upended what you'd always believed about Richard and me and told you something you'd always accepted about the world, the absence of magic, was false."

"That wasn't your fault." Like the dream figments Kate had believed Miranda and Richard to be, ghosts probably didn't drink anything. The impulse to offer her visitor some tea was likely pointless.

"Perhaps not, but if we had told you the truth earlier in your life, matters might have gone differently." Miranda shrugged. "All that's done.

Richard and I would like to resume our visits, but we wanted to be sure you'd come to terms with our being ghosts."

"I've had so much else to come to terms with," Kate told her, "that you and Richard being ghosts is next to nothing."

"I'm glad, and Richard will be as well. Sebastian may have told you I also am a seer. It was I who brought that Gift into the Mainwaring line. I may be able to help you master it."

"I need help." Cocking her head, Kate asked, "Has Sebastian or Rose told you about my lessons?"

"A bit about your progress but nothing about any personal information you may have shared with them."

"You know pretty much everything personal anyway." Kate mustered a smile. When Miranda smiled back at her, it eased Kate's nerves.

"Why don't you tell me what's difficult for you and what you've mastered, and perhaps I can make some suggestions."

"I would appreciate that."

"Before we begin, I've a piece of advice to offer. Don't try to rush yourself. This is the most contrary of Gifts, the most difficult to manage. Impatience will lead to frustration, and frustration blocks progress."

"Sebastian told me something like that." Kate blew out a breath. "What you said makes sense."

"I'm glad. Now tell me about your lessons."

Kate nodded. Now that Kate had had time to adjust to the idea, Miranda being a ghost didn't matter. What mattered more was that she'd been part of Kate's life, a supportive friend, since she could remember.

"It's hard not to be impatient," Kate said, and she told Miranda about the vision of boats on the French coast.

"That's worrisome indeed. Let us see what we may do to refine it and those visions you had of bombings and battles."

The warm water leached some of the pain from Sebastian's leg. He'd done too much walking in Guernsey. Had rested it too little. But his Gift warned him time ran short. The islands lay far too close to the French coast and its German occupiers and far too distant from the south of England to be defensible. Sooner or later, and he knew it would be sooner, the Nazis would pounce.

He took a small sip of brandy, savoring the heat as it went down. In his dressing room, he had a potion mixed by a Merlin Club doctor, Galen Wesley. It would fuzz his wits to disconnect him from the pain, and he didn't like not having his full senses. He took it only when he couldn't sleep otherwise.

This was shaping up to be one of those nights.

Not enough people evacuated. Not well organized and plagued by contradictory, confusing messages. Sign up, stay, sign up, stay, send children if you stay, don't send them, have to leave pets and homes. In the end, too many people had remained behind, either because of transport shortages or because they refused to go. Soon they would be beyond any help Britain might offer.

On top of all that, France had surrendered today. That had been inevitable, but having expected it provided no defense against its demoralizing effect.

The water was cooling. He could warm it again magically, but his fingers already looked like pale prunes. Perhaps he should get out.

Mulling over his choices, he took another swallow of brandy.

A shimmer at the foot of the tub heralded a visitor. When the form became clear, Sebastian's brows rose. "This is a surprise. I didn't expect you, Miles. Come to that, I've never had reason to expect you."

"Not since you were a babe, but you probably don't recall those visits." Sir Miles Mainwaring, captain of the *Queen's Honor* against the Armada of 1588, stood at the end of the tub. As usual, he wore the puffy breeches, thigh-high boots, and waist-length tunic with ruff of his era. "You were a cute lad, to be sure."

"Ah, thanks. What brings you here? The list of Wyndon properties?"

"Aye. I've been to their seat in Kent. Nothing about its wards seems unusual."

"Where are you going next?" Miles looked well, not at all as though he were fading. Still, perhaps Sebastian should visit the afterworld. See everyone. He hadn't lately.

"I haven't decided." Miles shrugged. "Your father's learning German. He seems to think one of us must, and it occupies his time. Your brother, too."

Yet another reference to needing the time filled.

Sebastian wasn't supposed to know about the fading, but perhaps he could come at the issue from the flank. "Are you growing bored? Is watching the world not enough to occupy you?"

"After a few centuries, any pastime palls." The ghost sighed. "In truth, lad, many of us are coming to think we may never be free. Edmund keeps to himself, likely out of guilt but possibly because some resent him more with each passing year."

"I'm sorry," Sebastian said. The words felt entirely inadequate. He couldn't blame his kinsmen for resenting the man who had cursed them all, but he knew Edmund regretted having done so. Not that his regret made anything better.

"I'm torn between my duty to all of you and my duty to king and country. Just now, the latter seems more urgent."

"And so it is." Miles nodded. "When the Armada assailed our shores, d'ye think any of us would've stayed home and let England burn? No sane man wants to be remembered for that."

"This isn't quite the same case." The water was definitely cool now. Sebastian shifted, trying to find a more comfortable position.

"If you turn your back on your duty to King George, you might save thirty or so of us. If the Nazis take England, they'll doom thousands to live under their cruel rule."

"That doesn't depend solely on me."

Was there some way he could search for proof to lift the curse on weekends? Would Rosie join the hunt? Archives had little appeal for her, but she was dogged in pursuit of any task. Or could Kate assist, once she mastered her Gift? There had never been two seers working together on the problem.

"Your duty, Lord Hawkstowe, lies first with your king, then with the folk of Hawkstowe, and then with everyone in these isles. Those of us trapped here, we've had our lives. If our afterlives have been not quite what we hoped, well, there's still a chance to redeem them."

He didn't sound convinced, though.

Sebastian sent a pulse of magic into the water to warm it.

Miles frowned at him. "I saw that. If the water's going cold, you should climb out before you make your knee worse."

He was probably right. Regardless, Sebastian was tired of being in the tub.

Miles's head swung suddenly to the left, toward something Sebastian couldn't see. He frowned but looked more worried than annoyed. "I'm coming, Richard. Straight away."

"Miles?" Sebastian asked. "What is it?"

What could worry Miles? Aside from the wraiths, the skeletal, ghastly remnants of souls doomed to stay in the afterworld until they atoned for their worldly sins, the shadow realm's only inhabitants were the souls of the cursed Mainwarings.

"Nothing to concern you, lad," Miles assured him, still frowning. "Don't fret."

With that, he disappeared.

"'Fret?'" Sebastian demanded of the empty room. "'Don't 'fret'? I may be a few hundred years younger than you, but I'm a grown man, a major in His Majesty's army. I do not 'fret.'"

At least his father, his most frequent visitor other than Richard and Miranda, acknowledged that Sebastian was no longer a child. Sebastian didn't know what his brother Reginald thought. Reg couldn't visit him because Sebastian was not his descendant. Too bad. At least they could see each other when Sebastian entered the afterworld. Not that he had much time for roaming the shadowland these days. Still, he should go soon. When his leg didn't plague him as it did now.

He climbed out, always an awkward process, dried off quickly, and shrugged into his robe. Bradshaw would've set out the mustard oil, other herbs, and flannel for a mustard plaster in Sebastian's bedchamber. He limped down to it. Bradshaw had, as usual, also turned back the bed and closed the blackout curtains, though fussing with the bed was no part of a butler's duty.

It was just as well Kate didn't expect a lesson tonight. Sebastian was in no condition to give one. If he missed her…well, that was a warning sign. A nudge about keeping a bit more distance.

As he poured himself a brandy, the phone rang. The Bradshaws were gone for the night, so he answered it. "Hawkstowe." He always answered with his title. Outside the army, his family name was only for friends.

"Hello, Seb. Is everything all right?"

Rosie. He swallowed a groan. Thanks to his bloody knee, he'd forgotten to ring her.

"Yes, thanks. I was soaking my knee. I'm sorry." He stretched out on the bed, straightening the aching muscles.

"It happens. John's working late, so I've nothing to distract me. The music on the wireless isn't doing the job tonight."

"I let you down." He fed magic into the poultice to soften the now-dried mustard and applied it to his leg. The warmth did help.

"I've become accustomed to having you and Kate here in the evenings, I think. Since you weren't having a lesson, she left this evening for Dorset for the Women's Land Army story."

"Should be straight up her street as a farmer's daughter. How did last night's practice session go?"

"You sound tired. How's your knee?"

"I'm managing. What about Kate?"

"Miranda and I worked with her every night. She can light or snuff a candle easily now. Controlling witchfire still challenges her, but she's gaining control over it and any unexpected visions. She seems to be hitting her stride."

"How long will she be away?"

"She won't return until tomorrow evening."

"Well, she can probably use some time away from all of it, time to let the lessons sink in. She's truly determined to master it. Not only to avoid having cascades of visions but because it's the right thing to do." He took a swallow of brandy. "Her concern about her family's reactions makes her perseverance doubly admirable."

A long silence, and then Rose said, "How much are you admiring it, Seb? You sound…"

"It doesn't matter. I would wager a great deal of money Kate intends to return to Missouri after the war and put away much of what she's learned, aside from how to control her Gift, like a forgotten trunk in the attic."

"That's truly a shame on both counts. I rather like her. She's no Millicent looking for a coronet. I doubt Kate gives a fig for your title."

"She *is* an anti-monarchist American, after all."

"Some of them would love titles, regardless of what they say, but that's neither here nor there. About your knee—you should take a dose of your tisane. Between juggling Kate's lessons, your duty at the War Office, and your Merlin Club responsibilities, you need your rest."

"I'll consider it." But she was right.

"You do that. I'll expect you for dinner tomorrow."

Will Kate be there? He bit back the words. Whatever personal interest he felt in her was doomed, so there was no use indulging it. "I'll see you then. Thanks."

"Always."

Sebastian sat with his hand on the phone. He should take the tisane, ensure a good night's sleep, and start fresh in the morning. Every concession to his blasted leg, though, felt one step nearer the next concession, which was one step nearer the next one, and so on, and he would not, absolutely would not allow the injury to dictate his life.

He took the vial out of his wardrobe and swallowed a single sip. Settling in the bed, he stared up at the canopy.

Don't be a sulky child. You're still in the army. Count yourself blessed and deal with your bloody knee.

The tisane did its work, fuzzing his wits and rendering the pain a distant annoyance instead of a throbbing nuisance.

Slowly, he drifted into sleep.

Instead of oblivion, though, he found himself amid the stinking, purple-gray mists of the afterworld. Mainwaring men hared back and forth through the fog calling, "Walter! Walter Hawkstowe!"

Sebastian frowned. He reached out to snag Miles, but his hand passed through his great-grandfather's form. So this was truly a dream, his role limited to observing.

"Walter Mainwaring," Charles Mainwaring, Amelia's father, stalked past clad in the cutaway coat, breeches, and top boots of the Regency. "This is not amusing!"

Under the men's irritation, however, rolled a current of fear. Why? The ghosts of his doomed ancestors could easily banish any of the wraiths that tried to prey on living intruders or newly doomed souls. Besides, living intruders were rare. Amelia, Countess of Aysgarth, and her husband had traveled there but with Richard and Miranda's help. A chance remark of Richard's had implied other living wizards had penetrated that realm, but he'd refused to explain. He'd told Sebastian to forget it.

But what if that had happened now? What if someone hostile to the ghosts… But surely mere magic couldn't kill someone already dead.

Robert Mainwaring, Richard's father, stalked through the distant fog. Like his son, he still wore the clothing of his era.

"Sebastian. Seb, wake up."

"Dad?"

Sebastian fought his way out of the dream, shaking off the fog of the tisane. Beside his bed stood his father. The features so like his own bore lines that looked deeper now. The loose trousers, open-throated shirt and jumper were what his father had favored in life.

"Are you awake, my boy?" Reginald Mainwaring eased down onto the edge of the bed. The bedposts and the room's furniture showed through his spectral form.

"What is it?" Sebastian pushed himself up in bed, fortunately with little complaint from his leg because of the tisane.

"We've a problem worse than fading. Walter Mainwaring, Edmund's great grandson and Miles's father, has disappeared. We can't find him anywhere, and I want you to help us look."

This must be the reason Richard had called Miles away earlier. "How is that possible? Where else could he go?"

"That's what I hope your Gift can determine." The elder Lord Hawkstowe's ghost shook his head. "He has been dejected about the prospect of lifting the curse. Has threatened…well, to do away with himself. To let the wraiths destroy him."

"Is that—can he do that?"

Reginald shook his head. "Wraiths are violent. If a wizard offered no defense…possibly they might rend his soul into irrecoverable shreds. I hope that isn't what happened."

The image made Sebastian faintly ill. "I'll try to See…but my wits are fogged. Tisane. Damn it."

"If he has given himself to the wraiths, we can do nothing about it now. If he has not, tomorrow will be soon enough."

"Can't you go back in time to find him? Isn't that how Amelia and her Julian broke the rule keeping you in the years of your lives and let you move through time?"

"Aye, it is. We've tried that." His father blew out a heavy sigh that had no actual breath behind it. "The Merlin Club has a library. If you cannot See what happened, perhaps something there will tell us how to find him."

"Why would he choose to end himself in such a dreadful way?" Unfortunately, Sebastian had an uneasy feeling he already knew.

His father shrugged. "Hope is a fragile thing, son. Walter has waited a very long time to move on, and he's one of those who've begun to fear we never shall. Everyone is searching, and Edmund is distraught."

Of course he was. Edmund had started the family curse and brought its effects on all of them. That he hadn't expected it to endure so long was understandable, but so was the resentment of some of his descendants. The afterworld was a ghastly place. The ability to travel anywhere, anytime and observe the real world seemed like an intriguing benefit, but anything could pall after hundreds of years.

"I'll come there in the morning."

"No, go to the Merlin Club. See what you can See, but don't waste time coming here unless you discover something. We'll continue searching, of course." Shaking his head, Reginald said, "If he has destroyed himself, it will be a blow."

"How's Miranda taking it? And Richard?" Of all his distant ancestors, those two were the ones to whom Sebastian felt closest.

"They're very worried. Richard never says so, but I believe he also fears there will never be an end to this." His father sighed heavily.

"Are you safe?"

"Reg and I are managing. It's wearing on Richard and Miranda, though their Robin keeps his chin up yet. Miles manages. Edmund…I believe the curse prevents him from fading. He seems unutterably weary, though."

"Yet no one told me all this?" He might've done something. Helped in some way. Now these kindred souls were gone. "Meanwhile, I—"

"None of that. This is no more your fault than it is that of any other Mainwaring in the past four centuries who failed to find the evidence that will release us. This is why Richard didn't want you to know about Walter. I see it differently. You're in this with all of us, and you've a right to know everything. I trust you to handle it. Do your duty, use your Gift to look when you've time, and protect England from these vile Nazis."

"Sounds as though you're doing your part. Miles tells me you're learning German."

"Well, someone must. What use is it to infiltrate their meetings if one cannot understand what they say? Sitting in on German classes at Cambridge is far less interesting than it would be if I could go to the pub with classmates after, but it will do. At least the classrooms at Cambridge are not warded."

"Thank you, Dad." The war office had translators, of course, but writing down words in a language one didn't speak, especially in one with words as long as some in German, was nigh unto impossible. And a highly error-prone process.

"We must all do our duty," his father responded. "Yours is to look after England. I should go now and let you sleep."

As though he could after all that. Sebastian bade his father farewell and lay staring up at the bed canopy again. Despite the persistent fuzziness from the tisane, sleep refused to return.

If only he had an idea of how to help. Miles's search seemed like a long shot, but at least he was doing something. Besides, it wasn't as though the Mainwarings had any surer bet.

CHAPTER 14

Fighting still raged in France though Sebastian had said he didn't expect it to last much longer. The project that had brought Kate here, the Women's Land Army, had been created in response to the war. At the moment, though, battle and politics took a back seat to the smells of moist earth knocked off the women's boots, the dry scent of hay in the barn behind her for the livestock, and the fields of wheat and barley waving toward the horizon. Standing here was a decent substitute for being home.

Pad and pen in hand, Kate took a deep breath to savor the familiar smells. The wheat would grow into the late summer before harvest, but the barley would mature sooner. Both would help feed this country.

"Sorry to keep you waiting." Finger-combing her brown curls, petite Ruth Kennerly hurried out of the barn. She wore the puffy, brown corduroy knee breeches, brown boots, fawn-colored shirt, and V-neck green pullover of the Women's Land Army uniform. "Just had to check the list for tomorrow while I thought about it."

"I didn't mind the wait," Kate assured her. "As I said, I'm a farm girl, and I haven't been home in quite a while. It's nice to be among growing things again." Would that sound silly?

Ruth grinned. "Innit, though? I'm used to city smells like petrol fumes and wet pavement and sounds like motors grinding and tires splashing through puddles on the street and horns beeping. Never thought I would like it somewhere so quiet."

"You can't beat the country for quiet." Kate uncapped her pen. "If you've things to do, we can walk while you work."

"I'm finished for the day, but thanks. I would've known you knew farms even if you hadn't said. You dressed for it."

"Habit." Sturdy shoes, dungarees, and a neat shirt fit the surroundings much better than a dress, or even trousers, and heels. If Kate had a pair of the knee-high rubber boots known as Wellies, she would blend even better. "Where are you from, Ruth?"

"I grew up in Manchester. Until last fall, I lived in Harrogate. Worked in a dress shop there." Ruth gestured to the baled hay beside the barn door. She and Kate seated themselves side by side with the view of the fields.

"Why did you join the WLA?" Kate asked.

"It wasn't for the dandy uniform, I can tell you." Ruth's mouth curved in a wry grin.

Envisioning the green neckties, brown felt hats, and loose khaki overcoats that went with the clothes Ruth now wore, Kate smiled in agreement.

"The uniform means something, though," Ruth said. "It says I'm doing my part. I go into town sometimes when I have a free day, and I see the other girls in pretty frocks and stylish hats. I miss it a bit, dressing like that. But then I think about what I'm doing. How important it is. That uniform tells everybody. I wouldn't pick it off a rack, but I'm proud of it."

Kate's pen raced. That quote needed to go in exactly as Ruth had said it.

"Why did you join the WLA? Why this and not something else?"

Ruth shrugged. "We have to eat, don't we?"

"We sure do. When I was growing up, my dad always said if we didn't work, we didn't eat."

"That sounds about right." Ruth looked out over the fields and sighed. "My brother's part of an air crew stationed at Duxford. You had probably best not put that in, though."

"How about saying you have a brother in the RAF?"

"That'll do. Anyway, the idea of flying into battles scares me, if anybody would let me. But they won't, and I don't know about motors like he does. But I figured I could learn this." With a nod at the fields in front of them, she added, "I plowed that. Me. Never did anything of the sort before, but I did that. I'm proud of it too."

"With good reason. Plowing straight is hard to learn."

"Yes, it is. Folks'll have bread because me and others did that. So I come out here, and I look at that, and it reminds me I'm doing my part. That's all any of us can do, right?"

"Absolutely."

Whether the task was plowing a field or developing an unwanted Gift, everyone had something to contribute. If only Kate's contribution were progressing faster.

The next day, concern for Walter Mainwaring's disappearance in the afterworld and what it might mean for them all intruded on Sebastian's thoughts from time to time. If no one updated him by tonight, he would go into the afterworld and see what was happening for himself.

Someone knocked on Sebastian's office door. When he looked up, Ken Gerald stood in the opening. "Good news, Mainwaring." He shut the door and seated himself in the lone wooden armchair across the desk.

"Secret news, I take it?" Sebastian raised an eyebrow.

"Indeed. The secretary asked me to inform you, as he believes your brother may've known the fellow involved." Leaning forward, Ken said, "The Earl of Suffolk has pulled off quite a coup. He arrived in Falmouth yesterday with Norwegian heavy water that'd been stored in France, a load of diamonds, and France's nuclear scientists. They'll reach London today. The secretary wants you to meet with Suffolk."

Quite a coup indeed. With luck, it would keep valuable resources for developing a nuclear bomb out of German hands.

"I don't know him," Sebastian responded, "and my older brother knew him only vaguely. They attended different schools. Why am I to meet with him?"

"To see what else he can do for us, of course."

"From what I recall, Charles Howard, the current earl, likes to follow his own path. I doubt he'll be amenable to any suggestion he's not already inclined to adopt. Isn't he attached to the Ministry of Supply?"

"Be that as it may, we need a liaison to Howard. He's daring and capable. We may have a use for him."

"I'll see what I can do."

"Excellent. I'll tell the secretary." Ken hurried out, leaving the door open.

Sebastian looked down at the papers on his desk, production reports from the different factories. Rifles, tanks, airplanes, all were growing in numbers…but so very slowly. Whatever Hitler's reason for not yet ordering an invasion, Britain needed it to continue.

From what he'd heard of Suffolk, the man liked to go his own way. Still, meeting him for a pint couldn't hurt. Sebastian called Suffolk House and arranged a meeting for July 1, the earliest open date, with the earl's secretary.

Meanwhile, he had a meeting that might be another cause for hope. Possibly. The Merlin Club was about a fifteen-minute walk from here. He would pay a price for that with his leg. This had better be worth it.

Sebastian met Lachlan MacGregor, Mage Laird of the Isles, in the lounge to the right of the Merlin Club entrance. In his fifties, the tall, dignified Scot had a generally thoughtful demeanor. Today he looked grave, perhaps a result of sending his son off to war.

He rose as Sebastian entered, and they shook hands. The small, round walnut table by Lachlan's chair held a pot of tea, cream and sugar, and an extra cup as well as a platter of his favorite ginger and treacle biscuits.

"Would you like anything else?" the porter, Albert Gray, inquired. "Or shall I put the sign on the door?"

Lachlan looked at Sebastian, who nodded. Lachlan responded, "We've all we need, Albert. Thank you."

The sturdy man departed and shut the door. He would hang a *Private Meeting* sign on the knob.

Sebastian poured tea and seated himself across from the other man. "How are you, Lachlan?"

"Well enough, thank you. Agnes sends her regards."

"Please convey mine to her as well."

With the pleasantries out of the way, the two men stared at each other, Lachlan waiting and Sebastian trying to think of the best way to approach his subject. Asking about someone else's magical Gifts was rude, but in dire need…

Finally, Sebastian said, "I must ask you something I've no right to know. Before I do, though, let me give you the background." He outlined

Kate's vision, ending with the thousands of ships massed along the coast of France.

"When?" Lachlan asked, frowning.

"I don't know precisely. Sometime this summer."

"Your question has to do with this? Ask it."

"When this invasion fleet launches, the Royal Air Force and the Royal Navy will be engaged by their German counterparts. I suspect they mean to wipe out both those services' capabilities before launching to improve their chances. Even if they fail, we could be left with too few bombers and naval craft to penetrate the German defenses and sink the invasion fleet. You and your order have skills the rest of us do not, so what I would like to know is whether you have any capability to sink a boat quickly."

"That depends on the boat." Lachlan frowned over his tea. "The larger the boat, the more power is required to breach the hull. Steel plating requires more yet. We haven't enough mages to sink a fleet such as you describe."

"What if you could move swiftly from one boat to the next? In, say, less than ten minutes?"

"We could sink quite a few. But not thousands. Given the resistance of warship-grade steel to magic, a bomb would be faster. When it's thousands of targets, though, against an enemy who will certainly fire on our mages, we can still destroy a mere fraction of their fleet."

"That might be enough. Depending. Will you write up a more precise estimate of the numbers you can bring to bear and the time they would need to sink a boat with an armored hull?"

Lachlan raised his brows, and no wonder.

"I will trust you with that information," Lachlan replied slowly. "You and no one else, not even Genevieve. Will you give me your word not to share what I divulge with anyone?"

"I will."

"I'll have your handshake on it."

Lachlan reached across the space between them. Knowing the import of the words, Sebastian braced himself as their hands met. A burst of the mage laird's magic rippled across their clasped hands and up his arm. With it came awareness of the bargain that hummed in his blood before fading away. That same awareness in Lachlan would alert him if Sebastian broke his word.

"I trust you," Lachlan repeated, "but I hold many secrets not my own. I must know if you play me false."

"Then you will also know when I don't. Fair enough."

When the time came, the support Lachlan offered could help turn the tide. If it was sufficient. Unfortunately, they might only learn whether it was after battle was joined. By then, if it wasn't enough to save Britain, they would all go down in defeat together.

~

That evening, Kate found Rose in the parlor near her bedchamber with a tea tray on the low table in front of her. Rose looked up from her book. "How was it?"

"Lady Denham was very obliging and very candid about her struggles to have the government take the Land Army seriously, though she said those were to be deep background only, not for publication. That's understandable. The girls were very glad to talk about their duties and their reasons for joining up. So I think it'll be a very good story."

"I'm glad. Tea?" Rose asked. When Kate nodded, Rose picked up the pot and a cup. "If you don't mind my asking, is all well with you? You seem a bit...low."

Kate shrugged. "I stopped in at the office before I came here. Everyone had gone home, but there were no messages for me. That probably means there's still no word from New York about whether they'll let me stay."

"Hmm. Perhaps they're waiting a bit longer to see." Rose passed the cup of tea over. "The house party this weekend might yield some interesting interviews. While Oswald Moseley, the head of the British Union of Fascists, and his most ardent followers are interned—for which we should all be thankful!—there are still plenty in society who sympathize with his views. Some of those will be at this gathering. Though with internment a real prospect, they may be reluctant to speak for publication."

"I might be able to find a way to interview them without attributing their views directly to them, though honestly, Rose, if they support Hitler, they ought to be interned."

"Indeed."

Footsteps in the corridor heralded Sebastian. Kate's heart skipped a beat. When had she learned to recognize his halting tread? And how could she hear the faint sounds it made on the carpet?

"Good evening, everyone." He dropped into the armchair across from his sister and laid his cane on the floor. Lines of strain marked his face, and fatigue had his shoulders drooping. "Rosie, if I might trouble you for a cup…?"

"Of course." Pouring, she frowned at her brother. "Seb, what is it?

His lips quirked in a wry smile that didn't reach his eyes. "In general? Or today in particular?"

"Any and all." Rose passed him his tea.

"Thanks." He held the steaming cup near his nose and inhaled deeply. "As to the general, production of planes, tanks, guns—large and small—proceeds, but not quickly. None of us knows what Hitler is waiting for. We can only hope squabbling between the Kriegsmarine and the Wehrmacht, and perhaps the Luftwaffe, if we're lucky, continues to delay them."

He took a long sip of tea and balanced the cup and saucer on his good knee. "As to the particular, I had a vision this afternoon of the Germans invading Guernsey. If they go in there, they'll take all the Channel Islands, and the people we had insufficient resources to evacuate or couldn't convince they should come away will all be under their yoke.

"Then there's the personal." He turned to Kate. "There's much more to magic and our family's situation with it than we've told you. Do you want to know, or would you rather not?"

"I want to know anything that affects me."

"This doesn't affect you directly, but very well. Between this world, once known as the realm of the quick, and that of eternal life, the realm of the dead, lies a shadow realm. Souls with penance to do must bide there, some forever. The ground is solid shadow, and it roils with purple-gray fog that reeks of rotten eggs. Most doomed souls become wraiths, skeletal beings with ghastly faces who're filled with rage and will destroy any living being who isn't protected. There is also some speculation that they can devour a soul that doesn't defend itself. Most souls go from life directly to the portal of judgment, which is sited in that realm, and so never face danger from the wraiths."

"Most. What about the rest?" If this had anything to do with her magic, he was taking a long time to come to the point.

"The rest. Ah, there's a tale. When Edward IV died, back in 1483, information about his marriage came to light. This information proved he was legally married to a woman not his queen before he met Dame Elizabeth Grey, or Elizabeth Woodville. That woman, Lady Eleanor Butler, was still alive when the king married Elizabeth, who became his queen. And therein lies our family's bane."

The story he told, a wizard's misplaced trust, murdered children, and a king betrayed and wrongly blamed for their deaths was astounding. The part where the wizard, Sebastian's ancestor, cursed his heirs was stunning.

"So this Edmund doomed all his line's heirs to make up for his mistake?" Kate shook her head. "If anyone else told me this, I would say it sounded like a bad movie. But you're clearly serious. I don't understand what it has to do with me, though. I'm a Mainwaring by blood, of course, but I'm not an heir."

"No, but Richard was," Sebastian said.

He'd been her friend all her life, and he'd never said. "Miranda?" she asked.

"That's also quite a tale, though I don't know all of it. During their life-times, they did something—they won't say precisely what—that allowed Richard to avoid this doom, to pass directly to judgment when he died. He declined, refusing to abandon his father and any children he might have to that fate. Whatever they did also gave Miranda a choice, to pass through or to remain with him. She chose her husband and, as it later turned out, their son."

Sebastian paused, sipping tea. "It doesn't affect you directly, but, you see, it does affect people you know."

"It's a lot to take in." Again, Kate shook her head. "They never said anything about it. Do you know why?"

"I can only guess," he replied. "You weren't raised a Mainwaring, and you eschewed magic. They meant to let you be."

"Until the war." Kate sighed. "I'm in this now, and if I can help, I will."

"That brings me to the point of all this. There are generations of doomed Mainwaring men's souls in the afterworld, all waiting for the proof that will lift the curse and free them."

"Proof no one has found in almost five hundred years," Kate said softly, driven by that eerie knowing within her. "Proof you don't expect find."

Sebastian shrugged. "Hope is running thin. So thin that some have faded away to nothing. Now we fear one of those souls, Walter Mainwaring, who would've held the earldom from 1545 to his natural death in 1581 if not for a little disagreement with Henry VIII over his divorce, gave in to despair and let the wraiths destroy him. The others can't find him, and one can generally find anything in the afterworld by wanting it."

"Tell her the rest, Seb. She'll figure it out, but you may as well tell her."

"Rosie—"

"She wants to know it all, and she should." His sister turned a defiant look on him. "Kate, if we can't find a way to lift this curse, the same doom awaits Sebastian when he dies."

The information struck like a punch to the heart. Fumbling for words, Kate gaped at him. "That can't be," she managed, suddenly cold. "It mustn't be."

He squeezed her hand, the touch warming the chill in her soul. "Let us hope it won't be."

"Hope is empty without actions to support it," she said.

"True, but…" He shrugged. "My country's in danger, and I'm in her service. That must come first. We know the evidence we need, Edmund's confession, existed as late as 1868, when the only seer who has ever managed to See it died. It's hidden, though, and we don't know where."

"You're a seer. Can't you find it?"

"Generations of seers have tried." Sebastian shrugged. "Miles, who was one of Elizabeth I's captains against the Armada, is dedicating himself to the search by a different method. Frankly, I don't expect him to resolve it. The lead he's chasing may be empty, but at least it keeps him occupied."

"So he too doesn't…vanish." The words coming out of her mouth seemed like a fable, impossible to believe, yet she *knew* this was all true.

"Anyway, I'm going to the afterworld," Sebastian said. "The seer Gift doesn't show anything about the living world when one is in that realm, but I've never tried to use it about events there."

"There being no true events," Rose put in.

"Usually. But Walter's disappearance is an event. So it's worth a try."

"You're not going tonight." Rose's stern expression dared him to challenge her. "Whether or not you admit it, you're tired. You need rest. As is too often the case of late. Whatever has happened or has not in that realm, discovering it can wait until tomorrow."

Sebastian shrugged. "If you say so."

Kate didn't believe him for a moment. Judging by Rose's glare, neither did she.

A gong sounded downstairs. Dinner was served.

Rose led the way down to the dining room on the ground floor.

Thank goodness, this household didn't dress for the meal. An image flashed into Kate's mind, a group of people around a dinner table set with silver plate and ornate candlesticks. All wore formal dress, including her and Sebastian. That could be a problem.

"At this house party," Kate said, "will people dress for dinner?"

"I imagine so," Rose replied. "I didn't want to bring it up, but you should take at least two gowns, preferably three."

Kate owned one. So much for fitting in.

"I don't imagine you generally require a great many gowns," Rose said. "If you need more, you're welcome to borrow from me."

A discomfiting idea, as Kate already leaned on Rose and Sebastian a great deal. Maybe one of her flatmates had a dress she could wear, though only Marge was tall enough.

They reached the dining room, and Sebastian stood aside for her to enter first. He was always courteous. He was also intelligent, a patient teacher, and dedicated to his country. If she could help him lift this family curse, she had to. No matter what that involved.

Hours later, Sebastian closed his bedroom door at home. Rose meant well in advising him to sleep, but worry for those in the afterworld precluded waiting. If he could find Walter or learn his fate, should it come to that, the sooner the better.

Using his bedchamber door as a guide, he cast argent power into a rectangle the same size and shape as the door. That done, he walked toward it, leaning on his cane. A barrier of cold resisted him. Pushing through it, he entered the afterworld. Shrieks warned of attacking wraiths as he drew power from the stinking fog to shield himself. The skeletal horde surrounded him, faces ghastly with slashing wounds or gaping holes that revealed the bones beneath.

Pulling more power, he blasted it back at them. Silvery purple flashes of magic struck them from the mass's other side. Screaming in outrage, the wraiths wheeled away.

Now he could see his father and his older brother, Reg, standing a short distance beyond him. Reg grinned. "Does Rosie truly expect you to do what she says?"

"No, but she apparently needs to try."

The three embraced, his father's and brother's bodies solid and even warm in this eerie realm. "It's good to see you," Sebastian said.

"Your arrival is always a pleasure." His father clapped him on the back. "Your sister, however, was correct. You need rest."

"Later. I've come to see if I can locate Walter. Whether I can or not, this won't take long. I don't suppose you've found him?"

"Not thus far," Richard's voice said from out of the churning mist. Smiling in welcome, he and Miranda walked clear of the fog. Despite their smiles, worry shadowed their eyes.

They also embraced him. Behind them, a thirtyish man with the typical Mainwaring features of blue eyes and clean-cut features raised a hand in welcome. He wore his dark brown, almost black hair pulled back in a queue. His garb, green knee breeches with hose and buckled shoes, a long, embroidered gray waistcoat, and a green coat with turned-up cuffs and fronts, all embroidered with white roses, was typical of what he would've worn in life.

"I see my cousin the dandy is here." Grinning, Sebastian embraced Richard and Miranda's son Robert, Robin to his kin.

"Military brown is so tiresome." Robin shook his head. "Truly, coz, you need a job with a greater range of wardrobe choices."

"You've enough variety for us all." The ghosts in the afterworld wore clothes conjured by its magic and their imaginations. They could "wear" anything they envisioned.

Richard frowned at Sebastian. "You shouldn't fret over this. If I thought you could help, I would tell you. Meantime, you've graver responsibilities."

"If one more Mainwaring tells me not to *fret*, he'll regret it." Sebastian scowled at them.

Miranda, of course, was fighting a smile.

"Let me see if I can locate Walter," Sebastian said. "If I can't, we're all no worse off. If I can, well, at least we'll know."

"Edmund is distraught," Richard said, his face grave. "This brings home to him, yet again, what his outraged sense of honor has cost us all."

If Walter's soul had been destroyed, according to research done by Amelia's husband more than a century ago, then that was the end. There would be no passage to judgment, no hope of salvation for him.

"Give me room." Sebastian walked a little way from the group and opened to his Gift. A kaleidoscope of images bombarded his mind, the lives and deaths of those around him.

Gritting his teeth, he drew more power from the fog and summoned Walter's image. He'd worn Elizabethan garb like Miles's but with an unusually ornate ruff decorated with lace and pearls. He'd apparently been fond of that little affectation.

Pulling that one image from the array of Mainwarings, though, required power and focus. Gradually, Sebastian managed it. Walter's face with its curly black hair, aquiline nose, and short, pointed beard and mustache became clear.

Unlike the times Sebastian had sought one of his kinsmen here, there was no pull, no prompting of a direction he should follow. Where had Walter last been?

The image didn't change. Bloody hell.

Walking, while unnecessary to reach a destination, helped one do so faster. Sebastian held Walter's image in his mind and started walking. If he moved back in time, would that help?

Doing so usually required focusing on a specific time, a year or a day. What was the day Walter had disappeared? Ah, yes, June 23.

Sebastian turned his attention to that date. He'd been on his way back from Guernsey, and Walter had been…

An image flashed into his mind. Walter paced through the roiling fog, his face grim. Tears ran down his face. With a shriek, he ran into the mist with his arms spread wide.

The wraiths surged. He leaped at one, embracing it. Its claws ripped into his soul, scattering translucent fragments of it. Shrieking in delight, the rest joined in.

Sebastian swallowed against nausea. As a soldier, he was no stranger to death. Had seen a good bit of it in Czechoslovakia. But this…a soul torn to shreds.

If he went back to that day, could he save Walter? An image of a soul was usually a guide. Focusing on Miles let Sebastian find him easily.

But there was still no directional tug. It was as though the destruction of Walter's soul wiped away all but that last, fleeting glimpse.

The death of hope was always agonizing. Even though Sebastian hadn't known Walter well, their shared doom created a bond.

Rubbing a hand over his face, he turned to face his kin.

Miranda's eyes filled. Perhaps she'd read his face, or perhaps some fragment of her seer's intuition survived. She reached for Richard, and his arms locked around her. Robin embraced them both.

Gently, Sebastian said, "It's no use. I can't find him because he's truly gone." He explained what he'd Seen. "We should—I suppose Miles, his son, would be his nearest kin. Or Miles's grandfather…"

"Francis. He's one of those who faded away. We'll tell them all," Sebastian father said. "Miles is off on his quest to see if any Wyndon property might hold Edmund's confession."

"We must keep a close watch on Edmund," Miranda advised. "He will blame himself all the more."

"As well he should," Richard commented, frowning. "Most of us have forgiven him, but there's no denying his choice brought us to this point."

"You and I should tell him," Miranda said. "We cannot leave that to Thomas."

No, because Thomas's father, the now-vanished Francis, Edmund's son, had resented his father's wish to clear the dishonor wrongfully laid on Richard III's name. His unwillingness to commit to the cause had spurred Edmund to impose this lunatic curse in the first place. The loss of Thomas's great grandson's soul would make that resentment so much worse.

Miranda continued, "Sebastian, you should go home and go to bed."

"Before you do, though," his father said, "I've news from Germany. A high-ranking officer, Raeder—"

"Admiral Erich Raeder?"

"Possibly." The elder Reginald shrugged. "I cannot yet read their rank insignia. But he and another fellow, von Blomberg, were arguing about something. They were in a private room at a restaurant, outside the wards around the government buildings. I didn't catch all they said, as my understanding of German is still rudimentary. But my impression is that they continued an earlier dispute about the resources needed to invade England. How wide the front should be. They kept using the term I don't understand. It sounded like *zeeloovuh*."

"I'll see if I can discover the meaning. Perhaps their dispute is the reason they haven't yet assembled their invasion fleet. Let's hope so."

But the memory of the invasion fleet Kate had Seen haunted him. The Germans were coming. Any reprieve would make a great difference in trained men and equipment.

Would it be enough?

CHAPTER 15

Kate knew she was out of her element at the Dravens' house party. Two earls and countesses, including the host and hostess, a viscount and viscountess, a barrister and his wife, and a doctor and his wife made up the rest of the party. All of them wore expensive clothing and seemed to know the Earl and Countess of Draven very well.

The surroundings reinforced the social gap between Kate and the rest. The salon where they sat had an ornate plaster ceiling divided into squares with elaborate floral medallions in the center of each. Thick Persian carpet covered the floor, and delicate furniture with upholstered seats and backs was scattered around the room.

This was vastly different from anything in Cobbettown, Missouri. Fortunately for Kate, her experiences as a journalist had given her plenty of practice at pretending to belong.

The Earl and Countess of Wyndon elicited the familiar feeling Kate now knew meant they were Gifted. Though both smiled broadly, their cold gazes sent unease prickling down Kate's neck and arms. Lady Wyndon grasped a martini glass marked with prints from the red lipstick that matched her nails.

The countess, whose hair was elaborately finger-waved, strolled over to where Sebastian and Kate stood chatting with the Earl of Draven, a tall man who had wings of silvery gray in his light brown hair. The slim, fortyish blonde said, "Excuse me for intruding, but I've a question for our journalist guest."

Above her thin, insincere smile, the woman's pale blue eyes glittered malice. Sebastian edged closer to Kate, who braced herself.

Arching an eyebrow, the countess said, "I understand Hermia—dear Lady Draven—has cautioned you about respecting our privacy, Miss Shaw. I would like your word that we may rely on your discretion."

Though Sebastian's smile didn't waver, his outrage made his shoulders stiff. He stayed silent, though, letting Kate speak for herself.

Kate smiled. "If you couldn't, Lady Wyndon, my saying you could would change nothing."

As the woman's expression chilled further, Kate added, "As it happens, however, you can rely on it." Turning her shoulder to the woman, she smiled at Sebastian. "We've kept our host long enough. Shall we find seats?"

"Straight away." Pride glinted in his eyes. As they walked toward a loveseat near the Viscount and Viscountess Whitestone, who'd said to call them Harry and Eve, Sebastian let his hand rest at the small of her back for a moment. The touch made her extremely aware of him, but judging by the approval in his eyes, it was meant to encourage. Only that.

Kate and Sebastian settled into comfortable chairs across from each other, with the Whitestones on the loveseat in between.

An elderly man in a black suit like Petersham's stopped beside Sebastian's chair. "What can I bring you to drink, sir, madam?"

"Gin and tonic," Sebastian requested.

The only drink Kate actually wanted was a beer. While she wouldn't have minded flinging her comparatively low, American origins in some of these people's faces, that might embarrass Sebastian. "Martini, please."

"Your job sounds so interesting," Eve said. "I look forward to asking you a great many questions about it."

"Thank you. I'm happy to answer whatever I can."

"Ignore Florence Wyndon," Harry said, his gray eyes warm. "Any friend of Seb's is a friend of ours."

Eve's blue eyes were warm and friendly. She too wore red lipstick and nail polish, but hers didn't create a predatory effect. "How did you become a journalist?"

While Kate explained, the butler brought her martini and Sebastian's gin and tonic.

"I worked at the Baltimore bureau until the opportunity to come to

England arose. I was delighted to be selected, but I don't think my bosses expected the situation to heat up the way it has. After the declaration of war, nothing much seemed to happen."

"Hence the term *Phoney War*, as some call it," Sebastian put in.

Kate nodded. "They didn't believe they were sending a woman into harm's way."

Now they didn't want to keep one there. Surely she could come up with something that would change their minds. The fighting in France had ended the previous Monday, but a country actively at war would produce stories regardless.

"Have you had interesting assignments, then?" Harry asked.

"Some, yes." Kate glanced at Sebastian, who was looking past her at the far end of the room, where the Wyndons sat. Odd. "I went to France with the BEF. Again, with no one expecting immediate trouble. They all mistakenly assumed Germany would have to attack across the Maginot line, which would allow plenty of time to evacuate civilians like me."

"Kate returned via Dunkirk," Sebastian said, smiling at her across his drink. "I've seen only her notes and photos, not the copy she filed. Given that the raw materials were detailed and poignant, I'm sure the stories must've been superb."

"Thank you, Sebastian." The unexpected praise warmed her.

As he nodded, Harry said, "I'm surprised to see you here, Seb. This doesn't seem like your sort of event. Especially all the emphasis on titles."

"Lady Draven serves on several charity committees with Rosie. I came primarily to shore up my sister's contacts, but I also thought Kate might like to see what goes on at this sort of gathering. A slice of English life."

"A minority's way of English life," Eve said, her voice dry. "A slice the Great War whittled down and this one may put paid to."

Her husband grinned at her. "You hope, at any rate, and never mind your own status and properties, viscountess."

Eve shrugged. "Fair is fair. I would imagine Kate, being an American, would have some sympathy for the cause of social parity."

Yes, but not enough to walk into a social minefield over it. "Not my country, not my concern. I wish you luck unraveling it." Kate toasted them with her glass.

The others chuckled and returned the salute.

"Again," Sebastian said, smiling, "well done."

They eyes met, and the warmth in his seemed to brush over her heart.

He looked away abruptly, leaving her with a vague jab of disappointment. To cover it, she said, "As Sebastian can tell you, I won't quote anyone without permission. Still, if anyone wants to give an interview, I'm certainly open to conducting it and writing it up. Provided they've something to say that will interest readers."

"What sorts of things do you have in mind?" Harry asked.

"Actually, what Eve said a moment ago gives me an idea. A huge segment of American readers are crazy for details about the British aristocracy. The change in lifestyles and customs since the turn of the century would interest a great many people, especially since more changes seem to be on the way."

Eve wrinkled her nose at Harry. "Told you this was important."

"But aren't those particular Americans keen for what they see as the aristocratic life?" Rubbing his chin, Sebastian continued, "I should think that would be akin to the fascination with Hollywood stars and their lives."

"I think it is," Kate told him. "But many Hollywood stars come from ordinary backgrounds. In contrast, the British nobility represent centuries of wealth and social power. Or so many Americans see it. That's ever so much more glamorous for being unattainable. Either you're born into the right circles or you aren't."

"Indeed." Sebastian shook his head. "The tax changes in the early part of the century seriously undercut the hereditary wealth possibilities, though. Nowadays, only those with diverse sources of income carry over their wealth from one generation to the next."

"I really would like to discuss this with all of you if we can find a time that won't be rude or set Lady Draven's teeth on edge."

"She lives with her teeth on edge," Harry muttered.

Eve shot him a stern look, which he ignored.

"Nevertheless," Kate said, "I don't want to give her any cause for complaint. Perhaps after dinner?"

She would need to do more research for the story, but a conversation with Sebastian and his friends, either on the record or as background, would be a great start. If she kept her job long enough to finish the story.

~

What the devil was Major the Earl of Hawkstowe doing at a Draven weekend gathering? He never attended such events. Pondering that, Gerald de Vere, Lord Wyndon, waited while his valet slipped cuff links into his shirt sleeves and knotted his black bowtie. The gold cuff links bore the Wyndon crest of a bear and a portcullis.

The man finished and stepped back. Gerald inspected his image in the mirror. A nod of approval, and the valet exited silently.

Florence entered from her dressing room and presented him with her back. "Do me up, please?"

Her maid could have done that, but this was his and Florence's little game. As she expected, he ran a finger down her spine and smiled at her shiver. Brushing his lips over her ear, he whispered, "Can't wait for later."

"Nor I," she moaned, sagging back against him.

Theirs had been a marriage of fortunes rather than passions, but it suited them both. Always having an eye out for the main chance united them far more thoroughly than any emotional tie could've. The bonus of their intense compatibility in bed had made the getting of their three sons a pleasure rather than an onerous duty.

Instead of a zipper, her gown closed with numerous small buttons down the back. The short-sleeved, ice-blue satin matched her eyes. It fit snugly in the bodice, the scoop neckline emphasizing her plump breasts, and flared gently from the waist. The diamond parure, consisting of dangling earrings, a cuff bracelet, and a necklace with a three-carat solitaire pendant, sparkled in the bedroom lights and declared his wealth for all to see. Florence was a clever and alluring woman, always a credit to him.

"I don't like Hawkstowe being here," he told her.

"Because he has never attended one of Hermia's gatherings before? Perhaps also because he's in the army?"

"Works at the war office, I believe. It won't do to have him become suspicious of our recent activities. Too much is at stake, but I must speak with Lemieux." He checked his light brown hair in the mirror. "Nobody ever mentions Hawkstowe's bad leg. Perhaps it's time someone did."

"His little American is clearly out of her depth here. Her dress this afternoon was not only off the peg but several years out of style. Given that she has such a poorly paid job, I doubt she has a single jewel to her name." Florence flashed him a cold smile. "If she's unhappy enough, he may take her back to London."

How like Florence to describe the American, who had a good five inches on Florence's five foot three, as small. Gerald bowed. "I leave that to you, my sweet."

~

After dinner, Lemieux and Wyndon adjourned to the billiard room. Considering that Lemieux was a friend of the now-interned Sir Oswald Moseley, head of the British Union of Fascists, that was worth investigating. Sebastian could've done so with his Gift, but that wouldn't advance his mission of ingratiating himself. Once he saw Kate settled with Harry and Eve, he strolled down to the billiard room.

In shirt sleeves, Wyndon leaned over the table. He acknowledged Sebastian's arrival with a cool glance before striking the cue ball. The targeted red ball banked off the cushion and rolled into the corner pocket.

"Nice shot," Sebastian commented.

Wyndon thanked him with a nod.

"Do you play, Lord Hawkstowe?" Lemieux asked.

"No, can't say I do. It's Sebastian, please."

"Then make it Algernon."

Wyndon sank, or potted, another ball. Lemieux frowned, his gaze intent on the table. Below thinning, graying black hair, his eyes were keen. Sebastian wouldn't have expected a successful barrister, a King's Counsel, the pinnacle of the profession, to flirt with fascism. Yet Lemieux was known to have expressed certain nationalist sentiments. Not enough to land him in an internment camp but enough to have him watched.

Wyndon missed, and Lemieux stepped up to take his turn.

Resting the butt of his cue on the Persian carpet, Wyndon stood beside Sebastian.

"Have you played long?" Sebastian asked.

"Since I was a boy. My father loved snooker." Wyndon cocked an eyebrow at him. "Wouldn't have thought you were close with the Dravens."

Lemieux sank one of the red balls. Wyndon extracted it from the pocket and rolled it across the table to him.

"Hermia and my sister serve on a couple of charity boards together." Sebastian watched Lemieux sink a blue ball. His turn would continue until he missed.

"You've an interesting choice of companion this weekend. How did you meet an American journalist?"

"I was on duty at Dover when she came off the boat from Dunkirk."

"She was in France?"

Sebastian nodded. "Turns out we're distant cousins."

"Indeed. Quite a coincidence."

Lemieux's turn ended. Wyndon stepped up to the table.

"I understand you're in the army," Lemieux commented. "It's surprising, your staying in with an injured leg. Perhaps the injury isn't permanent?"

"Oh, it is." Sebastian smiled despite his irritation. Being chosen as a KC required some degree of social polish, the sort that generally precluded exhibiting such overt rudeness to a nobleman. Lemieux's doing so therefore must have a purpose.

"Then it's a good thing you inherited your title, Hawkstowe," Wyndon said.

Recognizing bait when he saw it, Sebastian merely raised an eyebrow.

Wyndon continued, "Once the shooting starts, if it does, I don't expect the army will have much use for an officer who cannot lead. Managing the earldom will give you something to do."

The words burned, but Sebastian merely smiled. Were Wyndon and Lemieux trying to drive him away so they could talk? Like Kate, Sebastian had learned to deal with insults to his ability. "Fortunately, my other military contributions outweigh a bad leg. How're things at the Inns of Court, Lemieux? Lawyers and clerks joining up?"

"Eventually," Lemieux drawled.

"It's all a waste of time anyway," Wyndon said, lining up his shot. "Fighter Command is a woefully undersupplied joke, and the Royal Navy can't hold the line alone. We should seek terms before a great many men die for nothing."

That confirmed the war secretary's suspicions. The weekend wasn't a complete waste.

Sebastian shrugged. "Norway and the Netherlands each had an accommodation with the Reich, but they now have the Nazi boot on their necks."

Both King Haakon of Norway and Queen Wilhelmina of the Netherlands had fled their countries minutes ahead of German pursuit. Unlike Leopold of Belgium, they had avoided becoming Nazi puppets with their people hostages for their cooperation.

Wyndon potted a white ball. "They broke their agreements, or so I understand. One who makes a pact with a tiger had best not give it an excuse to pounce."

"If it's a tiger," Sebastian commented, "it doesn't require an excuse. Pouncing is what tigers do."

Lemieux shrugged. "Of course you would think that. Others are more inclined to be reasonable."

Or traitorous, depending on one's point of view.

Though Sebastian watched the game coolly, he wanted to swear. Britain had enough trouble without her own undermining her. He would lay this information and any more he gleaned during the weekend before Secretary Eden, who would pass it to MI6. They might decide to let Wyndon dangle, to see what else he might do, or to trace his contacts.

That strategy—every strategy—carried its own risks, of course. The trick to winning a war was choosing the right gambles.

Kate sat in the parlor and watched the whist players. The foursome included Lady Draven, Mrs. Lemieux, Mrs. Holsworthy, the doctor's wife, and Eve. Harry and the other men had disappeared. Kate had never played whist, but not having to talk to anyone let her start planning the story Eve had suggested and deciding what other research she needed.

The table was set up at one end of the room, near the empty hearth with a large portrait of some former Earl and Countess of Draven in a massive gilt frame above the mantel.

Lady Wyndon took the armchair beside Kate's and set a small plate of little cakes on the table beside it. Kate gave her a civil nod but went back to pretending to watch whist.

"So you work," Lady Wyndon observed. "Have you always?"

Snooty question. Maybe it was intended as a jab. In fact, that inner knowing assured Kate it was. The best way to handle that was to refuse to be irritated. No woman became a reporter on a city paper, let alone a war correspondent, without learning to handle conversational slaps.

Smiling, Kate answered, "I grew up on a farm. Everyone on a farm helps with the work."

"Good gracious, even children?"

"Sure. We start with small jobs like fetching eggs or feeding chickens when we're six or seven and take on more responsibility as we age." Kate shrugged. "It's a simple system."

"I suppose." Lady Wyndon cast her a doubtful look. "But the idea of, well, dealing with livestock…or plodding through the dirt in a field, why, it seems dreadful."

What a contrast to the girls of the Women's Land Army, who embraced their new jobs in farming or forestry with enthusiasm. Who saw the value of what they did.

"We all like to eat, don't we?" Kate responded. "If we're all to eat, someone must plow the fields and grow the crops and deal with the livestock. It isn't difficult. Of course, the world was simpler when everyone raised their own stock and their own crops."

"Well, not the better sort, of course." Lady Wyndon packed condescension into her smile.

"Oh, everyone had some responsibilities, even the feudal lords. As my dad always said, on a farm, if you don't work, you don't eat."

"That's absurd." Frustration and annoyance glinted in the countess's pale eyes.

Kate shrugged. *Gotcha.*

They watched the whist players, and Kate could almost feel her adversary recoup.

"That's a charming gown." Lady Wyndon nodded at Kate's champagne silk evening dress. "A couple of years out of date, of course, but I suppose one must make do."

She fingered the large diamond at her bust, possibly emphasizing that Kate's only adornment was her modest gold locket, her parents' gift on her college graduation.

"It is out of date, but I like it. In fact, I made it to wear to a charity ball I was covering, so thank you."

"Of course, dear. It's very clever of you to dress so well yet so inexpensively."

Sebastian arrived in time to hear that last. His eyes flashed, but Kate sent him a look that warned him not to interfere.

Giving the spiteful woman a sweet smile, she replied, "Thank you. It's so kind of you to admire my success."

"Kate." Sebastian stopped beside her. "Let's take a turn round the garden, shall we? We'll see you later, Florence."

"Of course," Lady Wyndon murmured. "Do mind your steps with that knee, Sebastian. The paths are uneven in places."

"I'm sure I'll manage." He gave her a cool nod and offered Kate his arm.

Surprised, she slid her hand into the crook of his elbow.

He led her down a carpeted corridor lined with framed portraits and landscapes. Halfway down it, they came blackout curtains hung on a rectangular frame three feet from the wall. Slipping through them, they found tall French doors that overlooked a terrace. Neither Kate nor Sebastian spoke until they were outside and he'd shut the door firmly.

"Don't let her distress you," he said. "I would've defended you, but you didn't seem to need my help. Or to want it."

"I know you would." Kate took a deep breath of the cool evening air. "I can handle her particular brand of spite."

"I saw that. You did well. But I suggested you come here, so I want you to enjoy yourself. Dealing with smug snobs isn't what I had in mind."

"I'm a woman photojournalist. I long ago lost track of the number of times I've been told I don't belong. It no longer bothers me." Yet this protectiveness was gratifying, especially since he'd reined it in to let her handle Lady Wyndon herself. "That was a nasty crack about your knee."

"Not the first of the evening," he admitted in a wry voice. He cast her a speculative look. "I wonder why they don't want us here."

"I think she just doesn't like me. But you...you're an army officer despite your injury. Maybe you shame them, seeing as how they appear to do nothing but indulge themselves."

As she spoke, a vision flashed over her sight. Lord Wyndon and Lemieux in a room where the German flag hung on the wall.

Startled, she gaped at Sebastian.

"What is it?"

Kate shook her head, clearing the last of the vision. "Or maybe they're up to something they're afraid you'll find out." Quickly, she explained.

Sebastian said nothing for a long moment. At last, he said, "Kate, I trust you not to quote anything I say without my permission. Can I trust you further, with secrets that are dangerous?"

CHAPTER 16

Kate's eyes widened and then narrowed. Sebastian said nothing, waiting for her to decide.

"Anything you ask me to hold in confidence," she finally replied, "I will. But I don't understand what you mean."

"Let's move a little farther from the house." He couldn't descend stairs quickly, but Kate didn't seem to mind matching her pace to his as they walked down to the wide lawn.

"I believe the landscaping is by Capability Brown," he said.

Kate smiled. "You realize I have no idea who that might be."

"He was a landscape architect. Perhaps the best ever. Lived in the eighteenth century."

"So he set the styles? For yards, I mean. Though this expanse is pretty big to call a yard."

"You could say that." They reached the bottom of the stairs and walked together toward the garden. Halfway down the path stood a low, wrought iron bench decorated with Baroque flourishes.

Sebastian stopped beside it. "This should do. We can see anyone coming long before they draw near enough to hear."

"This is all very mysterious," Kate commented, seating herself. "Journalists love a mystery."

"Of course you do." Sebastian eased down beside her. He would never admit it, but the time he'd spent standing in the billiard room hadn't done his leg any favors.

"This is a dire time," he began. "But it isn't the first for this country, nor am I so naïve as to believe it will be the last."

"I'm sorry to say we agree on that."

He nodded. "May I ask you something? When you return home, do you intend to pack away all you've learned? Aside from what you need to control your Gift, I mean. To forget this part of your life?"

She met his gaze without trying to hide the conflict in hers. "It's a tempting thought. It would make some things…simpler."

Her family, she meant.

"But I don't know if I can do that." Kate sighed. "I see the world now in a different way. It has depth and complexity I never suspected. I don't know whether I can stop seeing those things. Or whether I should."

There was that determination to do the right thing again. If he were betting man, he would wager on that principle keeping her in the ranks of the Gifted. So perhaps he should take a gamble.

"We've worked so hard to control your Gift that we haven't much discussed the organization of the realm's Gifted."

"Organization?" Kate's brows rose. "Just how many of you—of us—are there?"

"A couple of thousand." Although she looked stunned, he continued. "Our governing assembly includes us all and is known as the Conclave. Day-to-day governance is administered by the Council. They enforce the rules for our kind."

"Rules." Kate shook her head. "How many of those have I broken so far?"

"None, but there's one I…well, let's say I skirt it on a fairly regular basis. Because of treaties dating back to the reign of Alfred the Great and codified in Prague in the 1400s, our kind may not use our Gifts for tribal gain. National gain, we would call it nowadays. The Council have, for centuries, interpreted that to mean we must sit on the sidelines of any international conflict."

"But you don't agree." She was watching him now, so intently that he could almost feel her wondering where this led.

"There is an exception to the rule for defense of self or others. I consider everyone in my country to be *others* my abilities obligate me to defend. The Council would vehemently disagree, but I'm not the only one who feels this way."

He drew the line at explaining the Merlin Club. As one of the director's seconds, he had a right to share some information, but they had all agreed to reveal the club's existence only to their immediate families and possible recruits. He still hadn't decided whether Kate would make a good one.

She studied him for a long moment. "Are you asking whether I see it that way?"

"We could use your help, but I can't request it unless you know you may be violating a rule. The punishment ranges from a reprimand to the locking of one's Gifts."

"People can do that?" When he nodded, she shook her head. "You know I have mixed feelings about my abilities, but I find I wouldn't want to lose them."

"That's heartening." He smiled briefly at her. "But if you aren't willing to take the risk, this discussion can't go any further."

"So all this time, when I've been using my Gift to see what will happen, what the Germans will do, I've been breaking a rule I didn't know about?"

"Not precisely. You didn't use your Gift against German Gifted. The thinking behind the rule is that if wizards join in conflicts, they will escalate to the point of creating widespread destruction. In that, as in some other things, seers fall outside the rule. Scrying would also fall outside it, as mere knowledge does not, in the view of centuries of Councils, constitute action."

"Pretty picky distinction."

He shrugged. "I didn't make the rules."

They sat quietly. A breeze rustled the leaves of the bushes and trees and created flickering shadows in the moonlight on the ground.

Kate turned to him, her face grave. "We can't win this war without taking risks. How can I help?"

She'd vindicated his faith in her. He would do everything possible to shield her from any consequences. "There are...concerns about the Wyndons and Lemieux. If you see them in close conversation or if anything about them seems odd to you, tell me."

"I assume that goes doubly about visions."

"Yes. Rose and John know I do this. Don't mention it to anyone else." Harry and Eve Whitestone knew, as they were both Merlin Club members, but they didn't know about his surveillance of the Wyndons.

"Of course." She took another deep breath. "I suppose we should go in. Work to do and all that."

"Yes." He hesitated, but she deserved to know how her accomplishments appeared from the outside looking in. Especially as she struggled with what her Gifts might mean. "Kate, many wizards with unwanted Gifts would learn only as much as they must to keep them from being a nuisance. Few would do what you've done and use that unwelcome Gift to help others."

"It's how I was raised," she said simply.

The shadow flitted through her eyes again, and he swore silently. There must be some way to resolve her concerns about her parents. If they were the admirable people she believed them to be, surely they would accept the change in her and love her all the same.

If they were.

"Since we're being candid," she said, "you should know I appreciate your patience and understanding and your kindness toward me, even when I'm not the most apt pupil, your sense of responsibility, and your willingness to work until you drop for the sake of your country. Rose tells me you also invited your butler and your housekeeper to move into your home for the duration. I don't expect many whose staff don't already live in would do that."

With a grimace, she added, "Certainly no one in there other than Eve and Harry would."

Stunned, he stared at her. He'd had no idea she saw him that way.

The lights from the terrace caught a flush in her cheeks. Looking down, she smoothed her skirt. "I just thought you should know that, ah, your generosity doesn't go unnoticed."

"Thank you, Kate." He could've listed additional appealing traits of hers, but he hadn't wanted to risk embarrassing her.

They smiled at each other in the lamplight. Kate's face softened. Warmed. The temptation to kiss her became insistent.

She'll return to the States one day. Don't be an ass.

Sebastian wrenched his gaze away. Kate was not the sort of woman for a fling. If he and she became involved, it would be serious. In the circumstances, foolish.

Better to be wise. "Shall we go inside and plague the Wyndons?" he asked.

"Excellent idea." Kate stood and brushed off her skirts.

The champagne silk flowed around her hips and long legs, and the fitted bodice with its square neckline and elbow-length sleeves emphasized her slender form and its curves.

Longing threatened to choke him, but only a fool pined for what could not be. If he kept his good sense, his emotions would settle in time. They always did. Meanwhile, he and Kate had Nazis accomplices to trap.

The weekend dragged on. By Sunday, Kate had decided she'd never met so many tedious people in one place. Lord and Lady Draven were courteous enough but tended to prattle about their conservatory and their daughter the future marchioness. Mr. and Mrs. Lemieux and the Wyndons went out for a bracing walk each day but otherwise sat in the parlor and discussed the potential effects of the war on the markets. Sebastian sat with them sometimes. If Kate hadn't known better, she would've believed him to be enraptured by the discussion of allowing the war to proceed versus coming to terms with Germany.

Dr. and Mrs. Holsworthy, in contrast, looked for any excuse to proclaim how easily Britain would beat the Jerrys once the rogues found the spine to come calling. The German seizure of the Channel Islands earlier that day did nothing to deter them. While expected, according to Sebastian, the occupation was still demoralizing.

Sebastian's bland face plainly proclaimed his skepticism, but of course he couldn't say anything that might betray the true state of affairs. Kate tried to distract him when the Holsworthys started their rant.

The one bright spot was Harry and Eve. They were not only friendly but happy to sit in the shade under one of Capability Brown's lovely plane trees and chat.

When the group rose from dinner on Sunday evening, Kate started a mental countdown of the time remaining on this weekend. She had hoped to persuade either Lemieux or Lord Wyndon to discuss fascism with her, but they had ignored her conversational gambits. While the story on class differences would be popular with audiences, it wasn't the meaty sort of thing that would save her job.

"Oh, look," Isabel Lemieux nodded at the delicate clock on the parlor mantel. "It's nearly time for Lord Haw Haw. Do let's listen."

Lord Draven looked pained but acceded to his guest's wishes. "I'm afraid I don't know the station."

"It's Reichssender Hamburg. I'll find it, if I may?" Receiving a nod, Lemieux fiddled with the dial on the wireless. "—many calling, Germany calling" issued from the wireless. Lemieux sat back with a satisfied expression. "He's outlandish sometimes," he said, "but he does have a point. We should think carefully about the course we take."

"If you'll excuse me," Sebastian said, "I'm too restless to sit."

"Or too lacking in a sense of humor?" Lord Wyndon raised an eyebrow. "While this fellow occasionally makes a point, no one takes him seriously, Hawkstowe."

"Perhaps that's a mistake." With a slight bow, Sebastian turned away.

"I'll come with you," Kate said.

Harry and Eve followed them but turned aside at the doors to the terrace.

Out of earshot of the parlor, Kate asked, "Where are we going?"

"Good question." Sebastian stopped, glancing down the corridor. "Harry's brother is in the navy, so of course he doesn't want to listen to that rot. Harry would've joined up by now if not for a heart condition. He says he could manage, but the doctors won't pass him."

"That's a shame."

"Yes. As far as Haw Haw is concerned, there's a benefit to knowing what the enemy's claiming, but this propagandist being so popular..."

"It must rankle," Kate said quietly. Especially to a man who'd suffered a permanent injury in his country's service. No one had told her what happened to his leg, but his still being in the army spoke volumes about his dedication. "I much prefer the way *Hi Gang!* treats Lord Haw Haw." May, the CNU receptionist, loved that BBC program.

"Yes, ridicule can be very effective." Sebastian grinned. "Let's go to the conservatory. It's usually unlocked."

"I would like to see it, especially after Lady Draven has sung its praises. I'm surprised she hasn't dragged us through it."

Sebastian grinned. "That would involve going near actual dirt. Those of us who aren't quite so dainty find it appealing." He ushered her around the corner and toward the rear of the house. French doors fronted a dark space.

Sebastian tried the latch, and the door opened. He and Kate stepped into a humid area with a flagstone floor. The light from the corridor revealed trees, shrubs, and raised beds filled with flowers. The air smelled of damp earth and greenery.

Behind her, Sebastian said, "They painted the overhead panes black, and the curtains are closed. Good." He snapped on the overhead lights.

"This is lovely." Kate turned in place, admiring. Stripping off her elbow-length gloves, she gently stroked the feathery leaf of a fern in a waist-high bed.

"There's a bench a little way in on the right." He shut the doors.

A click came from the area near the door, and then low, soft ballads wafted through the air.

Kate hadn't seen the wireless when she came in. The music added a relaxing note, maybe what Sebastian had wanted.

She sank onto the bench, the skirts of her mauve chiffon gown, borrowed from Marge, settling in a cloud around her. Fruit trees laden with lemons, oranges, and peaches filled the bed behind the bench. Ferns bordered both planters.

"It must be grand to have such a supply of fruit," Kate commented, "especially as rationing is likely to expand rather than diminish."

"Undoubtedly." Sebastian looked down at her with an intent expression that made her breath short. Holding out his left hand, he said, "Dance with me."

He wouldn't ask her if he couldn't do it. Yet standing so close, moving in time with him…a wise woman would refuse, but she simply didn't want to.

Kate laid her gloved hand in his. He propped his cane against the low stone wall of the planter behind her.

When she stepped into his arms, he smiled. "Here we go," he murmured.

He led with short, sliding steps that were easy to follow. Probably easy for his leg to manage too. His aftershave smelled spicy, and the soft, black hair at his nape, falling just short of his collar, was on her eye level. Her fingers itched to touch it, to see whether it felt as soft as it looked.

While the woman on the wireless sang of love and hope and faith, Sebastian and Kate swayed together. Surrounded by greenery, they might've been dancing in a forest clearing. They gradually moved closer until his chin rested against her temple and only a few inches separated them. His shoulder under the black dinner jacket felt solid, and his right hand remained properly at her waist.

"I haven't danced since I came to England," Kate admitted.

"My fellow Englishmen are that blind?"

"I haven't been in many places where there was dancing." She drew back to smile up at him. "Too busy chasing stories."

The corners of his eyes crinkled with what might've been affection. "Of course you were."

If only those stories could save her job.

This wasn't the time to worry about that, though. She had on a beautiful dress and was dancing with an attractive man. Maybe too attractive, but that was also a worry for later.

For now, she should just enjoy this moment.

"What do you like to do?" she asked. "When you're not on duty?"

"I liked to ride, but that's over." His matter-of-face tone relieved her of any social obligation to offer sympathy. "When I'm at Hawkstowe, I visit the tenants. Mum does that when I'm away, and my brother, James, helps out. But I keep up with what happens on my lands."

He drew back to meet her gaze, his expression serious. "They're my home but also my responsibility."

"So you look after your lands and tenants at home and you look after your country here. When do you do something just for yourself?"

"Occasionally. I'm doing something just for myself now."

The warmth in his eyes made her feel like Cleopatra and Ava Gardner rolled into one. If she leaned in a little, if she gave him any sort of invitation at all, he would kiss her.

Which would complicate their relationship—no, their dealings, best not to use such a potentially intimate word—henceforth.

Kate smiled but didn't move any closer. She yearned to, though, and the softening of his eyes said he knew it. Yet he didn't move closer either. Of course he didn't. Such an intelligent man would see those possible complications as clearly as she did.

They danced in silence for a few more minutes until news replaced music on the wireless. The announcer's voice broke the mood.

Sebastian stepped back. "We should return to the parlor. That treacherous ass, Haw Haw, will surely have finished some little while ago. There may be a few sidelong glances because we've been away for so long, but you don't look in the least mussed, so no one will make much of it."

The lack of mussing gave her a pang, but staying friends was really the best choice.

Kate would never know how difficult he'd found stepping back from her. She wasn't a woman for trifling with, nor was he a man who did that sort of thing. Better to stay friends and cousins and ignore the potential for a romance with so much weighing against it.

He should've stayed to observe the reactions to Lord Haw Haw, but he could See them magically later and not have to school his face to endure them.

Sebastian took his cane in hand and gestured for her to go first. "Shall we?"

She'd taken a single step when Miles materialized in front of her. The plant beds behind him were clearly visible, though a little fuzzy at the edges, through his translucent form.

Kate halted, her eyes widening.

Sebastian set his palm at her waist. "Kate Shaw, allow me to introduce our many-times-great-grandfather, Captain Sir Miles Mainwaring, one of Queen Elizabeth's most trusted naval officers."

She needed a moment to find her footing. Then she smiled and, rocking both Sebastian and Miles, curtsied. "A pleasure to meet you, Sir Miles."

He bowed. "The pleasure is entirely mine, my dear." Glancing at Sebastian, he added, "She has mettle."

"Of course she does," he replied. "Kate, you may recall my mentioning our kinsmen who're trapped in the afterworld. Each of them can appear to those of us directly descended from him. Or her, in Miranda's case."

"Okay."

Miles's face bore lines of strain, and the skin below his eyes was shadowy. Apparently being a ghost didn't prevent grief from affecting him. Sebastian knew the feeling. His own father had died a few years ago, but despite visits from his ghost, the feeling of loss had never gone away. Never completely would.

Gently, he said, "Miles, I'm very sorry about your father."

"As am I, lad. I want to find this bloody confession so no one else follows his course. I have a promising lead."

The words brought a jolt of surprise and hope. "Hang on a moment."

Sebastian turned to Kate. "Would you mind rejoining the others? I can explain everything to you later, and it would be better anyway if we don't return together."

"That might be best." To Sebastian's surprise, Kate nodded to Miles. "I, too, am sorry for your loss."

She retrieved her gloves from the bench and donned them. With a last glance at Sebastian, she glided out of the room.

"That lass is a fine one, grandson." Frowning, Miles added, "'Tis a bit odd, her fondness for poking about in war zones, but the writing business is naught more than any gossip does, save that she shares it so widely."

"Kate is very talented." That was an understatement, but the last thing Sebastian needed was ghosts gossiping about him and Kate. "What have you found?"

"I've made it my business to visit Wyndon properties, as you know."

"Seeking a different sort of ward, one that blocks seers."

"Indeed." Miles looked grim. "I started with their seat at Wyndon, but the wards there had nothing unusual about them. Nor did the ones at his shooting box in the Highlands. Today, however, I visited Otterden Abbey. Edmund said it lay adjacent to Wyndon lands in his day. It became one of their residences after that disgusting swine Henry VIII dissolved the monasteries. It occurred to me that they might have put something in the abbey treasure room and then left it there. Easier to do that than to relocate it to that Baroque nightmare they call Wyndon."

If the matter weren't so serious, Sebastian would've taken the time to tease Miles about his taste in architecture. The former sailor had used his ability to move through time to see how ships were built, naturally, but also to see how people lived.

"I take it you found something worrisome."

"That's a good word for it. The usual warding such as we all use surrounds the house. In one corner, though, the southeast corner in the cloister courtyard, there's some sort of warding that…well, if I were alive, I would say it made my skin crawl. As it was, it gave me a feeling of unease bordering on nausea."

"That's very interesting," Sebastian said slowly. As a living wizard, he could go into the afterworld and pass through a structure with normal warding. Once within the ward, he could emerge from the afterworld, thus neatly bypassing the defensive barrier. Ghosts and living people trying to pass the wards in the real world couldn't penetrate them. Still, who was to say this strange sort of warding would have the same vulnerability?

Could this odd ward block a seer? No ward should, but if this one did, it would explain much.

"I'll try to See beyond the ward." Sebastian pinched the bridge of his nose. "I've a very full schedule the next few days. I might be able to manage something at night, though."

"I would say ye should wait, lad, but there are some among us who, well, a few days would make a difference."

What he meant was *all the difference.* "It's that bad?"

"Not yet. God willing, it won't be."

"Indeed. I'll meet you in the afterworld tomorrow night after Kate goes home. If I'm actually able to enter this place, there'll be less chance of discovery at night."

"A wise choice. Good night, grandson, and thank you." Miles vanished.

"I stand to benefit too," Sebastian said, even though he doubted Miles remained near enough to hear him.

If he could pierce this mystery warding, could find Edmund's missing confession…

Best not to get ahead of himself, though. Hope withering was bad enough. Hope dashed might be even worse.

CHAPTER 17

Sebastian hadn't been this nervous about the afterworld since his first journey there. So much rode on this expedition. Not thinking about that would be wise, but he couldn't help it. The possibility of finding Edmund's confession had been on his mind all day.

Trying to gird himself mentally, he changed out of his uniform and into street clothes. It wouldn't do to have a British Army officer lurking around a remote private residence like Otterden Abbey.

Even though Sebastian could form a portal without a reference point, he liked to have one. Tonight, the corridor door frame would do. He streamed argent power at it to form a glowing rectangle the same size and shape as the door. Walking toward it and leaning on his cane, he braced for the cold barrier that pushed back against him. He pushed through it and into the shadowland, where he immediately drew power from the roiling, stinking mists in a shield.

As expected, a flock of wraiths swooped toward him, all shrieking with ear-splitting shrillness. Their bony, claw-like hands reached out to seize and rend. The sight gave him a pang this time, and he couldn't help thinking of Walter. The idea of his kinsman's soul dying on these creatures' claws made his blood sizzle with rage.

"Begone," he roared, and slashed silver-purple power across the group.

He could no more destroy them than they could him, so long as he shielded, but the magic drove them away. Sebastian stared down at his hand.

"Seb?" His father walked out of the stinking fog. "What is it?"

"Why can't I wield magic that way in the living world? The Scots can do it. Why is the skill so difficult for others to learn? It would be bloody damned useful with a war coming."

The prior Lord Hawkstowe shrugged. "Richard says the technique is the same, but you need a teacher in the living world. Still, if you asked him, he might try to teach you."

"It would come in very handy against an invasion fleet." Sebastian sighed. "We've the Scots for that, granted, but still…"

"Is a fleet massing?"

"Not yet. They will eventually, though, I'm certain. Come, let's find Miles and see to this."

They set off in the mist together. "How is Reg?" Sebastian asked.

"Angry that he can't do more against the Nazis. Since he speaks French, he's watching their Paris headquarters. He can eavesdrop on collaborators at least but hasn't learned anything useful yet." His father hesitated. "I was home a couple of days ago to see James. He's planning to join up. Royal Navy, in honor of Miles and our other seafarers."

"I can't say I'm surprised." Yet the thought of his kid brother, his only remaining brother, under fire at sea… Sebastian tightened his lips against a curse.

At last, Miles's tall, broad-shouldered outline appeared in the fog. A few more steps, and he became clearly visible. He faced away from Sebastian and his father. With him stood Miranda, Richard, and Robin.

"No Edmund?" Sebastian frowned. "I would expect him to take a great interest in this."

"Edmund is…dispirited," his father replied.

Understandable. Miles turned, and Sebastian lifted a hand in greeting. Everyone exchanged embraces. In his kindred's set faces, Sebastian read wariness, perhaps a defense against hoping too much.

"Let's go to Otterden Abbey and see what we can learn," Sebastian said.

Miles took a couple of steps through the clouds in front of him and nodded. "There it is."

The others joined him. A low hall with a squat tower above the entry, likely the original abbey church, made up one side of a rectangle. The side abutting the hall's rear stood three stories tall, probably the main living area. Walkways that must've once been cloisters ran from it to the other front corner, where a blockish, three-story square tower stood, and from there to the former church.

Lights gleamed in a couple of the windows in the squat corner tower.

"How many in residence?" Sebastian asked.

Miles replied, "A caretaker only. He lives in that corner tower. From eavesdropping, I gathered the earl brings additional servants from Wyndon or else hires temporary help for the rare occasions when he's in residence."

"Not too many to worry about, then. Where was the ward you found so disturbing?"

"On the cloister side of the old church. I would wager there's an underground chamber in that corner of the courtyard. Why else would the ground itself feel warded?"

"Indeed."

Frowning, Miles stroked his short, pointed beard. "I discovered that ward by accident, walking across the courtyard to attempt entry in the old church. Amelia learned we could position ourselves above things in the living world, so I did that to go over the warded cloister. The disturbing ward on the ground is set back a little way into the yard from the corner where the cloister meets the hall, and I had no sense of it until I stood directly above it."

So the attempts in the last century to investigate all the Wyndon residences would not have found it. The wards around the perimeter of the old abbey and its cloisters would've kept out anyone who tried to pass through in the living world, and no one would have seen any point to investigating the center of a courtyard.

"I should be able to enter the old church," Sebastian said. "If the abbey had a treasure room, perhaps it's accessed from there."

He walked slowly through the fog. When he crossed the courtyard, senses extended to seek an underground passage, his stomach revolted. Sebastian hurried to the former church's side wall. The nauseating sensation faded with each step.

"Definitely dark magic," he told his waiting kin when they overtook him.

Trying to shake the effects, he blew out a breath. "Here goes. If I run into trouble...well, let's hope I don't." None of them could pass through the buildings' wards, and no other living Mainwaring except his mother knew how to come here.

Steeling himself, Sebastian walked toward the old church wall. He passed through it easily and let out a breath of relief. The cavernous space was dark, with faint light revealing stained-glass windows that had somehow miraculously survived Henry VIII's Dissolution of the monasteries and Cromwell's anti-idolatry Protectorate. Unfortunately, the dim outside light didn't penetrate far enough to let even Sebastian's Gifted eyes see them clearly.

Being in the afterworld, though, let him find anything by thinking about it and walking in the direction the shadow realm's magic tugged him. He imagined a door, and a subtle tug drew him toward the side, where a door in a wide, pointed arch led to the cloister. Sebastian passed through it, but the moonlight showed no sign of any access to the square other than another arch near the walkway's center.

He returned to the hall and made a circuit. One door led to the main building at the hall's rear, but there were no stairs. At least, no visible ones. Could there be a crypt?

With his mind on that question, he followed the subtle tug drawing him toward the dais where the high altar would've stood when this was a church. A long table of dark wood with armchairs around it occupied its center. He couldn't make out the carvings on the chair and table legs in the darkness. An ornate marble sideboard stood near the rear wall.

Standing on the raised, flagstone platform, he frowned at the floor. His seer Gift didn't work with regard to the living world when he was in the afterworld. No one had ever tried to see whether a living wizard in the shadowland could pass through a solid object thicker than a castle wall. If an object was too thick, the wizard might become trapped within it.

Perhaps best not to test it on this floor.

He formed a portal, pushed through the biting cold, and entered the hall in the living world. Now he could use witchlight to see what he was doing, though it might be better to wait. A light of any size might create a glow that showed through the windows.

Laying a hand on the flagstones, he opened his magical senses. No warding tingle brushed his hand, so he sent out a tiny tendril of power… into a hollow space. The crypt. Would it have a passage into the area below the courtyard?

Finding out required gaining access to the crypt. But how? His probing magic felt stairs, but there was no sign of an entrance to them. Could the stairs be concealed, perhaps behind the where the altar had once stood? The stairs he sensed seemed to be under the marble serving stand. If so, there should be something to trigger that.

Looking behind the tapestry revealed several carvings he couldn't make out in the dark. Rather than trying each of them, he laid his hand on the wall at shoulder height and sent a pulse of magic across the stone. Something clicked, the sound echoing in the vaulted space. With a grinding noise, the carved sideboard slid toward him.

Sebastian hurried around it. Crouching behind it, he risked a tiny flame of witchlight.

Shadowy stairs came into view, and he stifled a shout of exultation. Before stepping onto the stair, he opened his senses fully. The air smelled musty and damp, but there were no cobwebs.

At the stair's bottom, he risked a brighter flare of witchlight. It revealed a low-ceilinged chamber the width of the old church. Coffin-sized niches lined the walls, most of them occupied by ornate caskets. In the open floor stood a number of what appeared to be above-ground tombs topped by carved figures in various styles of garb. Some wore clothing resembling the fashions of Miles's day while other effigies were dressed in Elizabethan and even Georgian styles.

Definitely the crypt, then. But did it have any other exit?

Summoning a mental view of the layout, he walked down the left-hand wall, the one that bordered the courtyard. In the far corner, he poked his head into a space where the side niches stopped short of inter-secting those across the rear.

A low, narrow door set into the left-hand wall filled the space between the side niches and the rear one.

Sebastian smiled. If his sense of space was accurate, he would have been directly above this in the cloister. The warded space in the courtyard would lie about seven or eight feet from here.

This was the way into it. It must be.

Whether the treasure it guarded included what he needed was a different question, and there was only a single way to answer it.

He reached toward the door. About two feet from it, warding magic seared his palm. The power in it traveled up his arm and into his body. His gut knotted, and his heart thumped wildly.

If the Wyndons didn't want anyone to see this, it was well worth a look.

Gritting his teeth and taking care not to release any magic, he forced his hand forward, pressing against the glowing ward. Heat seared his arm. His gorge rose. Sebastian tightened his lips and opened to his Gift.

Images flashed through his mind. A murdered man in garb like Edmund's. Blood pooled along the floor. Magic glowing.

Someone's laughter, so cold and ugly in tone that he shuddered from it.

The warding magic clutched at his throat, and he couldn't breathe.

Gasping, he stepped back. He reeled against the end of the niche tombs and nearly lost his balance.

The farther from this ward, the better, so he limped well clear of it and leaned back against a standing tomb. Given that ward's behavior, his touching it might've alerted someone, but he couldn't form a portal to reach the afterworld until he caught his breath.

Gradually, his heart rate and his breathing settled. He shoved to his feet and climbed the stairs to the dais again. Locating the carving behind the tapestry that triggered the stairs took only a moment. The sideboard slid smoothly back into place.

Sebastian formed a portal and stepped back into the afterworld. This time, Richard and Robin beat off the attacking wraiths.

Miranda put a hand on Sebastian's arm. "Are you injured? You look dreadful."

"Need a moment," he managed.

"Sit down, son."

Before he could drop to the glassy, fog-covered ground, a chair materialized behind him, courtesy of his father. With a nod of thanks, Sebastian sat heavily.

"You found something," Miles rasped.

Sebastian explained what had happened. The gleam in everyone's eyes could only be hope.

At last, Richard asked, "You couldn't See anything beyond the ward?"

"No, only what may have happened when the ward was set. Murder and blood magic might offer an avenue to defeat Sight, though I've never heard of that happening before. Whatever they're hiding matters a great deal to them, though, to guard it with dark magic. Or at least, it did about four hundred or more years ago."

"Why four hundred?"

"The murdered man's clothes resembled Edmund's."

Richard and Miranda exchanged a glance. She knelt beside Sebastian's chair and put a hand on his. "Sebastian, my dear, you are not the only seer in your generation. You couldn't reach past the ward alone. If you and Kate combined your magic, could you do so?"

"No!" He shot to his feet. "I won't subject her to that. It was painful and terrifying and ugly and gut-churningly revolting. I won't have her anywhere near that bloody ward."

He was breathing hard again, both furious at them and terrified for Kate.

Miranda rose slowly. "She is a seer. That means something." She held up a hand to stop his hot interruption. "She is also a woman determined to do what it is right, so perhaps this is not your decision to make."

~

Lack of sleep made for a dreadful start to the day. Sebastian stared at his hollow-eyed reflection in his shaving mirror. Miranda had a point, however much he might want to deny it.

He also couldn't overlook Kate's determination to do the right thing. He had a hunch she wouldn't balk even when the right thing meant dealing with something revolting, frightening, and literally sickening. She was a novice, though. Flinging her against something like that would be not only unkind but reckless.

But perhaps necessary.

He argued with himself as he made his way to his office. At least it was on the ground floor, sparing him the staircase. Last night's activities had not been kind to his knee.

He put his cap and blouse on the coat tree and seated himself at the desk. Rather than deal with the stairs, he rang Ken Gerald in Secretary Eden's office.

Ken answered, and Sebastian said, "Mainwaring here. I had a pint with Suffolk yesterday. He thanks us for our interest, but he declines." The earl's adventures made for an interesting tale, so the time hadn't been wasted.

"You couldn't convince him?"

Sebastian grinned at the memory. "I believe we're rather too tame for him. He's going into bomb disposal and expects learning that and dealing with explosive ordnance to occupy all his time."

"I see." A pause, and Ken sighed. "Thanks for trying, Major."

"Of course."

There, that was done. Opening the top folder, a report on fighter production, Sebastian began reading.

Some time later, someone knocked on his door. Ken rushed into the office.

His pale face had Sebastian rising half out of his chair. "Ken, what is it?"

"The Italians. We only just had word. Hundreds of them are dead."

"What Italians?" Sebastian gestured to the chair across from his desk. "Sit down, take a breath, and tell me what's happened." There were Italian internees at Ascot, others in Scotland, but they weren't the War Office's province.

"Sorry." Ken dropped into the chair and ran his hands over his face. "The Italians who were interned have been held in various places."

Sebastian gave him an encouraging nod. No matter how much Sebastian sympathized with those who'd been caught up despite having no ill intent, this wasn't the time to debate the fairness of the internments.

"There was a decision taken," Ken said, "I suppose by the Home Office's Aliens Department, to ship some to Canada. Along with some German prisoners of war. Several ships transported them. One, the *Arandora Star*, departed Liverpool early this morning. Off the coast of Ireland, a U-boat spotted the ship. Sank her. Doesn't look good for survivors."

"Sank her? They fired on a civilian ship?"

"Apparently she wasn't marked with the red cross to indicate civilian transport. She was painted gray as a holdover from her naval service."

Sebastian stared at him. "We're at war, and no one thought to paint a red cross on the bloody ship?" A vision shoved at his mind, a sinking ship with people in the water. Screams splitting the morning air. Swallowing hard, he pushed it aside.

Ken shrugged. "It's shaping up as a dreadful tragedy. The secretary asked me to be sure everyone knew, and you're always in early."

"Right. Thanks."

Ken left the office. Sebastian stared at the papers on his desk without actually seeing them. All those men. Many of them innocent of any wrongdoing.

The vision flashed over his sight again. This time, he let it come. Saw the gray ship without the recognizable civilian marking. Saw the torpedo streak through the water. The explosion. Desperate people scrambling to board lifeboats. Frightened shouts mingled with curses.

Feeling faintly sick, he put his head in his hands. These were only the first. Marked or unmarked, no ship could be assumed safe. Not with the *Lusitania* sinking still in living memory.

A U-boat had sunk the passenger liner off the coast of Ireland, resulting in hundreds of casualties, during the last war.

What was it about U-boats and the Irish coast, anyway?

Regardless, there would be worse to come.

Another vision rolled into his sight, this time of bombs falling on London. Buildings exploding. The air rent with people's screams that the explosions drowned out seconds later.

Sooner or later, London's civilians would be in this. There was no avoiding it. He'd known that, of course, but he'd managed not to think about it until now.

Acknowledging it, Seeing it coming, brought clarity. He would have another go at the ward below Otterden Abbey. If he failed, he would ask Kate's help but only after warning her how dreadful it would be and giving her ample chances to refuse. If she agreed, they would attack that as soon as possible. Get it out of the way. If she demurred, so much the better.

Either way, when they had that matter settled as best they could, he was sending her home.

CHAPTER 18

Something was on Sebastian's mind, Kate thought, walking up the stairs at Rose and John's with him. He'd been very quiet at dinner despite his brother-in-law's attempts to draw him into conversation. On top of that, he had avoided making eye contact with her, and the one time she'd caught him looking, he'd had a speculative, worried expression on his face.

They settled into the upstairs parlor, Sebastian in an armchair and Kate on the loveseat. Tonight, the low table in front of her held a plate of cheese squares and wheat biscuits, a couple of small plates, and neatly folded blue linen napkins as well a crystal pitcher of cider and low glasses. In this country, cider was alcoholic. Her cousins must think she was doing well at mastering her magic if they thought she could handle that with her lesson.

Lessons could wait, though. Kate stared at Sebastian. "What's on your mind?"

He blew out a hard breath. "We have a lead on the family curse. One that might require two seers to follow it effectively. Assuming even two of us can manage that."

"Okay. What do you want me to do?"

"Understand, I don't actually want you to do this. It's dangerous. No one would think less of you if you declined. But I've tried twice to breach it alone and failed. I believe it's my duty to our trapped kinsmen to ask you."

"If you feel that way, this must be very important. Will it lift the curse?"

"I don't know." He took a deep breath and launched into a fantastical story. A crypt with hidden stairs, a warded door that sickened and seared and terrified him when he touched it.

"It's a blood ward," he told her, "the darkest of dark magic. Very dangerous."

His grim expression reinforced the dreadful sound of the whole business.

"No one would hide something that way unless it were very important," she commented, trying to shrug off the chill his description had given her. "Something they didn't want anyone ever to find, but why do you think his has to do with your family curse?"

"Our many-times-great-aunt Amelia, Lady Aysgarth, had a vision in 1815 of the document that would free us all. Edmund wrote a confession. He thought it burned in a fire at Hawkstowe in 1605, but when Richard and Miranda attempted to go back in time through the afterworld—"

"You said that place touched all times, but I didn't realize that allowed travel to different eras."

"Yes, but that's a tale in itself. When Miranda and Richard tried to retrieve Edmund's confession, the space where he'd stored it, below the hearthstone in the room where they kept valuable items and records, was empty. The confession was gone."

"I thought you said being in this afterworld and thinking of something enabled you to find it easily."

"As a rule, that's true. But not this time. None of us has been able even to locate the day Edmund wrote it. Someone stole it."

"Could he have imagined writing it?"

"Possibly, but Amelia's vision says not. Due to the surrounding circumstances, she and her husband, Julian, deduced that a branch of the de Vere family, the ones holding the Earldom of Wyndon, had the document hidden somewhere."

"Are you certain the missing document is this confession?"

"Oh, yes. Amelia showed the document she had seen to Edmund by putting her vision into the fire, like a scrying. He confirmed that it's his confession."

"I'm still learning to do that."

Sebastian nodded. "You'll catch on, I'm sure. The de Veres having the confession makes sense because Edmund and others helped convict Roland de Vere, then Earl of Wyndon, of treason against both the Gifted and unGifted. King Edward IV, not knowing of his magical antecedents, sentenced him to death in the late 1470s, and Roland's family vowed revenge."

"Yet you can't find any trace of them taking this confession?"

"No, and I would dearly love to know how they did it." He shook his head. "Anyway, Kate, we Gifted can share magic through a hand clasp."

"As you do when you help me control wayward visions."

"Precisely. Miranda, who has had several hundred years to pay attention to magic use in general and the seer Gift in particular, thinks that if you and I combined our magic and tried to evoke a vision of what's beyond the ward at the same time, we could pierce it with our Sight if not in fact. Could know whether it's concealing the confession or something that's nothing to do with us."

"If it's the confession, what then?"

He shrugged. "We'll need to steal it."

"You make that sound so simple." Kate raised an eyebrow.

"It won't be, not if we must break or circumvent that ward."

"Yet it's important enough to try that. If it's a confession, would it clear Richard III's name?"

"It should. If we can publicize it."

"And that would save everyone. Release all those trapped souls."

"In theory. It might be necessary to persuade people to believe it. No one knows."

It would free him too. Interesting, how he didn't mention that.

"You're a novice, Kate. All of this might be much worse for you than it was for me. No one will think less of you, as I said—"

"I'll do it." She didn't need to be a seer to know he would try again alone if she didn't help him. The idea of his facing that kind of torment by himself, especially when she could possibly lessen it, was unbearable.

He didn't look pleased. "That's very generous, Kate. Very kind."

"They're my kinsmen too." *As are you.* Though she knew only a few of them.

"We'll work on melding magic before we try this. Then we'll practice using that technique to See through a ward." Sebastian ran a hand through his hair. "Remember always that you may change your mind at any time. No one will—"

"Think less of me. I heard you the first two times."

"Right. Of course."

Yet he still eyed her warily.

"Sebastian, this has been a long day. If there's something else, let's deal with it."

"There is something else, something you won't like. You know about the internment of Italian nationals."

"Yes, and it's appalling. They lost everything, yet that ass, Lemieux, strolls around free extolling the idea of *accommodations* with the Nazis, by which, of course, he effectively means surrender to them."

"It gets worse. Several hundred of these Italian nationals were on a ship bound for Canada. Early this morning, a U-boat sank her. The casualty count is…high."

Kate gaped at him. When she spoke, her voice emerged rusty. "All because they were Italian."

"For the most part. Some of them were active in fascist movements. Not many. Other passengers were German prisoners of war."

"Dear God," she breathed. She could see the ship sinking, the terrified people floundering in the water. Tears stung her eyes, and she clenched the lids shut.

"There will be worse before things get better. I suppose you remember the *Lusitania*? No matter what symbols one puts on a ship, no matter what her cargo, the Kriegsmarine will sink whatever Herr Hitler tells them to. Just now, they're feeling very powerful. Peace overtures are coming. I've Seen it. When they're rejected—please, Lord, *when*, not *if*—there will be hell to pay."

"It's war." Proud of her even tone, Kate shrugged. "I didn't expect it to be tea at the palace."

"Nor should you." He leveled an intent stare on her, and warning chills raced down from her nape. "Kate, my dear, this isn't your fight. I want you to go home."

Surely she hadn't heard him correctly. Kate cocked her head. "What did you say?"

"I want you to go home. Where you'll be safe."

She had heard him right, and the words were like a slap in the face. "Maybe I would be for a while," she managed. "Not forever."

They stared at each other, and Kate swallowed hard. "I thought you understood how important my career is to me. How much I need it. The important stories are here, not back in Baltimore or wherever CNU might send me."

"The bombs will be here too. The fires. The falling buildings. I want you out of that."

"You said you needed my help." She'd meant to give it even though what was to come would be terrifying. She jumped up to pace to the window. Unfortunately, the blackout curtains blocked the view. "Yet now you're sending me home?"

Kate marched back to stand in front of his chair.

Sebastian pushed himself to his feet. "Kate—"

"Do the British government and the Allied cause need my help? Or not?"

Sebastian glared at her. "That's beside the point."

"Not to me. Especially not when you'll be caught in what's coming. I care about you," she cried.

Their gazes locked. The shock in his face equaled the shock in her heart as her words hung in the air between them. Heat rose in her cheeks.

Sebastian's expression softened. "Do you indeed?" he murmured.

Surprise and joy roared through Sebastian's veins. But Kate, looking appalled, wheeled back to the window.

"Of course I care," she blurted. "I care about Rose and John and all my friends here and—and, really, Sebastian, you shouldn't take that as meaning I expect—that you need to do anything—I, oh, please forget I said it."

"A bit late for that," he replied over the happiness humming through him. He should pretend he didn't care. Maybe that would convince her to go home.

But it would be a lie about something so fundamental as to be almost sacred.

He took a single step closer, so he stood directly behind her. "Kate, will you look at me?"

Hesitantly, she turned, her face still very red. He waited until she raised her eyes to meet his, and the trepidation in hers tore at his heart.

"I can't forget you said that," he told her, "because I care about you as well."

She searched his gaze, and the dread in hers slowly faded. When her lips curved up in a smile, he smiled back at her.

He leaned in, and she met him halfway. The soft, tender kiss gave way to longer ones and then deeper ones. At some point, he and Kate moved to the love seat.

The kisses and touches grew more intense until Kate pulled back to smile up at him. "I won't leave you, especially not to protect my own skin."

"All right. We'll figure out how to work together." He stroked her cheek gently with his knuckles. "You've made me very happy, Kate."

"I'm glad, because I'm happy too."

Though she smiled, a shadow lurked in the depths of her eyes. He had a pretty good idea what it could be. Her heart might lead her to him, but what would her beloved family think of a man who was not only a foreigner with a title but magically Gifted?

The story Kate was developing would be great. Eager to work on it, she hurried into the office in the early afternoon. May smiled at her. "Lew wants to see you, Kate."

"I want to see him too. I spent the morning developing a lead on a terrific story."

Rose had introduced Kate to a friend of hers, Lady Elspeth Douglas, youngest daughter of the Earl of Stornaway. Lady Elspeth had befriended several members of the Polish Air Force who'd fled to Britain to fly for the RAF. She and Kate had hit it off, and Kate's notebook now contained pages of background information on these men.

As usual, Lew's door was open. Kate tapped on it. "You wanted to see me?"

"Yes." The grim look on his face froze her insides as he continued, "Close the door, honey, and have a seat."

Honey? Lew never called her honey. This was going to be very bad. Was it her job? Please, not her family.

Mouth dry, Kate sat across from Lew's desk.

"Sugarcoating this won't make it any better," he said. "New York is adamant that you're to come home."

She bit back a cry of protest.

Shaking his head, Lew added, "The stories you've done since France were all great. But you're a woman in what's sure to be a war zone, and that makes them nervous."

The old bitterness lay sour on her tongue. Once again, she was being told she didn't belong—this time, by someone who could enforce that.

"It doesn't make me nervous," she said, her voice flat. "At least, not especially, and I'm the one whose neck will be on the line."

"Sorry, but that's it." He peered across his desk. "You're not gonna cry, are you?"

"I stopped crying over baloney like this years ago." At least where anyone could see, she had. Later, in private, was another matter, as the ball of pain above her heart warned.

"They're offering you the congressional beat." Lew beamed at her.

A plum assignment, but… "Jim Halliday has that beat."

The tightening of Lew's features betrayed him. Anger bloomed hot and hard inside Kate. She didn't need magical Sight to know what was happening.

"Jim's being reassigned here. Isn't he?"

"Now, Kate—"

"Save it, Lew. Nothing you say can make me okay with this." She took a slow breath in and let it out. "I appreciate what you tried to do."

"I'm sorry I couldn't do more. You're booked on the *SS Olympic Star* out of Southampton on the fifteenth."

"So soon…"

"They want you home. The Brits might come to some arrangement with the Jerrys, but the way Churchill's talking makes that unlikely. This situation could blow up any day."

"Given the sinking of a refugee ship yesterday, I don't know that being on the ocean is any safer than being here. Especially given the *Lusitania's* fate in the last war."

"That was a fluke."

Kate shrugged. "I've started work on a fabulous story. An exclusive. I don't know that I'll have time to finish it, but I want to try." Those men, like so many others, deserved to have their stories told. Maybe doubly so because they were fighting to take their country back.

"If you like, sure." Lew hesitated. "Take whatever time you need to, ah, pack and such. New York is letting your flatmates' bosses know, but you might want to go ahead and tell them."

"Of course I will." To do otherwise would be inconsiderate.

He didn't even ask what the story was.

Kate stood. "If that's all, Lew?"

"Yeah. I'm sorry, honey."

"Me too." Kate marched out of his office and down to the bullpen. Instead of taking off her hat and gloves and stowing her bag, she sank into her desk chair and stared around the room.

I'm a better writer than Halliday.

She would never say that aloud, but it was true. She was also more dogged in pursuit of a story. She'd had to be, to prove she could play in the boys' sandbox.

Her eyes stung, and Kate squeezed them shut. Angry crying might make her feel better, but she wouldn't do it here for anything.

I could go freelance.

The thought came out of nowhere. Was it practical? It might mean depending even more on Rose and Sebastian for contacts. That would be uncomfortable, especially given her and Sebastian's new relationship. But surely getting a story here was the same as anywhere. You landed a story, did a good job on it, made a favorable impression, and developed contacts. People wanted word to get out, and they brought it to you.

She couldn't hang around the pub and down multiple pints in the hope of accosting a government minister, but there were other methods.

But maybe she was overreacting because she was mad. Maybe the smart move would be to take the congressional beat and make the best of it.

But everything inside her said no, both because of Sebastian and because she had her share of professional pride. So what could she do instead?

CHAPTER 19

I can't believe they're shipping you home this way," Rose said over dinner. "They consider your work exemplary, so can't they let you make the decision?"

"Apparently not." Kate picked at a pretty summer pudding that contained strawberries, raspberries, and black currants. The berry juice turned the bread casing a deep, beautiful pink. "Looking back, I should've expected it. They sent me here originally with the idea of my going to France with the BEF, taking a look at the training, shooting some photos, and being back home before everything blew up. I've actually been on borrowed time all along."

The candlelight picked up furrows of concern in John's lean face. "Still, it's a shame. Though I understand their desire to be chivalrous."

Carefully, because he meant well, Kate replied, "Unfortunately, men barring women from the dangerous or the ugly to protect us has also kept us from seizing opportunities."

Rose looked down the table at her husband, who nodded. Turning to Kate, she said, "If you decide not to go, you're welcome to stay here, of course."

"That's very kind, but if I don't go, I'm sure to lose my job. I wouldn't be able to pay you, and I won't impose." She managed to speak calmly though disappointment burned her throat. Leaving wouldn't only cost her career opportunities. It would be the end for her and Sebastian. There was no guarantee they would both live through the war or, if they did, that they would feel the same after months or years apart.

"It's not an imposition when you perform a valuable service, such as helping with the war effort," Sebastian noted.

"You would be company for me," Rose added. "Charity work occupies only so much time. Once the war heats up, the time I'm home will be spent alone even more than it is now."

"I fear she's correct," John said. "If you need help with your visa until you find work, I can probably help you. Still, you should think long and hard about whether staying is wise. The Luftwaffe are mostly harassing shipping at present. They won't limit themselves forever, though, and let's not forget your vision of invasion craft on the French coast." Looking to his brother-in-law, he added, "Wouldn't you say so, Seb?"

Sebastian nodded, his gaze on Kate's face. "I want you safely at home. I also want you here, both because I would miss you and because I think you could help. As I said last night, though, this is not your fight. At least not yet."

"If I'm helpful enough, maybe it won't ever be my country's fight."

They all knew that was unlikely, given Hitler's drive to conquer, but no one argued.

As everyone resumed eating their desserts, Kate eyed them surreptitiously. Rose had seemed delighted when she walked in on Kate and Sebastian kissing last night. She must've told John, who hadn't mentioned it but also hadn't changed his attitude toward Kate.

"I apologize for tying up your evening with this," Kate said. "I hope you'll bear with me a while longer. I'm wrestling with whether I want to stay—personal interests aside—for my career or to help the war effort or just because I'm angry at being so easily replaced."

"All three are valid reasons," Sebastian said. "You're a seer, Kate. If you trust your instincts, you'll know what you should do."

That was the problem. She'd trusted her instincts all her life. Now that she knew they were special, though, doubt of her interpretations could be paralyzing.

~

Later, Kate and Sebastian sat in the upstairs parlor together. Last night's lesson hadn't been anything new, only practice using witchfire. Sebastian had wanted her to practice pushing out power, which he described as the basis of magic use, and he considered that a good way to do it.

He held out his left hand. "Take my hand, Kate. I'll feed magic to you the way I did to push back your visions."

She complied, and he channeled power into the grip.

Kate frowned. "It feels…warmer than it did." In fact, awareness of his power flowed through her entire body. Awareness of him came with it and made her fidgety. She hadn't felt that when he helped her control her visions.

"That's because I'm not funneling it against your own power but simply into it. Now think of the way you feed witchfire into a candle wick and imagine the stream of your power rolling into my hand."

"Like this?" The sensation of power moving out of her chest and down her arm had become familiar. She channeled it farther, into his hand, and his fingers tightened on hers.

His eyes darkened. "Very good," he said, his voice clipped.

Shifting to sit on the table facing her, he held out his other hand. "Let's try it this way. You feed power into my left hand while I feed it into your right."

Her awareness of him deepened until the urge to squirm became almost unbearable. Judging by the darkening of his eyes and the tension in his face he felt the same desire.

"Sebastian…" she choked.

He muttered something she couldn't understand, dropped her hands, and reached for her. Kate almost dived into his arms. His mouth caught hers in a long, deep kiss. She dimly felt him tug her onto his lap.

His knee…

Her breasts flattened against his chest, and she forgot his injury. His tongue stroking hers set up a matching pulse deep within her.

Groaning, he pressed kisses along her neck. Her hands slid into his short, soft hair, and she pressed closer to him.

He pressed his face into her neck, his hold tightening, and Kate gasped.

"Sebastian—wait."

Raising his head, he met her gaze. "Too fast?"

"No." She swallowed hard. "Too distracting. Is it…is this sharing of magic always like this?"

He shook his head. "It's like this for us because of our feelings for each other. I'm not…filtering the power, for lack of a better phrase, the way I would with anyone else."

"I don't even know how to filter it."

"It's instinctive." He kissed her quickly. "Perhaps you should practice this with Rose. For now, we can move on to reading past a ward. Let me fetch something."

She switched back to the loveseat. "Am I, um, too heavy?"

"My knee's the problem. My leg above and below it is sturdy enough."

He limped to the desk in the corner and retrieved a wooden box about three inches deep and six inches on a side. "I had John ward this earlier tonight. You and I will now try to See what's in it."

"Do you know already?"

"No. A seer's Sight should defeat any ward. We needn't break the ward to see past it, which is fortunate because breaking a ward often alerts the wizard who set it and requires a very fast escape to avoid serious trouble."

"I thought you said we had to go to this crypt to see past the ward."

"It's an unusual ward. None of us has been able to See past it to the document itself, save Amelia. Perhaps she could See its image because she caught a flash of it from the Lord Wyndon of her day. A seer can usually See through any ward without going anywhere near it. However, it's supposedly possible for a seer to push magical Sight physically through a ward. Or so Aunt Amelia's Julian suggested in the books of his I've read."

Sebastian set the box on the table and seated himself beside her. "Turn your full attention to the box, and will the contents to appear to you."

"You do remember that I can't summon a vision the way you do?"

"It isn't that you can't but that you haven't yet mastered the trick. Have a go at this, and let's see what happens."

Could it really be that easy? Kate stared at the box. *What are you hiding? Show me.*

Nothing came to her.

After a couple of minutes, she looked back at Sebastian. "Do you know what's in there?"

"I do now." He stared at the box. Slowly, he said, "Let's try something different. Move your hand toward the box until you feel the magic in the ward. Then hold it there."

Kate complied. When power tingled across her fingers and palm, she paused. "I feel it."

"Good. Now think about what it's hiding. See whether you can summon the image."

Kate tried. A current like electric shock jabbed her palm and knocked her hand a foot away. Kate choked back a cry.

"Darling, are you all right?" Sebastian caught her hand and ran his fingers gently over her palm.

"It stings, but it's fading."

"I suspect you fed magic into the ward. It shouldn't react that way to passive magical presence."

"Isn't summoning visions magic?"

"Yes, but it's internal, puts no magic into the world." He squeezed her hand. "Try again."

Kate did as he asked. Again, the ward stung her hand.

"Game for another go?" he asked.

She did but with the same result. "I'm obviously not doing this right."

"Let's try something different. Put your hand against the ward and think about the magic in it. Open your mind and your senses but don't reach for anything."

Steeling herself, she tried again. This time, she caught an image. Vague and fleeting, it brushed across her mind. She closed her eyes and tried again.

When she opened them, Sebastian raised his brows. "Find something?"

"Sort of. I…there was an image of John with his hand over the box, a sense of magic flowing around it. But nothing about what the magic hid."

"That's progress. Let's take a break."

Sebastian poured water while Kate set ginger biscuits on a small plate for the two of them to share.

When he put his arm along the back of the loveseat, she leaned into his side. Sebastian kissed the top of her head.

"You will get the hang of this, Kate. It simply takes time."

"I may not have time." Sighing, she nestled against him. "I thought about freelancing, but building a network of contacts and a reputation, especially enough to make a living, is a slow process. If I can't support myself, I'll have to take the job CNU is offering in DC."

"I would miss you, but I would be glad to have you out of harm's way. As for your Gifts, Miranda has trained seers for more than two hundred years. She can help you master your visions and carry messages between us. For that matter, I could visit you from time to time."

"How do you figure? It's four or five days to New York by boat and then a day on the train to reach DC, and then the same in reverse. Can you be gone that long?"

"You're forgetting the afterworld. I can travel from here to anywhere in the States in under an hour."

"You would do that?"

"To see you, yes. As often as possible."

They kissed again but broke the kiss before it became too intense. They had work to do tonight.

"Let's try something," Sebastian said. "See whether you can lay your hand on the box if you use no magic whatever. Like this." He demonstrated.

"That's how you carried it over here from the desk." She hadn't noticed that at the time.

Since it hadn't stung him, it probably wouldn't shock her. Kate stretched her hand out carefully and laid it on the smooth wood. "So far, so good."

"Now open yourself, like opening your senses, and tell me what comes to you. Open your senses first."

Kate tried. The box stung her hand. With a yelp, she pulled it back and shook it. "So much for that."

Sebastian shook his head. "Give me your hand." Holding it, he said, "Now open your senses... Hmm, I feel your magic like static against my palm. You used your Gift in unorthodox ways for so long that you may not approach your magic the same way the rest of us do."

"Are you saying I have to unlearn what I didn't realize I'd learned at all?"

"More or less." He gave her a wry grin. "Let's stop for now. When you go home tonight, open your senses on the train. Try to pinpoint everyone in the car with you. Do the same on the street between the station and your flat. If you like, I'll go with you and hold your hand."

"This is that big a problem?"

"It could be. At least when we go against that ward together. It may be that I can handle the ward with you simply feeding magic to me, but we'll have a better chance if we both channel our seer Gifts at whatever's beyond it. That aside, I hope you'll never be in danger from another Gifted, but if you are, leaking magic when you open your senses could betray your location. You should learn this for your own safety anyway."

"You're serious." When he nodded, she shook her head. "Do you truly expect that I'll need this someday? That some Gifted person might attack me or something?"

"Thanks to the secret magical work I mentioned, I sometimes make enemies. If you work with me, possibly even if you're known to be part of my family but inexperienced, you could become a target."

"That's lovely." Really not. In fact, it was chilling.

He shrugged. "No one ever expects an emergency. That's why it's an emergency."

~

Returning to her flat the next afternoon, Kate paused at the door and opened her senses. A tingle at the nape of her neck signaled human presence, two people in the flat who were probably Marge and Janet. No one in the flat they shared this floor with or in the one below it. Pigeons on the roof, though, and a mouse in the stairwell wall.

At least she could pinpoint who was here, but how could she learn to do it without what Sebastian called *leaking* magic last night? Really, not a flattering term.

She unlocked the door and walked in. Sure enough, Marge and Janet sat at the little table in the parlor having tea. Kate smiled a greeting, but her heart wasn't in it.

"What's wrong, honey?" Marge asked.

"Have some tea," Janet urged. "We pooled our sugar ration to make chocolate biscuits. At least chocolate's not on ration yet."

"I could use some chocolate." Kate sat down by Marge on the sofa.

Her friends said nothing while she fixed tea and put a couple of chocolate cookies on a plate. Now that tea had gone on ration, they reused the leaves. It was bound to be weak, but sharing it would be a comfort.

After she taken her first sip, they both stared at her.

"Well?" Janet asked.

Kate shrugged. "I'm developing a dynamite story. Ties to the war effort, human interest, brave heroes. Lew says the censors likely won't pass it."

Marge shifted to face Kate. "Tell us more."

"A friend of my cousin Rose has befriended some Polish Air Force pilots."

"I'd heard some of them were here, along with some of their army," Janet said.

"According to Rose's friend, Poland had one of the best air force training programs on the continent. Her husband's airplane mad, which is how they became interested in these pilots. First the Germans rolled into Poland, and then the Russians. Both had many derisive things to say about the Polish military. Rose's friends in the army, though, say that's propaganda, that the Poles fought valiantly."

"So are they with the RAF?" Marge asked.

"Not exactly." Kate frowned down at her cup. "The RAF took them in, but they treat them abysmally. Most of them don't speak English, and it's as though the higher ranks in the military assume that makes them stupid. They've had accomplished fighter pilots practicing maneuvers on tricycles. Tricycles, for goodness' sake!"

As Janet and Marge exchanged a glance, Kate finished, "All they want to do is fight for their country, and they're apparently well able to do so. Yet no one will give them a chance."

"No wonder Lew doesn't think the censors will clear it," Marge said. "Do you disagree?"

"No, but I had to try. They deserve to have their stories told."

"Did you, ah, talk to anyone from Fighter Command?" Janet asked.

"I tried. They brushed me off." Kate blew out a hard sigh. "I'm sure they have a very different take on the situation, and I would've liked to hear it. But I got the distinct impression they didn't take me seriously."

"Yet again," Marge said, her voice dry. "Someday, some woman is going to break the story of the century and all the men who stood in her way will have apoplexy."

Kate and Janet toasted her silently with their cups.

"Have you decided about Washington?" Janet asked.

"Unless something comes up, I'll have to go. I need a job, and I don't think I can earn enough here to live on. I just don't have the contacts."

"Probably right," Janet said. "I would help if I could. There might be openings at smaller papers as the men're called up. You might even get a job that qualifies you for a work permit. If you can hold out."

"Rose offered me a place to stay, but I hate to impose. She's a very distant cousin, and I just cannot mooch off her."

The thought of never seeing Sebastian again physically hurt her chest. Yes, he would try to visit through this afterworld, but as the war rolled onward, how much time would he truly have for that? She should enjoy being with him while she could. It would take a miracle for their new relationship to last once she returned home.

"He's a lord of some kind, isn't he?" Marge asked. "Didn't you say his sister married an earl? Maybe they know someone who can help you stay here. If that's what you want to do."

"I don't know," Kate said. "They haven't mentioned anything like that."

Marge hesitated. "I put in for a transfer home today. If things get ugly, or *when* they do, I want to be near my family. Or at least on the same continent. My boss is pretty sure it'll go through. Our home office isn't as antsy as yours about a woman in a war zone, but that could change. Regardless, I want to go home while it's still fairly easy to do that."

Betty's arrival interrupted them. They exchanged a flurry of greetings while she fixed a cup of tea and a few cookies. Janet poured hot water into the teapot to brew more.

"We were just discussing Kate's situation," Marge said.

Betty shook her head. "I know you want to stay, and more power to you even if I don't understand. I mean, I do understand because war is always a big story. But it comes with falling bombs and flying bullets, and that is just not for me."

"It's not a prospect I like much," Kate conceded, "but I feel as if I might be able to help."

Janet said, "Don't give up too soon. Let's see what develops. It might not be enough to live on, but perhaps you could earn enough so you could live with your cousin and contribute something. Not feel like a mooch."

"What's this?" Betty perked up. "Live with her cousin the earl?"

Heat fairly blazed in Kate's cheeks. "No," she managed. "His sister."

"Just teasing you." Betty patted Kate's knee. "You're the only one of us who really wants to work for a paper long term. For me, it's a stopgap. I mean to have fun with it, but when I walk away, I won't have any regrets."

"I know." Unfortunately, every man Kate had dated, including the one man she'd been serious about, had assumed she would give up her job to be a homemaker. There was nothing in the world wrong with that, as Mom and Dad's happy life and family proved, but Kate loved chasing stories, landing interviews, and showing people a truth they maybe hadn't recognized before. She might give that up for a family but not for a man who insisted on it.

"I'd better pack some more," she said. Regardless of what she decided, she couldn't stay here without a salary. She set her cup, saucer, and plate in the bin they used to carry dishes down to the common kitchen for washing.

While she packed, maybe she could come up with some idea that would let her stay in England.

CHAPTER 20

On his way home, Sebastian stopped in at the Merlin Club. Genevieve would've informed him of anything urgent, but he liked to stay in touch.

They met in her office, as usual, with tea and cinnamon biscuits. "I intended to send you a note today," she said. "We've news from Berlin."

"Important news?"

"It could be." Pouring tea, Genevieve shook her head. "This is both the peril and the benefit of sending young agents. If I'd known Algernon meant to try this, I would've absolutely forbidden it. But I must admit he managed it brilliantly."

"Managed what?" Sebastian blew on his tea to cool it.

"He walked into the Chancellery, pretty as you please, with no protection other than an invisibility glamour."

"Good God! Is he safe?" The building that housed Hitler's offices surely had tight security.

"For a miracle, yes. He has news, which I read in a lengthy missive on his desk this afternoon." Frowning, she stirred her tea. "I wish we had a better way to communicate. If anyone had seen that before he destroyed it, they would've killed him."

"Indeed. But we've wanted better communications a hundred years and more."

"Very true. Anyway, the Nazis are working on their invasion plans, which they're calling Sea Lion. By the way, I passed your query about *zeeloovuh* to him, and that's what it means. Sea Lion."

"If only we'd known the significance sooner."

"We do what we can. They've chosen harbors on the coast of France for massing their transports. Hitler has ordered the Wehrmacht and the Kriegsmarine to figure out how his army crosses the Channel in the teeth of the RAF and the Royal Navy. The suggestion being put forth is that the Luftwaffe must destroy the RAF, especially Fighter Command, by destroying the airfields as well as shooting down as many planes as they can."

"And damage the navy as much as possible, I suppose."

Genevieve nodded. "Hitler's making a big speech in a couple of weeks. It's to be an ultimatum."

"Well, of course it is. Damn it." The figures on aircraft production streamed through his head. The total rose daily. In fact, the RAF were headed toward having more aircraft than pilots. Ramping up production of objects would always be far easier than ramping up training.

"How's our new seer?" she asked.

"Coming along. Training her presents unique challenges, though. Because she was unaware she possessed magical Gifts, she used some of them unwittingly—along the lines of wishful thinking—and so has an unconventional approach. Habits to unlearn."

"Will she help us?"

"She's trying, but her employer has recalled her to the States. Doesn't like the responsibility for putting a woman in a war zone."

"I suppose, though there will be plenty of us where bombs are falling soon enough." Genevieve frowned. "You know, we could use someone to index the books in the library. I should think a reporter would be fairly good at that. We could pay her. Of course, she would have to join the club."

"Of course." Kate in the Merlin Club was easier to envision than it once had been. Many of the codices and grimoires in the library had no indices. The librarian leafed through them hastily and wrote their topics in a file, but that wasn't the same as having a comprehensive list of what each book covered.

"I think she'll go," Sebastian said. "If she doesn't, I'll keep that in mind."

∼

How's your packing coming?" Sebastian asked Kate that evening. They'd had dinner at his house for a change, to the delight of the Bradshaws, and now sat in his personal library. It couldn't compare to the one at Hawkstowe or even to the Merlin Club's. Sitting here among all the books, though, was always restful. Having Kate sit beside him on the sofa was a pleasure not to be squandered, as their time together was running out.

"It's mostly done. I turned in what I think will be my last story today. Unless the Luftwaffe starts targeting passenger liners. In which case, I probably can't sail home."

"I'll take you home, Kate. Going through the afterworld won't be pleasant, as it's a ghastly place, but we must go there anyway to tackle that ward."

She looked at him thoughtfully. "Should I know more about this place?"

"I can tell you more if you like, but it's easier to believe when you've seen it."

"All right then." Kate dropped her head against his shoulder. "The days are ticking away, and I need to allow time for travel to Southampton. I think we shouldn't wait much longer to tackle this ward. If we wait, only to fail the first couple of times, we might run out of time. Then you truly would have to take me and my baggage home."

"Baggage?" He pretended to shudder. "No one said anything about baggage."

"Well, what do you expect? I've been here for months. I have clothes, my cameras, and a few other things. A couple of steamer trunks full."

"Then we'll practice again tonight and try tomorrow. Then, whether or not we succeed, I'd like to take you out to dinner the next evening."

They would have at least one real date before she left. "Sounds good. So let's practice."

Hand in hand, they walked to the desk. Three boxes varying in size from a foot long to a few inches sat on it.

"I warded these," he said. "Pick one and see if you can read through the ward."

Kate held her right hand, palm down, about half an inch above the largest box's lid. That was about where she should feel the ward, so it was a good start.

"It's… I can see you, in my mind, see you raising the ward. You make it look so easy."

"One day, so will you. Can you See past it?"

"No…" She turned startled eyes to him. "I see you putting a letter opener in the box."

"So you saw the box before the ward surrounded it. Interesting. Come over here." He lit the fire in the library hearth with a stream of green witchlight.

The night was warm for a fire, but Kate didn't protest. She must've realized where this was going. The heat warmed his face. He would be sweating shortly, so best to have this done.

"Direct your magic at the fire, Kate." He didn't see it, but he felt it. If she didn't need to use witchlight, to make the power visible, her skill was improving. "Good job. Now feel the fire's movement. The crackling, the flickering. The igniting bark on the logs."

When she nodded, he said, "Now think of the vision you saw and push it along your magic into the flames."

The power behind her effort washed outward, brushing his magical senses. But the flames remained unchanged. The mantel clock ticked off minutes.

When sweat appeared on her upper lip, he touched her arm lightly. "Wait. Let's try something else. Think of something familiar. Perhaps the orchard you mentioned to me once. Imagine seeing that in the flames."

Kate bit her lip. Again, the effort she made leaked magic. The flames flickered for a moment, a flash of sunshine coming through green leaves to make dappled patterns on the grass below the trees. Then it vanished.

"You almost had it." He squeezed her waist. "Try it again."

She tensed in his hold. "It's no use. It doesn't work for me the way it does for you."

He'd Seen this moment before, weeks ago, in Dover, though his vision hadn't exactly matched reality. But he hadn't Seen how the situation would resolve.

Gently, he said, "Sometimes we trip over our own doubts. How many times did someone say you would never be a journalist? Yet here you are. Because you wanted that badly enough."

"It's not the same thing."

"Come and sit down a minute." A wave of his hand snuffed the fire.

He poured them each a glass of cider and handed her one. Rose was so much better at this sort of thing than he was, but she wasn't here. He had best not botch this.

"I tried," she repeated, looking anywhere but at him.

"I know you did. I felt the effort. May I ask you something?"

"Sure. Of course." Yet she still wouldn't look at him.

"You worry about how your family will react to your magic, I know. I hoped that would decrease as you became more comfortable with the power. It hasn't, though. Has it?"

"No."

The answer to this next question might be painful, but he needed to know. "Is being with me making that worse? Is it adding to your worries?"

"Maybe some, but…if they accept me, they'll accept you. You're a good man, Sebastian. The kind they would want for me." With a feeble smile, she added, "Aside from the title, I mean. Nobody in Missouri expects their daughters to date an earl."

"I suppose not, but let's go back to what you said a moment ago, the bit that started with 'if they accept' you. You needn't tell them about your Gifts if you would rather not, but you've always been close. You don't like keeping secrets. Have I interpreted that correctly?"

"Yes."

"And now that you're going home, you face that decision."

"Among others." Another feeble smile.

She tried so hard to keep her spirits up, to keep from lowering his. How could he not be smitten with her? How could he not send her away if that would make things easier for her?

"I need your help at Otterden Abbey with that ward. After that… Kate, I don't want to lose you. To lose the chance to find out what we might have together. But even more, I don't want to cause you a moment's unhappiness. If you'll be happier without me—"

"No. No, Sebastian." Finally, she turned to look at him. "It's a weird, painful jumble of feelings, but I always felt I was different. The hunches, as you called them, the weird knowing I felt sometimes, the…uncanny skill at hide and seek. Nobody else I knew had all that. You do. Rose and John understand it. So even though I worry about how to deal with Mom and Dad and my brothers, walking away from the people who understand all of me would make things worse. I would feel as though I'd cut off part of myself."

"The other night, you said you couldn't go back to seeing the world as you had before."

"Yes. That applies here, too."

When he extended his arm, she settled against his side. They drank their cider in silence, and the tension gradually left her body.

Sebastian pressed a kiss against her hairline. "Kate?"

"Hmm?" She looked up at him.

"What did the letter opener look like?"

"It's silver metal with an engraved handle. The inside of the box is blue velvet or something like it."

"That's right. Could you sketch it if you had to?"

"Maybe. What are you thinking?"

"If I can gain even a brief look at the contents of the room behind the ward in the abbey crypt, I should know whether Edmund's confession is there. But it may be that I won't gain that. It may be that you do."

"How can that be? I've failed every time."

"We'll be working together, and shared power can filter through in odd ways. If we can see through the ward, focus on a document with a heavy, red wax seal in the lower right corner. Assuming it's there, of course. Pay as much attention as you can to the seal. If you sketch it for me, I'll know whether or not it's Edmund's. If I'm not sure, Edmund may be able to tell us."

"I'll try, of course."

"I know you will. There's one other thing. So far as I know, there have never been two Mainwaring seers in the same generation. Nor any two seers working together. Because the Gift is so rare, it hasn't been studied much. If we join our magic and wield our Gift together, the magic may work in a way we cannot anticipate."

"That's kind of scary."

"It is." He looked directly into her eyes, willing her to feel his sincerity. "But it's unlikely to do anything harmful. Some sort of odd vision is a more likely result. Regardless, I trust you, Kate. I'm happy to have you at my side."

"I'll do my best." She took a deep breath. "Things are jumbled up inside me, my emotions, dealing with magic, worry over my situation. But I do trust you."

"Then we should manage well enough, even if we fail."

If they did, though, what else could he try?

CHAPTER 21

Kate complied with Sebastian's request by dressing for activity. Her dungarees, short-sleeved, flowered blouse, and brown lace-up oxfords would've sufficed for roaming outdoors at home.

When his butler, Bradshaw, ushered her into the upstairs parlor, Sebastian eyed her with approval.

"Is this all right?" she asked, setting her purse down by a chair.

His trousers, open-throated blue shirt, and brogans proclaimed that he had also dressed to be practical.

"That will do nicely. Let's sit a moment."

They sat on the sofa. Taking her hand, he said, "This will sound very strange, but no description can match the reality. I told you about the afterworld and the wraiths who infest it."

"Doomed souls."

"Yes. What I didn't tell you because it didn't matter at the time is that they attack any living being stepping through a portal into that realm."

Stunned and suddenly anxious, she stared at him. He tightened his grip on her hand.

"I know how to protect us and to drive them away," he assured her. "The important thing is to avoid panic and stay close to me. Richard and Miranda will be waiting for us on the other side. Perhaps my father as well, and I would wager Miles will be there."

"Miles from the house party?"

Sebastian's grin was warm with affection. "The very same. By the way, his father lost our lands and titles for disagreeing with Henry VIII about his divorce, but Miles's valor against the Armada and in the years after induced Queen Elizabeth to restore them." Sobering, he added, "It was Miles's father who gave himself to the wraiths, so Miles likely won't be at his best for a time."

"I understand."

"I'll use magic to create a portal. Then we simply walk through it. There will be cold, and the air will resist, like walking into a headwind. We must push forward. Once we clear that resistance, we'll have made the crossing. To return to the real world, you'll need an anchor, a natural object like a rock or a twig not shaped by human hands. I picked up a stone for you in the garden earlier. Any questions?"

"I don't think I know enough to have questions." She blew out a hard breath. "You've done this before, I take it?"

"Many times."

"Well, you're still here, so I suppose that's okay."

"I won't let anything happen to you. I promise."

"I know you won't." Of that much, at least, she was certain. She kissed him, and the kiss softened and lengthened.

When Sebastian raised his head, his eyes searched hers. "We're all right, so long as one of us has an anchor and we're together. But it's good to have two in case we drop or lose one."

"I don't think I want to know how the *losing* part might happen in a place like that."

He kissed her quickly. "Hang on to your pebble, and all will be well.

I hope so. "Lead on."

Still holding hands, they stood. Sebastian steered her so they faced the door. To her surprise, he passed her his cane. "Hold this. I need a hand to make the portal and one to grip yours so you come through with me."

"Can I beat off wraiths with it?" No matter what he said, the idea of such beings attacking was nerve-racking.

"You won't need to." He raised his hand. Argent power streamed from it to form a rectangle in front of the hallway door. "That's a portal. Don't let go of my hand."

As he'd said, they walked into cold air that grew dense, as though it tried to push them back. Sebastian drew her closer so they forced their way through as one.

The cold stopped, and purple-gray mists roiled around them. The air stank of rotten eggs.

Shrieks split the fog, so shrill and angry that Kate jumped. At least a dozen ghastly, skeletal shapes swooped out of the clouds with claws extended. She instinctively pressed close to Sebastian as silvery power tinted with purple formed a nimbus around them.

"Begone," he shouted. Silvery magic streamed from his hand, this time tinted with purple. He made a slashing motion that whipped the bolt of power across the charging horde. Still shrieking, they wheeled away.

When they vanished, the quiet seemed eerie.

"Welcome," Miranda said. Smiling, she and Richard walked out of the fog. The mists hovered around their lower legs, but gaps in the fog occasionally offered glimpses of ground like solid shadow.

Sebastian embraced them. Hesitantly, so did Kate. Neither held her for long, as though they knew this felt strange to her.

Richard smiled. "It must seem odd to embrace someone you're accustomed to seeing through."

"A little. But I can't see through you now."

"In this realm," he replied, "we manifest as solid. We choose our appearances, our clothing, and so on. But the veil between this realm and yours filters out some of the power that makes us seem substantial."

"I see. Um, thanks."

"Of course." He patted her arm, and the touch carried surprising warmth.

"Miles said he'll meet you at Otterden," Miranda told Sebastian. "Your father is with him. Reg and our Robin are in Paris."

Sebastian took his cane from Kate and caught her hand again. "We travel this realm by thinking of the place in the living world we want to reach and walking. Edmund says walking isn't really necessary, but I like the feeling of movement it gives."

"Edmund? The one who, ah…"

"Cursed us all. Yes," Richard answered in a dry voice.

They all set off through the fog. In a few minutes, the mists thinned, revealing Miles's tall figure. Next to him stood a man in simple trousers, a white, open-throated shirt with the sleeves rolled up, and a sweater vest. Like Miles, he bore an uncanny resemblance to Sebastian.

And to Richard. Kate raised an eyebrow. "Do all the Mainwaring men look alike?"

Richard grinned. "We're fortunate that way."

Smiling, Kate shook her head.

Sebastian greeted both men and introduced Kate to the other man, his father. Miles pressed her hand between his and bowed over it. "I'm deeply grateful for your help, my dear."

"He speaks for us all." Sebastian's father, Reginald, shook her hand. "A pleasure to meet you, Kate."

"Thank you. It's good to meet you." Struck by a sudden thought, she cocked her head. "I've never met so many of my natural mother's kin. I never thought I would."

"We are also your family," Richard said, "and we're so very glad to have you among us."

Kate hugged him again.

"We should set about it," Sebastian said. "We'll go to the corner and into that building over there." He pointed at a square, stone structure with a courtyard in the middle and covered walkways on two sides. Its outlines were faintly hazy, as though viewed through a purple-gray veil.

"Is that a church?" she asked.

"This was once an abbey, and yes, what's now the hall was its church. Traveling through here, we can pass through the wards around its walls and into the structure."

"I cannot do that," Miles grumbled. "It's permitted for the living only."

"I was coming to that," Sebastian said. "Walking through a wall will seem very strange. You won't feel anything physical, but mentally, it's…weird."

"Okay." This entire business of magic still felt weird, so what was a bit more?

"Good luck to you," Miles said.

Sebastian led Kate across the front of the building to the door of what had been the church. They passed through it—definitely weird, though she felt nothing physical—and into a darkened hall. Only faint light filtered through the stained-glass windows.

Although she'd always been able to see better than her family in the dark—a benefit of her Gifts, Sebastian had explained—Kate waited for her eyes to adjust.

"There's a dais at the far end," he said. "A marble serving stand near the rear slides aside, allowing access to the stairs below it. They lead to the crypt."

Horror movie, Kate thought, but she said nothing. This whole business seemed like something out of a horror movie.

"The stairs are below the serving stand. It grates when it moves aside, so I'll muffle the sound magically. You never know when someone who can't sleep will be strolling about."

He paused, peering into her face. Witchlight formed at his fingertip, casting strange shadows over his features. "Are you with me, Kate? Is any of this too much?"

It was all very strange, but there was no avoiding the task. "If you say this will work, I believe you."

"Good. No one in the living world can see my witchlight while we're in this realm. Once we step out, however, it will be visible if I'm still using it. So we go out in the dark. I can see well enough to find our way, though barely. Once we're in the crypt, we can have light."

"Okay."

A gleam that might've been admiration lit his eyes before he extinguished his light. "Then let's go."

~

They re-entered the living world in front of the dais. Sebastian opened his senses and verified that they were alone. "Wait here," he said.

He stepped onto the dais and pushed the stone that triggered the serving stand. It slid aside, revealing the stairs. When he beckoned to Kate, she joined him.

"I'll go first," he announced. He set a green globe of witchlight floating before them. Holding her hand, he followed the light down the stairs.

"This place feels like something out of a horror movie." Kate frowned at the crypt. "Nothing good ever happens in these places."

"That would make it the perfect spot to hide something." He squeezed her waist. "Ready to have a go?"

"Lead on," she replied.

He led her to the corner where the warded doorway stood. They had to squeeze into the space at the end of the wall tombs. "We're now under the corner of the cloister beside the building. Extend your hand until you can feel the ward, then draw it back."

"Okay." Her face looked pale, but perhaps that was only the effect of the witchlight. She did as he asked. "What next?"

He laid his cane on the floor. "I'll put my hand alongside the ward. When I do, feed power into me and concentrate on learning what's behind that door. If we can summon a vision, we'll know whether further burglary is warranted."

"Maybe it's a silly question, but if Edmund's confession is here, why can't you just buy it from Lord Wyndon? Why didn't someone down the generations do so?"

"Old family feud, at least for a couple of centuries. The Lord Wyndon of 1815 would never have parted with it. By now, the feud may be less important. The current earl may not even know what he has. But he's the sort who, if he knew it was important to us, would never part with it. Their family have always been that way."

Kate nodded. "Got it."

"Ready?" he asked.

When she nodded, he extended his hand until the warding magic tingled against his fingers and palm. This was no faint prickling but much like being jabbed with tiny needles. Careful not to reach, he opened his senses but Saw nothing.

"I can't See beyond it. Feed me the power," he said, "and concentrate."

Kate's magic slid into his fingers, then up his arm. Into his temples? Was something wrong? That had never—but he'd never done this with a seer. Perhaps...

Her lips tightened, but she said nothing.

Sebastian summoned power, reaching. "Feeding you some as well," he ground out. "Joining our Gifts."

The sight of the door flickered, then reappeared. Flickered again.

"Maybe if we created a circuit?" Kate laid her hand over his near the ward and gripped hard. Now shared power coursed through them both in a closed loop, amplifying itself.

Again, he reached.

Show me, he insisted, not because a ward could answer but because the question focused his will without pushing magic into the ward itself.

Oh, come on! came a mental voice. Shocked, because that also had never happened, he recognized it as Kate's.

His eyesight winked out, overlaid by Gifted Sight. Darkness. A small room lined with shelves that held books, scrolls, and small chests.

Pushing down his excitement, he reached for more.

"I see the seal," Kate murmured. "Table with things on it."

In that instant, he Saw it too. Sharing power had let them share their Gifts. Atop a long table in the room's center, two low stands held a sword parallel to the tabletop. A pair of ornate candlesticks flanked it. Various documents lay scattered on the table, and shelves lined with chests, books, and scrolls lined the wall beside it. On the lowest shelf lay a document with a glass cover over it. Sebastian focused his Gift on the papers. Hard to get a good enough look.

The ward was growing hotter, though. If he'd felt this heat near a stove, he would've moved his hand.

"Kate, we should—"

With a sizzling *bang*, the ward flung them backward. Sebastian's bad knee slammed into the edge of the tomb shelving. A loud *crack* announced bone shattering. Agony roared through his veins and crashed behind his eyes. He barely swallowed a yell.

Passing out had a great deal of appeal, but— "Kate?"

Luckily, his witchlight still glowed above them.

He rolled toward her. His knee screamed as it moved on the pavement, and his left shoulder protested. Kate lay sprawled on her back beside him, her head turned away.

If he'd gotten her killed, he would never forgive himself *No. No, not that. Please don't let her be—*

She moved her head and whimpered.

"Easy," he said. "Easy, sweetheart. Let me see. Did you hit your head?"

"Hurts." Cloudy with pain, her eyes opened. "There are—there's two of you."

"Lie still." He was no healer, but he knew the basics of checking someone. Opening his magical senses, he held his hand about six inches above her and slowly ran it over her body. Moving to examine her legs sent searing pain through his leg and jabbed into his side, but he had to know how badly she was hurt.

"Nothing broken," he realized in relief, "but you've banged your head good and proper. How many of me now?"

"Two...no, three for a second." She blinked at him. "I have a concussion, don't I?"

"Most likely. I've friends who can fix us in no time, but they're in London."

"Are you hurt?"

"Not badly," he lied. Considering the difficulty of hauling himself off this floor, returning to London seemed a herculean task. "Stay still. I'll stand and then help you up."

He reached up for the edge of the nearest tomb niche, positioned his good leg under him, and pulled himself up.

"Sebastian, you don't look good. Any of you."

"I'll do. Can you sit up?" He should've helped her. Hadn't been thinking, and if he went down again, returning to an upright position would be nearly impossible.

Kate pushed herself up to sit. Blinking at him, she said, "I can manage."

She shifted sideways, got her legs under her and stood. A moment later, her eyes rolled up. She sagged against the tomb.

Sebastian lunged for her, and his bad leg gave way. Only clinging to the edge of the tomb saved him from another fall.

Kate caught herself on a tomb niche. Breathing hard, she held a hand toward him, palm out. "'s all right. Just…need a minute."

"Is the room stable?"

"No."

Hellfire and bloody damnation. No one knew they were here except the Mainwarings in the afterworld. They didn't know what was happening because they couldn't cross the wards around the building. He and Kate had to get themselves out of this. But how?

CHAPTER 22

W e'll rest a minute," he said. "Lean on the wall. Let your brain adjust to being upright."

"You're leaning on that tomb. You can't stand, can you?"

"Not at the moment."

She bent down for his cane, gasped, and jerked upright again. "I'm okay," she choked. "Just…bending's not a good idea."

"No. Rest, Kate. Breathe deeply."

Despite the pain, he managed to use his bad leg to reach his cane and roll it across the floor within reach. He had to shift his position to be able to stand on his good leg and not overbalance. Leaning down carefully, he grasped the cane.

Having it in his hand bolstered his confidence. He could walk. Without two functioning legs, though, he couldn't carry Kate. *Damn it.*

What could they do? She couldn't form an afterworld portal. Even if she could, they were below the level where they'd started, so would they enter the afterworld lower than the part where they'd left it? Were there even levels below the glassy shadow that passed for ground? A comment of Miles's implied they could change levels at will, but perhaps he'd misunderstood.

"Told you," she mumbled. "Nothing good in…places like this."

"I humbly apologize."

"Darn right." Her eyelids fluttered.

"Don't go to sleep, darling. Stay with me. Listen to me. We must return to the afterworld." He would simply have to hope the cellar-to-ground-level change wouldn't be a problem. Regardless, they couldn't stay here.

"Okay." She frowned up at him. "You said wards…when a ward breaks…it causes trouble." Casting an owlish look around, she asked, "Are we in trouble?"

The door ward still glowed. No one had come to investigate. At least, not yet.

"Not that sort of trouble," he said.

He'd always formed portals six to eight feet away from him, but there was no rule about it. He and Kate would never say upright for six feet.

The space between the wall niches, the nearest standing tomb, the ceiling, and the floor formed a rough rectangle. If he formed the portal there, roughly three feet away, they could probably make it that far. He would have to avoid passing out if they fell through, as none of the Mainwarings in the afterworld could find them or protect them from the wraiths until they passed out of the wards around this structure.

He told Kate what he was going to do.

Frowning, she slowly straightened away from him. "I can stand. If I can steady myself on your shoulder, I can walk. A couple of steps, anyway."

She sounded certain, but she couldn't be, not with dizziness plaguing her. There had probably been many times when she'd had to sound more certain than she was to make her way in a man's world. She must've pushed herself through on sheer will. If so, she could do this, too.

"I don't know whether I can walk through," he confessed. "I'll hop, but I may not be able to keep my balance. If I fall, stay close. No one can help us until we pass the wards around this property. I'll shield us and send the wraiths away, and then we'll go look for our family."

"Okay." Her face was pale, but she set her jaw. "Whenever you're ready."

Her eyes were still not focused. No help for that now, though. They would simply have to push themselves through this.

Sebastian formed the portal. That much, at least was easy. This close to it, however, the cold air was chilling. A single step would likely bring them up against resistance. Would they be able to push through it in their condition?

Only one way to find out.

Leaning heavily on the cane, he straightened. "Ready?"

Kate set her hand on his shoulder. "Go."

He hop-walked with the cane. Each jolting landing seared his leg. That couldn't matter, though, not now. She tottered into him but didn't fall.

The cold pushed against them, shortening his already awkward steps. Sebastian set his jaw. He couldn't send her through first because she couldn't protect herself.

"We—can do this," Kate panted.

"Lean into it and push," he told her.

They did, and the sudden breaching of the barrier threw them both off balance. Sebastian fell into the afterworld, and Kate crumpled beside him. The pain threatened to blind him, but triumphant shrieks jerked the world into focus. He coated himself and Kate in silver-purple shielding magic as a horde of wraiths swooped in.

Lacking the breath for *Begone*, he gathered as much magic from the mists as he could and flung it at the wraiths. When they swirled away, shrieking, he gave himself a mental pat on the back. He still had a bit of bite left in him.

"Now...what?" Her eyes looked even more unfocused. Her head drooped.

"Now we drag ourselves past these wards. Can you do that, darling?" He absolutely wouldn't leave her. The shielding he'd put around her might not last until he returned.

Her lips tightened. For a moment, her eyes focused. "Lead on."

"Let's think of Richard. I'm sure he's waiting with Miles just beyond the wards. If we think of him, the magic of this realm should lead us to him." If there wasn't some change of levels involved.

She nodded, only to wince.

There was nothing for him to pull himself up against. "I can't walk," he said. "Can you?"

"I could...I could help you." She picked up his cane. Holding it, she rose to her knees. "Use the cane and my shoulder."

It was a crazy idea, but it might actually work. If he didn't pull her off balance.

Holding the cane seemed to steady her. He rocked forward onto his good leg with the injured one off to the side. When he tried to rise, though, he pulled Kate over. She caught herself on her elbow. He sat down hard.

He'd had to do this in Czechoslovakia, but there had been trees and rocks and crude furnishings for leverage.

That had damaged his leg permanently. If this reinjury made it worse...but this wasn't the time for that worry.

"Hold the cane," he said. "I'll use that."

Sitting cross-legged, she gripped it with both hands. "Okay."

Sebastian rocked forward and then back so he crouched on his good leg. He pushed down on the cane, shoved up with his leg, and gained his footing.

Kate grinned at him.

"Now I'll hold it steady," he told her, praying he could, "and you stand."

Leaning on his good side, he managed to help her up. They were both breathing hard by the time she wobbled to her feet.

"Think of Richard," he reminded her, and they set off through the stinking fog.

It carried them up through the warded building as though it were a ramp, so they emerged from its wards in the courtyard. The shortest way out from there was through the covered walkway. They stumbled through it, clearing the wards. But their companions weren't in sight.

Kate wobbled, clearly trying not to lean on him. "Sebastian, where are they?"

"We must be close."

"God's feet," Richard's voice exclaimed. Then his many-times-great grandfather was there, bracing him.

"'Tis good that we heard the wraiths shriek." Miranda peered into Kate's face. "Look at me, Kate."

"She hit her head," Sebastian managed. "Concussion."

Miranda frowned and laid her palm across Kate's forehead. The frown deepened. Not a good sign.

From his left, his father said, "You've done a proper job on yourself as well, son." He and Miles emerged from the fog. Worry lined both their faces.

"We may've found it," Sebastian began.

"Later for that, lad," Miles told him. "The two of you need tending."

Miranda cast a worried glance from Kate to Sebastian. "I've listened to lectures in your medical schools, but I haven't healed anyone in more than two hundred years. I'm afraid to try healing it lest I make it worse. There're fragments of bone around your knee, Sebastian. As you move, you could jolt one of them into a blood vessel, and that could kill you. That, at least, I'm confident I can prevent."

Considering what he and Kate had done to escape the crypt, perhaps he was lucky that hadn't already happened.

Miranda continued, "I can magically immobilize all the bone around your knee. Neither of you has the strength to deal with returning to London as you are anyway. Richard, make a tent, if you please, with a couple of pallets inside. We don't need the distraction of wraiths just now."

The fog around them solidified, becoming blue canvas. Sebastian gaped at it. He'd never seen that particular magical feat.

"Help Sebastian lie down," Miranda said. She supported Kate, easing her onto the pallet that formed under the new tent.

His father and Miles helped Sebastian down as Richard finished their temporary home. He wanted to protest. He'd worked so hard to gain his feet, but Miranda knew what she was about.

As he lay on the pallet, his father gripped his shoulder. "All will be well, Seb. Don't fear."

The words were meant to comfort, but the look in his father's eyes was anything but reassuring. Sebastian knew his leg was bad. If he'd made it worse than it was before, if it wouldn't heal, what would he do?

~

S ebastian? Come now, Major. Let's have a look at you."
The gruff voice drew Sebastian out of a haze of pain. His surroundings at least were familiar. His nephews' London bedchamber. Not the afterworld. Good.

He squinted at the stocky, gray-haired wizard bending over him. "Galen?"

"The very same." Dr. Galen Wesley patted his shoulder. "Let's cut these trousers off and see what we have."

Sebastian blinked. They'd been in the tomb. The ward—

John stepped into view and offered the healer a pair of scissors.

As Galen took them, Sebastian managed, "Kate—?"

"I've seen to her," Galen said, his voice now soothing. "She had a mild concussion. I've eased it, and your sister's keeping an eye on her. Now we must see to you."

Galen made fast work of cutting Sebastian's right trouser leg off above the knee. Eyeing the joint, which was probably as bruised as a boxer's face after a bout, he gave the scissors back to John.

John leaned over the bed. "Seb, shall I stay or go?"

"You can stay." John's presence wouldn't make any difference.

Galen assumed his usual carefully neutral expression, but this time, it evoked a surge of foreboding. The healer held his hand out, palm down, about six inches from Sebastian's right knee. Warm magic eased the pain.

"You banged it good and proper," Galen said, his voice flat, "but you surely know that."

"I guessed," Sebastian muttered.

The flow of magic continued, easing the pain.

Galen shook his head. "Whoever stabilized these bone fragments likely saved your life. There's a jagged one very close to the popliteal artery. Wouldn't have taken much to push it right in, and then you would've bled to death in short order."

"Can you fix it magically?"

"Not any longer."

Galen's grave voice stirred Sight, an image. Dread.

Sebastian pushed them away. "The fragments will have to come out, then," he guessed. He'd assumed as much when Miranda—

"No," the older man said softly. "No, we're beyond that. The joint is shattered." He looked back at Sebastian with eyes full of regret. "The only course now is amputation."

Kate opened her eyes to a yellow and cream bedroom with sunlight muted by flowered curtains. Where...? Oh. Rose's guest room.

Memory flooded back. She and Sebastian had emerged from the afterworld in Rose's parlor. Thanks to Miranda, Rose had already summoned a Gifted healer.

Kate's headache was gone, along with her concussion and the aches from various bumps and bruises suffered in the fall. The room was in focus. But Sebastian...

Miranda had been able to do only so much. Apparently, the afterworld diluted healing along with other Gifts. He'd still been badly hurt when they came back.

She had to find him. But first she needed clothes. The nightgown she wore was Rose's.

Someone tapped on the door.

Kate called, "Come in."

Rose opened the door and smiled. "Good morning. How are you?"

"I feel fine. I'm sorry you had to keep getting up to wake me up last night."

"A simple precaution with a concussion, and I'm always able to fall asleep again easily. Probably a side benefit of having two boys. If you've no headache now, you should have no further problems."

Kate acknowledged that with a nod. "How's Sebastian? Can I see him?"

"Of course. He's in the boys' bedroom. I can take you down there when you've dressed. Your clothes are in the armoire. It's after nine. Would you care for some breakfast?"

"Thanks, but after I've seen him."

Now that her head was clear, she remembered flashes she'd gotten when they merged their Gifts. Sebastian in Czechoslovakia with an injured leg, barely able to limp along with a tree branch as a crutch. Urging his comrades to leave him. Frustrated, guilty, and yet grateful when they refused.

Rose's smile faded. "His leg is badly damaged."

"The healer—Galen?—couldn't fix it?" Kate had a vague memory of a stout, middle-aged man checking her over. He'd sent a warm wave of magic through her head and told her she should be right as rain.

"That's complicated. I'll let Seb tell you."

That sounded ominous.

Rose stepped out so Kate could dress in private.

Kate pulled her clothes from the armoire and shed the nightgown. If Sebastian was still in bed, his leg must be in a very bad way.

Now that her head was clear, she remembered his struggles to stand and the lines of pain in his set face. She'd been so afraid for him, but the concussion had made the fear hazy at the time. Now, however, it came roaring back.

So did other memories. A younger Sebastian rode a black horse over the hills near Hawkstowe. The wind riffled his dark hair, and a wide smile brightened his face. The mental image had been tinged with grief, and he'd said once that he couldn't ride any longer.

The same taint marred the memory of the young officer in army brown saluting his king at his Passing Out ceremony after graduation from Sandhurst.

She'd never seen him smile that way, and a sense of loss tightened her throat. He'd had so much potential, and now he sat on the sidelines.

Kate bit her lip. He had already lost so much. If his leg injury meant losing more…

She couldn't leave him. Couldn't return home while he struggled to walk or while he fought to save his country. Her unwelcome Gift could help with that struggle, so she had an obligation to do so.

Where Sebastian was concerned, the obligation was even deeper. Being with him made her feel complete in a way she never had before. He was the piece of her she'd never realized was missing.

The knowledge hurt. So did all that came with it. Staying with him meant accepting her magic. Risking her family's love.

Risking her heart if he didn't love her in return.

But that was a worry for later. The first priority was finding out about his leg.

Kate opened the hallway door and found Rose waiting for her. "I'm ready," Kate said.

~

Sebastian picked at the food on his breakfast tray. With his leg, and thus the future of his army career, in jeopardy, he had little interest in food.

He glared at the mound his bandaged leg made of the covers. There must be some way to fix the damn-and-blasted thing.

But if a Gifted healer couldn't…

A tap on the door came with Rose calling, "Seb, may I come in?"

"Yes."

Rose stuck her head into the room. "Kate wants to see you."

His heart lifted at that. She'd still been sleeping when John brought his breakfast. "Let her come in, then." He set the bed tray aside.

Rose stepped back, and Kate hurried past her. The worry on Kate's face dissolved when their gazes met, and he found himself smiling despite the dark cloud over his hopes.

She rushed toward him, skirting the other narrow bed easily. Sebastian opened his arms just in time. Hers closed around him, and he buried his face in her soft hair.

"I was so worried," she choked.

"I was as well." When he kissed her cheek, she turned her head for a proper kiss.

The kiss started in tenderness and relief but became passionate and possessive. Her mouth opened under his, her tongue teasing his lips. He groaned and deepened the kiss.

Untold minutes later, Kate pressed her face into his neck.

Stroking her hair, he said, "Galen said you should recover by this morning. Did you?"

"Completely." She raised her head and kissed him quickly. "I know there's something about your leg. Tell me."

The words stuck in his throat. His lips tightened. Whatever she saw in his face softened hers—in sympathy? Or in pity? He would literally rather die than have the latter from her.

"Last night," she said, settling onto the bed by his hip, "when we were struggling to stand, I caught something from you, a memory or maybe a vision. This was like Czechoslovakia."

He went cold inside. "That's not relevant."

"I don't mean to pry, Sebastian, but if talking about it would help—"

"I don't need comfort," he snapped. The hurt look in her eyes made him instantly ashamed.

Before he could apologize, she quietly said, "Maybe I do. Last night, I was afraid for us both but especially for you. You were obviously in pain, and I could do nothing to help us escape from that place. That needs to change. I have to learn how to do what you did. The next time we go up against that ward, there'll be two of us who know how to travel the afterworld. We also need to be better prepared now that we know it can fling us around that way even when we don't leak magic into it.

"Speaking of that, do we need to contact Edmund about that document? Or Richard? I got a very good look at the seal, though it may not be the right one. I'm sure I can sketch it."

He stared at her. Everything in him revolted at idea of her dealing with that ward again. With the revulsion came clarity. He would do anything, anything at all, to protect her.

Because he loved her.

Sebastian drew a painful breath. So be it. He would do what was best for her, no matter what that meant for him.

Frowning, Kate cocked her head. "Sebastian? Did you hear me?"

"I did. But you needn't learn any of that because your part in this is done. You're going home, remember?"

"That was yesterday. Now I've made up my mind. I'm staying."

"Bloody hell, you are. You're sailing from Southampton on the fifteenth."

"You can't recover the document without me, and you know it. The two of us barely managed a brief look at the inside of that room. How do you propose to get in there so you can take the confession, assuming the seal I saw is on the document we want, without help?"

"There are other Gifted who can help."

"Oh, yes, that secret group you mentioned." Kate's eyes narrowed. "However, I distinctly recall your saying we are the only two seers in this generation. If you thought you could do that without another seer, you wouldn't have asked me in the first place."

"I was too hasty." He was also feeling as he had during war games simulations when his unit had been pushed into retreat.

"That's absurd." She actually sniffed at him. Put her pretty nose up in the air.

"Kate, damn it, you're going home, where it's safe."

"I'm not." She crossed her arms. "That's final."

"You haven't a job or anywhere to live. I'll ask Rose not to let you stay here."

"I bet she will anyway. Rose likes me."

She also liked Kate for her brother, so he had no chance to prevail there.

"Speaking as an experienced sister," Kate continued, "I'm sure she also recognizes that you're pigheaded."

"I am not pigheaded," he roared. "I'm right, and you damn well know it."

"You need my help. Do you think I can live with going home if it means Richard and Miranda and Miles and the others will cease to be? How can you ask me to deal with that?"

"We'll find a way to prevent it." Sebastian sighed. "I want you to go because you could've been killed last night and the most important thing in the world to me is your safety."

Now confusion furrowed her brow, but hope was dawning in her eyes.

"I want you to go," he said, bracing himself, "because I love you."

Kate looked stunned for a moment before she smiled. "That's good because I love you too."

They reached for each other, and Sebastian drew Kate against his chest. Having her in his arms lifted his heart. The long, deep kiss, the pressure of her breasts against him, and the tight circle of her arms around him felt like finding his place at last.

When the kiss broke, she sighed and nestled against him. His chin rested against the smooth hair at her temple, and she stroked his pajama-clad chest idly with one hand.

Sebastian pressed a kiss into her hairline. "So you'll sail on the fifteenth."

Sitting up, she looked at him as though he'd suddenly announced that the Crown was painting Buckingham Palace bright red. "After what we just said? I'm not going anywhere."

~

Sebastian's tender look became an exasperated glare with astonishing speed. "Darling, have you not heard a word I said? I want you gone because I want you safe."

"I want you safe too. If I go, you come with me."

"You know I can't do that. Kate, be reasonable."

"I am." She reached for his hand, and his immediate lacing of his fingers through hers was reassuring. "You want me to go home because you think it's safe. How safe will it be if Britain falls?"

"Safer than it will be here."

"Maybe. For a while. But maybe having two seers feeding intelligence to the British, working with these secret wizards you mentioned, whom I'm happy to help, could make a difference. How can I go home knowing I could've made a difference if I stayed?"

"We don't know that."

"Nor do we know the opposite. Then there's the family curse. You need my help, Sebastian. We found out more together than you'd managed alone."

"Yes, and I damn near got you killed. You're not going near that ward again."

That dictatorial tone… Kate raised her eyebrows. "Are you under the impression that being in love with me allows you to dictate my choices?" Saying the words *in love with me* gave her warm fizzing inside, but letting him know it would be a tactical mistake.

"Of course not, but I know more about these matters than you do. The final calls on strategy should be mine."

"You're not objective." Kate sighed. "Let's not fight about this. You're doing what you think is right. Can't you let me do the same? A week ago, you were okay with my staying."

He leaned back against the pillows, a tacit concession, and shook his head. "I didn't know I loved you. That changes everything."

"Not for me. The job needs doing—both jobs, the war and the confession. You can manage them better if there are two of us. You know that, and it's not only our lives at stake. It's everyone's."

He ran a hand over his face. His eyes lost focus, as though he were thinking. "I'll strike a bargain with you," he said. "You stay for now, but if —when—the war gets sticky, you allow me to take you home through the afterworld."

Kate studied him. He looked tired, and his face still held lines of pain. And worry. For him, this was a large concession. Mom always said a good relationship required compromise. Sebastian was offering one.

"Okay," she said, squeezing his hand. "Deal."

He smiled and raised her hand to his mouth. "Thank you, Kate."

The brush of his lips over her knuckles sent a rush of heat into the depths of her body. Her hand tightened on his.

"Thank you, too." She leaned in to kiss him quickly. "I don't like arguing with you."

"I don't like it either."

Yet the worry in his face remained. Maybe it wasn't only for her.

An image flashed into her mind, the short, silver-haired healer standing by this bed shaking his head.

"What did the healer say?" she asked.

"It isn't good. Did you hear Miranda say she was afraid to work with my leg lest she cause more damage?"

"I vaguely remember that, but I wasn't fully aware of what was happening. I thought your father supported you as we returned because your leg wasn't fully healed."

"It wasn't healed at all. She repaired only my cracked ribs."

His flat voice and dispirited look said the news was very bad. Kate braced herself.

"Galen says it's shattered. He magically reinforced Miranda's stabilization of the bone fragments so they won't shift and pierce an artery, but he doesn't think he can fix it."

"I thought magic could fix anything."

"If the knee had been healthy, he could've done. But it was already deformed from that old injury. Magical healing, in essence, returns the injured part of the body to its normal condition. My knee has been damaged for so long, as he explained it, that my body has no sense of what's normal for it. As it is, the body's signals about that knee are confused. A jumble. With a less severe injury, he might've patched it together, but I wouldn't have been hurt so badly if the joint weren't already fragile. He can't fix it."

That sounded ominous. "What about army doctors?"

"He suggested I try them. Because he's also a licensed physician, he's arranging to have it x-rayed this week. He isn't holding out much hope, though."

"What does that mean? Will it heal badly?"

"It will heal as a bloody useless mess." Anger flashed in his eyes but faded into despair. "He recommends amputation."

CHAPTER 23

The word tasted bitter in Sebastian's mouth. He'd survived Czechoslovakia, eluded capture, and returned to England with a leg that worked, after a fashion, most of the time. Now dark magic had finished it off.

"You have money," Kate said. "You can see other doctors. Even go to someone in the States. Maybe a wizard healer there."

"I could." He drew her down against him. Having Kate's warmth snuggled against him and her arm around his waist offered some comfort. "I doubt they would have any better suggestions. Galen is superb at what he does. He's one of the few healers who also practices medicine. Rose did well to call him in."

"Will you have to leave the army?"

"I don't know. I talked my way into my current assignment, but everyone could maintain the fiction that my leg might eventually recover. Amputation would scuttle that. But there are things I can do, as I have been, to free up those fit for combat." If that was a bitter thought, he would deal with it. Restrictions were nothing new, after all.

They said nothing for several minutes. Finally, Kate asked, "Does Rose know?"

"John was with me when Galen was here. He told her."

"What does she think?"

"That I might be better off with a working prosthetic than an unreliable leg. But Rose isn't in the army, of course, and never wanted to be."

"Whereas it was all you ever wanted," Kate said softly.

"Precisely."

Again, they sat in silence. Stating the prognosis, forcing himself to face it, was actually something of a relief.

"Galen told me to rest in bed with my leg supported for a couple of days to bring the swelling down," Sebastian said, "but you probably have things to do."

"Nothing more important than this. Though I could sketch that seal from last night if I had some paper. And a pencil."

"Richard said he would bring Edmund by to see if he recognizes what you draw."

"I want to be here for that. At some point, I should go to the office and resign. Tell Lew they can cash in my ticket."

She sounded matter-of-fact, but the shadow in her eyes said she didn't feel nearly so calm as she sounded. No wonder. She'd fought hard for the position she held.

"Kate, are you certain? Perhaps you could have a leave of absence."

"Lew was clear. If I don't go home, they'll fire me, and I'm not going. Besides, having them slide me into a plum beat isn't nearly so rewarding when it's only open because the guy who has it now is taking my place here." She mustered a wry smile. "I've never been fired. I would rather resign and keep it that way."

"Understood. There's probably a pencil and paper in one of those desks. Help yourself."

Kate found what she was looking for quickly. No surprise since Rose and John's sons kept their room tidy and organized.

Kate laid the paper and pencil on the desk. "Can I get you anything? A book, maybe? A magazine?"

"You could hand me that collection of Sherlock Holmes stories off the bookcase, please. And tell me what was on the seal?"

She passed the book to him. "The seal was a man's hand holding an upright sword with a bird flying toward it. In...red wax."

A bubble of hope pushed into Sebastian's chest. He tamped it ruthlessly, lest it lead to disappointment.

"Sebastian?" Kate prodded, staring at him. "What is it?"

"We no longer use the old seal, but I've seen it many times. You just described it."

Kate grinned at him, and he grinned back. "Sketch it anyway for Edmund," Sebastian suggested. "We can show him that, and I can project what I Saw into the fire."

"Of course." Kate sat down to work.

The Holmes stories didn't hold his attention. That little kernel of hope kept trying to bloom. He kept forcing it back. While he couldn't think of any other document the Earls of Wyndon might have that were signed by an Earl of Hawkstowe, that didn't mean there weren't any.

When Clara, the maid, came to remove the tray, he thanked her absently.

When he wasn't fighting hope that could lead to disappointment, his attention strayed to Kate from time to time, to the intense focus she turned to her task. The way the morning light gleamed on her hair and cast shadows in the open vee of her shirt.

He couldn't have said how long they'd been sitting quietly when awareness of a presence rippled across his magical senses. Richard and Edmund appeared in the center of the room. Sebastian hadn't seen Edmund in a long time, and he needed a moment to master his expression.

Edmund looked thin, almost emaciated—and even less substantial than usual. Was he fading? Probably best not to ask, so Sebastian mustered a smile of greeting.

"Kate, we have company."

She looked up and blinked. "Hello, Richard."

"Good afternoon, my dear. Sebastian. We're all terribly distressed about your leg."

Probably not as distressed as he was, but that was a petty thought. Sebastian thanked him. Since Kate could see Richard, Edmund's descendant, she should be able to see Edmund as well.

"Edmund, this is Kate Shaw from America. She's my very distant cousin."

Kate smiled at Edmund and greeted him warmly. Curiosity bloomed in her eyes, though, and Sebastian knew questions for their ancestor were rolling through her mind. His shoulder-length hair, green tunic and hose, boots, and sword belt—without the Sword of Hawkstowe, which remained at the manor—must be entirely strange to her.

"What happened in the crypt last night?" Richard asked.

Sebastian explained, detailing their progress until the time they left the wards and reached their family. "Kate has sketched the seal," he said. "I'll light the fire and show you the chamber I Saw through the ward."

"May I see your drawing?" Edmund asked.

She extended it toward him, then froze. "Sorry. I forgot you aren't actually in here with us." Instead, she raised the sketch so he and Richard could see it.

Both of them suddenly tensed. They glanced at each other, then at Sebastian, who nodded. "Red wax, as Kate noted," he told them. "We both glimpsed the seal and a corner of the document that bears it. Kate had a better look but doesn't yet know how to transfer a seer's vision into a fire to share it. Kate, if you'll sit beside me, I'll show you."

"Again," she mouthed silently, but she sat beside him on the bed. Using witchfire, Sebastian lit the wood fire in the hearth. Most households used coal nowadays, and a few had switched to gas, but wood worked best for scrying.

To Kate, he said, "Put your hand on mine and feel what I do."

When she nodded, he directed a stream of power toward the fire with the vision of the chamber in his mind. Her magic surged, joining his, and the image forming in the flames came clear. On the corner of the lowest shelf above the table, the Hawkstowe seal dangled from the document in the glass case.

"Kate, did you—?"

"I don't know how it happened."

"Whatever you're doing, don't stop," he replied. "It—"

"That's it," Edmund cried. "That's my confession. But how did the bastards come to have it? How did they arrange it so we found no trace of my ever having written it?"

The image flickered. "We don't know, Edmund," Sebastian answered. "We can let this image go for now, though it's worth looking at it again to see if we can make out in detail in the chamber."

Kate lifted her hand from his, and her power withdrawing into her brushed across his hand. The image winked out.

She frowned at him. "Sebastian, is it possible to learn something from a ward? About the ward itself?"

"Sometimes." The bloody images he'd seen the first time flashed into his head. "What did you See?"

"A woman dying with her throat cut and a man pouring blood out of a goblet." She nodded to Edmund. "The man wore clothes like his."

Richard rubbed his jaw. "That's odd. Otterden Abbey was a consecrated friary until Henry VIII dissolved the monasteries in 1536. Who would've raised a blood ward there? Besides, if that was the abbey's treasure room, the ward effectively barred the monks from their valuables."

"It's on Wyndon land," Edmund said. "Perhaps the abbot owed the earl of my day a favor. Or perhaps there's another treasure chamber. Miles did find a similar chamber, unwarded, in the next corner of the courtyard as he walked along the hall's wall. If the abbot of the day and those following weren't Gifted, they wouldn't have sensed anything about the ward the Wyndons raised but might've felt its compulsion to stay away from that area."

"The warded one is back in a corner," Sebastian said.

"The dying woman was involved with the man who killed her," Kate said. "I didn't see that, but I'm sure."

"Anything about the man?" Sebastian asked.

She frowned, concentrating. Before she spoke, what she had Seen and unconsciously known flashed into his mind. Because they were holding hands? Or because they were both seers and sitting close together?

"He's…a bastard," she said. "Not in the sense we use it, as an insult, but…as a status."

"Good lord," Edmund choked. "Anthony de Vere."

"Who's that?" Richard asked.

"His father was Roland de Vere, the Earl of Wyndon whom the Conclave Council and King Edward IV condemned. On evidence gathered by our family."

"The de Vere who was executed?" Richard asked.

Edmund nodded heavily. "I felt sorry for the lad. Born under the bar sinister—"

"Heraldic emblem for a bastard," Richard put in, likely for Kate's benefit.

"—and resented by his legitimate brothers. They shunned him after their father died. I took him in. He…was there when I wrote my confession. He—oh, God's wounds, what have I done?"

Edmund vanished.

"I must see he doesn't harm himself," Richard said. "I'll tell you anything I learn."

Richard vanished.

Kate and Sebastian looked at each other. "Now what?" Kate asked.

Sebastian studied her for a long minute. "I told you about the secret group of wizards working to help England. Would you like to join them?"

~

"I don't know. What does joining them involve?" Judging from the look on Sebastian's face, it wasn't a decision to be made lightly.

"First, promising to be loyal to the group and to Britain. Second, using your Gifts to support her cause and never to hinder it. Third, keeping the group's existence an absolute secret from everyone except the members' families and the club's financial supporters. For example, Rose and John are not members but are in my confidence."

That all sounded reasonable, but… "What if I want to go home at some point? To stay, I mean."

"You're still bound by the secrecy. You can be released from the loyalty and magical support requirements. I ask because the group has a library full of badly indexed codices, grimoires, and other magical texts. One of them may contain, buried in its jumbled contents, the answer to lifting that ward."

"You want me to look."

"And to index as you go. This would be a paid job but one you do at your convenience. We've contacts who can get you a work permit, and you could still pursue story opportunities."

"I could pay Rose something toward expenses. And I can have my ration book assigned to the shops she uses, of course."

"You said you couldn't impose." He shrugged. "Until I can convince you to go home, I would like you to be comfortable, to not feel obligated, for lack of a better way to put it."

"That's so sweet. Even more, it's…respectful. You're helping me make my own way instead of encouraging me to depend completely on you."

"You're made your desire to pull your weight plain."

The warmth in his face faded. He looked down at the mound under the covers. "I may be the dependent one shortly."

The bitterness in the words stung her heart. "Only for a while, Sebastian. Once you heal and become used to the prosthesis, that will pass."

"I suppose." He swallowed hard, and the grief in his eyes had her tightening her grip on his hand. "You see," he continued, "as long as I have the leg, even though it didn't work well before and is an unholy mess now, I can hope magic—or perhaps even the doctors—will find a way to repair it. Once it's gone…that hope dies."

She didn't know what to say. She would've hugged him, but the stiffness of his demeanor warned against that. His gaze remained locked on that mound of cloth.

"I hate this for you. Anyone would be distressed over losing a limb, but I know you can manage this, Sebastian. I'll be with you through it all. I'll do anything you need me to do."

Maybe it was because she was holding his hand, but that odd *knowing* bloomed in her brain. She scowled at him. "Let's please not make this into a maudlin movie. Having your leg amputated will not change my feelings one whit. You insult me if you think it would."

He had the grace to look embarrassed. "I may be sorry I taught you to share power."

"I'm not, so don't you be. Do you think that's why we pick up flashes from each other, even when we're not sharing?"

"Two seers working together is a new phenomenon. I don't know if that's why, but it's as good a guess as any. Once we shared our magic and then our Sight within the magic of that ward, it's possible our Gifts… melded or became attuned in some way."

His lips curved up in a wry smile. It didn't reach his eyes, but he was trying. "There may be something in the library jumble to explain that, too. The librarians made a hasty list of what the books contained, but they didn't pretend to be comprehensive. Anything at all could be in those books."

"I like research. Sometimes the difference between a solid story and a weak one is the background research. So tell me about this organization."

"Come sit with me." He held out his arm.

Kate shifted to snuggle against his side.

Sebastian pressed a quick kiss into her hair. "The group is actually a club. We have headquarters in St. James's, off Charles II Street. It looks like any other gentlemen's club that has been there for centuries, but this one is special. All the members are Gifted, and they include women."

"Well, I should hope so." She wrinkled her nose at him.

This time, his smile was genuine. "It's called the Merlin Club."

When her eyes widened, so did his smile.

"After the bird?" she asked. "Or the wizard?"

"Very good. Thinking of questions like that, you should be a reporter. It's named for the wizard but uses the bird as its emblem. I'll take you there to join. If you don't want the library job, of course you needn't take it. If you do, though, we can help you start on it. We'll go the day after tomorrow."

How did he intend to do that when he was supposed to rest in bed? That might be a sore subject, though, so it could wait.

Leaning into him again, she asked, "Tell me more about this library."

~

Quitting? What do you mean, you're quitting? You can't quit!"

"Actually, Lew, I can. I am." This was even tougher than Kate had expected. Her job at CNU and then her posting as a foreign correspondent had been a dream come true. A level of the profession few women reached.

Yet she was chucking it. *It's the right thing to do. Keep your chin up and remember that.*

"Look, honey, I know you're upset over being sent home, but there's no call to overreact here. The congressional beat is a prize."

Every time he had bad news, he reverted to *honey*, as though that would soothe her. He and the other men in the profession had no idea how patronizing that was.

"You think I'm having some kind of tantrum? Do you actually believe that, Lew?"

"Well, honey—"

"In my shoes, what would you do? Tell me that."

His face fell. She had him.

Taking the office key and the one for the flat out of her purse hurt, but there was no going back. Kate set the keys gently on his desk. "I know you went to bat for me, Lew, and I appreciate it. However, great as the congressional beat is, we both know the best stories are here."

He stared at the keys as though he couldn't believe she'd actually done that. "Where will you go? How will you live?"

"I've distant cousins here. They've offered me a room and helped me find work. We moved my things to their house this morning." The two hours since she left Sebastian had been busy. "I also have contacts who can help me sell freelance pieces." Not many, and there was no guarantee, but pride had its demands here, too.

"If I need to reach you, how do I do that?

Kate squelched a small, foolish blip of hope. Lew wouldn't contact her professionally unless New York approved it, and they wouldn't.

"I'll be staying with Lord and Lady Borrowdale in Belgravia." She gave him the address. "You can send my last paycheck there."

"Nice place to land," he commented.

"They're nice people." Kate stood and offered her hand. "Thank you for everything, Lew. I hope great stories come your way."

"Thanks, honey." He shook her hand. "You take care of yourself."

"I'll say goodbye to May on my way out, but there's no one in the bullpen. Please give the guys my best."

Kate marched out of his office and up to the front.

She could've done well on the congressional beat. It would've solidified the reputation she'd worked so hard to build. Feeling as though she'd deserted her friends here, deserted the Allied cause when she might've made a difference, however, would undercut any sense of pride in whatever professional recognition she might gain.

As Dad had said when she told him farm life wasn't for her, sometimes you had to close the door on the old to embrace the new.

I thought you said women went in the back door." Kate stepped onto the low stoop of the Merlin Club and waited for Sebastian to do the same on his crutches.

He wore his uniform today, as usual, but with the leg of his trousers split from his knee splint downward. Knowing how much that drab brown suit meant to him and that he might soon lose the right to it made her ache for him.

"That's women members arriving alone," he said. "A woman with a man appears to be his guest."

A gleaming brass plate to the right of the door bore an engraving of one of the small, fierce falcons known as merlins and the words *The Merlin Club*. The bird looked over its shoulder toward the door.

Anchoring his right crutch under his arm, Sebastian put his right palm against the engraving. The tiny pulse of magic he released shivered over Kate's magical senses. A moment later, the door clicked.

She moved toward it, but he said, "Don't touch it. Anyone can use the knocker, but only a member can safely open that door."

So the house had more defenses than it appeared to. Interesting.

Sebastian pushed the door open and gestured toward the interior with one hand. "Welcome to the Merlin Club, Kate."

She stepped into a foyer lit by a crystal chandelier overhead. A carpet runner in rich blue, maroon, and gold lay along the center of the hallway's polished parquet floor. Doors to the left and right opened onto sunlit rooms. The one on the left held square dining tables topped with snowy linen while leather-upholstered chairs and small side tables filled the one on the right. Just past the doorway on the right, a staircase rose before curving gracefully across the foyer to the second—no, first, this was Britain—floor.

As the door clicked shut, a stocky, middle-aged man hurried through the black, paneled door at the foyer's rear. "Sebastian! It's good to see you, cousin. Alice and I are very sorry about your injury. Genevieve told us."

Sebastian seemed to take that in stride, unlike the way he bristled when most people mentioned his leg. He drew Kate forward with his hand at the small of her back.

"Kate, this is Albert Gray, the club's porter. Alice is his wife, who isn't here at the moment. Albert, this is Kate Shaw. She'll be joining today."

"Isn't that fine?" Albert beamed at her. "Welcome, Kate."

"Thank you. It's so nice to meet you." She extended her hand, and he shook it heartily.

"With the Jerrys on the march," he said, "we need all the talent we can recruit, eh, Sebastian?"

"Indeed we do."

The slender, gray-haired woman who was the club's primary director emerged from behind the stairs at the right. Hand outstretched, she said, "It's good to see you again, Kate."

"Thank you, Genevieve. It's good to see you, too." They shook hands, the older woman's grip strong and professional. Genevieve, the Earl of Aysgarth, and Earl of Havelock had met with Kate and Sebastian at his house two days ago and approved Kate's membership.

For the occasion, Kate had donned her favorite suit, navy blue with a waist-length, vee-necked jacket worn buttoned and a white hat with navy trim. Her white cotton gloves and leather clutch completed the ensemble. It was a professional look. Kate knew it. Yet something about Genevieve, despite her warm manner, made Kate feel as though she should check that the seams of her stockings, one of her few remaining pairs of the now-scarce lingerie, were straight.

"We swear in new members in the library," Genevieve said. "If you'll give Albert your hat, gloves, and bag, we can go up. The lift is this way."

Sebastian also passed his uniform cap to the porter.

Genevieve led them to the rear of the foyer and opened a paneled door on the left. Behind it lay the brass gate of the lift. Smiling, the club's director said, "Squeezing a lift into an old house presents a certain challenge, but we've managed."

"It's beautiful." It was also a very snug space for the three of them and would've been even without Sebastian's crutches. The mahogany paneling and stained-glass panels bearing merlins against green leaves made the small lift elegant.

They emerged on the second floor, the first to her hosts. Sebastian had said the library occupied half the space with the rest given to bedchambers available to club members.

"Lachlan is still here," Genevieve said to Sebastian. "He said you wanted him on hand for a while. He'll join us this morning."

"Very good," Sebastian said.

A murmur of voices came from the room ahead of them. Genevieve led the way into it, and the voices fell silent. Kate found three men and two women of varying ages regarding her with friendly curiosity. Bookshelves lined the walls, and a long table with chairs around it dominated the center of the room. Against the far wall stood five portraits on easels. She recognized Richard's and Miranda's but not those of the other three men.

"These are our founders," Genevieve said, indicating them with an outstretched hand. "You may be familiar with Richard and Miranda Mainwaring, Lord and Lady Hawkstowe. Beside Lady Hawkstowe is Christopher Grayson, Lord Havelock." Kate studied the dark-haired, gray-eyed man. "Next we have then-Rear Admiral of the Blue Sir Cabot Winfield and the Reverend Doctor Jeremy Winfield, a future Archbishop of York."

The two men looked much alike, with brown hair, square faces, and aquiline noses. But the one in the clerical collar was slightly thinner, not sun-browned, and wore a more thoughtful expression. His brother was broader of shoulder with sun streaks in his shoulder-length hair.

Genevieve steered Kate to the corner of the table nearest the portraits. A long parchment covered in florid writing rested on end of the table near the portraits. From one corner dangled a green wax seal bearing a merlin like the one on the door plaque. Halfway across the table stood an ornate silver candlestick holding a fresh, yellowish taper. At the table's far side, a large, thick book bound in brown and gilt leather lay beside a silver hand bell about four or five inches high.

As the club's director moved around the table, two figures slowly became visible beside Richard's portrait. Kate shot a quick look at Sebastian. His tiny smile and nod confirmed her guess. Now translucent but fully visible, Miranda and Richard smiled at her.

The five people who were in the room took places beside Genevieve. The two middle-aged men had salt-and-pepper hair. The younger one, who looked to be about forty, was fair-haired and solemn. One of the women, a twentyish brunette, wore clothes as simple but elegant as Rose's. The other woman, slightly older with graying blond hair, dressed more like people back home.

"These are the witnesses," Genevieve said, standing behind the bell. "We will introduce you all around afterward."

Sebastian had told Kate that. He'd also told her every new member required a sponsor, and he was hers.

Now he moved closer to her side.

Genevieve glanced around the room. "Are we all ready?"

Everyone nodded, and she said, "Sebastian."

He used witchfire to light the candle on the table. The sweet scent of beeswax drifted through the room. He didn't look at Kate, but when he took his place beside her, his fingers brushed hers.

Kate knew what to expect, but she'd still been nervous. Now nerves gave way to anticipation and a strange, almost detached sense of rightness.

"Madam Director and members," Sebastian said, "I offer for membership Katherine Shaw, a Gifted woman of integrity and honor. As I place my faith in her, so may you place yours."

Genevieve nodded to him. "By the candle burning now, all will witness this solemn vow. Kate, raise your right hand and place the fingertips of your left on the document before you. It's the Merlin Club's charter."

Kate complied, and silver magic drifted from Genevieve's fingers. It wreathed the document, which took on a soft glow, and tingled against Kate's fingers.

Genevieve raised her right hand and laid her left on the book in front of her. "This is the record of all the club's members. Repeat after me: 'I, Katherine Joan MacGregor Shaw, do solemnly swear…'"

The middle-aged man on the far end seemed to perk up at that, but Kate ignored him and repeated the words. Next came "…that I will use my Gifts in the defense of Britain and to stop the abuse of magical Gifts as set forth in the club's rules and directives…that I will wield them with honor and integrity… I further pledge to keep the secrets of the Merlin Club as required by the club's rules… In this cause, I pledge my faith…and make this solemn vow."

Genevieve held eye contact. She lowered her right hand but didn't move her left. Kate followed suit. The parchment under her fingers still tingled.

The older woman picked up the bell and rang it once. "By the tolling of this bell, you are sworn against all magic fell."

She passed the bell to the older woman, who also shook it once. "As this bell rings strong and true, you are one with us, and we with you."

The younger man came next. "As this bell sounds bright and clear, we stand united in the face of fear."

The man set the bell gently on the table.

Genevieve looked back at Kate. "By the candle, book, and bell, a bond is formed. May it hold well."

The tingle under Kate's fingers died.

Genevieve smiled. "Congratulations, Kate, and welcome."

Sebastian squeezed her hand. Miranda and Richard gave her broad smiles before they vanished.

"Come sign the book," Genevieve said, "and we'll go down to the morning room for a small celebration. Your magic is now melded with all of ours, so you can enter unaided and scry through the club's wards."

Kate walked around the table to sign her full name and list her Gifts as magic and Sight, as the seer Gift was known.

Genevieve introduced her to the five witnesses. The last, an older man named Lachlan MacGregor, spoke with a Scots accent when he congratulated her.

"A MacGregor, are you?" he asked.

"I have MacGregor kin." Perhaps it was unfair to the man who sired her, but she couldn't call him her father when she had no memory of him. Her parents, wanting to honor her birth family, had simply added the Shaw name to the end of hers.

The older man's blue eyes twinkled. "Perhaps you've the MacGregor Gift as well."

Sebastian sighed. "Lachlan—"

"What would that be?" The last thing Kate needed was another magical skill to master.

"Why, Cousin, it's what the less enlightened call stubbornness. We MacGregors, though, we know it for what it truly is—determination." Under his light air lay a serious current.

Kate smiled. "I think I do have a bit of that."

"Cartloads of it," Sebastian corrected. "She has cartloads of it."

Lachlan grinned. "May it serve you well, Kate Shaw."

Kate thanked him. The group moved out of the library. Most went down the stairs, but Kate, Sebastian, and Genevieve took the lift.

"Welcome to the Merlin Club family," Sebastian said softly.

Kate smiled, but the words gave her a pang. In embracing this family, was she walking away from the one she had always known and loved?

Sebastian insisted on taking her out to dinner despite his crutches. Kate suspected he was thinking this might be their last chance before his weeks or months of convalescence, so she didn't argue that he was supposed to be resting. Instead, she wore her best dress, a dark green organza that was almost black.

Restaurants weren't yet subject to rationing. The Dorchester Hotel meal of tomato soup, sole, roasted chicken, peas, and potatoes seemed like pure luxury compared to the meals Kate and her flatmates scraped together.

"We should enjoy this while we can," Sebastian said as they dipped their spoons into their dessert, a creamy trifle. "There are already rumblings that it isn't fair for those who can afford to eat out to have unlimited choices, and I can see the point."

Kate smiled. "At home, we don't have multiple courses. We might have a salad with the meal and then a dessert on Sundays, but fancy appetizers and a cheese course and more than one entrée still seem like an embarrassment of riches to me."

"We all expect what we're used to, I suppose." Smiling, he glanced around the room. He hesitated for a moment but kept scanning.

His smile slowly faded, and he leaned across the table. "Lord and Lady Wyndon are here. Table at nine o'clock from your seat."

"We don't have to talk to them, do we?" Still, the location reference seemed odd.

"It's better if we don't. You're Merlin Club now, Kate, so I can tell you this. There are some questions about his loyalty."

"During the house party, I thought there might be. You did a good job of not revealing any interest."

"Good. I don't recognize the people with them. Do you?"

Kate glanced where he'd indicated. "I've seen that man before. He's Hugo Arbuthnot." Not certain how much she should say here, she carefully added, "He's in steel."

"Is he indeed?" Sebastian pursed his lips. "If you're finished, we should go somewhere that allows us to…conduct research."

"I've had enough. Let's go."

~

They returned to Rose's by taxi. The nearest Tube station to the hotel, Hyde Park corner, wasn't on the same line as Victoria, the one nearest Rose's house. Even from Victoria, the trek to the house would've been long for a man on crutches. Sebastian hated having to plan around his infirmity.

Maybe that was why he'd found himself growing reconciled to the amputation. Adapting to his leg's restrictions had been annoying before. Now it was a bloody nuisance.

The day was waning as he and Kate arrived at Rose's.

"Do you mind if I change before we do this?" Kate asked.

"No, go ahead. I'll meet you in the upstairs parlor." Did she truly need to change her clothes, or was she giving him time to make his slow way up the stairs? He would be damn glad not to have such questions hanging over them.

When he gained the first floor, Kate was walking toward the parlor in her blue slacks and the loose, cream shirt he liked because it draped her curves.

She smiled at him. "Perfect timing."

"It's good the blackout hasn't started yet," he said. "Having the curtains closed and the fire going—if we decide to scry—would make it hot and stuffy in here."

They sat in chairs facing the hearth.

"What do you want me to do?" Kate asked.

"Give me your hand. We'll see what Wyndon and Arbuthnot are up to together."

"You surely don't need my help for that." She gave him her hand anyway.

"I don't, but you Saw more when we were working together in the crypt than you usually do on your own. Doing this together may help develop your Gift."

"You say that oddly. Saw, I mean. As though you capitalized the word."

"Because I'm referring to a seer's Sight. If I tell you I saw a boy flying a kite, it's a different emphasis."

"Yes." She looked doubtful. "I hadn't thought of it that way."

"You needn't unless you want to. It clarifies things amongst us Gifted, but no one cares whether you observe the custom or not."

"I know you're trying to make this easy for me, and I'm grateful. But what to call things isn't the hard part."

"I know." He tightened his grip on her hand. "I don't mean to presume, so forgive me, but I wonder whether the difficulty lies in taking another step away from the world you share with your family."

"That's it exactly." Her throat moved in a hard swallow. "I need to do this, Sebastian. I can't turn my back on it, but I don't want to turn my back on them."

"Or have them turn theirs on you." He brought her hand on his lips. "You're the sort of person who faces her fears, Kate. We can face this one, too. Together."

"What do you mean?"

"I told you Missouri is no more difficult to reach than Otterden Abbey. Once I've dealt with this situation about my leg, I can take you home to see your parents."

～

The idea made Kate's stomach roll. "I'm not ready for that. I wouldn't know what to say. How to…how to bear it if they—"

"There's no hurry." One corner of Sebastian's mouth crooked up in a wry smile. "I see the surgeon in the morning, and I expect they'll schedule the surgery. If we don't go before the operation, I doubt I'll be able to take you for some weeks."

Above that self-deprecating smile, his eyes were dark with grief. And likely with the same physical pain that cut lines in his face and made his shoulders stiff.

"You're facing your fear," she said softly. "You make me ashamed to hide from mine."

"We tackle things when we're ready. Unless life gives us no choice."

As he now had no real choice. "I suppose so."

"All right, then. Let's see what these odd allies are up to. Think of seeing them in the hotel and then think of them now. Did they go some-where after dinner, or was that their only meeting?"

Kate imagined Lord Wyndon's face. *Where is he?*

An image formed in her mind with gratifying speed. Lord Wyndon sat in a book-lined room with a snifter of brandy in hand. "Sebastian, do you see it?"

"Yes. Keep going."

The door opened. Lady Wyndon entered in a lacy, pink peignoir.

"Unless they have some odd habits," Kate said, "Arbuthnot isn't there."

"Likely not. Let's eavesdrop on their dinner conversation."

She shifted the image to see the table at dinner. The Wyndon-Arbuthnot conversation revolved around house parties, the tediousness of rationing, and an upcoming polo match. Kate let it play out. Sometimes exercising patience and enduring boredom led to the information she wanted. Sebastian didn't urge anything different, and she sensed his agreement in the magic flowing between them.

The vision's Kate and Sebastian left the restaurant. The conversation rolled into the stupidity of not evacuating Princess Elizabeth and Princess Margaret to Canada months ago. Queen Elizabeth had said her daughters would not leave without her. She, however, wouldn't go without King George, and he refused to go.

Arbuthnot snorted. "They should ask King Haakon how much he enjoyed rabbiting out of Norway just ahead of the Nazis. No harm in exercising a little prudence, as he should've done."

The two women left to "powder their noses."

Sebastian asked, "Do women actually powder their noses in the lav, or is that only a euphemism?"

"Mostly the latter, though we do tend to check our makeup and lipstick."

Arbuthnot lit a cigarette and leaned across the table. "I'll have cargo outside Dungeness on Tuesday. Tell your contact."

"Tuesday. Will do."

Sebastian said, "Let's see what that cargo is."

"I can't... I'm not getting it."

"Let me try." Through the magic, Kate felt him will the images to change. The hotel restaurant became a warehouse with crates stacked high. Again Sebastian shifted it, this time to the packing of those crates.

"Steel ingots?" Kate asked.

"Steel goes into tanks, warships, and a wide range of weapons. You can make almost anything with those ingots."

They returned to the restaurant and picked up the conversation where they had left it, but the two couples departed without any further conversation of interest.

Sebastian let the image fade. "Dungeness. Interesting."

"Why? Where's Dungeness?"

"It's in Romney Marsh, a hotbed of smuggling in Britain for centuries." The vision faded. Sebastian and Kate grinned at each other. "Before I see the surgeon in the morning," he said, "I believe I'll stop in at the office."

"Weren't you going to the Merlin Club first?"

He nodded. "It'll be an early morning. If we can put a snag in a bit of treason, though, it's worth it."

CHAPTER 25

The next morning, Sebastian insisted on going to the Merlin Club and the hospital alone. That left Kate with nothing to do until she met with the Merlin Club librarian that afternoon. So she sat in the parlor scanning her list of contacts for one who could yield a useful, saleable story.

Yet her thoughts kept returning to yesterday's ceremony. Everyone had welcomed her, and Lachlan MacGregor seemed to regard her as a favored niece. He was an earl, yet he seemed as comfortable with one of the witnesses, Della Benfield, a shopkeeper, as he was with Sebastian. After so many months in the stratified society of Britain, the egalitarian informality was astonishing.

The Merlin Club…what an amazing thing.

What would Mom and Dad make of it?

Maybe Sebastian was right about facing her fears. He was facing his, the complete, final loss of the career he'd wanted since childhood and built for more than a decade. He had no choice. Even if he stayed in the army, he would never be a battlefield leader.

She could hide, of course—hide the truth from her parents, hide from the consequences of her Gifts. Having them wasn't her choice, but using them surely was. But she'd never kept any big secret from her family and didn't want to start now.

Petersham tapped on the parlor door. "Excuse me, miss, but you've a visitor. A Mr. Dwight Shaw. He says he's your brother."

What? For a moment, Kate sat frozen. Had he really said—?

"Shall I send him away?"

"No! Oh, no." Kate shot to her feet. "Sorry, Petersham. I was just surprised. He is my brother. I'll go down and see him."

"I can bring him up if you like."

"He's not used to the, ah, formality. Thank you."

He stepped aside for her, and Kate rushed down the stairs. A few steps from the bottom, she realized she hadn't asked Petersham where Dwight was.

"Dwight?" she called. "Dwight, where are you?"

"I'm here." Grinning, her tall, sandy-haired younger brother stepped out of the parlor on the left of the entry. He wore the blue suit that was his Sunday best. "Bet you're surprised."

Kate flung herself into his arms, and they held each other tightly. "It's so good to see you," she said into the collar of his suit jacket. Until she'd seen him, she hadn't realized how homesick she was. In a way that had nothing to do with magic or family fears.

"I brought you a letter from home. Glenn wanted to mail it, but we figured I'd get here as fast, maybe faster."

"Come upstairs," she said.

Petersham had joined them. Kate introduced Dwight, who offered his hand.

Without missing a beat, the butler shook it. "A pleasure to meet you, sir. Ring if you need anything, Miss Shaw."

"Uh, thanks," Dwight said. "Likewise."

Petersham marched back toward his domain under the stairs. Dwight mouthed, "Butler?"

"It's a long story," Kate answered softly.

As they climbed the stairs, Dwight looked at the portraits on the walls, the landscape in the foyer below, and the thick carpet with open curiosity. "This is a very nice house," he commented.

"Yes, and the people who live in it are lovely." Kate showed him into the parlor and closed the door. Once Dwight started asking questions, he would keep at it until he was satisfied, and she didn't want to risk Rose overhearing.

Dwight sat in one of the chairs by the loveseat. "Kate, what's going on? I went by your apartment, but no one was there. Then I tried the CNU office. They said you didn't work there anymore, that you were staying with some lord and lady, and sent me here. Is that…like a lord and lady in that movie *The Prince and the Pauper?*"

Their whole family had loved the Errol Flynn film. Kate nodded. "Yes, but not villainous, of course."

"I should hope not." Dwight frowned. "What're you doing here?"

"It's kind of a long story. Before I launch into it, why're you in London?"

"I'm joining up." His jaw had the stubborn set that meant he expected argument.

"Joining what?" Even as she asked, that weird knowing told her. Chilled her.

"The Royal Air Force," he answered, as her Gift had warned. "What else would I come here to join?"

Oh, no. Kate needed a minute to take it in, and fear slowly wrapped itself around her heart. "You're not a British citizen. America's not in the war."

"Not yet, but we will be, soon as folks wake up. Dad says this Hitler guy with his *lebensraum* nonsense is just like those ranchers who wanted to drive farmers off their homesteads back in the last century."

The 1800s? "Sorry, but you lost me."

"Land grabs, Katie. Some folks never have enough."

She'd said almost the same thing about Hitler, but… "Any Americans who violate neutrality can lose their citizenship. Are you certain you want to do this?"

"I've been through this with Mom and Dad and Glenn. If they couldn't change my mind, you won't either."

"I suppose not." Kate sighed. "You always were the stubborn one."

Now he would be the endangered one. Given her decision to stay here, even when the bombs eventually started falling, however, she was on thin ice for arguing.

"Now it's your turn. Who are these people, and why're you staying here?"

"They're distant relatives of my birth mother. I met Rose's—Lady Borrowdale's—brother in Dover when I came back from France."

"I s'pose it's natural you'd want to know more about them," Dwight said.

Concern shadowed his eyes, and Kate's Gift told her it was fear she would prefer these fancy people to their shared family. Would he feel the same if he knew about her magic?

"I never was particularly curious about that," she told him. "My family is you and Dad and Mom and Glenn, but I like these cousins, and they've been very helpful."

"With what?" At least he didn't look worried now.

"In a nutshell, CNU decided, despite admitting I did an excellent job in France with the BEF—under enemy fire some of the time—they didn't want to be responsible for placing a woman in a war zone."

"Darn right."

Kate gaped at him. "Says the man who wants to go up against German Messerschmitts. Don't be a hypocrite, Dwight."

"I'm a man. You're a woman. It's my job to fight, not yours."

Kate glared at him. "I can't enjoy being relatively safe at home—relatively because, as you say, sooner or later the US will be in this—while my friends here are in danger."

"And your kin?" he demanded, again looking worried.

"Yes, Mr. Baconbrains, and that includes you. If you think I'm scampering home while you stay here to be shot at, you'd best think again."

He scowled at her. "You always were the stubbornest girl. Don't add stupid to that."

Kate bit back a shriek. "I already went through this with Sebastian," she snapped. "The subject is closed."

"Sebastian?" Dwight's eyes narrowed. "Who the dickens is he?"

Oh, hell's bells. She hadn't intended to tell Dwight about Sebastian until he adjusted to the idea that she was here to stay.

Someone tapped on the door, and Rose stuck her head in. The worried look on her face wiped away any thought of arguing with Dwight.

"I'm so sorry to interrupt," Rose said, "but Sebastian just rang. They're putting him in hospital straight away and plan to operate tomorrow."

Sebastian sat upright in his narrow bed and glared at the lump of his splint under the covers. He'd had a plan for this, a way to prepare himself. It had been progressing nicely. Now he'd been preempted—with the connivance of Galen, curse him!—and he would go into surgery tomorrow with too much left undone.

Too little time to brace himself for it.

That was the real problem.

He'd kept the dread and the loss at bay by focusing on preparations for after. Now *after* was rushing toward him with his plans incomplete.

The ward encompassed a dozen beds. Only a couple of others were occupied, one by a man with his bent arm in some sort of hoisting rig. The other man lay dozing.

The door at the end of the ward opened. Kate hurried in, and his heart lifted.

She came directly to him, and then her arms were around him. Sebastian held her tightly, turning his face into her soft hair.

"Dearest. I'm so sorry. They've torpedoed your plan." She pressed a kiss into his hair, and he tightened his hold.

"Bloody single-minded arses." Despite his anger, he kept his voice down so it wouldn't carry. "When I said I needed a few days to wind things up, Captain Thurston, the army surgeon, gave me all sorts of dire warnings about bone fragments shifting and severing an artery and causing me to bleed to death. I couldn't tell him the fragments were magically stabilized. Then Galen, who was there, said he'd told me all that and I wouldn't listen, so they called Secretary Eden."

"And he ordered you to the hospital."

"Yes." Eden had said the war effort needed Sebastian's mind and tactical sense and he mustn't risk depriving his country of his skills. And never mind that the skill he'd most developed, battlefield leadership, was sidelined forever.

"They insisted I come in so if the bone fragments caused a problem, they could amputate immediately."

"Well, I have to admit to some sympathy with their goal." Kate sank into the metal chair by the bed but caught his hand.

The warmth in her eyes brushed over his heart. He mustered a smile for her.

"Rose came with me," she said, "but they would let only one of us on the ward at a time."

"Well, of course." He made his voice as dry as possible. "Wouldn't want to overcrowd the place."

Kate chuckled. "What can I do for you, my heart?"

Keep thinking of me that way. But that was a maudlin thing to say. Instead, he asked, "Did you bring a notepad?"

"Are you kidding? Of course I have a pad."

As he'd expected. She'd once said no good reporter traveled without one.

"Some of the things I'd meant to do in the next few days must now fall to Genevieve. Will you go and see her tomorrow?"

"Of course. After you called, I postponed starting in the library until tomorrow, so I'm going there anyway. I'll do that after your surgery." Kate paused, eyebrows rising. In a low voice that wouldn't carry, she asked, "To enter the club, I put my palm on the merlin, release a little magic, and then open the door?"

"That's it."

She uncapped her pen and opened the pad to a clean page. "Ready when you are."

Keeping his own voice equally low, he said, "I'd planned some things to keep up with what the Nazis are doing, particularly with regard to their invasion plan. I'll need her to prepare the agents involved so I can pick up the reins whenever they let me out of here."

Kate's pen raced across the narrow sheet of paper. Oh, yes, shorthand. Good.

"First, she should contact Flight Lieutenant Athol Shelby of the Photographic Development Unit at Heston and tell him he's to report to her. She should coordinate his findings with what our Berlin agent reports." The Berlin agent would tell her which ports the Nazis meant to use, and she could pass that to Shelby, who was also a Merlin Club agent. He would be already on alert when the Germans began assembling their fleet.

"What about the Mainwarings in the afterworld?" Kate asked softly.

"I can coordinate them once I'm home. Meanwhile, you'll contact them for any information they might help Genevieve obtain. Though she can't know about them."

"Right."

The Merlin Club was always prepared. He would have to trust them to keep things moving until he could return to his duties there.

At least he had that to go back to. Simple as his tasks at the War Office had been, they'd contributed. Not being able to do that, even in a small way, not having any sense of purpose, would tear him apart.

～

The walk from Victoria Tube station to Rose's house wouldn't take long. For both Kate and Rose, their shared worry about Sebastian discouraged conversation. They were within sight of the house before either spoke.

"Your brother is welcome to stay with us, of course. The only vacant chambers are the ones on the second floor. They're a bit smaller, as they used to be part of the schoolroom, but we can make him comfortable."

"That's very generous. I don't know what he'll do." Kate sighed. "I think he realizes I didn't tell him everything about Sebastian—I said he was your brother, my cousin, and in the army—and Dwight is nothing if not persistent. I just don't want to get into it with him."

"You're concerned enough about your family already. Should I not have invited him to dinner?"

"No, that was very kind. Thank you again for that. I didn't realize I was homesick until I saw him. But anything I say to him will go straight back to our folks in his next letter." She glanced at Rose, who didn't look disturbed or offended.

Just in case, Kate added, "It's not that I'm not proud to be seen with Sebastian. I can't believe I'm lucky enough to have him care for me. It's just… I wanted to keep that private from my family until I straightened out some of these other things."

"All that makes perfect sense. I sent Mum a telegram. I expect she'll come as soon as she can. Our younger brother, James, will probably come with her. Sebastian undergoing such drastic surgery, especially after we lost Dad and Reg so suddenly…" Rose shrugged. "We all worry a little more than we used to."

"That's understandable."

They passed Eaton Square Gardens and turned down Rose's side of the square. Kate checked her watch. Rose had suggested Dwight return about four thirty for tea. It was now almost five, but they'd stayed with Sebastian, taking turns, until visiting hours ended.

When they walked into the house, Petersham greeted them. "Mr. Shaw is in the upstairs parlor, madam. I offered tea, but he preferred to wait for his sister. Will you be joining him?"

"Yes, but let's give Kate a few minutes with her brother first."

Petersham acknowledged that and departed.

Rose squeezed Kate's shoulder. "Brothers are sometimes pains in the arse, but the good ones do want us to be happy."

"I'll try to remember that. Otherwise, I may kill him."

Trying to decide on the best way to handle him, Kate climbed the stairs and put her hat, gloves, and bag in her room.

When she entered the parlor, Dwight was pacing in front of the cold hearth. He looked tremendously relieved to see her. "How's your cousin?" he asked.

"He's doing about as well can be expected of a man who'll lose his leg and probably his career tomorrow morning. Before you ask, he injured his knee a couple of years ago. A bad fall last week finished it off."

"I'm sorry to hear that."

As they settled onto the sofa together, Dwight asked, "What is he to you?"

Kate gave him her best wide-eyed stare. "I told you. He's my cousin."

"Um-hm. But you got the same guilty look as when you let Billy Prescott kiss you in the orchard in high school."

"I have no idea what you mean."

"The dickens you don't." He frowned at her. "You didn't fool me then, and you don't fool me now. What I want to know is why you won't just 'fess up if you're dating the guy. You ashamed of him or something?"

"Certainly not," Kate snapped. "Stop looking as though you're a cat who fell into cream. Yes, all right, Sebastian and I are seeing each other. We don't yet know where it's going—" *Not entirely, anyway.* "—and I would like to figure that out before I start getting letters from Mom and Dad and Glenn wanting to know who his people are and what are his prospects."

"They're reasonable questions."

Kate shrugged.

Dwight looked around the parlor, his thin face thoughtful. "His people seem to be pretty well off and, so far, pretty dadgum decent. If he's an earl, I guess his prospects are good."

"He has an estate in northwest England, a house in a very nice part of London called Mayfair, and some other properties. He and his family are respected socially. Sebastian appears to have a good reputation as an officer." Not that it could bring him what he wanted any longer.

Much as she loved her brother, she would rather be at the hospital to distract Sebastian or offer whatever comfort she could. Hospital rules made that impossible, though. At least she and Rose and John would see him tomorrow before the operation.

He'd put up a brave front, but the desolation in his eyes told its own tale, one her Gift confirmed. Once the lights went out in the ward tonight, he would lie alone in the dark with his dread. *Oh, my dear one.*

"Katie? Are you listening?"

She looked up to find Dwight frowning at her. "Sorry. What did you say?"

He stared at her for a long moment before his face softened. "You look worried. Does he have good doctors? I expect an earl would."

"He does, but it's still difficult, and there's nothing I can do to make it better."

"You can stick by him, but I reckon you already mean to do that."

Kate sighed. "Dwight, I just don't want to go into all this with the folks. Or with Glenn. Can you not just keep everything about us dating to yourself for now?"

"I guess I can," he finally said. "But he pulls any funny stuff with you, he'll answer to me."

"I count on that," she replied, and he hugged her.

Rose joined them, followed by Clara, the maid, with a tea cart. Rose drew Dwight's attention by explaining what all the little sandwiches were.

Kate barely listened. The best gift she could give Sebastian was information. His body might be sidelined, but his mind would work perfectly well once he didn't need pain medication. The sooner she began at the Merlin Club, the better.

CHAPTER 26

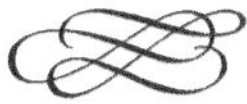

The headline on the front page of the *Times* screamed, "U-Boat Sunk Off Dungeness." The headline below read, "Contraband Cargo Seized."

Gerald swore and crumpled the paper. "What bloody bad luck."

Seated at the breakfast table across from him, Florence frowned. "Perhaps Arbuthnot isn't as careful as we've been, my love. It's sad for him, really. If he weren't so far in debt, he wouldn't have fallen for the German scheme."

"Perhaps not. Or perhaps…" Hawkstowe and his American had been at the Dorchester that evening. Had they overheard? Gerald and Hugo had kept their voices low. Not being Gifted, Hugo didn't know about the heightened senses of the Gifted.

"What is it?" Florence asked.

"Nothing. Never mind."

Hawkstowe worked in the War Office. He would have been in a position to scupper any plans he overheard.

"I know we needed that cargo delivered to help your credibility, but there will be other chances," Florence said. "For instance, isn't there another, ah, landing this week? Once that goes off, all will be well."

It had better be. His neck was on the line.

"I'll arrange another dinner. At least when we're with other British agents, we needn't bother with all that tedious *sieg heil* business. It's showy and changes nothing."

The Earl of Hawkstowe was supposedly in hospital. Not even he could cause problems from there. Amputation, the gossip said. Too bad for him, but Gerald wouldn't lose any sleep over it. The entire Mainwaring family were a bunch of meddlers. They deserved to be pulled up short.

Of course, Hawkstowe wouldn't be in hospital forever. When he emerged, with magic to aid his convalescence, he wouldn't be sidelined as long as most men.

He would definitely bear watching.

CHAPTER 27

The group gathered for dinner at Rose's made an effort to keep their spirits up, but it was a struggle. The surgery had gone well, according to Captain Thurston, the army doctor. Sebastian, however, seemed listless and disinterested during his brief post-operative visits with Rose, John, and Kate.

Sebastian's mother and his brother, James, had arrived that afternoon. James had the same Mainwaring features as Sebastian but with dark brown hair like Rose and their mother instead of black.

James paced the parlor while they waited for his mother to change for dinner. "Seb's not himself," he said. "He's so pale. So despondent."

"It's the drugs," Rose said. "It must be." Yet the fear in her eyes undercut her effort at certainty. She sat beside Kate on the loveseat.

"He was making plans," Kate told James. "For afterward. He hadn't finished setting things up when they insisted on operating immediately."

"That could throw him. He always was a planner," James replied.

"Yes," Lady Hawkstowe agreed as she entered, "he is." She sat in the chair across from Kate. "He's not himself," she echoed flatly, "but he perhaps he simply needs time."

"I hope so," Kate said. If only the planning for action against Sea Lion were further along, but they didn't have enough intelligence on German intentions to come up with a strategy.

Sebastian's mother turned to her. "Kate, I understand you were with

Seb when he suffered this drastic injury. Will you tell me what happened?"

"Yes, ma'am." At least there was no accusation in the words or in her face.

"Eleanor," the countess corrected. "Please."

Kate acknowledged that with a nod. As she started talking, James settled in the chair opposite his mother's. They listened impassively until she reached the part about the struggles to return to the afterworld and seek help. Sebastian's mother's eyes glistened, and his brother's face went tight.

"He saved us both," Kate concluded. "I wish I could've done more to help."

James glanced at his sister. "You did very well for a novice, Kate. I hear you're coming along well."

"I try." Had Rose discussed her with him?

"You've done more than that," Eleanor said. "We all appreciate your willingness to help our embattled country."

Kate didn't know what say to that, so she settled for, "I'm happy to do what I can."

"Not everyone would," James said. "Remind me after dinner that I have something for you. Seb wrote to me a couple of weeks ago and asked that I send this set of books to London for you. What with one thing and another, I didn't mail it, but it's in my bags at his house."

"What kind of book?"

"It's the earliest published defense of King Richard. It was written by Sir George Buck, Master of Revels at the court of James I, and published after his death by his nephew. It's five volumes called *The History of the Life and Reign of King Richard the Third*. Since you're helping us with this blasted curse, Seb thought it might interest you."

Rose added, "We have a copy of Horace Walpole's *Historic Doubts on the Life and Reign of King Richard the Third*. You're welcome to borrow that as well."

"Thank you. I would like to learn more about it." She would welcome any tool that would free Sebastian and their kindred from this curse.

~

The next day, Sebastian was no better. Worried about him, Kate curled up at bedtime with the first volume of the set he'd sent her. She had read only a little when Miranda appeared in the parlor.

"Would you like to see Sebastian?" Miranda asked.

"Of course, but scrying…it isn't the same."

"Not scrying. If you come through here, it still won't be the same, but you can stand beside his bed."

"I don't know how to come there." When the ghost raised her eyebrows, excitement burst through Kate. "Are you going to teach me?"

"If you want to learn."

"I sure do!"

"All right, then. This is easiest to learn when you've someone in this realm to teach you, but it's still difficult. You, however, have already passed through with Sebastian. You know what happens, and your seer Gift may have also picked up the magical steps involved."

"I still have my anchor. And then…I need to make a door."

"Your unorthodox way of working magic may help you with that. Fetch your anchor, and I'll meet you in your chamber."

As Kate hurried to her room, she tried to remember how she'd felt watching Sebastian create a portal. She found the pebble in her dresser drawer. When she turned around, Miranda stood in the center of the room.

"I'm not sure what Sebastian did," Kate told her.

"I think you can do it differently. Find a space that forms a rectangle. The hallway door will do, and tell your magic to make a portal. In other words, do as you do when you summon your glamours or your healing abilities."

"Make a portal," Kate said, staring at the door. "Make a portal, make a portal, make a—"

A rectangle of silver light flickered into view, then winked out.

"Almost," Miranda said. "Again."

To Kate's amazement, the third attempt produced a glowing portal.

"Hold it steady," Miranda advised. "In your mind, see it hanging there. Then walk through. Reach for me as you do so. You felt what Sebastian did. You know how to do this."

"What about the wraiths?"

"I'll see to them."

Kate tried to push through the intense, resistant cold but failed. The rectangle winked out, and she ended up standing against her bedchamber door. She tried twice more, three times, four.

On the fifth try, she pushed through.

Miranda immediately coated her with purple-gray magic and banished the wraiths.

"I need to learn to do that," Kate said.

"All in good time. We'll practice. For now, though, let's go see Sebastian."

~

They walked through the churning mist to the darkened hospital ward.

Faint light from the windows showed Sebastian lying in his bed, apparently asleep. She'd seen him this way, with the drape of the bed covers over his legs much too short on the right, during the vision cascade at the Officers' Sunday Club. Then, when he hadn't mattered to her, the vision had been distressing. Seeing it made real now tore at her heart. It had this afternoon, too. It probably would until he mastered his prosthesis.

"What can I do for him?" she asked Miranda.

"His instinct always is to take command. With time, that will rally. Bring him any information about the German plans. Engage his mind, and he will come back to himself all the faster."

"I can do that."

"Of course you can."

They stood by the bed for several minutes before Kate whispered, "Sleep well, my heart," and turned away.

"This probably should be our secret," Miranda said. "He doesn't like the idea of your traveling through here."

"Nor do I," Richard announced, emerging from the fog. "It's dangerous."

"But sometimes useful," Miranda replied.

"I'm not only talking about danger to her, and you know it. It's bad enough Sebastian taught his mother so she could visit his father and brother. The people who know—"

Miranda shrugged. "If we can't trust our own kindred, who can we trust?"

"You must not teach this to anyone else," Richard told Kate. "I want your word."

Miranda tensed at her side.

"Why?" Kate asked.

"I can't tell you that."

Kate studied him. "I think it's more you won't, so I won't promise."

"God's wounds, Kate—"

"No. I'm sorry. I haven't any plans to go spilling these beans, but I won't promise blindly."

Richard glared at his wife. "I hope we don't regret this." He stalked into the fog.

"You know," Kate said, frowning. "I've never seen him angry before." It was vaguely unsettling.

"That's not anger. It's worry."

"Why?"

Miranda smiled. "I cannot tell you either. Let's walk."

At least Miranda didn't try to extract promises. Instead, she said, "We once thought coming to this realm required communication with someone here. That's how we've taught our kinsmen, one in each generation. But we learned there are other ways to master the crossing—fortunately, ones that rarely succeed."

They walked in silence, and Kate's room at Rose's appeared out of the fog.

"I'm pleased you're reading about King Richard," Miranda said. "He was not a perfect man, but he was a good one. He had no illegitimate children after his marriage and was apparently loyal to his wife. Even at great risk to himself, in exile and war, he supported his brother Edward IV though others turned away for their own advantage. His motto was 'Loyalty binds me,' and he appears to have lived it."

"That's good to know."

"I'll keep watch on Sebastian, but I'll also come and see you each day. Now let's make an exit portal."

That proved to be much easier. In moments, Kate again stood in her bedchamber. The sense of Miranda's presence faded.

What Miranda had told her about Richard III was not only interesting as a matter of history. It had also given Kate an idea. First, though, they had to recover that confession.

~

A week after the surgery, Sebastian sat in the hospital garden in the summer sunshine. Other injured soldiers also sat out in the garden, but he'd chosen a spot away from everyone else. Idle conversation held no interest, and talk of battle would've been painful reminders of all he'd lost.

Thanks to Galen's surreptitious magical treatments, he was done with skin traction and had his wound closed. This was definite progress. But progress toward what?

He still groped for a sense of himself. Lachlan was recruiting members of a strike team, but they didn't yet have enough intelligence on the German plans to form one of their own. Perhaps when they did, he would wake up from this stupor that seemed to enshroud his mind.

Galen came down the path toward him. Sebastian watched him come and felt...no interest in why.

"Still angry with me?" the healer asked, stopping before Sebastian's chair.

Sebastian shrugged. "You did what you thought best." Besides, much as he hated to admit it, his landing here had been inevitable from the moment he and Kate touched the ward.

Galen nodded. "I've come to offer you something to think about." He paused, but Sebastian had nothing to say.

"Magic can shorten your recovery—if we can pull you out from under the army's supervision. It can put you into a prosthesis months before you ordinarily would reach that point. Come to that, you have advantages in using a prosthesis," Galen said quietly, "that others do not."

A prosthesis was still an artificial limb. No matter how his fellow wizard painted it, Sebastian would never again be fit for active duty.

Galen continued, "Wielding magic through our hands isn't a biologic imperative. It's tradition. It's also the path of least resistance, the easiest to learn, since we manipulate the world around us with our hands."

"I don't need a magic lesson." Sebastian stared at the shrubbery across from his chair. Were they boxwoods?

"In this, perhaps you do. Sebastian, nothing about our bodies or our magic precludes our using magic through our feet. Our legs."

Of which Sebastian now had one each. Besides, who the devil cared? His hands at least remained unimpaired.

"My boy—"

"I'm not your boy."

A pause. "Of course not. My apologies." Galen sighed. "I'll come to the point. Once your leg heals and you've adjusted to the prosthesis, I believe you can use your magic to manipulate it so that it moves—when you mount a horse, for example, or climb in and out of a car—just as a natural leg would."

"With my remaining foot?" Sebastian snorted. *Is that possible?*

"No, with magic flowing out of your amputated leg."

"That's daft." But if that were possible…

"I wouldn't advise you on infantry tactics, Major. Nor should you argue with me about magic and physiology."

False hope was worse than none. Sebastian shook his head.

"If you try it before your leg heals, you'll make matters worse and prolong your recovery. Once you're ready for a prosthesis, you can practice channeling power through your left leg and foot. Then, when you've mastered that, through the stump."

That sounded too logical. Sebastian swallowed hard. "What would be the point? I'll never be able to return to duty."

"The point, of course, is to give you more of your life back." Impatience laced Galen's words. "As for active duty, if that's what you mean, you haven't been fit for that for nearly eighteen months. There must be plenty of other contributions you can make. What with there being a war on and all that."

The sarcasm poked at Sebastian, but arguing was too much work.

"Think about it." Galen clapped him on the shoulder. "The RAF put Douglas Bader back in a cockpit with double leg amputations. That's not the same as charging over terrain, but Secretary Eden seems to think he can put your mind to good use. He's the war secretary. If he wants you in uniform, you will be."

Trying, if he failed… Sebastian rubbed his chest.

"I'll be back." With those faintly ominous words, Galen walked away.

He exchanged nods with a sandy-haired, blue-eyed man in his early twenties who was coming down the path. The young man wore a blue suit and a gray fedora. His suit showed some wear, but the way he carried his sturdy frame spoke of confidence.

"Major Mainwaring?"

The visitor stopped in front of Sebastian's chair and doffed his hat. "I'm sorry to bother you at such a time, but I'm signing up tomorrow. I need to say this before I go let Jerrys shoot at me."

American accent. Joining up. With something urgent to say. A chance remark of Kate's about one of her brothers popped into Sebastian's mind.

"Make it Sebastian." He offered his hand. "It's good to meet you, Dwight. Thank you for what you've come to do."

Kate's brother blinked but gave his hand a firm shake. "Ah, thank you. I'm, um, sorry about your situation."

That made two of them.

Before Sebastian could reply, Dwight added, "But you might want to hold your horses on the *good to meet* part."

Interesting. "How can I help you?'

"It's about Kate. I'm sorry as I can be to have to say this when you're still recovering, but… You seem like a decent fella from all I've heard. But every guy wants his sister's boyfriend to know she's got brothers. You know?" His face flushed. "I'm making a mess of this, but—"

"I know precisely what you mean. My brothers and I had the same chat with Rose's beaux."

"Oh. Right." Dwight took a deep breath. "Kate's a good reporter, a sharp one. She has a sense about when someone's lying to her, and she'll dig until she finds the truth. In her personal life, though, she's more trusting."

He paused, his gaze assessing. When Sebastian nodded, Dwight continued, "I'm going off for training somewhere, but if you're not good to Kate—if you hurt her or upset her—I'll find out about it sooner or later. Then it'll be me and you, and I don't care what titles you hold or what you wear on your uniform epaulets."

The army reference stung, but Dwight was pushing on with, "Do you understand?"

"I do indeed." Sebastian held the younger man's gaze. "I realize words count little here, that actions matter far more. I will, however, tell you Kate is very important to me. My primary aim is to keep her safe and happy. As I trust you'll eventually see."

Dwight's expression relaxed, but his eyes still held a keen, assessing look. At last, he donned his hat. "Well, I should get going. Let you rest."

He didn't ask Sebastian not to tell Kate, but that didn't matter. They were both brothers who looked after their sisters. This would remain between them.

"When you have leave, you're welcome at my house. We'll talk further."

"That's really swell of you. Thank you."

"Of course. Good luck to you." They shook hands.

Sebastian watched him go. Dwight had a sense of purpose, on his sister's behalf and for himself.

It was time Sebastian recovered his own. The first step was getting out of here.

CHAPTER 28

Sebastian?" Kate smoothed his hair back gently. "Richard has news, and I think you'll want to hear it."

He blinked at her. "Must've dozed off." The mystery he'd been reading, Marjorie Allingham's *The Case of the Late Pig,* lay against his good hip as though it had slipped off his lap.

"Well, it's no wonder, with the medicines you're taking." Kate settled on the mattress beside him.

He'd been out of hospital two days and still had to take powerful painkillers. At least he'd convinced the doctors he should recover and undergo rehabilitation at home.

"The army owes you this care," his doctor, Captain Thurston, had insisted.

"Before long, it will begin owing such care to a great many other men," Sebastian had replied, "ones who cannot afford private care. I can, and I would prefer to be home anyway."

At least Galen had supported his plea. The wizard healer had already done much to decrease the swelling in Sebastian's stump.

Pushing himself up in the bed, he stifled a wince. His missing ankle ached, and there wasn't a thing to be done about it. *Phantom pain,* the doctors called it. Not even Galen's magic could banish it. At least Mum and James had felt sufficiently reassured to go home.

At the foot of the bed, Richard appeared. Sebastian's father stood beside him, but of course Kate couldn't see Dad.

"I came because Reginald cannot alert Kate," Richard said. "Now that you're awake, you don't need me for this." He vanished.

"What is it?" Sebastian asked.

"Hitler's to give a big speech tomorrow," his father said. "I still can't enter the Reichstag or the Chancellery, but I followed one of the aides home. His house isn't warded, and he had much to say to his wife about how Hitler would give the British one last chance to be reasonable."

"Meaning come to terms," Sebastian said flatly. They already knew the Wehrmacht and the Kriegsmarine had been arguing over how broad a front they could sustain in an invasion, what tidal conditions would be best, and even what hour of the day they should launch.

"So I gather." His father nodded. "This fellow is rather hoping we won't. He feels we're entirely too arrogant and in need of a good trouncing. Unless we bend the knee, the Luftwaffe are to lure out the RAF and destroy it."

"Winston will never accept that." Nor would Fighter Command, and their ability to resist grew daily. Or had been doing so, the last Sebastian had heard.

The lack of access to information burned. He had his own sources but nothing so immediate as the War Office.

"No," Sebastian's father agreed, "but there are still some ministers who would. If we're to stand against the Nazis, Winston must persuade these men that war is the better course."

A tough job.

Sebastian rubbed his hand over his face. "If they're going ahead with Sea Lion, they'll start massing boats. Perhaps Kate and I can figure out where."

"Start planning early, eh?" His father nodded. "Your man in Berlin has taken to waltzing in and out of the Chancellery under an invisibility glamour as though he lives there. Genevieve might want to caution him against becoming cocky. It would be a shame to lose him."

The ghost bade Sebastian farewell and vanished.

Sebastian relayed the conversation to Kate. "You'll talk to Genevieve tomorrow?" he requested. He didn't actually need to ask. In the time he'd been convalescing, Kate had handled matters with Genevieve exactly as he would've wished. He'd come to see Kate as his partner, a dangerous development for his peace of mind.

"Of course." She moved his book to his nightstand and climbed onto the narrow bed on his undamaged side. "It's good to have you home. With Galen magically helping you heal faster and bring the swelling down, you should be ready for a prosthesis before much longer."

"I hope so. I'm sick of lying in bed." Moving to the chair was a huge undertaking and the only relief for the monotony of his day. Still, he was out of hospital, and that was a relief.

The only hitch was that his entire family, living and dead, had put down their collective foot at the notion of his returning to his own house. Being with Kate, who would become the object of gossip if she stayed there with him unchaperoned, was an advantage to being here, but he missed his own things. His own routine.

Or whatever he could salvage of it.

Meanwhile, there was work he could do. "Kate, let's see if we can determine where they're to begin massing those ships."

They tried for half an hour but came up with nothing except Dunkirk and Calais.

"Shouldn't we find something else?" Kate frowned. "Admittedly, I'm inexperienced and you're a little woozy, but I've done better than this before."

"It may be that they haven't decided beyond these two. If our man in Berlin doesn't come up with something in a few days, we'll try again. They can't bring together the thousands of boats they'll need that quickly. We have a little time. Just not much."

~

On July 19, Hitler made the expected speech to the Reichstag. He promised death and destruction to Britain if she resisted and friendship if she acquiesced. Peace overtures began again the next day.

On July 22, Lord Halifax, who had been an advocate for discussing accommodation with Germany, delivered the British government's answer. His speech soundly rejected any idea of coming to terms with Nazi Germany.

Members of the Merlin Club knew what the government likely did not, that September 21 had been set as the date for Operation Sea Lion, the invasion of Britain, before Halifax delivered his response.

All that ran through Kate's head as she skimmed the pages of an ancient grimoire. The aged paper crackled, and a musty smell rose from the pages. The combination made her deeply aware of the book's age.

She'd finished cataloguing the contents. Now she was exploring the section on wards.

Hmm. This segment discussed blood wards, at least as well as she could tell from the faded, ornate writing. Nothing about how to lift one, though, and many dire warnings against creating them.

The Wyndon who raised that ward must've learned how from someone. Was it a family secret? Or was the information in some obscure volume they might never find?

She'd first become interested in lifting the curse out of fondness for Richard and Miranda and because she believed it was right. Since she'd learned Sebastian's soul lay under the same cloud, lifting it had become doubly important.

I would do anything to help him. With each day that passed, his courage in dealing with his infirmity and his pretense of being calm inside about it impressed her more. She knew, either because of the bond created by trying to probe beyond that blood ward or because of her Gift, that he was far from settled about it. He'd done what he must. Accepting it fully was another matter entirely.

From the corridor came the faint whirr of the elevator rising. Kate noted it absently while she traded the book for the next one in her stack.

"Hard at work, I see," Sebastian said.

Kate started. He sat in the doorway in his wheelchair.

"Are you supposed to be here?" she blurted. *Oops. Probably not the best greeting.*

"No one said I couldn't come, though I did pressure Wilson to drive me while no one else was home," he replied, wheeling himself in. "I thought perhaps you could use some help."

"Your help is always welcome."

"Good. I'm sick of being in one place." The space between the shelves that lined the walls and the chairs around the table would be tight for his chair. He managed it, though, and rolled up to the corner of the table. "Would you move that chair, love?"

"Of course." She dragged it to one side and made space for him. In his lap, he had a notepad. A pen protruded from his shirt pocket, and his trousers were folded neatly around his stump. He truly had come to work.

"Did you have this planned this morning?" she asked.

"No, but I wanted to talk to you without the chance of Rose or John interrupting us."

"All we need to do for that is go into your bedroom and close the door."

"Yes, but I can't keep them out of their sons' bedroom. It isn't right." With a wry grin, he said, "When I stop to think about it, the kissing and such we've done in the boys' bedroom feels…inappropriate."

Kate's cheeks heated. She stood to gain leverage for lifting the heavy, oversize books and set three in front of him. "Now you can be useful while we talk."

"Happily." But he didn't open a book. "I want to go home, Kate. To my own house. I'm recovered enough to manage, and Bradshaw will help me in any way I need. Perhaps he has an elderly uncle or someone like that who can serve as my temporary batman."

"You probably are well enough. You've been so diligent about your physical therapy." She looked down at her tablet and then back at him. "I'll miss you, but I can understand the need to go home."

Sebastian folded his hand around hers and waited until she looked at him. "Come with me, darling Kate."

"I want to. So much. I really shouldn't, though. Especially now that Dwight's over here. Back home, no decent unmarried woman would live in a single man's house."

"I know, and I'm not doing this well." He brought her hand to his mouth. First his soft breath and then his lips whispered over her knuckles.

The touch shivered through her body, and the tenderness in his eyes set her heart thumping.

"I love you, Kate. I always will. Marry me and come to Charles Street as my wife."

For a moment, she wasn't sure she'd heard him correctly. "You…you're serious."

"Entirely."

"I… Sebastian, I love you with all my heart. You know that, don't you?"

"I do." His gaze remained steady on hers. "But you planned to return to the States, and you're worried about your situation with your family. Now I'm adding another problem to the mix."

Kate choked out a laugh. "You're not a problem. Not ever. You're a boon I never expected. It's just…so much of my life is unsettled, and the idea of marrying an earl seems, if you'll forgive me, like something that happens to other people. Not to farm girls from Cobbettown, Missouri."

"I understand, darling. Take all the time you need. I won't change."

They leaned in and kissed each other. The kiss deepened, and the embrace tightened.

"Lap," he murmured against her lips.

"I don't want to hurt you."

"I'll manage. Come here, please." He settled her onto his good leg with the incomplete one behind her. When he pulled her close this time, Kate flicked his lips with her tongue. He sighed and opened them.

His hands slid over her body, across her breasts, and down to her hips. She stroked his shoulders and chest and his back above the chair's back.

Breathing hard, they cuddled each other. Sebastian kissed her brow.

"My life has been dark since we were injured in the crypt," he said quietly. "You've been my light, Kate. You've supported me and comforted me and helped me do something that matters instead of just lolling around Rose and John's house between therapy appointments. Whatever you decide, never forget that."

"I won't." She kissed him softly and settled against him again.

Minutes drifted by. Voices came up the stairs.

Reluctantly, Kate stood up. "Someone could come in anytime."

"We're lucky they haven't already."

She returned to her seat, and they set to work. From time to time, though, she sneaked looks at him. The image of him sitting there, his dark head bent over the ancient book, his pen scratching notes, slipped into her heart. His face was pale and drawn from the pain that still plagued him. If only she could ease it.

Aside from being tied to England, he was everything she had ever wanted. Why was she hesitating?

Because of Mom and Dad? If they could accept her, they could accept him.

But what if they couldn't?

He'd faced his fear. Perhaps it was time to face hers.

"Sebastian?"

"Yes, darling?" He looked up with a smile, and her heart turned over.

"When you're well enough, I would like to take you up on that offer to go to Missouri."

"Of course." Although he nodded, the shadow was back in his eyes.

Kate laid her hand over his. "Whether I marry you won't depend on their reactions. But I've always known they were behind me. Before I can move forward, I have to know whether they still are."

"I understand. We'll go as soon as we can."

Kate thanked him, and they went back to work. The idea of facing Mom and Dad brought all her misgivings to the fore. Her feelings for Sebastian made it necessary, though, and the sooner the better.

～

Two days later, Lachlan MacGregor met Kate and Sebastian for lunch at the Merlin Club. The staff set out the meal in one of the bedchambers so they could eat in private. Sebastian had insisted Kate join them. Whether or not she married him, she was his partner in the planning for Sea Lion.

"We need to rethink our plan," Lachlan said as soon as the staff left them alone. "Our mages can blast through a stone wall, even a thick one, in moments, but steel is much denser, and hull plating, even more so. Penetrating it requires three of us exerting full power for just under ten minutes. The process, unfortunately, is not quiet."

Sebastian grimaced. "I was afraid of that. I have some news, though, that should move us along in logistics anyway. Our best information presently is that the Germans will begin massing boats for their invasion fleet next month. They'll use Calais, Dunkirk, Ostend, Boulogne, Antwerp, and possibly a couple of others."

"How did you obtain this information?" Lachlan asked.

"Some by scrying. Other bits by means I won't share, but it's reliable."

When the Scotsman nodded, Sebastian continued, "I want to wait until they're all at their launch ports, then scuttle two or three big ships at the harbor mouths. Some of the waterways are too wide for that, but as we said before, we needn't stop them all if we stop enough. Bomber Command can then do the rest."

"So you need engine room crew and a pilot or helmsman, all Gifted, as well as your wizards and my mages." Lachlan shook his head. "That's a challenge."

"What if they don't have to scuttle the ships with their magic?" Kate asked. "What if we sneaked bombs onboard? Maybe with an invisibility glamour?"

Sebastian nodded to her. "My alternate plan."

"Is this a suicide mission?" Lachlan asked, his face grave. "I won't ask my folk to undertake one without knowing what they face."

"I hope it isn't," Sebastian said. "I can transport them on and off the ships." That involved a risk that they would figure out afterworld travel, but it couldn't be helped. That fleet simply could not be permitted to launch. "We'll tackle one harbor, then the next, and then the next, and so on. I would like to wait until the boats are full of Nazis, but if they decide to load immediately before launching, we won't have time to destroy as many boats. So we should attack as soon as the convoys are gathered at their embarkation points."

"Logical," Lachlan commented. "Just how will you do this transporting, Sebastian?"

"You have your secrets, and I have mine. Our teams will learn a bit of what's involved, and I'll need them sworn to secrecy."

"We can do that. Anything else?"

"What do you know about blood wards? I need to go past one, and any use of magic near it triggers a wave of magical force."

"I know nothing about them," Lachlan answered. "I'll see if any of my folk have any ideas. Beyond that, I can't help you."

"That'll do." Sebastian thanked him.

Lachlan would offer whatever help he could, but would it be enough?

Purple-gray fog swirled around Kate in the dreamscape. She was in the afterworld, but why? How had she come there? And where were her kindred?

For that matter, where were the wraiths?

Since she and Sebastian had tackled that blood ward, she'd intermittently dreamed of the dead woman she'd Seen in the magic. If she thought of the woman, would the afterworld lead Kate to her?

The fog churned as she walked. A few minutes later, it rolled to the side, revealing an elegant chamber. The paneled walls, ornate hearth with heraldic carvings of a bear and a portcullis, the cushions on the wooden settle and X-shaped chairs, all proclaimed an affluent family lived here.

A door across the room opened. A woman walked through it. Her disheveled brown hair hung almost to her hips, and her long shift hung crooked, baring one shoulder. She walked to a table under the window to pour wine into a slim, silver goblet. The darkness outside proclaimed that it was night.

A naked man entered behind her. Kate's cheeks heated, and she had to resist the urge to look away. She'd never seen a naked man and had no desire to see this one. He slid his arms around the woman's waist and nuzzled her neck. Sighing, she leaned back against him.

"I thought you were joking about being Gifted," he murmured. "But no, you're very powerful."

"And I know how to use those Gifts on a man, do I not, sweet Anthony?"

Eyes sparkling, the woman turned to embrace him. Her hand slipped down between their bodies, and his face tensed.

"You do, my pet."

Anthony? Was this the man Edmund had tried to help?

He kissed her lightly. "In fact, I've a surprise for you. Close your eyes."

He walked across the room and opened a cupboard in the corner. The woman waited with her eyes closed and a small smile on her face.

When he turned from the cabinet, Kate gasped. He held a long, gleaming dagger in his right hand.

"No," Kate said, watching him glide toward the unsuspecting woman. "No, no, no. Oh, look out!" She knew what would happen, what had already happened, yet everything in her cried out in protest.

Of course the woman couldn't hear. The man stepped behind her, cupped her chin in his hand, and slit her throat.

She fell, wide-eyed and gasping. Accusation filled her eyes.

The man shrugged. "Such Gifts are wasted on a whore." He hurried to the cabinet and drew out a small, shallow silver basin. Holding her bleeding neck above it, he let her blood fill it.

Then he poured it into a flask, stoppered it, and sealed it with magic.

Cleaning his hands magically, he strode to another door and opened it, revealing a corridor. "Edward," he called, "it's done."

A man who resembled him but was burlier and looked slightly older stalked into the room. He wore a velvet tunic in rich blue with dark hose and soft boots. A gold necklace of bears and portcullises with diamonds and emeralds interspersed between hung around his shoulders.

"Very good," he said. "Remember, pour that around the foundations of the Mainwaring house before you go in and perform the incantation. If you forget, it won't work. Are you certain Mainwaring will do as you wish?"

Anthony smirked. "I've sown such discord between him and his son that they're barely speaking. He's worried and ashamed. He'll do it, and then I'll bring the confession to you."

Edward's eyes gleamed. "You know how to tamper with his memory. You have enough blood?"

"Of course. The fool will curse his entire line. He won't outlive the Tudors, and when his grandson however many generations from now goes to retrieve the confession that could save them all, it won't be there. Edmund will be certain he wrote it, for, indeed, he will have done, but he won't know what happened. He's damned forever, and all of his line with him."

"As he so deserves," Edward said. "You've shown you're truly Father's true son, Anthony. The manor outside Ashford will be yours, as agreed."

Anthony flashed him a satisfied smile. "I'd best be about it, then."

The fog rolled over the dreamscape. Kate paced. Was she in the afterworld? Or only dreaming it?

Or was she Seeing it?

Richard and Miranda hadn't been able to spot the confession from the afterworld. But they also hadn't known to look for the woman. Just as subsequent seers, not sensing the image of the confession through its possessors, couldn't regain the Sight of the confession Amelia had summoned more than hundred years ago. Perhaps not having the woman's image to draw their power prevented Miranda and Richard from finding her.

Her blood had blocked the ability to scry or See Edmund writing the confession. Or, apparently, Anthony carrying it away.

If they knew the words Anthony said, would that enable them to undo the concealing spell? Even to break the ward?

What had Anthony done?

The churning fog thinned. Kate saw Anthony pace around a house set in a field. Outside of London, it must be. When he completed his circuit, he entered the house. But the words he said were unfamiliar, guttural. The sounds sent a chill down her back and into her arms.

She also didn't See him depart the house. What had he done after going inside?

Wondering that, thinking of his face, Kate let the power draw her. Anthony and Edward rode toward Otterden Abbey. Anthony carried a narrow wooden box across his horse's back behind the saddle. Seeing it, Kate knew it contained the confession.

"What are we doing here?" Anthony asked. "I thought we were going to the manor."

"We are, but first we must put that where no one will ever expect it to be. The abbot owes me a favor. He'll let us hide it here and raise powerful warding to conceal it."

They dismounted and walked into what was now the hall. Light shone through stained-glass windows depicting the Genesis story and the Last Supper.

A cowled monk who looked to be in his mid-forties greeted them. "Welcome, my lords. Father Gregory has asked me to open the crypt for you." He led them to the dais and pointed to the right end of the altar. "Stand here, if you please."

In place of the carved serving stand, but closer to the front of the dais, stood a stone altar. Instead of a large tapestry, a smaller one the width of the altar and decorated with crosses and lilies hung behind it.

The monk reached behind the tapestry and touched something, and a section of the floor slid to the left, revealing the stairs. "When you complete your business, touch the carved lamb behind the wall hanging. The stairs will close."

"Very well," Edward replied.

The two men waited while the monk walked out. Only when they were alone did they descend into the crypt.

Edward led the way to the back corner where Kate and Sebastian had found the ward. The door there, unwarded in this era, opened smoothly. Edward created witchlight and entered, Anthony behind him. They traveled down a low passage angled toward the center of the courtyard. At its end, they walked into a chamber that was about ten feet square. Shelves around the walls held small chests, likely reliquaries and possibly money. A worktable stood in the center.

"Let us spread the thing out," Edward said, "so we and those who come after us can admire it."

They did so, weighting the curving edges with small chests and a couple of candlesticks. Set into red wax, the Hawkstowe seal dangled from the corner.

Then they stood back, admiring their handiwork.

"You've done well, Anthony." Edward hooked his left arm over his half-brother's shoulders. Smiling, he walked his brother to the door. "After you. I'll close this up."

Anthony stepped into the passage. Edward jerked a dagger from his belt sheath, caught his brother's jaw, and slit his throat so quickly than Anthony had no time to react. Blood sprayed on the stones. Edward drew a shallow bowl from beneath his tunic and magically directed some of the blood into it.

Standing over his dying brother, he said, "You truly thought I would share my inheritance with a bastard? Your mother was a whore, and you're a burden. But you'll be useful for this."

The light died out of Anthony's eyes.

Kate choked against nausea. Tears ran down her face. She'd seen war and death, but watching two cold-blooded, hate-fueled murders in so short a time was more than she could bear.

A flash of witchfire obliterated the corpse and cleaned the blood from the stones. Edward dripped blood down the passage to the door, where he magically directed it around the door frame. His lips moved, but he used the same blood-chilling, guttural language that Anthony had earlier.

He stepped out and closed the door. The frame glowed the red of a coal in the hearth. Its magic felt in the dream in the same way it had when she and Sebastian battled it.

So that was a blood ward. What a vile, wicked, nasty thing. No wonder blood magic was forbidden. Kate's tears came faster now, fueled by shock and anger.

She jolted awake.

The memory of the dream was as clear as the experience had been. This was no mere dream, then, but a vision. As she'd suspected.

She climbed out of bed to pace but couldn't shake the chill and the fury at what these men had done. Perhaps writing it down would help. She drew her pad out of her bag and sat at the desk.

But writing didn't help. Instead, it brought it all back in vivid, wretched detail.

Kate put her head in her hands. Somehow, she had to banish these images. Go back to sleep. She had work to do tomorrow. As a reporter, she'd covered the courts and local government and city hall. She knew people did unspeakable things to each other. Except in France, though, she'd never actually seen it done.

If she was lucky, she never would again.

Someone tapped at the door, and she jumped. A moment later, she smiled. She knew who had knocked.

"Just a minute," she called softly. Shrugging into her cotton robe, she hurried to the door.

As she expected, Sebastian stood on the other side on crutches, his own robe hastily tied and his hair disheveled.

"Is something wrong?" he asked. "I woke up feeling as though you needed me."

"I do. Oh, I do, but I didn't mean to awaken you."

"Never mind that. What's happened?"

They sat on the bed together. He propped his crutches against the wall and put his arms around her. Holding on to the warmth and security he offered, Kate told him about her vision.

"I couldn't hear what Edward said," she told Sebastian. "Or what Anthony said when he blocked Edmund's memory and hid the confession. I didn't think of it at the time, but…the monks would've have been able to enter their treasure room either, would they?"

"Perhaps they ceded it to the earldom. If they did have access, though, we might be able to do whatever they did." He tucked her head under his chin. "Show me what they said again?"

Kate complied.

When she finished, Sebastian shook his head. "I have the standard classical education. That's no language I ever heard, and it feels…evil."

"It does."

"Once I can move easily again, we can go back to the crypt and see whether this new information helps. I hope that won't be long."

"With magic to speed your hard work, it likely won't be." She had helped him too. Galen had taught her how to magically reduce the swelling and speed the healing daily.

"Meanwhile, we've other jobs to do. But this should give our kinsmen renewed hope, and that's very important indeed."

They smiled at each other, and his eyes warmed. He leaned in to kiss her.

Kate kissed him back, holding him close. He brushed his tongue against her mouth, and she took the kiss deeper. The warm, solid width of his shoulders tempted her hands to roam, and she let them. Apparently taking that as license, he stroked her back and ran his hands over her hips and breasts.

Kate arched into his touch. Sebastian sighed. She pressed slow, tongue-flicking kisses down his neck, and he groaned. When he brushed his lips over her ear, the rush of pleasure blinded her.

"My beautiful Kate." Sebastian thumbed her aching nipple. He dragged his open mouth down her neck to her shoulder and then to the cleft between her breasts.

Panting, Kate fell back on the pillows with him.

Sebastian groaned and pressed his face into her breasts. His warm breath penetrated her thin nightgown and teased her further.

When he raised his head, his eyes were hot and dark. "I should return to my chamber, but I don't want to. I want to touch you, Kate. To make love to you."

The ache between her thighs urged her to agree. But she wasn't sure their love would last. Doing something irrevocable…

Hoping he would understand, she brushed his hair back. "I want to touch you, too, but I've never gone all the way, and I don't—I'm not ready."

"Then we needn't do that." He kissed her quickly. "There's a wide range of pleasure we can share without it."

Relieved, Kate smiled. Letting her fingers wander down his neck and into his pajama shirt, she said, "Maybe you should take this shirt off."

"Will you do it for me?"

They sat up. Kate scattered kisses over his chest while she unbuttoned his shirt. It and his robe landed on the floor.

Settling into a position that was comfortable for his still-healing stump took them a minute, but they managed. Kate lay with her head on his arm. He held her gaze while he slowly unbuttoned her nightgown.

Each time his knuckles brushed her skin, anticipation built bubbling heat deep in her belly. Kate shifted restlessly.

"Say stop," he told her, "and I will. Straight away."

"I know." If she didn't, they wouldn't be doing this.

At last, he slid the front of her gown aside to bare her left breast. "So beautiful."

Kissing her, he molded the sensitive flesh with his palm, rubbing until she whimpered. He continued caressing her while he kissed his way down her neck and over her breasts again. When his mouth closed over her taut nipple, she gasped, clutching him to her.

Sebastian groaned. He sucked and licked until she writhed against him.

Her legs fell open. He stroked her thigh, his hand moving upward, under her gown, and she ached for him to touch her. When he did, she bucked under his hand. He lifted his head and brushed her sex with one finger. Pressed gently.

"Yes or no, darling?"

"Yes," Kate gasped.

His finger slid into her, then almost out and in again, and her hips rose to meet it. This was too much. Too much feeling to bear for long, far too much to bear alone.

She slid her hand down and found the opening in his trousers.

"Darling—you needn't."

She closed her fingers around his hard length, savoring the thrust of his hips against her hand. When she tugged his head down with her free hand, he detoured to lick her other breast.

His attention to her breast and the relentless slide of his finger inside her soon had her hips pumping to his rhythm. The tension on his face and his harsh breathing as he thrust into her grip gave her an intoxicating sense of power that pushed her pleasure higher.

The pleasure tightened like a shrinking spiral, focusing on the tiny spot between her thighs. Kate panted, "Sebastian—"

He sealed his mouth over hers and pressed against that tiny, sensitized spot.

The spiral burst, rolling outward in a blinding rush of heat. She cried out into his mouth.

Sebastian groaned and shuddered against her.

As their breathing settled, he rolled to his back. Kate nestled against him, her hand resting on his bare chest. The intimacy of the moment wrapped itself around her heart.

She'd never loved anyone this much. But could she give up everything familiar to stay with him?

CHAPTER 29

I t's odd not having Kate here," Lachlan said. He and Sebastian sat at the desk in Lachlan's chamber at the Merlin Club. A diagram of Antwerp harbor, which Sebastian had made by scrying, lay on the desk.

"What I mean to propose is dangerous. She'll want to be involved, and that isn't acceptable." Indeed, when things heated up, as everything in him felt they would soon, he would send her home somehow. Making plans that depended upon her therefore made little sense.

"There is a world that lies alongside this one," Sebastian said. "I know how to traverse it. By doing so, we can pass through wards and solid objects. We'll board the Nazi ships without ever being seen."

"That sounds too good to be true."

"It's not a walk in Hyde Park. There are deadly wraiths who will tear us apart unless we protect ourselves with the magic of that place."

"Which you also know how to do."

Sebastian nodded. "Have you had any luck with explosives?"

"We have indeed." Lachlan's teeth showed in a wolfish grin. "Using magic to explode a shell augments the explosion exponentially. It blew apart a piece of warship-grade steel we obtained by methods I won't explain. It should penetrate anything the Nazis have."

"So if we do that in the hold, the lowest deck, the ship will sink quickly?"

"You could drive a train through the hole." Lachlan's smile faded. "It's risky, though. Whoever explodes the shell must escape before it actually detonates. Failure to do so means dying in the explosion."

Sebastian thought about that for a couple of minutes. "We'll need to rehearse. If we can exit quickly enough—"

"Via this mysterious realm?"

"Yes. If we can, those explosions will do the trick nicely. But we'll need more than one team to move enough ships to block a waterway before the Nazis can react. Let's practice exits by blowing up much smaller charges. If we can make the timing work, I'll train you and a couple of others to make that transit."

Staring at Lachlan, he added, "I'll be trusting you with a dire secret, so I'll need your word not to reveal or teach what I'll show you."

Lachlan said nothing, studying him.

"I'll want your handshake on it," Sebastian said. "And theirs, if we get to that."

Lachlan reached across the table. "You have it."

Gripping Lachlan's hand, Sebastian sent magic down his arm. It passed through his and Lachlan's clasped hands and echoed deep in his body. Awareness of their bargain hummed in his blood and slowly faded.

"Well. Back to work," Sebastian said. He and Lachlan said their farewells.

Sebastian watched the Scotsman go. In the last couple of weeks, the Luftwaffe had stepped up the air war. They attacked shipping convoys, ports, airfields, radar stations, and defense industries. The Kriegsmarine mined the waterways to further curtail shipping. All of these felt like a prelude to invasion. The RAF and the Royal Navy were responding, and Bomber Command was targeting launch ports for Sea Lion, but Britain's fate hung in the balance. The Merlin Club-Mages of the Isles joint teams could help tip that balance.

If they pulled off their plans.

Sebastian drew his crutches under his arms and departed, closing the library door behind him. This time of day, he could take the Tube back to Rose's. Soon, though, he was going back to his own home.

He pressed the button for the lift only to hear Richard's voice behind him.

"Sebastian. I'll have a word."

Nodding, Sebastian followed him to the library and hung out the

Private Meeting sign. He'd known they would have this confrontation, but he'd hoped to be better prepared for it.

As soon as Sebastian closed the door, Richard ground out, "God's bleeding wounds, man. Are you daft? You cannot teach anyone how to traverse this realm."

"It's necessary." Saving his strength for the Tube, Sebastian sank into one of the library chairs.

"Nothing is that important."

Did Richard not understand? Carefully, Sebastian said, "England's fate is at stake."

"I don't care. Sometimes there are bigger stakes than that."

Sebastian stared at him. "I've no idea what you mean."

"You put the timeline at risk if you teach anyone to travel here. You cannot imagine the terrible results that flow from a change in history."

"That's what you did," Sebastian said on a flash of Sight. "Someone changed history, and you and Miranda fixed it."

Richard's face stiffened. "Do not do this."

"If we don't, we watch England fall to the Nazis. No." Sebastian stood. "I'm sorry, Richard, but that realm will be our staging ground. It's the only way to accomplish this quickly. If there are problems after, I'll deal with them."

Scowling, Richard glared at him. "Don't think I won't hold you to that."

A moment later, he vanished, leaving Sebastian with grave misgivings.

There truly was no other way, though. He would simply have to see that he and Lachlan chose their teams well. First, though, he and Kate had an important errand to run.

Three days later, Kate and Sebastian stood in the afterworld but also in the back yard of her family farmhouse. A thin layer of purple-gray mist, like a veil, gave the house and barn and the gently rolling hills in the distance a fuzzy look in the twilight. They'd had to come at this time of day to be sure her father would be home instead of in the fields.

Sebastian gripped Kate's hand, but even that warm reminder of his support couldn't stop her stomach butterflies. At least he seemed steady on his cane and new leg.

"You needn't do this today if you'd rather not," he reminded her.

"Putting it off won't make it any easier." It would only give her more time to dread her family's reaction.

Silvery magic with a faint purple tint streamed from his hand to form a portal in the fog. They walked through it together, past a brief curtain of intense cold, and into the back yard. Lights from the kitchen and the parlor cast a warm glow into the fading light. Mom moved across the window, probably preparing to start supper.

Kate took a deep breath.

"Are you certain you should do this alone?" Sebastian asked.

"I have to. They don't know you, and that will influence what they say. Maybe."

He cupped her cheek. "The house isn't warded, darling. I'll be near you at all times."

"That helps."

They kissed quickly. When Sebastian raised his head, Kate tugged it down again. His arms locked around her, and she leaned into him. He loved her as she was. Whatever happened here wouldn't change that.

"Kate?" Mom's voice.

Kate's heart leaped in mixed joy and dread. She and Sebastian took a single step apart.

Sebastian squeezed her waist gently before he let go. "You can deal with this," he said softly.

"Oh, my stars, Kate!"

Mom dashed down the back steps like a teenager. Dad bolted after her. Sebastian couldn't return to the afterworld now without revealing his magic.

Kate ran to meet her parents. Her mother's arms closed around her hard, and then her father's. Dad let go after a moment, though, and marched to Sebastian.

The two traded measuring looks before Dad stuck out his right hand. "Caleb Shaw."

"Sebastian Mainwaring."

They shook hands as Kate's brother Glenn dashed out of the house.

"Katie, it really is you!" He enveloped her in a hard hug.

"Guess you'd best come in the house," her father said to Sebastian.

Mom slid her arm around Kate's waist. "Honey, how did you get here? When did you leave London?"

"It's a long story, Mom. There's something I need to talk to you about."

Her stomach was doing the jitterbug now. "I would rather talk to you and Dad alone. Sorry, Glenn."

"Glenn can show Sebastian around the farm," Dad decided. "After we talk, you'll stay to supper."

Kate looked to Sebastian, whose slight raising of his eyebrows said that was up to her. "We'll see," she answered.

"Come on in the house," Mom said, her gaze probing Kate's, "and let's talk."

Kate walked in with her parents. At the door, Mom and Dad exchanged a worried look. If they had any idea what Kate was about to reveal, they would be much more than worried.

They walked into the kitchen where a metal colander full of pole beans sat beside half a dozen shucked ears of corn on the counter.

"Honey, do you want some iced tea?" Mom asked.

"No, thanks."

"Then let's go in the parlor."

The snug little room had a low sofa with rolled arms, a rocker, and two overstuffed chairs. A low, oblong table of dark wood with a small rim around the top stood in front of the sofa. The rocker had no cushions, and the sofa was worn horsehair but comfortable. Faded, flowery chintz in green and blue covered the chairs. Faint indentations in the seats spoke of long use.

It was all so familiar. So dear.

Kate chose the nearest chair while her parents settled on the couch.

"Honey, don't look so worried," her father said. "Whatever this is, we'll face it together, like always."

"I really hope that's true." Cold with nerves, Kate continued, "I love you so much. I never want to let you down. To disappoint you. But sometimes…things…happen."

"What kinds of things?" Mom asked quietly.

On a flash of insight, Kate knew what they thought. They feared she might be pregnant.

That might be easier for them to accept than this.

What she said next would change everything. The only question was, how much?

"I—that is—" Her voice rasped. She cleared her throat. Best to go straight to the point.

"I'm not who you thought—who *we* thought—I was. I'm different. It's

—there are things I can do that, well, they seem impossible. I always thought they were, but now…"

"Katie, just tell us," Dad said.

"It's…you know how we always said magic wasn't real? That fairy tales were fun but were just that, tales?"

"Of course," Mom said. She looked baffled.

"Well, they're not," Kate said. "Magic is real."

Her parents looked blank, as though she'd said something in another language. Carefully, her father asked, "Honey, have you been drinking?"

"If only it were that simple." Maybe starting at the beginning was best. "In England, I met some very distant relatives of my birth mother. They explained—Sebastian did, the man who came with me—some things I've done all my life and not thought about. Things I did in France that seemed strange."

Her father scowled. "If this is some trick to entice you—"

"It's not. I promise it's not."

Mom laid a hand on Dad's knee. "What sorts of things, Katie?"

"When I was little, calling animals. Being really good at hide and seek. Having, ah, hunches about what would happen next. But things really came to a head when I was in France after the invasion."

She detailed it all for them. What had happened, how odd some of it had seemed, and how it had all made sense when Sebastian explained it. They listened intently but with bewilderment growing in their eyes.

When she finished, they sat in silence. "Say something," Kate pleaded.

Her parents looked at each other. "I don't know what to say," her dad admitted. "It sounds so…like something out of a movie."

Or a fairy tale. Kate took a deep breath. "I can prove it to you." Concentrating hard, she thought, *Don't see me. Don't see me. Don't—*

Mom gasped in surprise as Dad blurted, "What the—?"

Kate released the glamour. Their bewildered, disbelieving expressions made her heart hurt. "Please don't look at me like that. I can do things we didn't know I could. Otherwise, I'm still me. Still your daughter." Her voice wobbled on the last word.

"Of course you are," Dad said. "We love you, honey. We always will. It's just…it's a lot to take in."

"Do your brothers know?" Mom asked.

Kate shook her head. "I had to tell you first. I can—if you like, I can show you some of the other things I've learned to do."

Her father shook his head. "I don't think we're ready for that, baby."

The *baby* was reassuring, even though the unhappy looks on their faces weren't. Would they ever be able to fully accept the new her?

~

"I never met an earl before," Glenn said. A blond giant in his early thirties, he had a deep voice and a keen gaze. He slowed his steps to match Sebastian's careful, cane-dependent pace over the uneven ground. "You have a fancy title, yet you raise sheep?"

"I don't," Sebastian said, "not personally, but we breed them on our lands. Supporting the estate requires a lot of money."

Although Kate had planned to introduce him to her parents if all went well, she'd been right to advise against wearing a suit and dress shoes. The soft trousers, open-collared shirt, and brogans served much better for tromping over the fields. Especially in the twilight, with his balance on the prosthetic leg still a bit dicey.

Sebastian added, "I've friends who raise cattle, as you do, but a different breed."

"Sure." Glenn leaned on the top rail of a wooden fence and stared across a field of seedlings coming up. "My dad'll want to know your intentions toward my sister, what with you kissing her like that in front of God and everybody, but you can go ahead and tell me now."

So the Shaw brothers were united at her back, at least for now. Good. Depending on how the talk with their parents went, Kate might desperately need them.

"I've asked Kate to marry me."

Glenn's blue eyes narrowed. "What'd she say?"

"She hasn't yet. Marrying me would involve a great many changes. It isn't as simple as it would be if I lived on this continent."

"You could move. Give the title to somebody else."

"It doesn't work that way." Life might be simpler if it did. Aside from his duties to his tenants, though, he had a duty of stewardship to Dad and Reg, to protect what they'd so abruptly left behind.

"Huh. Don't seem fair for Kate to do all the giving up."

Despite the curt manner, Sebastian read between the lines. Glenn wasn't happy with the idea of his sister living so far away. For that alone, Sebastian liked him. He would like him even more if the big man could accept the truth about her.

"It isn't," Sebastian said. "I'm well aware."

"That's something, anyway."

"Glenn!" a woman, likely his mother, called from the house. "You and Sebastian come in now."

Glenn shrugged. "Let's go."

They walked back to the house, again slowly as Sebastian negotiated the rough ground. He couldn't wait for the day when he could walk something like normally.

"You better hope Mom and Dad like you," Glenn said with a sidelong look, "or they'll make it tough for you with Kate."

"I'll take my chances." As long as they didn't make it tough for her, he could deal with anything.

~

I wish you would stay to supper," Mom said. "It's roasted chicken. I can always shuck more corn and pick more beans." She looked miserable.

They'd had a shock, including Kate's explanation that she and Sebastian had come via magic, but they were trying to accept it. To pretend things were still normal.

Yet their hesitation hurt. That didn't change the school programs they'd attended or the skinned knees they'd bandaged or the bedtime stories they'd read. But neither did those things change the pain of seeing the looks on their faces.

Sebastian and Glenn walked out from behind the barn. Sebastian moved with more assurance than he had a week ago, but he still had to take care. In typical Glenn fashion, her older brother slowed his steps to his guest's. He also stood near enough to help if Sebastian stumbled.

The furrow between Sebastian's brows hinted that he picked up her feelings. She tried to smile for him and got a smile in return that didn't reach his eyes.

Dad said, "What with everything else, I didn't get a chance to ask what he is to you. He must be important if you brought him home with you."

"I love him. He's asked me to marry him."

Her dad straightened his shoulders. His face went blank. Mom's eyes widened before her face also went blank.

"Are you going to accept?" she asked.

"I don't know yet. It's hard to make such a crucial decision when you're afraid your family can't accept what you are. When the man you love is the same."

"Kate…" Mom made a helpless, fluttery gesture with one hand. "Honey, we love you. We just…we need some time to get used to this."

"I needed some time too," she admitted. Maybe she was overreacting to their dismay.

"We would like to get to know your young man," Dad said quietly.

She met his gaze, and her Gift reinforced everything her parents had said about loving her. She had wanted them to give her a chance once they knew the truth. Shouldn't she do the same for them?

Kate took a deep breath. "We can stay to supper."

The smiles on their faces made her throat close. She cleared it roughly. "Before you ask, his people are English nobility going back hundreds of years and are well respected socially. They're generous in looking out for others. He's my very, very remotely connected cousin—about twenty generations back—on my birth mother's side. His prospects are good, as he owns a productive estate in northwest England in addition to a couple of other properties. So can we please not have that inquisition over dinner?"

Her dad grinned. "Kate Shaw, when have I ever fallen for that? We'll make our own judgments, thank you."

"He sounds like a fine young man," Mom put in, as she had so often. "But of course we want to see for ourselves."

Kate met Sebastian's gaze. He studied her face, and she knew he picked up on the turmoil inside her.

"We're staying to dinner," she told him, going down the steps to meet him.

His arm closed protectively around her. "Whatever you want," he replied. "I'll enjoy becoming acquainted with your family."

"You haven't been through a round of Dad's questioning," Glenn muttered.

"He can hold his own," Kate said. So could she. With the Shaw family behind her and Sebastian at her side, she could do anything.

Kate and Sebastian went from the farm to his house, arriving long after the Bradshaws, who were still living in their own flat for now, had gone home. Kate wanted privacy while she tried to come to terms with her parents' reaction. She and Sebastian would return to Rose's after everyone had gone to bed.

Meanwhile, should he offer to discuss the situation? Find something to occupy himself and leave her in peace?

Or should he suggest they forget returning to Rose's tonight and sleep here together?

He liked that last idea a great deal, but he wouldn't take advantage when she was feeling low.

Perhaps work would offer a distraction.

As they sat on his parlor sofa with glasses of wine, he asked, "Feeling any better?"

"A little." Kate sighed. "I'm so relieved they still love me, and I know they didn't mean to hurt me. But they did, so much."

"I know." He slid his arm around her shoulders. "We can see if there's music on the wireless, we could call it an early night, or we could work. You choose."

"Let's work. What did you have in mind?"

"I want to know what Wyndon is about. We haven't melded our Gifts since the crypt. The result then was astonishing, so let's see what happens when we tackle something more ordinary."

He'd had Genevieve set Merlin Club agents to watch the bench in Berkley Square by scrying, but scrying couldn't penetrate the wards on Wyndon House. For that, the club needed him or Kate.

They settled on the sofa together. Kate fished her pad and pen out of her bag and set them on her knee.

Frowning, she asked, "How much of what we caught through the ward that night do you think was due to our Gifts combined with its magic?"

"That's an advanced question. You've been studying."

"I do work in a library these days. So what do you think?"

"I've no idea, but perhaps we can figure that out." He offered her his hand, and she laced her fingers through his.

He continued, "Your dream vision about the creation of the wards may have been remnants of information you caught from the ward but didn't realize you'd sensed. I'm more inclined, however, to think the fragments we Saw spurred your Gift."

"Why do you think that?"

"Because you heard what they said, and a vision from a ward wouldn't usually carry sound."

Kate nodded. Her gaze had sharpened, and life had come back into her face. "How do you want to do this?" she asked.

"Let's think of Wyndon with Germans and see what happens."

Kate closed her eyes. Sebastian simply let his lose focus. Purple-gray fog rolled over his sight, and the rotten-egg smell, as usual, stung his nostrils. The fog rolled back, revealing Wyndon, Lemieux, and their wives in the foyer at Wyndon House. Isabel Lemieux thanked Florence Wyndon for a lovely evening. The butler opened the door, revealing a twilight sky. This was earlier tonight, then.

"What do you See?" he asked Kate.

"Lemieuxes leaving Wyndon's house."

The guests departed. The Wyndons climbed the stairs, the earl unknotting his tie as he went. He probably wouldn't leave the house tonight.

"Let's see about last night," Sebastian suggested. "Can you control the time frame that precisely?"

Kate's brow furrowed. The fog rolled over the scene again. Finally, she asked, "How's this?"

The stinking vapors parted to reveal a group of men in suits and women in cocktail dresses standing in a paneled room with a faded gold and brown Persian carpet on the floor. Ornate wall sconces lit the space. Across the room, Lady Wyndon stood in a group of other women. All wore elegant, below-knee dresses accented with glittering jewels.

Wyndon wasn't immediately visible in the crowd. Sebastian could've found him but refrained. Kate was guiding this.

The vision slowly shifted, the viewpoint moving into the crowd. Wyndon stood by the bar with a tall man whose light brown hair was receding and going gray at the temples. Each sipped what appeared to be a martini.

The babble of conversation obscured their words.

"I can't catch it," Kate said. "Can you?"

Sebastian had more experience, so he was able to home in on the two men in question. "I'll recommend that to my friend," the stranger said, idly scanning the room. "He wants to do a bit of traveling while he still has the leisure for it."

"I'm glad I could help." Wyndon wished the man a good evening and wandered away.

"Did that exchange seem a little off to you?" Kate asked. "I can't pinpoint a problem, but it's disquieting."

"Perhaps. It feels off in a way I can't explain. Let's hear more of it. Think of the two of them meeting somewhere in the room. It may have been at the bar but wouldn't necessarily have been. Simply think of their meeting."

Reeking fog rolled across the scene again. When it cleared, Wyndon joined the other man at the bar. They exchanged greetings, chatted about their families, and discussed the American ambassador's comments in Belgium about food shortages there, which were partly due to British blockades.

Finally, the other man said, "I've a friend who wants to travel a bit while he can. Perhaps explore the countryside. Can you recommend somewhere picturesque? Perhaps in an area not heavily traveled?"

"There's an old hill fort in Shropshire, Caynham Camp. Has to do with the Romans. The views there are spectacular, and there's nothing round it."

"Hmm. He's interested in antiquarian sights, though God knows why."

"This hill fort might be just the thing, then."

"I'll recommend that to my friend," the other man said.

Sebastian and Kate watched for a few more minutes, but nothing in the vision drew them to anyone in particular.

"Now what?" Kate asked.

"I'd like to know why he's recommending Caynham Camp. He previously sent a message about Stonehenge, which is on Salisbury Plain in Wiltshire. Is it for a drop of men or equipment? A rendezvous point? Or a landmark for something more sinister? Both places should be discernible from the air on a moonlit night, but the hill fort would be harder."

"Should we see if the other man did anything with the information?"

"Definitely. Let's do that first."

Sebastian summoned the vision of the cocktail party, this time centering it on the man who'd spoken to Wyndon at the bar. He circulated through the crowd, having a word here or there, his path seemingly idle.

"He's heading toward the back corner," Kate observed. "Taking his time about it, but he always ends up going in that direction."

"Yes, he does," Sebastian said softly.

Their target at last reached the corner. A man detached himself from a nearby group and joined him. Sebastian narrowed his eyes. "Well, well. That fellow picked up a message from Wyndon on a bench in Berkeley Square a while back. He took that message to his home and destroyed it. He then transmitted that to someone over a radio in a secret closet.

Someone in Germany was on the other end of the conversation—speaking German, unfortunately."

He explained about his earlier vision. "I tried to See why he wanted to use that place, but nothing came to me. It may be his contacts hadn't yet decided why they wanted to use it."

"Should we try that now with Caynham Camp?"

"Yes, let's." They laced their fingers together. Sebastian thought of Wyndon's contact at the bar and the Caynham hill fort.

Purple-gray mist blotted out the room, and the stink of rotten eggs stung his nostrils. Kate's, too, he felt in the link between them.

The fog thinned, revealing the hill and the ring of trees circling the hill's wide, bare top on a moonlit night.

"It's beautiful," Kate murmured.

A faint, droning noise marred the quiet of the night. It grew louder, and the moonlight glinted off the wings of a small, low-flying plane. It barely cleared the trees as it homed in on the particular hill.

"Trying to fly below radar," Sebastian said. "But the Chain Home Low system would've picked them up before they crossed the coastline."

Kate's brow furrowed. "Then how did they get this far without being intercepted?"

"I imagine fighters scrambled, but if the Nazis glamoured the plane with invisibility, our pilots wouldn't be able to spot it. Radar doesn't intercept this far inland, so no one's looking for it now. They don't need the glamour any longer."

As he spoke, the plane's nose came up to a sharp angle, and it ascended.

"What're they doing?" Kate asked.

"Gaining altitude for a parachute to open safely, I'd wager."

The plane soared above the circle. A figure emerged and dropped like a shadow against the moonlight sky. A few seconds later, the white canopy of a parachute bloomed above it. The figure drifted down.

A man's shadowy form emerged from the trees ringing the hilltop. A moment later, the jumper landed near him.

The jumper gathered his chute. He and the other man exchanged the Nazi salute. Together, they walked down the hill and across a field to a car on the narrow roadway's verge. They climbed in, and the car pulled away.

"Can we see where they're going?" Kate asked.

The vision shifted to a town square. Beyond loomed the dark walls of a ruined castle. To one side stood a tall, half-timbered building.

"Ludlow," he said. "That's Ludlow."

The car drove through the narrow streets to a squat stone building. The passenger climbed out, took a bag from the back, and walked inside.

"Has this happened yet?" Kate asked. "I can't tell."

Sebastian considered the imagery. "No. The moon won't be full for another few days. Yet the images are so definite, I think this plan is certain. What comes after that may not be. I'll alert Secretary Eden, and he can pass the information along. The Secret Intelligence Service supposedly have an eye on Wyndon, but it can't hurt to tell them what we know."

"That's a good ending to the day," Kate said.

He squeezed her hand. "Feeling better?"

"Definitely. Mom and Dad were shocked at first. Even though I expected that, it hurt. But the most important thing is that they love me as much as ever. I needed time to get used to the idea of magic. It's only fair to give it to them."

"What about accepting me?" he teased. "Your father has a bit of barrister in him, the way he asked those questions. Did I pass muster?"

"You know you did. If you hadn't, he would never have shaken your hand and said he hoped to see you again."

"So one worry off our plate."

"Definitely." Kate paused, studying him. "Do you think we could sleep here—only sleep, for now—and go back to Rose and John's early in the morning? Even though things went well at home, I want you beside me tonight."

"Of course, darling."

As they prepared for bed, though, her use of *home* for the farm stuck in his mind. Could she make a new home with him, or was she too tied to her Missouri roots for that to happen?

They climbed into his bed and snuggled together. Kate fell asleep almost instantly, probably exhausted from the emotional stress of the day, but Sebastian stared at the ceiling.

They made a good team. She knew that as well as he did. Together, they could contribute to the war effort and perhaps, with luck, lift the family curse. With luck—and time, if she needed it—perhaps she would see that they could be so much more.

CHAPTER 30

The air war continued. The skies over southern England were often filled with dueling squadrons of airplanes. Knowing that was happening yet being unable to affect it strained everyone's nerves at Rose's house.

On top of that, the Merlin Club's Berlin agent had a list of the harbors in use for Operation Sea Lion. The Germans were already assembling their fleet.

John buried himself in work at the Home Office, Rose grimly set about organizing charity drives, and Kate and Sebastian spent hours researching the family curse at the Merlin Club.

"The answer could be in any of these books," Kate said, eying the stack of thick volumes bound in cracked, aged leather. "But finding it could take months."

Seated across the library table from her, Sebastian set down his pen. "It could," he agreed, "but there's no one we can pull in to help. As the war effort ratchets up, there will be fewer and fewer of us here in London."

"We've gone through, what, a couple of dozen volumes so far?"

"Something like that."

"Hunting for something. Something that may or may not be there." Kate hesitated. What she was about to say was either very clever or very naïve. "Seers find things, don't we? Can we try to find which book has the spell we need?"

"Hmm. I never thought of it that way. We've nothing to lose by trying. Do you want to have a go, or shall I?"

"I'd rather you do it. You have more experience."

"You're learning fast, though."

His eyes lost focus. A minute ticked by and then another before he shook his head. "Either there's nothing in these books or our Gift doesn't work that way. You could—hang on. Kate, give me your hand."

She darted around the table to lay her hand in his. His magic rolled up her arm, pulling her into his vision.

In the slanting light of afternoon, Lord Wyndon leaned on the parapet that fronted the Albert Embankment. The brick and stone of Lambeth Palace loomed behind him. Holding a cigarette in his hand, he appeared to enjoy the view of the Houses of Parliament, with Westminster Abbey's towers just visible beyond, across the river.

A tall, lean man with a newspaper under his arm strolled up to the bench behind Wyndon, one of many dotting the embankment, and dropped his newspaper on the bench. He and Wyndon exchanged nods. The man pulled out a pipe and a tobacco pouch.

"Caynham Camp is done," Wyndon said casually, still staring at the river. "I recommended the Ludlow hotel."

The man tamped the tobacco and lit the pipe. He puffed it a couple of times. "They'll take the bait?"

"Almost certainly."

"We'll keep watch." The man puffed a bit more. "We've hauled in the Jerry who dropped at Stonehenge. His disappearance could make them suspicious. Watch your back."

"Sinking the bloody U-boat off Dungeness could make them suspicious too."

"You can blame the Royal Navy for that. They saw a U-boat. They fired on it." The man shrugged.

"This doesn't sound like he's working with the Nazis," Kate said.

"No, it doesn't. Let's find out who that fellow is."

Purple-gray fog obscured the scene. When the mists thinned, the man from the embankment had his newspaper under his arm and was strolling up a narrow street with Westminster Abbey in the background.

"Tothill Street," Sebastian murmured.

Caught up in the vision, Kate felt, rather than saw, him tense.

"If he's going where he seems to be..." Sebastian's intensity in the tie between them deepened.

The man turned right. The street sign above him on the stone building's corner read *Queen Anne's Gate*. He turned right at the next corner, where Queen Anne's Gate continued, and walked down to a townhouse of dark brick with an elaborate iron canopy over its small stoop. He opened the door and went in, and Kate sensed that there were guards beyond.

"Sebastian, what…?"

The vision faded. Staring at nothing, Sebastian sat back in his chair with a look of shock on his face.

"Sebastian?"

He shook his head. "It seems Gerald de Vere does not, after all, run true to the family form."

"What does that mean?" Kate fought back a strong urge to poke him.

"That's 21 Queen Anne's Gate," he finally told her, not that he needed to, as she'd Seen the street sign on the corner and the number over the door. "It's the entrance to the headquarters of the Secret Intelligence Service, MI6."

She gaped at him. "But that would mean…"

"Yes. The Earl of Wyndon is a double agent."

They sat in silence for a minute, digesting that.

"Okay," Kate said. "I mean, good for him. He's a jerk but a patriotic one. But what does that have to do with the family curse?"

Sebastian shook his head again. "I wish I knew."

Fat, olive-green Heinkel bombers marked with bar cross markings roared toward the airfield with fighter escorts around them. On the ground, pilots on duty scrambled for their fighters. Others rolled out of bunks, shoved their feet into boots, and raced after their mates.

One after another, Hurricane and Spitfire fighters marked with the RAF red, white, and blue concentric circles rolled across grassy runways and took to the skies. They banked into turns to engage the oncoming enemy.

The scene in Kate's dream shifted to a radar installation under attack by bombers. On the ground, spotters spoke frantically into radios, and fighters appeared out of the clouds. Firing on the invaders, they zoomed past the tower.

A word flashed into her mind, *Adlertag*. But what did that mean?

The scene turned into a kaleidoscope of besieged airfields and radar towers with fighters dueling in the air above as wave after wave of German planes roared across the Channel.

Cold with sweat, Kate jerked upright in bed. The horrific vision slowly faded. Breathing hard, she lay down again and pulled the covers over her.

What she'd seen was today. Later today. Was there any way to warn the RAF?

What about Dwight? He hadn't completed his training, but he could be at an installation under attack.

Someone knocked softly on her door. Sebastian. She snapped on the bedside lamp to avoid running into the door and hurried to admit him.

He carried his robe but was using his crutches. Of course, since he didn't sleep with the prosthesis. His gaze searched hers in the dim light.

"You Saw it too," he said.

Kate nodded. "It's going to be dreadful. I think...I feel, they're throwing everything they can at us."

He studied her for a long moment. "I agree, so it's time you went home."

"Oh, no, you don't. You need me here. How will you transport your bomb teams onto and off of all those ships if only you can move through the afterworld?" The fact she was scared spitless about doing it couldn't be allowed to matter.

His brows knitted. "How do you—did Miranda or Richard tell you?"

"Miranda thought I should know what you were up to."

He stared at her, as though mentally cursing, before he replied. "Well, it doesn't matter. I'll manage. We have a bargain, remember. Besides, you can't cross into the afterworld by yourself." The room winked out, replaced by a sunny yard where he taught Lachlan and Harry, Viscount Whitestone, to travel the afterworld.

So that was how he planned to handle transport without her. Chivalry and protectiveness were all well and good, but there was a war on.

Kate smiled at him. "Oh, but I can. Miranda taught me while you were hospitalized."

"She *what?*" His knitted brows became a thunderous scowl.

Kate shrugged. "We both thought it made sense in the circumstances for me to know how to do that. But we didn't see the need to upset you by telling you unless it became necessary."

"Upset me?" His voice had a dangerous edge.

"If it helps, Richard didn't want me taught either, for the same reasons as you. But now I know what to do, which means I can be useful, and sending me home doesn't make any sense. Especially since you're training Lachlan and Harry. Eve would be joining you if Harry hadn't talked her out of it."

A flicker in his eyes confirmed her accusation. "We have a bargain," he repeated. "I mean to hold you to it."

"While you risk your life, our friends risk theirs, and your country's fate hangs in the balance. Having me help transport the teams could make the difference between success and failure." Kate set a hand gently on his chest. "I love you. I know you love me, and that means the world. But this is the time to do your duty, my heart, and that means letting me do mine."

His lips tightened. He took a turn around the room, his crutches thumping softly on the carpet. Then he took another. Then another.

At last, still scowling, he stopped in front of her. "Damn it to bloody hell, Kate."

That meant she had him. Laying her hand along his stubbled cheek, she said, "I'm sorry to worry you."

"That isn't much help," he grumbled. "You're a woman. It isn't your place to fight."

"Oh, really?" Kate raised an eyebrow. "I suppose that's why your government is training women as well as men to parachute into France and help the Resistance? Special Operations Executive, I believe you call it?"

"That's Top Secret. How did you—oh, of course. Miranda again." Shaking his head, he added, "She has been a great deal too busy of late."

"She has time on her hands too, and this is still her country. You can't blame her for wanting to know how the war is going."

Sebastian sighed. "I suppose not." He lowered his brow to hers, and Kate slid her arms around him.

"Bloody crutches," he muttered. "Grab the left one, will you?"

When she did, he hooked his left arm around her and pulled her closer. They stood holding each other, the warmth and comfort of their embrace pushing back the chill of the dream visions. Sebastian kissed her temple, and Kate raised her face to his. Long, deep, and tender, the kiss swept away awareness of anything but him. When it broke, Kate pressed her face into his neck and sighed.

A faint chirping started beyond the curtains. In moments it swelled. With their dawn chorus, London's birds greeted the day.

"I can't go back to sleep," Kate said.

"Nor I." He glanced at her bedside clock. "It's almost six. The trains will be running shortly if they aren't already. Let's go to the club and work. Our agents in the RAF will be too busy to report today, but those in the countryside won't be. If they can safely reach their village phone boxes."

"Of course." Even after months in England, she wasn't accustomed to the relative scarcity of residential telephones.

Sebastian said, "I'm a member of the In and Out, though I haven't—"

"Wait. 'In and Out'? What's that?'

He grinned. "The Naval and Military Club. It's in Piccadilly across from Green Park. Active-duty personnel won't be there, of course, but many retired members still have connections. Someone may know something. I haven't been there since I went to Dover in May, but that won't matter."

"Should we eat first? I can fix breakfast if Mrs. Jarrett isn't in yet."

"Let's eat at the Merlin Club. We managed to have our kitchen classed as a restaurant, so it's not yet affected by rationing. It's also well supplied because many members contribute meat and produce. We should eat some of it."

"So we're doing the club a favor by eating there," Kate teased.

"Of course, darling." He kissed her quickly. "Let's dress and be about it."

He took back his crutch and returned to his room.

While Kate dressed, she thought about what had happened. He'd backed down on sending her home to keep her safe. He was flexible. Did that mean he would accept a wife with a career?

There was only one way to find out.

No longer being linked to the War Office with its constantly updated reports rankled. Sebastian tried not to think about it. Better to note how much longer he could wear the prosthesis before it irritated the skin of his stump. He was making progress and took pride in it despite slightly guilty awareness that he had an advantage over unGifted amputees. Still, by the time he saw Kate to the Merlin Club, walked after breakfast to the Piccadilly Circus tube station, took the tube from Piccadilly Circus to Green Park, walked to the In and Out, and repeated the process in reverse, he was ready to sit in the Merlin Club library and go over old books for a while.

Kate sat at the table's far end, frowning. He paused in the doorway to look at her. Working together in this oasis of quiet would push his frustrations aside. Give him a sense of doing something. And, perhaps, given how well they did work together, tick a box on her Reasons to Marry Sebastian list. If she had one.

She looked up. "How was your other club?" she asked.

"Familiar." He limped down the table to sit beside her. His pad and the waiting stack from yesterday still sat on the table in front of his chair. He dropped into the seat gratefully, laying his cane on the floor. "The absence of younger officers was conspicuous. They're all at their posts this morning, of course."

As he would've liked to be. Kate squeezed his hand as though she knew. Perhaps she did. She was, after all, a seer. He linked his fingers with hers on the tabletop.

"I don't know whether this will help," she said, "so forgive me if it doesn't." She waited for him to nod before continuing. "What we're doing here can save our family, and the work you've done on the invasion fleet may make a very big difference in the war. To me, not having a military background, this seems like your post."

"I hadn't thought of it that way." He'd been so focused on what he'd lost that he hadn't considered the military nature of what they were doing.

"Can I ask you something?" Kate looked solemn now, and his magical senses caught tension in her that had his heart beating faster.

"Anything," he replied.

"What does a countess do?"

She wouldn't ask unless she was thinking of becoming his countess. Tamping a rush of hope, he said, "Whatever she likes. Rose handles the boys' day-to-day activities. Now that they're away and John works so much, she spends a great deal of time on charity work. Her latest project is communal kitchens to help those who can't cook at home for whatever reason. There will be more of those as the war goes on. Especially once the Jerrys turn to bombing the cities, as they're bound to do eventually. She supports several arts organizations as well."

Kate nodded. With her gaze intent on his face, she asked, "What do you see your countess as doing?"

"Whatever she likes," he repeated. "Kate, are you asking whether I would object to your continuing in your career if we married?"

"I have to know."

She was trusting him to be honest. They were holding hands, so she would know that he was.

"The short answer is no, I would not object." A broad smile broke over her face, and joy flowed in the link between them. The hope within him surged again. He continued, "I want you to be happy, and I know your career is important to you. You've honored me by sharing some of your struggles. Your determination is one of the things I love about you. So you must do as you like about the job. I will support whatever choice you make."

Kate grinned at him, and everything inside him felt incandescent.

"If you still want to marry me," she said, "my answer is yes."

Sebastian returned her grin. They rose to share a long, passionate kiss. He planted kisses along her jaw and down her neck. Her hands slid up and down his back, caressing and arousing.

Kate sighed, pressing closer. "There are bedrooms here, right?"

"Yes, but darling—"

A discreet cough came from the doorway. They reflexively jerked apart but kept their arms around each other. Kate blushed furiously as they looked to the door.

Lachlan MacGregor shot them an apologetic glance. "Sorry. I've news, but it can wait if this is a bad time."

"No, come in," Sebastian said. He and Kate resumed their seats but kept their hands joined.

Lachlan sat across from Sebastian. "Several of my mages are now in London with more on the way, women and men too old to be called up. I wondered whether you had news."

"Not yet. Thanks to our agent in Berlin, though" Sebastian said, "we should soon know which harbors they'll use for embarkation and launch. If we can bottle all their boats up in their departure harbors, it'll be too late for them to make other plans."

A week later, Sebastian had the information he needed. He called a council of war at the Merlin Club for the morning of August 23. He sat at the head of the library table with a large chalkboard behind him. Kate sat to his right side to take notes.

The air war still raged as the Germans tried to destroy the RAF airfields and fighters. "It's a good sign," Sebastian said to Kate as they waited for their Scots allies. "It means they haven't yet reached the level of dominance they want for Sea Lion. We have time to prepare."

"I hope so. I've tried several times to See what Wyndon being a double agent means. So far, I have nothing."

"That may mean the events that will make that matter haven't yet been set in motion."

Kate shook her head. "I still can't figure out how he has anything to do with either passing that ward at Otterden or lifting the family curse."

"Nor have I. Perhaps that means he isn't as much of a bastard as his predecessors. Or it could be an omen that he might sell us the confession. When we have time, I'll test those waters with him."

Voices in the corridor heralded Lachlan and his cadre from the Mages of the Isles, five women and three men. The women appeared to range in age from their thirties to their fifties, while the men all appeared to be over sixty. They filed into the library. While most of the Scots were not Merlin Club members, the club's extensive warding and other defenses made it a more secure location for planning than any other.

Behind the Scots came a similar mixture of Merlin Club members. The teams totaled two dozen in all.

Harry Whitestone, who would deal with the afterworld for the third team, followed his fellow Merlin Club agents in and sat. His family had given loyal members to the Merlin Club for more than two hundred years. If they could trust anyone with the secrets of the afterworld, they could trust him.

"Thank you all for coming," Sebastian said. "I'll give you the background, and we'll introduce ourselves. Those of you who are not members must swear not to reveal anything about this club."

"We'll do that together," Lachlan said.

Sebastian continued, "Our strategy for this operation also requires exposure to a dangerous place and the use of a rite you must not make any attempt to learn how to perform for yourselves. My family have kept this secret for hundreds of years for good reason."

"What reason?" a man down the table asked.

"It's too dangerous to share. Anyone who objects must leave now."

No one spoke. Sebastian looked to Lachlan, who nodded. The Mage Laird would keep his cadre in line.

"Well, then," Sebastian said, "Let's introduce ourselves. I'm Sebastian Mainwaring, Earl of Hawkstowe." He turned to Kate, who gave them her name. The introduction process went around the table from her, with Lachlan coming last.

"A few days ago," Sebastian told them, "the Merlin Club obtained the list of embarkation and launch ports for Sea Lion, the proposed German invasion of these islands."

"Rotters," one of the women on the left muttered.

Ignoring her, he continued, "The Nazi fleet will launch from the ports of Rotterdam, Antwerp, Ostend, Nieuport, Dunkirk, Gravelines, Calais, Boulogne, and Le Havre. They're already moving their invasion craft into place." His Sight and Kate's earlier vision, combined with scrying, confirmed the report from the Merlin Club agent in Berlin.

"So we've a bit of time," Lachlan said.

"A bit, yes. They're using a wide range of vessels—freighters and passengers ships for troop transport, along with barges, tugboats for the nonpowered craft, motorboats, motorized fishing boats, pusher boats, and coasters. We have large diagrams of the embarkation ports. Once the boats are all assembled, we'll scuttle several in each harbor, either to block the entrance or simply to make a big mess that will take a great deal of time to clear."

With a nod to Kate, who'd made the large diagrams of the embarkation ports, he said, "Some of the harbor mouths are too wide to block that way, but Lachlan and I agree we need not stop all the boats, only bottle them up so they can't launch in the force they need. We'll execute these raids over a period of three days," Sebastian said.

"Won't the first one alert them?" a fortyish brunette woman named Iona asked. "They'll likely post a light watch before their soldiers embark, but if they have trouble, they'll tighten that."

He smiled at her. "That would matter if we were boarding via the gangplanks, but we're not."

She raised an eyebrow. "The secret you mentioned."

"Yes. Lachlan, how's the stock of black powder coming?"

"We have it in abundance along with three dozen outmoded shell casings from the last war. We expect to have eight or ten more in the next couple of weeks."

"Excellent. Have you tried triggering a shell magically, and if you have, what's the effective range?"

Lachlan nodded. "Twenty feet is optimum."

Sebastian looked at Kate and read agreement in her eyes. That was far enough away for one the Scots to loose a bolt to detonate the shell and dart through a partner's open portal into the afterworld ahead of the shock wave.

"Very well." Sebastian and Kate clipped her large drawing of the Port of Antwerp to the blackboard frame. "We'll start here," he said, "and this is how we'll do it."

He laid out a plan for sabotaging the lock at Antwerp. "To do that," he said, "we'll travel from here through a ghostly realm outside of the real world and emerge in the lower hulls of our target ships in the harbor."

"Hang on," someone said. "Ghostly realm? Are you joking?"

"I wish I were," he replied. "One team will conceal themselves with an invisibility glamour and release the moorings so we can cast off. I have a navy veteran from the last war studying the troop transport controls. He'll teach us how to move those where we want them."

"It's barmy," an older man down the table announced, rolling the R with his brogue, "but it just might work."

"Let's hope so," Sebastian said.

CHAPTER 31

They finished in the late afternoon. Kate waited until everyone had gone before locking her arms around Sebastian's waist. "You were brilliant. You sold them on the plan."

"Lachlan helped a great deal." Sebastian put his arms around her and tightened the embrace. His expression softened and warmed, setting her heart thumping and creating bubbly heat deep within her. "Do you still want that bedroom?" he asked.

"Oh, definitely."

"Then let's go to Charles Street, let the Bradshaws make tea for us, and then send them home early. They'll be happy for us, but I should tell my family first."

"An excellent plan." She toyed with his shirt collar. His family would be glad for them. Would hers?

"Kate?" He waited for her to look at him. "Do you want to go to Missouri?"

"Yes and no. Whatever they say, though, I don't want to delay the wedding."

His brow furrowed. "You deserve all the frills and ceremony. The Earls of Hawkstowe usually marry in All Saints' Church at Hawkstowe, but St. George's, Hanover Square, here in London is also a possibility. Even with materials growing scarce, Rose can help us pull together something nice."

"I'm sure she would be happy to, and I welcome her help." Leaning against him, Kate sighed. "We're planning something extremely dangerous. I want us to be married before we actually execute that plan. While I want us to have a lovely day, that doesn't mean lots of frills and furbelows, not when we have such pressing concerns confronting us."

Struck by a thought, she looked up at him. "Unless you want them?"

"All I want is for the world to know you're my wife. Hawkstowe Church suits me well if it's enough for you."

You're enough for me. But that would sound sappy, so she said only, "Hawkstowe Church, then, as soon as we can arrange it. We'll go to Missouri. If Mom and Dad and Glenn won't come, well, maybe Dwight can get leave and come give me away."

"They'll come," Sebastian said firmly.

Kate tapped his chin with her index finger and gave him a stern look. "No threatening. I mean it."

The flash of guilt in his eyes betrayed his intention, but he shrugged. "They raised you, so they're likely as fair-minded and affectionate as you are. You're their daughter. They'll come."

She hoped so. Before she put that to the test, though, she wanted an evening alone with Sebastian to enjoy their love and their new commitment. To spin castles in the air.

To hope they could survive this war and see their dreams come true.

After dinner that night, Rose asked Kate to meet her in the parlor she and John shared. Walking into the small, cozy room, Kate couldn't help being a little nervous. Had Rose changed her mind about Kate for Sebastian? They'd celebrated the engagement at dinner with a bottle of Rose and John's precious store of Champagne. What could this be about?

A narrow, rectangular wooden case about two feet long and a couple of inches deep rested on the table between the chairs. Odd. Was this another magic test, maybe?

She and Rose settled into the two armchairs. Rose snapped on the light between them.

"I won't keep you," Rose said. "I know you and Sebastian want some time together, and that's important. But so is this." She picked up the wooden case and turned it so the clasp faced Kate. When Rose opened it, a sheathed dagger with a foot-long blade and a plain hilt rested in the velvet lining.

"This belonged to Miranda," Rose said. "It was Richard's gift to her. For the last two and a half centuries, this dagger has gone to the oldest daughter in the line of the Hawkstowe earldom. The next such daughter will be yours, God willing. So I'm giving the dagger to you to hold in trust for her."

Kate gently ran a finger along the worn, plain leather sheath. "Why now? We may not have a daughter, you know." *We might not live long enough to have any children.*

"We're in a war. Who's to say I'll survive long enough to pass this on as has always been done? I want you to have it now. Especially because you and Seb are about to do something incredibly dangerous. I want you to wear the dagger in France. Will you do that for me, Kate?"

Kate's throat closed. She looked into Rose's solemn eyes and saw not only trust but love. Kate nodded and cleared her throat. "I would be honored."

∼

Kate's stomach felt tight when she and Sebastian emerged from the afterworld in her family's back yard. It was early morning here, the sun just peeking over the horizon. Everyone would be having breakfast before Mom tended to the chickens and Dad and Glenn started the chores of the day.

Holding hands, she led Sebastian up the wooden steps to the back porch. He managed the stairs better than he had. He was growing more adept with his new leg every day.

They stood at the back door, and she bit her lip. Once, she would've gone right in. Now...should she?

"Do not knock," Sebastian said in a low voice. "You'll wound them if you do."

He tugged open the screen. Kate reached for the door, only to have Glenn open it first.

His eyes widened, and then he swept her into his arms. "Katie! Mom, Dad, Katie's home! I thought I heard something. Come in the house." Glenn released her and shook hands with Sebastian.

Dad rose from the table, which was set for three, and Mom turned from the stove. For a moment, tension hung in the air. Then they rushed forward to greet her.

Their arms locked around her, and tears of relief stung her eyes. Both of them kissed her on the cheek.

"Come in and sit down, both of you." Mom wiped her eyes on her apron. "Oh, I'm so glad you're here. Sebastian, it's nice to see you."

Dad shook hands with him, and Mom embraced him. Glenn dropped an arm around Kate's shoulders. "He being good to you? Dwight's last letter came yesterday. Said he hadn't seen you."

"He's been busy."

"God help the RAF." Glenn grinned, and Kate smiled back at him.

"I had a letter from him a few days ago," Kate said. "He's loving his flight training. There are some men at his base from the Caribbean, Black men. He says they're crack pilots, but he and they took a while to understand each other. What did he say…? Oh, yes. 'Those fellows speak British English with a Jamaican twist, and I speak American.'"

"That sounds like Dwight," Mom said, smiling. "I think he sees all this as an adventure. I wish it was just that."

Silence fell in the kitchen.

Glenn cleared his throat. With a stern look at Sebastian, he asked Kate, "This here earl, he treating you right?"

"Sebastian has been wonderful."

"He's 'wonderful,' huh?" Glenn glanced at Sebastian. "Well—"

"Glenn, don't tease your sister," Dad said. "Set another couple of places. Kate, Sebastian, coffee?"

The flurry of taking seats and Mom fixing more bacon and eggs took a few minutes. When they were all around the table, though, and Kate had said grace, an awkward silence fell. Her parents looked uneasy, and the tension in the air jangled over her magical senses. At her side, Sebastian sat braced.

Her mother looked at her father. He cleared his throat. "We're glad you're here. Both of you. Katie, I know we didn't take things so well last time."

"I did," Glenn put in, pointing at her with his fork. "I don't care if you fly on a broom. You wouldn't do anything wrong with that."

"No brooms, but thanks." Kate shot him a grateful look.

"The thing is," Dad resumed, "we'd had a right big shock. But as Glenn says, you're our Kate. No matter what abilities or powers—or whatever you call it—you have, you'll always do what's right."

"It's a strange thing to us," Mom said, "and hard to believe, but we're trying. When you left, we knew we disappointed you. We were afraid you wouldn't come back." With an apologetic look at Sebastian, she added, "Especially since you got on so well with your natural kin. Maybe you didn't need us anymore."

"I'll always need you," Kate protested. She reached for Sebastian's hand, and his fingers closed around hers. "I especially need you to come to our wedding. In England. On September fifth."

They looked stricken. "Oh, honey," her father said, "we can't afford that."

"There's a faster way to travel," Sebastian told them, "and it's free. It's just a bit, ah, hair-raising."

He explained traveling the afterworld. As he talked, the looks of incredulity and dismay on her family's faces deepened. Kate's heart twisted. She'd already asked a lot of them. Now she was asking so much more.

When Sebastian finished, Kate's mom looked at her. "Katie? Is all that right?"

"It is. I've traveled that way too. It's scary at first, but if Sebastian is with us, we'll be safe."

"You haven't known each other long," Dad said. "Maybe you should wait a bit."

Give her family time to adjust, he meant. Unfortunately, that would probably require more time than she and Sebastian had before they confronted Sea Lion.

Sebastian looked to her, and she knew he would back whatever she said.

"The war is pretty intense," she replied. "Maybe you've heard about it on the news."

Dad nodded. "We would like you to come home. Sebastian, you're welcome, of course. We know you would eventually go back to England because of your obligations there, but you would both be safe here. You could get married at Cobbettown Methodist."

He meant well, but he'd unknowingly insulted Sebastian.

When Sebastian replied, though, his voice sounded relaxed. "That's very generous, Caleb, but I can't abandon my country. Although I'm not certain about my future with the service, I have duties to the war effort. I would be delighted if Kate returned here, but she refuses."

That was a sneaky trick. She answered the innocent look he turned on her with narrowed eyes.

Before anyone else could speak, she said, "I don't see the point in getting married and then not living together just so one of us can avoid the risk. It's one thing for people in the service to be apart. Sebastian and I don't have to be, and I don't want to be."

"Katie, baby," Mom began.

"You're wasting your breath," Glenn said. "She's the stubbornest girl in the State of Missouri, and her mind's made up. I'm coming to the wedding. I don't care if we have to walk through some Halloween spook house."

"Thank you," Kate answered, her throat tight.

Glenn continued, "Sebastian, welcome to the family. You be good to my sister, or it's me and you."

"And Dwight," Sebastian answered, grinning. "He made that plain weeks ago."

Kate's eyebrows rose. "Oh, really? This is news to me."

"Brother business," Sebastian informed her. She rolled her eyes.

"Then we're square." Glenn forked up eggs. "He know you're getting married?"

"I haven't seen him to tell him. I thought Mom and Dad should know first."

"And me, 'cause I'm the big brother. Now we should eat before everything gets cold. You know I hate cold biscuits. Somebody pass the honey, please."

Sebastian handed the small pot to him and watched with interest as Glenn buttered his two steaming biscuits.

"Like scones," Sebastian said, "but fluffier."

"If you say so." Glenn drizzled honey over the biscuits. "You ever had red eye gravy, Sebastian?"

"What's that?"

"Oh, man, you gotta come back and have country ham and grits and biscuits with red eye gravy. Mom makes the best. It's black coffee and ham drippings."

"I see." Sebastian looked doubtful. Kate would've bet putting black coffee in food was a new and not very welcome idea.

But she couldn't enjoy the byplay between her brother and her fiancé because Mom and Dad still hadn't said anything. Kate looked from one to the other of them.

Dad turned to Sebastian. "Do you swear to me this is a safe way to travel?"

"Sir, I wouldn't risk Kate if it were not."

Never mind that they both would risk themselves in the ports of France in a few weeks.

Sebastian continued, "We've come here both times by that route. If you'll trust me, I'll see that you can be with us to give the bride away."

Another sneaky move. Judging by the way Dad's eyes widened for an instant, he hadn't stopped to think that refusing to come meant some other man would walk her down the aisle.

Her parents exchanged a look.

"All right," Dad said. "We're honored to come."

Kate smiled at them. They would do their best, but the afterworld was not for the faint of heart. It was also unlike anything even the worst scary movie offered. They were strong people, though, and they wanted to see her married. Surely they would persevere.

Despite wedding preparations, the war was never far from Kate's and Sebastian's minds. August 29 was a brutal day for Fighter Command, and the Germans continued to escalate. All the while, Sebastian watched the preparations for Sea Lion by scrying and with visions. Fighter Command was taking a pounding, but they were slowly turning the tide, inflicting steep punishment on the Luftwaffe. All the while, ships continued to arrive at the embarkation ports in France.

Sebastian set all that aside for the ceremony. Kate's family had dealt with the afterworld better than expected, though they weren't looking forward to the return trip, and Dwight had obtained leave to come. Around the small group of their families clustered a throng of spectral Mainwarings led by his father, Richard, Miranda, their Robin, and Miles.

His brother James stood at his side with Dad's ghost on James's other side. Reg was probably watching too, but Sebastian couldn't see him because he wasn't his brother's descendant.

Candles cast a warm glow over the small stone church's antiquated box pews, the fading medieval drawings on the plaster walls, and the Victorian stained-glass windows depicting New Testament scenes. Wearing her champagne silk gown and her mother's lacy, hip-length veil, Kate walked down the aisle to Sebastian on her father's arm.

For one fleeting moment, as they faced Father Marston, he was glad he still had the right to wear his uniform to honor the occasion. Then her father placed Kate's hand in his, and nothing else mattered.

Now, after a wedding banquet and an evening of family, he stood in the antechamber to the earl's suite and waited for Kate to call him. Earls of Hawkstowe had brought their brides to the adjoining bedchamber for more than five centuries. He'd already removed the false leg, so he propped himself up on his crutches. The lord's chamber lay above the end of the now empty hall. Everyone had tactfully moved to the adjacent tower to continue their celebrations.

The bedchamber door opened. "Sebastian?" Clad in a rose silk peignoir, a gift from his mother, Kate opened the door. The warmth and excitement in her eyes lifted his heart. The war could wait. Tonight was for them.

He hobbled in and shut the door. Beeswax candles on the mantel and the bedside table cast a soft glow into the room. The manor had electricity, but the candles were a tradition. Even here, though, blackout curtains kept the light in.

The four-poster bed behind her, with its wooden canopy and elaborately carved headboard, footboard, and posts, was almost as old as the chamber. The brocade hangings, though new, were blue, as the family tradition mandated for this particular bed.

Kate kissed him, her body pressing against his, and Sebastian teased her lips with his tongue. She parted them for him, deepening the kiss, and he lost himself in their intimacy. His arm around her waist, he stroked her back. The thin silk under his palm did little to hide her warmth.

The kiss broke. She clung to him and sighed.

"Nervous?" he asked. They'd been intimate these past weeks, but they'd saved the ultimate act of love for this night.

Kate smiled up at her husband's face. "A little. And curious. And eager. I love you so much."

"I love you too, Lady Hawkstowe."

She slid her hand under the knot in his robe's belt and raised her eyebrows. He leaned down to kiss her, and she untied the knot. Shrugging out of the robe didn't require breaking the kiss, though the crutches made it awkward.

When he cupped her breast with his free hand, heat flashed through her. Kate gasped and arched into his touch. Sebastian kissed her neck while he slipped his hand around to her back, then down to her buttocks to draw her against the hard bulge at his groin. Another flash of heat, stronger this time, had her clinging to him.

They had done this before, but they'd both known they would stop. Now there was no reason to.

He nipped her ear and tugged on the string tie of the peignoir. "Let me take this off."

"Please."

They looked into each other's eyes while he tugged the end of the simple bow. The garment gapped open. She wouldn't have thought his gaze could heat further, but it did.

"The bed," he said. "I want both my hands on you."

"I do too." Running her palms over his lean torso, she added, "And mine on you."

They left the peignoir in a rosy puddle on the floor and dropped his crutches by the bed. As he scooted over the creaking bed, Kate said, "Wait." She unbuttoned his blue pajama shirt and licked his flat nipple. Sebastian groaned, his body arching, and she exulted in her ability to please him. As she kissed and stroked her way down his torso, his muscles tensed and relaxed. His trousers tented below, and she nipped at the covered mound.

He made a choked sound. "Love, you're destroying me." When he pulled her up for a kiss, Kate let her hands roam. She knew his body now, as he knew hers, and she knew how to make him groan.

When he squeezed both her breasts, she cried out with pleasure. Then his mouth replaced his hands, and he eased her down to the mattress.

Writhing in a haze of pleasure, she barely felt cool evening air on her moist mound. Then his hand replaced it, stroking. He slipped one finger inside, then a second one, and Kate gasped. Her hips bucked in time with his rhythm. Everything narrowed to that one small spot, tension coiling inside her. She groped for him, but he jerked his hips back.

"Not this time," he ground out. Then he pressed hard on the sensitive nub of flesh.

The tension blew out. Kate gasped, her body arching, as she clutched him tighter and went temporarily blind.

As the pleasure faded, she found herself cradled against his side. Sebastian kissed her brow.

"You cheated," she murmured, and she kissed his shoulder.

"No, I wanted you to go first this time. It'll make our joining easier."

She drew back to look at him. "Rose said it might hurt."

"It might, but only this time and, I hope, not for long."

She stroked his cheek. "I trust you."

He pressed a kiss into her palm. "I want this to be all you ever hoped for, Kate, and I'm not as mobile as I would like to be. I think you should be on top."

"If you think that's best," she said, though that seemed odd.

Sebastian tugged on the gown's thin shoulder strap. "Will you take this off for me?"

"If you help me." They'd seen each other naked, so there was no need to be shy, but she liked having him touch her.

Removing the garment required only a moment. Kate straddled Sebastian's lap, and his arms locked around her. His kiss was searing and passionate, their tongues sliding together and their breathing harsh. He planted a hot trail of kisses down her neck to her left breast and sucked it into his mouth.

Kate's back arched on a wave of pleasure and craving. His fingers teased the other breast until she was writing, rubbing the hardness jutting against her stomach.

Sebastian shifted her hips and looked into her eyes. "When you're ready," he said, "ease down onto me. It'll feel strange, so go slowly."

Excitement fluttered inside her. Holding his gaze, watching his tender smile grow more intense, she gripped his hardened flesh and eased down on it.

The feeling of being stretched did seem odd, but having him inside her —oh, yes. "My heart," she gritted out. "Always."

"Love you. Always."

The temptation to go faster grew. Her breathing became choppy. So did his.

"Sebastian, I—I can't—it's—"

"Stop if you—"

Stop? *Never.*

Kate gave up restraint and let herself slide down on him, sheathing him fully. A jab of pain, a little burning, and they were fully joined.

"All right?" he asked.

She leaned down and kissed him. Locking his arms around her, he drew her down on top of him. "Take a minute," he rasped out. "Give yourself time."

She turned her face into his neck. The burning soon faded, replaced by awareness of his hard, full flesh inside her. He stroked her back. With each pass of his hands over her body, his touch became more insistent. More enticing. Her awareness of his lean body under hers and the soft chest hair tickling her breasts urged her to rub herself against him.

Sebastian kneaded her breast, and her hips bucked in response. She sat up for better movement and was rewarded with a flare of pleasure. When she rocked above him, pleasure became craving, only to have pleasure return, more intense and hotter, as she took him into her again.

Sebastian's hands at her hips guided her. "So beautiful," he groaned.

He sat up again to suckle her. As she writhed, he pressed his thumb to the sensitive spot between her legs. Kate cried out as the building need burst, flooding her with light and pleasure.

He gripped her thighs, pulling her down, and thrust upward. He shuddered between her legs. She forced her eyes open for an instant to see his face taut with pleasure.

His lips curved in a lazy smile, and she grinned at him.

Caught in languorous relief, she snuggled down onto him again. He kissed her hairline and pulled the bedclothes over them both.

"Forever and always," he murmured as they drifted into sleep.

Purple-gray fog rolled across Kate's vision. When it cleared, she was standing by the river, looking at what she knew to be the London docks. The drone of engines overhead drew her gaze upward. German bombers and fighter escort flew over the capital in broad daylight. Bomb bay doors opened, bombs falling on the East End. Her heart pounded.

This is a dream. I don't need to find shelter. I'm not really here.

Then Sebastian appeared beside her and took her hand. He wore his army uniform. "You pulled me in with you."

His gaze turned skyward, assessing. Counting? "Look for a newspaper."

For the date. Right. Kate peered around them. Someone had dropped a paper on the ground. She let go of Sebastian's hand to grab the paper before the wind could blow it away.

The first bombs hit, knocking her off her feet. "We're not here," he shouted. "Keep telling yourself that."

He locked his arm around her, steadying her, and Kate shook out the paper. It was the *Times*, and the dateline read September 7, 1940.

"Kate. Wake up, darling. Come back to me."

Slowly, she opened her eyes. The candles had guttered and gone out, but the blackout curtains were open. He must've done that somehow. The faint predawn light let her see the grave expression on his face.

"Not the sort of dream I wanted for our wedding night," he said.

"No, and not one I expected."

She laid her head on his chest, and he stroked her shoulder. "We were together, though," he said. "Without trying."

"Maybe because we're married, because we're, as the vicar said, one flesh."

"Perhaps so." Sighing, he rested his head against hers. "Whatever comes, we'll face it together."

"Always."

In a war, though, *always* might not be very long.

CHAPTER 32

"Tomorrow will be bad," Kate said. "Maybe worse than anything yet." Nine days after their wedding, she and Sebastian sat in the fall sunshine in the garden at Hawkstowe. Each of them had a book, hers on Richard III's life. As they had Seen, there'd been a large-scale bombing of London's East End on September 7, and that had been just the beginning.

Sebastian closed his volume of John Donne's sermons, marking his place with one finger. "Why do you say that?"

"I feel it. It's going to be...bad. It's as if...maybe it's their last-ditch effort."

The bombing of London continued nightly. The Luftwaffe pounded the southern cities while the Royal Navy fought the blockade and the U-boats.

"If they can't shatter the RAF," he said, "they may not launch Sea Lion."

"*May* not. Do we want to count on that?"

He shook his head. "If we can cripple their fleet, we should. Tomorrow isn't the best time to return, obviously, but we have work to do."

"We'll go early in the day. Before things heat up."

Lachlan and Genevieve had recruited retired merchant marine sailors who'd figured out how to operate the bridge controls on the troop transports. The engineers could start the engines, but the team still needed a crew to keep the engines running for the little time necessary. The more locations on any ship they had to evacuate, the riskier the operation became. Everyone had to be off before the bombs blew.

"I wrote to Wyndon," Sebastian said. "I asked if I could discuss a matter of business with him when we return to London. I expect to find his answer waiting when we return home."

"I can't See whether he'll agree to a sale." Kate frowned into the sunshine.

Sebastian turned his face up to the warm light. "It's a contrary Gift, as I said. It sometimes shows things that might happen in one's own life, but never the things one actually wishes to know."

"That's annoying. Do you think—"

"Kate." Again, he caught her hand. His power flowed into her, rising up her arm, and the familiar fog obscured her the garden.

The fog died away. She needed a moment to recognize the location because she'd only seen it in the dark. "Otterden Abbey?"

"Apparently."

Outside, tires crunched on gravel. Wyndon walked out of the hall and down the shallow front steps as a large, green car pulled up before the entry.

"Welcome to Otterden Abbey," Wyndon said. He offered the Nazi salute, which his visitor returned. The man's thin, seamed face would be completely forgettable. His thick, brown hair was cut as any banker might wear it. But his eyes were cold and hard.

"You took your sweet time arriving," Wyndon said. "I've expected you for more than a week."

"Some of us must be careful in our movements." No hint of a German accent tinged the words. The man was good. "Did you bring the money?"

"Yes, and I'll want a note for it."

The visitor laughed. "Come now, my lord. You know better. When the Führer controls England, you'll have your money. With interest."

Wyndon looked glum but didn't argue. He and the visitor strolled into the hall. "Beer?" Wyndon asked. "We have a light luncheon prepared."

"Why not?" The man tossed his hat onto one of the tables and followed the earl onto the dais.

"I could offer you better if I'd brought servants. The housekeeper prepared the food at Wyndon."

"It's important this meeting be private," the man said, his voice as hard as his eyes.

"So you said."

The two men sat opposite each other at the table. Wyndon poured beer into glasses, and they toasted Hitler's health.

"What's so important that we must meet here?" Wyndon demanded. "I've interests in the City that require my attention."

"That's unfortunate." The man reached into his suit jacket and extracted a gun. He aimed it at Wyndon and cocked it.

The earl jumped to his feet.

"Do not move," the man ordered. "One of the operatives who dealt with you has disappeared. He's in British custody. Or so your little conversation on the Albert Embankment a couple of weeks ago informed us."

"Damnation," Sebastian said. "They could only know that if they had wizards working with them. No one was near Wyndon or the agent he met. Unless they used an invisibility glamour or had a seer on their side."

"Or the agent betrayed him," Kate pointed out, feeling faintly sick.

"We'll check for that later," Sebastian replied.

"That's ridiculous," Wyndon snapped, though his face paled. "I don't know what you're talking about."

"You smoked a cigarette and spoke over your shoulder with a man from MI6. You know there are ways we can learn these things, wizard."

At the word, Wyndon's face went ashen. "Now, see here—"

The German fired.

Kate jumped, and Sebastian's grip on her hand tightened.

"Steady," he murmured.

Wyndon fell over the table, then crumpled to the floor. The assailant walked calmly around the table and shot him again.

"Dying from a gut wound is a slow and wretched process." The German gave him a cold smile. "Your reward for betraying the Reich."

He walked back out to his car and drove away.

"Sebastian—"

"I can't tell when this is, but the urgency of it implies it's now. I'll fetch my swordstick and my sidearm while you retrieve your dagger. Then we must go, darling. We may be able to save him."

The journey through the afterworld seemed to take forever, though Kate knew it was very little actual time. Richard, Miranda, Robin, and Sebastian's father accompanied them.

As Otterden Abbey appeared out of the fog, Sebastian said, "Let's see whether I'm right about the time."

"Be careful," Richard said. "If German wizards are involved, this could be a trap to see who aids him."

With a nod, Sebastian extracted the sword from his cane. He held it in his left hand and his sidearm in his right. Kate drew the dagger at her waist.

They walked through the wards on the cloister and then entered the hall. A groan came from behind the dining table. Kate and Sebastian hurried to the end of the dais. From there, they could see behind the table. Wyndon lay on the floor, his bloodied hands clutching his stomach. The fronts of his shirt and trousers were dark red.

"We have to help him," Kate said.

"Agreed."

Kate created a portal. She and Sebastian stepped through it and onto the dais.

She dropped to her knees beside the wounded man, laying down her dagger. Sebastian sank into a chair beside him and opened his senses. No one here but the three of them. But he still held his weapons ready.

Wyndon opened his eyes and blinked, as though he couldn't believe what he was seeing.

"You're the healer," Sebastian said.

"Napkins. Where are the napkins?" She might have healing skills, but there hadn't been much time to develop those while tending to more pressing matters. "I don't know how to remove a bullet magically." Miranda might, but she couldn't pass the wards to come in here and explain.

"Stop the bleeding, and someone with more experience can worry about that." Sebastian passed her the napkins from the table.

Kate folded one into a pad and pressed it to the wound. *Stop bleeding, stop bleeding, stop bleeding.*

Blood soaked through the heavy linen. "Come *on*," Kate snapped.

Wyndon groaned and opened his eyes. "You're…what?"

"Never mind that now," Sebastian told him. "Have you a telephone? You need a doctor."

"Damned Nazi wizards," Wyndon muttered. "No telephone."

"The bleeding is slowing," Kate said. "He's too pale, though. I think he must've lost a good bit of blood."

"I'll stay here with him," Sebastian said. "You go have, er, our family send a doctor."

That would mean having one of the ghosts appear to Rose or any relative who might live closer and have that person send a doctor. It was a clumsy method but better than nothing.

"All right," Kate said. The pad was saturated. She took the second napkin, folded it, and placed it over the two bullet holes in Wyndon's abdomen. "Hold this in place. The magic probably makes more of a difference than the cloth, but it can't hurt."

She kissed Sebastian quickly. "Keep your eye on him."

With that, she ran out of the building and out of Wyndon's sight to create her portal.

⌇

Sebastian stared down at Wyndon. "I have very basic healing abilities. Shall I try to relieve your pain?"

The wounded man nodded.

Sebastian sent a pulse of magic into the fabric and imagined it spreading like a soothing balm inside the wound.

"Better," Wyndon croaked.

Sebastian did the same thing again.

"What…are you…why here?" Wyndon asked.

"Following a hunch." The injured man seemed to be trying to talk. Frowning, Sebastian added, "That's as much as I'll say, so don't waste your breath."

"You…" Wyndon said, "…last person…I want to be…indebted to."

"We can't always have what we want." Sebastian shrugged. "I would rather be reading in my garden with my wife than sitting here with you."

"Same."

"You know," Sebastian said, "there's a way to clear this debt."

"What?" The other man shot him a suspicious look.

"Your family has a document signed by one of my ancestors. We would like it back, and we've reason to believe it may be in this building."

"Mostly…old papers…more likely."

"Perhaps it's one of them."

"Nothing…worth…anything here."

"I would like to look. Allow Kate and me to do so, let us take the docu-

328

ment if we find it, and we're even." Of course, there would still be the problem of passing the ward to enter the chamber.

"If val-val'ble...should keep."

"You can, of course." Sebastian shrugged. "By the same token, my wife and I can subtly mention that we happened to be passing, heard a gunshot, and saved you from what appeared to be a bungled robbery." Even though the hall lay about half a mile from the road. Society wouldn't question their story closely enough for that to be a problem.

The injured man scowled. "Very...adroit... S'prising."

"I don't play the gossip game because I dislike it. That doesn't mean I don't know how."

Wyndon nodded. He drew in a breath. "Where...?"

"In the room off the crypt, under the courtyard."

Wyndon's blue eyes narrowed. "Just...guessed...did you?"

Sebastian shrugged. "Yes or no?"

"Yes, damn you... I...pay...debts." His throat worked. "Water?"

"When Kate returns. I shouldn't leave you alone."

The wounded man nodded. His eyes turned toward the bloody napkin Kate had dropped on the dais. "Need...that," he said. "Blood ward... Wyndon blood. Passes...passes the ward."

"Thank you." Sudden realization struck Sebastian. He'd tried to See the answer to lifting the curse in the Merlin Club library. Instead of a book, he'd had the vision that revealed Wyndon as a double agent. That status that had led to this encounter and, at last, to the solution. The cryptic vision had paid off after all.

Wyndon closed his eyes. "Debt...paid."

Kate returned about twenty minutes later. She and Sebastian waited until the ambulance attendants drove away with Wyndon. His caretaker would lock the building when he returned in the evening. Kate scooped up the bloody napkin, which the ambulance crew had ignored.

Sebastian triggered the entrance to the crypt. "Odd," he commented, "that he knew it was a blood ward but claimed not to know what was in the room."

"Not if his father told him there was nothing worth much in there. He doesn't strike me as a guy with an interest in antiquities or history, particularly."

"True, though you'd think something as rare as a blood ward might've made him curious. I don't suppose it much matters, though. We're done with him." Sebastian set a ball of witchlight floating. "Coming down here without sneaking seems a bit strange."

"It does, but it saves time."

They made their way between the standing tombs. She'd brought back the outer part of Sebastian's cane. Now it made a faint tapping sound on the flagstones.

He held out his hand. "I need the napkin to tend to the ward."

"You don't think I can handle it?" Kate tightened her grip on the bloody cloth.

"That isn't why I offered. I don't want that ward flinging you across the room again."

"Same to you, so maybe we should do this together."

"Christ, you're stubborn," he said, frowning.

Kate gave him a sweet smile. "Again, same to you, Lord Pighead."

They reached the corner where the warded door lay.

"If I can't talk you out of this," Sebastian said, "at least humor me and stand behind me."

Kate rolled her eyes but complied. She had to reach around him with the handkerchief. Together, bracing themselves, they slowly pressed it to the ward.

Its glow faded and slowly died.

"It's still there," Sebastian said, "but I think the blood…disarmed it, for lack of a better word."

"Then let's get inside before it rearms itself. Or whatever it does." She reached for the door handle, but he grabbed it before she could.

"No magic," he commented. For once, he didn't hold the door so she could go first. Ducking under the low, beamed ceiling, he marched down the passageway.

Was he using the cane to deliberately bar her way? Kate scowled at his back.

The passage ended in a low, boxy room. The table at its center held the sword, the candlestick, and the small chests they'd Seen earlier. But they scarcely noticed.

On the corner of the lowest shelf above the table, a glass case held the document bearing the Hawkstowe seal. As they had Seen. Sebastian hooked his arm around Kate's shoulders. The document was perhaps a foot square, parchment discolored by age and wrinkled at its borders.

"It looks like such an insignificant thing to have so much depend on it," Kate said. Miranda and Richard and the rest would be so relieved. So happy to have their long confinement ended. Edmund would doubtless welcome the lifting of his guilt, though the lost souls meant he would never be free of it.

Sebastian hefted the case carefully and cradled it against his chest in a way that kept the document level. "It isn't heavy. We'll take the case to protect it. If Wyndon wants the case returned, I'll send it."

"What next?" Kate asked. He wasn't using the cane now. It had definitely been a ruse to keep her from charging ahead.

"Now we have it authenticated by someone not related to us. Then, when that's done, as I'm sure it will be, we publish it. And hope for the best."

~

You can't publish it," Richard said when the jubilant congratulations of the Mainwaring spirits had died down. "Not yet."

"What?" Edmund cried. "Are ye daft, lad?" Others around them grumbled.

Richard ignored him. "If you publish it before the war's end, and if it's accepted, we'll all go. We don't know how quickly, but I suspect it will be very fast. As the curse is all that holds us here, its end may immediately release us."

"Why is that bad?" Sebastian asked around the pang in his heart. He looked across at his father and brother, whose affection for him shone in their faces. "You deserve to have this done."

"Aye, lad," Miles said, "but some of us have been your eyes and ears in this war. If we go, you lose that. Tuck the paper away until the war's done. Knowing we have it at last will sustain us until then."

"No more fading?" Kate asked, staring hard at him.

"I think not," Miles said, glancing at Richard. Standing beside them, Miranda and Robin nodded. So did Dad and Reg.

Sebastian looked down at the confession. Kate slid her hand into the crook of his elbow, a signal that she would support whatever he chose.

"We're at war," he said slowly. "London has been bombed nightly, each day worse than the last and tomorrow sure to be dreadful. The Merlin Club vaults are deep and secure, but I can't guarantee they would survive a direct hit." With a glance at his wife, he added, "Or that either of us will survive. If we don't, what happens then? You go to Rose? Her boys? James? What if they don't make it?"

He took a deep breath, painful because goodbyes always were. "No, as the Bard said—he had a way with words despite his slander of King Richard—'if 'twere done, 'twere best done quickly.' We authenticate it first. Then Kate and I come to say goodbye before we publish."

He glanced at her, and she gave him a slight nod.

"We'll bring this long nightmare to a close," Sebastian said.

They still didn't know, though, whether publication would suffice without also making people believe. Could a nation so steeped in Shakespeare's libelous portrayal of Richard III be persuaded to doubt it?

CHAPTER 33

I have bad news," Lachlan said, "and not much good."

Two days after Sebastian and Kate secured the confession, they joined Lachlan and Harry Whitestone for a working lunch at Lachlan's hired estate near Watford. The Dover sole suddenly seemed less appetizing.

"Let's have it." Sebastian laid down his fork.

"There are wizards guarding the embarkation ports. My agent believes they've been there since the ships started arriving."

"That's a problem," Sebastian said slowly, "but not necessarily a fatal one, depending on where they're stationed."

"In the harbormasters' offices at present. I suspect seeing a ship moving without authorization will draw them out quickly."

"No denying that," Kate said, frowning.

Harry nodded. "They can't fly, though. So if we move the transport away from the dock fast enough, they can't actually stop us."

Unless one of them knew how to pass through the afterworld. Richard and the rest hadn't reported incursions, though, so the strike teams would have to hope for the best.

"So speed is essential," Sebastian said.

He glanced at Kate and found his concern mirrored in her eyes. He wasn't very fast on his prosthesis yet, but he was supposed to lead one of the ship teams. Not only Richard but Miranda and Edmund had thrown fits when they learned he planned to teach Harry and Lachlan how to enter the afterworld. If he pulled himself off portal duty, requiring yet another person to learn, that might spur them to stop the strike teams. But a leader had to face up to his own weaknesses, not only his team's.

"Perhaps I should be ground crew," he said, "not on a ship." The ghosts would simply have to understand.

Lachlan shook his head. "I disagree. The ships aren't crewed yet, so we've no one to worry about there. Their bridges are less exposed than the docks. Farther away from any Gifted interference. The engine rooms, even more so. A protected location cuts down the need for haste."

"Stay with the plan," Harry said. "My uncle served in the Royal Flying Corps in the Great War. He always said last-minutes changes were the best way to make a dog's dinner of any scheme. There's always someone who doesn't fall in with the change."

"I agree," Kate said. "I don't have the experience you and Lachlan do, Sebastian, but practice matters. We've drilled on this. We're ready."

"Very well," Sebastian said. "I checked again with our navy man. He says once these ships are moving in the right direction, inertia will take over. We can abandon both the bridge and the engine room and convene on the lower deck, as we practiced. Once we're all together, the team leader brings everyone back to the afterworld, goes to the lowest deck and creates a portal there, and brings the bomber out before the shell blows."

"Let's hope no one's timing is off," Harry said.

Lachlan's mouth curved up in a wry grin. "Indeed. Anything else?"

Sebastian stood. "We'll convene here tomorrow evening. We go at midnight."

Harry had moved into the manor for the duration, but Kate and Sebastian wanted one more night alone before they did that. Lachlan and Harry escorted them downstairs. A buggy waited in the drive to take them to the rail station.

Sebastian regretted the breach with his ghostly kin. If all went well, he would lose them soon enough anyway. Having their last times together marred by a quarrel was a bitter draught.

He'd stored Edmund's confession in the magically secured and warded steel vault at the Merlin Club. Dr. Edward Montague Faversham, a retired Cambridge professor and a Fellow of the Society of Antiquaries, was handling the authentication. Albert admitted the professor to the Merlin Club each morning, established him in the library, and took the document away when the professor finished with it. Anyone he wanted to have see it would have to follow the same procedure. The Mainwarings were taking no chances.

~

Charges are set. Sandy's on her way back," Callum MacGill, one of the two demolitions experts on Kate's team, said softly. He stood close so his invisibility glamours merged with Kate's and those of the other four Gifted on the team, allowing them to see each other. They couldn't see his partner for the night, Sandra Ross, crossing the lock gate structure of the Kruisschan Lock, the one nearest the sea. She and Callum had wired explosives to the lock and its infrastructure. When it blew, it would generate debris that should block the passage for several days. Bottling up the invasion ports, even for a while, would give Bomber Command more time to destroy the transports.

Kate let her hand rest on the dagger sheathed at her waist. Wearing it, she carried a symbol of her new family's love and acceptance. It meant more than she had first realized.

Moonlight glistened on the water, and the dark hulks of transports loomed against the night sky. The scent of motor oil hung faintly on the air. Most of the port structures were dark, but lights shone in the ground-floor windows of a three-story stone structure with four corner towers ending in peaked roofs. This was the harbormaster's office.

Three locks separated parts of the harbor from the Schelde River, their access to the sea. The other teams should finish wiring theirs any moment. While the timers ticked down, each team would drive a transport into the middle of the passage along the Schelde itself, which had no locks on it, and scuttle them, barring that passage as well.

If they were lucky, the explosions at the locks would draw any guards, including Nazi Gifted, away from the transports long enough for the teams to get them underway.

Sandra arrived a moment later. "Timers set for thirty," she reported.

"Then let's go."

Kate took them back through the afterworld, where a disapproving Richard and Miranda guarded the supplies for the next phase, the transports. No one spoke. Gifted couldn't help picking up the ghosts' displeasure, but there was a job to do.

They waited until all four teams returned. Each person picked up a fresh load of charges, and each team shared the weight of a laden shell.

Sebastian steered them to their ships. Harry and his team of three men and two women had the fourth boat. Harry would take the pilot and two others from the afterworld to the ship's bridge and into the hold. Harry and the other man would then travel via afterworld to the dock, emerge in the real world, cast off, and then join the others on the ship, again via the afterworld. Each team followed a similar plan.

Lachlan had the third ship, while Kate took the second and Sebastian, the lead. Speed and silence were essential. As Kate created an exit portal for her team, Sebastian stood at her shoulder.

"I'll see you soon," he said.

"Before you know it," she agreed, and she stepped through.

Sebastian watched her go and hated it. If anything happened to her, it would be the worst loss of his life. He had faith in her, in all of them, but so few of them had experience under fire. He would simply have to hope their nerves held steady.

And that the enemy didn't surprise them.

Reaching his team's ship required only a few steps and a couple of seconds. "Here we go. Morag, Bruce, and Flora, you first." That way, they wouldn't have to lug the shell around.

He took them to the hold by the simple means of staying in the afterworld while walking down the nearly vertical ladders that passed for stairs on a ship. Relying on the diagrams they'd studied, Sebastian opened the portal. Morag, Flora, and Bruce stepped out, straining with the shell. Morag would guard it now and blow it when the time came. Flora and Bruce would handle the engine room.

Sebastian closed the portal. He, Iona, and Brice made their way back to the bridge via the stairs. As expected, it was deserted. The entire ship felt deserted, and Sebastian hoped they all were. He opened a portal. Brice stepped through and took his place at the helm.

Sebastian released the portal and thought of reaching the dock. When he and Iona started walking again, the moorings appeared.

"A handy trick," she observed, her brogue rolling the R.

"I've been doing this a long time," he said, creating a portal. He and

Iona stepped out, immediately forming invisibility glamours. As agreed, she ran to the stern while he took the bow.

The explosions on the locks would be the signal to get underway and, everyone hoped, a diversion. Once the ships were headed in the right directions, the engine room crew and the pilots could evacuate. Inertia would carry the ships where they needed to go. Last to come off would be the teams who exploded the shells in the holds. Their timing would be critical. The ships had to sink close together but slightly spread to block the passage. Or else this would all be for nothing.

With her heart in her throat, Kate rejoined Ailish, her pilot, on the bridge. "I'm here," Kate announced before walking up to the retired teacher and merging their glamours.

"Engine room ready?" the older woman asked.

"They say they are." The cold engine start, for them or for any craft that might pursue once the Nazis realized their boats were moving, wouldn't take very long. What would delay any pursuit the longest was getting crews out of their bunks and aboard the craft. By the time they could do that, it should be too late to stop the assault teams.

Of course, the port personnel did have rifles, and even a blind shot could hit something.

The two women waited in silence.

A thunderous *boom* ahead and to the right broke the night silence. Bright yellow and red lit the night. A moment later, a shock wave rocked the transport. Kate and Ailish grabbed consoles to hang on.

"I hope the engineers are okay," Kate muttered.

Another explosion lit the night, the one their team had set. Then another roared immediately ahead of them and made their ears ring. Men poured from the barracks area toward the ruined locks. A secondary explosion rocked the Kruisschan one. Callum loved his explosives.

When the sound and the vibration died away, Kate's Gifted senses picked up a rumble deep in the ship. Rhona and Brice had the engines going.

Kate grinned at Ailish. "Step one."

Ahead of them, Sebastian's ship pulled away from the dock, turning into the channel.

Ailish tightened her hold on the wheel. "Here we go."

~

Standing at Brice's shoulder, Sebastian watched the Nazis scramble. So far, the diversion was working. But any minute now…

A figure silhouetted against the flames took aim at the ship.

"Down," Sebastian warned. *I hope Kate and the rest see them.*

A bullet *spanged* off the steel bridge housing, then another.

"Brice?"

"A moment more."

More bullets struck the sides of the ship. The Nazis had figured out what was happening.

Brice popped up his head to look. "We're on course."

"Then let's go."

Sebastian created a portal, and they leaped through it. As they entered the afterworld, his father and brother drove off the wraiths. Sebastian returned to the real world in the engine room and evacuated Iona and Bruce. Then he headed for the cargo hold, where Morag waited with the black powder shell. All that transit took less than a minute, but it felt like an eternity with bullets striking the hull and Kate in danger somewhere behind him.

He stepped out of the afterworld beside Morag. "It's time."

She watched him open a new portal. Because this would be tricky, he hooked his arm around her waist and stood so close to the portal that its chill prickled over his neck.

"Now," he said.

Morag shot a hand-wide bolt of bright, blue magic at the shell. In the same instant, Sebastian shoved through the resistant barrier to the afterworld.

A tremendous, booming roar sent shock waves at the portal as it closed. They knocked him and Morag off their feet. Unfortunately, falling onto shadowy ground hurt almost as much as falling onto dirt. He landed on the hip of his bad leg, jolting the prosthesis.

Hellfire.

His cousin Robin offered him a hand up. "Good job, coz, but I expect you'll have a bruise on that leg."

Sebastian waved that away and helped Morag stand. "Thanks. Where's Kate? And the rest?"

"Not back yet."

Just a few seconds more.

Despite the bullets bouncing off the hull, Kate peered out the front windscreen. Sebastian's boat drifted ahead of hers. Suddenly, it rocked. A muted explosion boomed, and she flinched. *Please let him be safe.*

Sudden, green light split the darkness. A bolt of magic slammed into the side of the boat.

Ailish's lips tightened. "Well. Now we know the bloody Nazis can do that too."

If so, perhaps the Scottish mages should reconsider their refusal to teach the skill, but that wasn't Ailish's call.

"How much longer?" Kate asked.

Ailish gauged the distance to the foundering craft ahead. "In a moment...now."

Kate created a portal, and they rushed into the afterworld and down to the engine room. She would evacuate the engineer, then go to the hold to bring Callum out when he blew the shell. Another magic bolt rocked the ship, and then another. Two Gifted? Or more? Would they throw the transport off course?

Nothing she could do if they did.

Sebastian watched from the afterworld with his heart in his throat. Kate couldn't see the magic bolts denting the hull. There were three wizards blasting at her now, trying to stop her from reaching the channel. As Lachlan had warned, the process wasn't quiet. It was, however, effective. As he had also said.

Hurry, Kate. Please hurry.

Another trio attacked Lachlan's ship. How could the bloody Nazis use magic that way when the English couldn't? That must change as soon as possible. In ordinary times, he would respect Lachlan's tradition, but he couldn't now.

A muted boom came from Kate's transport. The boat rocked in the water.

Where the bloody hell was Kate? He gritted his teeth to keep from calling her.

A minute later, she emerged from the fog with Miranda and Miles.

Her team followed her. "That was an unpleasant development." She glared at the scene visible in the real world.

"Yes, and we must plan for it next time," he answered.

Miles said, "I'll go watch for Harry." He disappeared into the churning fog.

The Gifted who'd attacked Kate's boat ran to attack Harry's. Now those who'd attacked Sebastian's joined them. Blue and green light slammed into the hull.

Beyond the veiling mists, Lachlan's boat rocked with its explosion. Would they make it off?

The charge in the hold of Harry's craft went off. The boat shuddered.

Minutes ticked by. Escorted by Reg, Lachlan emerged from the fog with his team. He and Sebastian exchanged nods.

Where was Harry?

More minutes ticked by, and Sebastian's unease grew. Through his odd link to Kate, he knew she felt it too. The seer Gift didn't function here with regard to the living world, but intuition did.

At last, Miles walked out of the fog, his face grim. With him came four members of Harry's team. No Harry, though, and no Ophelia.

Sebastian went cold. "Miles?"

The Elizabethan captain shook his head. "All was going well until they triggered the explosion. The magic attack rocked the ship at just that moment, and they didn't make it through the portal before the bomb went off."

"They're dead," Sebastian said through his suddenly tight throat. He clenched his fist to avoid rubbing against the hard, hot, choking boulder of grief and helpless fury in his chest. "No one could survive that close to such a blast."

"Aye. 'Tis merciful that way, at least."

Better than drowning. But...Eve would be devastated. And Sebastian had lost a friend he'd trusted all his life.

Kate slipped her hand into his and leaned against him. He hooked his arm around her, but this was no time for grieving.

"The Nazis know what we're about now," he told the group, "and they've a skill we didn't know they possessed. We must strike again before they can double the watch on the other ports."

"We've enough shells with us for tonight," Lachlan reminded him. "Do you still want to hit Le Havre?"

"Yes. We should finish well before dawn. Then we'll go to Boulogne and hit the barges there. We'll take black powder aboard, blow it, and run. The hulls are thinner, and they're jammed in together. With luck, each explosion will take out several of them. We'll do the same tomorrow night. I'll be damned if the bastards will stop us." They owed it to Harry and Ophelia to see this through.

Lachlan looked at him for a long moment.

Sebastian frowned. "What is it? You know we need to talk about the Nazis' magical skills."

"So we do. But that isna what I had in mind." The Scotsman gripped Sebastian's shoulder. "The army's loss is the Merlin Club's gain. No general could have done better, and I'm proud to follow you."

"We all are," Kate said.

Sebastian's throat closed. Yes, his plan had worked, but... "Tonight cost us. We lost two of our comrades."

"What general," Lachlan asked him gently, "has not?"

The hardest call Sebastian had ever made was his visit to Harry and Kate's townhouse in Cavendish Square later that morning. The Gifted butler, Lawrence, admitted him with a glum countenance. When his gaze met Sebastian's, the older man shuddered as though from a blow.

He swallowed hard. Though his blue eyes filled, his voice was steady when he said, "I'll tell Lady Whitestone you're here, sir." He showed Sebastian to the parlor by the door and departed.

Instead of Lawrence, Eve came rushing down the stairs, her face pale and her eyes full of fear. Sebastian turned to meet her, and she checked on the threshold.

Her face turned paler, and her eyes darkened. Her lips trembled.

Sebastian froze. Should he go to her and risk shattering the composure she fought so hard to maintain?

Eve gestured to him to sit on the sofa behind him. With her eyes glued to his face, she walked slowly and carefully to the other end of the sofa and sat. She clenched her shaking hands into fists on her knees.

"I hadn't the nerve to scry." Her throat worked in a hard swallow. "Tell me."

Sebastian did. The telling was even more difficult than he'd expected. After everyone had gone home, he had traveled back in time and watched

Harry and Ophelia in those last moments. He'd owed that to his friend. Describing it all to Eve brought it vividly back to him.

"The Nazi Gifted's magic bolts rocked the ship as Ophelia detonated the bomb. She and Harry lost their balance. Missed the portal."

She stared at him for several seconds. "I should've been with him." Her voice seemed unnaturally calm. "I would've been, but he convinced me not to go."

Eve, like Kate, lacked the skill that had detonated the bombs, but saying that would only wound her further. "My dear, I imagine he was glad you were not."

"Yes, well. His opinion..." Her lips trembled. She pressed them together. At last, she said, "That's neither here nor there now."

"Eve, I'm so very sorry. What can I do for you?"

She raised an eyebrow. "Kill as many bloody Nazis as you can. Better yet, put me on your teams, and I'll do it."

That would never do. Killing Nazis might be satisfying to all of them, but the Sea Lion counter missions couldn't focus on that. "Eve, that isn't what we do. If you wish to join a team, I'll take it up with the rest, but our job is to block the harbors. Trying to do more would cost us the edge of surprise. It could ruin everything." He took a deep breath. "If you give me your word—"

"I can't do that." Eve rose, so he also did.

"Sebastian, dear friend, you gave him a chance to strike a blow, something his heart condition would never have allowed him to do otherwise. For that, I'm grateful. I thank you for coming, as I know you loved—loved him too." Her throat moved in a hard swallow. "Now, though, you should go. Please."

"Of course. Eve, if you need anything..."

She nodded and made a shooing motion with her hand. Her eyes filled. Since she didn't want him there when she wept, he did the decent thing and left.

On the sidewalk, Sebastian took a deep breath and sought his own composure. *Harry, my friend...we will finish this job. For you and Ophelia and all our British dead.*

CHAPTER 34

Over the next week, with help from the Mainwaring ghosts, the Merlin Club and the Mages of the Isles hit every embarkation harbor for Sea Lion. They lost three mages and one Merlin Club member to the magic bolts of the Nazi Gifted. But they sank several dozen transports and a couple of hundred barges and bottled the craft up in their harbors.

In between raids, Sebastian magically investigated Wyndon's MI6 contact. He confirmed that the man had not betrayed the earl. One of the Germans had, and MI6 was in pursuit.

RAF Bomber Command and Fighter Command also executed daring raids, sinking barges, transports, and other craft. Algernon had reported from Berlin that Sea Lion was postponed, perhaps indefinitely, but the Merlin Club was taking no chances.

Kate and Sebastian returned home after dawn on the last day. As they undressed to climb into bed and sleep for a while, she asked, "What are you thinking? You have an odd smile on your face."

"I've felt…satisfied by what we've done. It's not the army, but it's important. It gives me a chance to use all those years of training and make a difference."

Some of the worry inside her eased. After his amputation, he'd seemed so depressed. Lost, in a way. Now he had his purpose back.

"Are you going to take Lachlan's suggestion? Make this alliance a permanent guerilla force?"

"If my fellow directors, Genevieve and Aysgarth, go for it, then yes. If they won't, I'll do it without involving the club."

"But either way, you're doing it?"

He nodded. "I feel called to it, so yes, but I think we must limit ourselves to extraordinarily urgent situations. If we involve ourselves too often, that could spur the German Gifted to respond in kind. Once that sort of tit-for-tat business starts, it could easily lead to the escalation the Compact of Prague and the agreements before it were designed to avoid."

"That makes sense. So you'll resign your commission? Or not apply to return to duty, whichever?"

Sebastian shook his head. "I can't go from blowing up ships to sitting behind a desk, but there's a middle ground. One that would leave me time to work with the Merlin Club. The Home Guard train at Osterley Park, and they have secret units based in the countryside. I mean to ask for a return to detached duty but with an assignment to help train them."

"I admit I'm surprised." Kate peered at him. "Will this satisfy you? Can you be happy with this?"

"I think so, yes. I'll speak to Secretary Eden when enough time has passed for me to have recuperated without magic. It wouldn't do to give the game away."

"Then I'll do all I can to help you." She kissed him quickly.

Sitting at her dressing table, she picked up her hairbrush. "I spoke to Eve yesterday. I meant to tell you. She seems very...brittle. I'm worried about her."

"We all are. Thank you for checking on her, darling. I wish I knew what to do."

"Not much else we can do until she finds her feet again. She made it clear she wants to be left alone to do that."

While Kate brushed out her hair, Sebastian flipped through the mail on the secretary.

"That can wait, can't it?" Kate asked.

"Yes, but this thick envelope has me curious, so..." He froze. "From Faversham."

Kate came to stand beside him while he opened it. With the flap slit, he paused. Tension darkened his eyes and his shoulders. "We know that document is Edmund's authentic confession, but if we can't prove it..."

Abruptly, he pulled a letter and a sheaf of documents from the envelope. He scanned the typewritten sheet, and his tension fell away.

"He supports us?" Kate asked.

"Yes. He says he has enclosed his affidavit and those of the experts he consulted. Two executed copies of each."

Sebastian grinned and threw his arms around her. "Kate, we truly may do this thing!"

"I hope so. Now we need to spread the word. Get people's attention. I have some ideas about that."

He stroked her hair back from her face while she explained. "When people hear Richard III's name, they think of Shakespeare's character. From what I've learned from the family, the king was nothing like that. I can prepare some press releases explaining who he truly was. I'll bet Faversham will help me."

"That's a marvelous idea. There may be other help as well."

"Really? Who?"

"For a couple of hundred years, the descendants of those who supported King Richard, including some whose ancestors died with him at Bosworth Field, held a banquet in the king's honor on his birthday, October 2. But that tradition died out during the Napoleonic Wars. Only recently has another group convened, a much smaller one called the Fellowship of the White Boar in honor of King Richard's white boar emblem. A physician, Dr. Saxon Barton, helped found it and serves as their secretary. They may have contacts who will work with us. I don't think they've been active in the last year or two, but we can hope their sentiments haven't changed."

"I'll write my press releases, then, and we'll take photos of the materials Dr. Faversham sent and the confession. Then, if you don't mind, I'll contact this Dr. Barton and ask to meet with him."

He raised an eyebrow. "You don't want me along?"

"You have a guerilla force to form. Our trapped kin are my family too. Let me do this part and ask you for help if I need it."

"Fair enough. Thank you, darling." He kissed her quickly.

As they climbed into bed, Kate was already planning what she would write. So much depended on this, and he was trusting her to manage it. She had best not botch it.

∽

A little more than a week later, Kate sat on a train pulling into Liverpool Central station. She'd tried not to think of all that rode on this meeting. If they couldn't persuade the secretary of an organization founded to combat the traditional view of Richard III as a murderer that the confession was genuine, could they win over anyone? She clutched the envelope under her arm tighter.

Though the military leaders and the Führer continued to discuss Sea Lion, the Merlin Club's Berlin agent doubted they would try again. Meanwhile, the RAF and the Royal Navy maintained the security of their skies and seas. They took damage, but that was unavoidable. The important thing was that they prevented the Germans from gaining superiority in either realm.

Kate hurried out of the three-story, brownstone station. In this day of fuel rationing and scarce taxis, she appreciated Dr. Barton's offer to meet her at a nearby tearoom. The chilly wind off the River Mersey had her hunching her shoulders in her green wool coat and walking faster.

As directed, she turned left out of the station and walked down a block and a half to the Hanover Street tea room, a modest shop with an uncurtained glass panel in the pale green door and cheerful yellow café curtains in its plate-glass window. At least she hadn't had to walk far in the cold. She slipped out of her coat and hung it on the rack beside the door.

A sturdy, bearded man who might've been in his fifties rose from a table beside the door. "Lady Hawkstowe?"

"Kate, please." She offered her gloved hand, and he gave it a firm, businesslike shake. She'd written that she would wear a burgundy suit trimmed with blue and a blue hat.

He seated her without comment on her being obviously American. "What will you have, Kate? And please call me Saxon."

Stripping off her gloves, she nodded her thanks. "Tea and whatever biscuits you think are best here. I appreciate your making time to see me. I know you're a busy man." He was an adviser to the Bureau of Pensions and a painter as well as a physician.

"I expect we're all a good deal busier these days."

The waitress came and took their order.

Barton said, "For sixteen years, my friends and I have devoted ourselves to restoring the honorable reputation King Richard possessed for his entire adult life. Now, with the war on, we have less time to devote to that, but we've never lost interest in it. We simply…ran out of leads.

Especially after that dreadful forensic examination of the bones in the abbey."

Westminster Abbey he meant. An urn in Henry VII's Lady Chapel contained bones purportedly those of the Edward IV's sons, Richard III's nephews, the "Princes in the Tower." A forensic examination in 1934 had led to the conclusion that they were, in fact, the boys' remains.

Barton scowled. "Starting a scientific examination with a foregone conclusion in mind is not precisely true to the scientific method. Even if they were correct, that says nothing about how the children died. But of course, everyone lauded this as proof Shakespeare and that overly revered Thomas More were correct."

"They're not, and I have proof." Kate slid the envelope across the table. "In this envelope is a photograph of a confession written by a nobleman, an ancestor of my husband, detailing the ways he unwittingly helped the Duke of Buckingham's agents murder those boys. As you'll see, the bones in the abbey, the ones found under a staircase, cannot be those of the Plantagenet boys because the murderers weighted down the bodies and dumped them in the Thames."

"Why is this only now coming to light?" Barton asked. But he opened the envelope and drew out the photos of the confession and authenticating documents and carbons of Kate's draft press releases.

"The document was believed lost and has only recently been recovered. You also have an affidavit from Professor Faversham of the Society of Antiquaries, who authenticated the document, affidavits from those he consulted, and press releases I wrote in case they may be of use. Before the war, I was a journalist. I still am from time to time."

Thanks to Sebastian's connections and her own, she had been accredited to submit stories through the censors to file for American news bureaus.

"You're serious about this." Barton studied her, weighing her.

"Entirely. All my husband and I ask is that you look over these materials. The *Yorkshire Clarion* has promised to run the story as soon as we give them the go-ahead." Thanks to her former flatmate Janet.

"King Richard was much loved here in the North," Barton noted.

"Yes, I know. We would like to have you and your fellowship in our corner, but we will proceed regardless. As you note, there's a war on. None of us can be sure of surviving it, or even of this document surviving. So it's important to our family that King Richard be cleared of his nephews' murders as soon as possible."

The waitress brought a teapot and a plate of ginger biscuits. She poured for them, milk first in Kate's and then the tea. Barton took his tea plain.

"Do you mind if I take a quick look?" he asked.

"Not at all. If you have any questions, I'll do my best to answer them."

They sat quietly sipping tea and munching cookies while he leafed through the pages. At last, he looked up. "I'm familiar with Faversham's work and with some of these he consulted. Let me read through these at my leisure."

Despite his calm tone, his eye gleamed. He knew the significance of the papers in front of him. He simply didn't want to commit without being sure.

"Of course." Kate smiled at him. "Those photos are for you. We have the originals, of course."

"Of course. If I may ask, where is the confession?"

"It's in a secure vault."

He nodded at that. "The Jerrys have paid us a few visits lately. These will make for interesting reading in my bomb shelter. I'll contact you when I've made up my mind."

They chatted idly about the shipping industry and his love of painting.

As they finished, she checked her watch. "I need to leave to catch my train. Thank you again for your time, Saxon." She pulled her wallet out of her bag.

"Oh, no, please allow me, Kate. You've given me an interesting conundrum. I expect to enjoy it."

She thanked him, and he walked her to the station, the precious envelope held close to his chest. His caution was understandable, but she couldn't wait to hear what he decided.

The more people who would proclaim King Richard's innocence, the better the odds for all the ghostly Mainwarings. And for one living one who had quickly become her world.

Would the censors pass a story about the women of the Air Transport Auxiliary ferrying Spitfires from the factories to the airfields where they were needed? Or would they see letting the world know as some kind of admission of weakness?

Pulling the story together in her head three days after her meeting with Barton, Kate hopped up the one step to the stoop of the Charles Street house and opened the door. Bradshaw emerged from the door below the stairs, moving quickly without appearing to. That really was a good trick. Since Petersham also did it, it must qualify as a basic butlering skill.

"Good afternoon, madam. Welcome home."

"Thank you, Bradshaw." As he helped her out of her coat, she asked, "Is my husband here?"

The butler nodded. "His lordship took the post upstairs. It arrived shortly after he did."

"Thanks!" Unpinning her hat as she went, she trotted up the steps to the first floor. In the parlor, Sebastian sat at his desk looking over some papers.

"Anything interesting?" Kate asked, leaning over to kiss him.

"Reports on the villagers at Hawkstowe. All's well so far. There's a letter for you. From CNU."

"Huh. I wonder what they want?" She hurried to put her hat and gloves in the bedroom.

Curled on the sofa behind Sebastian, Kate tore open the letter. As she read, her eyes widened. On the one hand, this was a great opportunity. On the other…*how dare they?*

"Something the matter?" Sebastian turned in his chair to face her.

"Yes and no." She waved the letter at him. "They're offering me a slot as a regular correspondent, stories left to my discretion, pay by the piece. It's a good offer. But Mr. J. Cartwright Gillingham, Vice-President of Personnel, makes it plain that since I'm married to you and living here, they would no longer be responsible for my delicate female presence in the war zone."

Her husband grinned. "Does he know you at all?"

"We've never met, but I can tell he's a weasel, splitting hairs that way. On top of all that, he thinks my position as a countess would 'increase interest' in my pieces, and he hopes I'll have time to address the ways London society has adapted to the war."

"You did tell Eve and Harry, at the Dravens' house party, that the American audience hungered for inside looks at the peerage. Or something of the sort."

"Yes, I did, but I don't want to focus on things like that." Yet CNU would offer a wide readership for, say, the story on the women pilots. If it passed the censors. Kate bit her lip.

"What is it?" Sebastian asked.

She explained. "I want to tell them to go jump in the lake, but if I do, am I cutting off my nose to spite my face?"

"It depends on which form of satisfaction you want more. Having them give you a platform—indeed, begging to do so—or putting them in their place? I don't care whether you use your title on your work or not. It's yours to use as you please, but it must be doubly galling that it increases your prestige in their eyes."

"I wanted to earn my own prestige, not marry it." Realizing how that sounded, she began, "Sebastian—"

"Relax, darling. If I wanted press coverage, I, too, would rather earn it than marry it."

"Okay, then." Kate scowled down at the letter. "So…"

Bradshaw tapped on the door. "I beg your pardon, but there's a telegram for you, madam." He handed her the yellow envelope.

Kate thanked him and shot a worried look at Sebastian. Had something happened to Dwight? Or back on the farm?

She ripped open the envelope, jerked the paper out, scanned it, and grinned.

"What is it?" Sebastian asked.

Kate's eyes stung. She blinked to clear them. "Your material best chance ever to clear king's name. Stop. Suggestions follow by letter. Stop. Warmest regards Barton."

Sebastian's smile had an incredulous aura. "He'll help us."

She launched herself at him for a hard hug. He settled her on his lap and stared down at the telegram she still clutched.

"Step one is on, then," he said, still sounding as though he didn't entirely believe it. "Lord Aysgarth has already said he'll introduce *Titulus Regius* and use that as an excuse to speak in the Lords. The Earl of Havelock will support him."

"What's *Titulus Regius*?"

"The Act of Parliament proclaiming Edward IV's marriage bigamous and his children bastards. The act also proclaimed Richard III, then Duke of Gloucester, his brother's rightful heir. Henry VII had it repealed unread because his queen was one of those children from the bigamous marriage, and he needed her to be legitimate. Fortunately, George Buck, whose book you read, found a copy in a monastic chronicle."

"That's amazing."

Sebastian grinned. "Indeed. Genevieve knows a couple of MPs who'll speak in the Commons. When Barton's letter arrives, we can decide how to proceed and when to set all that in motion."

Shaking his head, he added, "I hope it does the trick. If it doesn't, our quiver is empty."

As Sebastian and Kate laid their plans for publicizing the confession, he permitted himself the tiniest bit of hope. In the week after her return from Liverpool, they had firmed up their plans. Professor Faversham, who had authenticated the confession, convinced a friend at the *Times* the story would be an interesting diversion from the war. He also had numerous friends involved with academic journals, including two devoted to medieval history. Janet had the *Yorkshire Clarion* ready to go. Saxon Barton's BBC News contact agreed to consider the story, and one of his fellowship knew a curator at the British Museum. Everyone also had other suggestions.

Kate and Sebastian outlined a plan including everyone's ideas. After all, the more publicity, the better. They sat together in their parlor with the list on the table in front of them.

Sebastian looked at Kate, and she nodded. "You want to go tell them," she said. "In case there isn't time after all this starts happening."

"Yes." Around the heaviness in his heart, he added, "They've always been there, Richard and Miranda, and even Miles. Then Dad and Reg. Losing them in life was ghastly, but still being able to see them made it bearable. Now..."

"I know." Kate hugged him. "I'll miss them all too. I'm sure there are hundreds of stories among them that I would love to know, and if this works, I won't have time to ask about them."

"It's for the best. It's justice long delayed, but...well, you understand."

"Let's go see them, love."

They entered the afterworld and drove away the wraiths to find their family waiting. Richard and Miranda stood at the front. Miles, Robin, Edmund, and Sebastian's father and brother stood with them.

"You have news," Richard said. Despite the hope in his eyes, he wore a solemn expression. They all did.

"Yes." Holding Kate's hand, Sebastian explained. "This may not do the trick. If it doesn't, we'll try to think of something else."

Miles shook his head. "There is naught else, so let us hope. I'll miss you, though I cannot wait to see my sweet Margery again. You're a good man, Sebastian, Lord Hawkstowe, and you married a remarkable woman."

"I want to thank you." Tears glazed Kate's eyes, but she pressed on. "Even when I didn't know who you were, you befriended me, Miranda and Richard. You watched over me. You're responsible for my meeting Sebastian, and you've all given me something I never thought to have, time with my birth mother's family. I'll always remember you."

"You're a superb member of this family," Richard told her. With a glance at his wife, he added, "Even if you are rather strong-willed, you come by it naturally."

Everyone laughed.

Sebastian's father stepped to his side. "God willing, my son is the last cursed Mainwaring, and I couldn't be happier. He's a fine man, and his steadiness set us all free."

"We all did that together," Sebastian protested.

"But some parts of it, we could never have done. Thank you." Richard stepped forward to embrace him. A round of hugs and memories and bittersweet laughter followed.

When everyone had said what they wanted to, Kate looked around at them. "The publicity we've arranged may need a while to reach people, to change their minds. There is, after all, a war claiming the headlines. While we wait, come see us whenever you can. Please."

"You may depend upon it," Miranda promised.

Sebastian's eyes burned as he and Kate returned to their parlor. Would this be the last time he saw his father? Painful as that thought was, the idea that they might fail, that the Mainwarings might remain trapped, was worse.

"We'll do all we can," Kate said softly, leaning into him.

He nodded. There was, after all, nothing else to do.

~

I'm telling CNU to jump in the lake," Kate announced over tea in the parlor about a month later.

Really, there was nothing like feeling vindicated to lift a woman's day.

This letter also offered a welcome diversion from wondering whether their campaign to clear King Richard III's name was succeeding or falling flat. Articles and interviews had been appearing regularly, and nothing had changed.

Sebastian's brows rose. "Do tell, darling Kate."

She grinned at him. "My old flatmate Marge told her friends at UPI about me. I suspect she laid it on pretty thick, but they've made me an offer similar to the one from CNU. Without the insulting cracks about responsibility for a female in a war zone." She handed him the letter.

As he read, his lips curved upward at the corners. "They also seem pleased about possibly having the Countess of Hawkstowe write for them."

"Yes, but they're not insulting about it. Read what they said."

"I did. 'If you choose to use your title, it will add a note of authenticity to your pieces for our readers and will underscore your understanding of both the American and the British positions.' A very different slant there. The choice is, after all, entirely yours to make."

"Yes." Kate plopped onto his lap and locked her arms around his neck. "I wonder if Marge coached them on what not to say."

"Do we care?"

She thought about it for a second. "No. The money's not quite as good, but the respect is better. I'll take it."

"Congratulations, Countess London Correspondent." He lowered his head toward hers.

"Sebastian. Kate." Richard's urgent tone had their heads jerking toward the hearth, where he and Miranda stood with their arms around each other.

"It's time," Miranda choked. "You've done it."

Sebastian said, "We'll come—"

He and Kate leaped to their feet, but Miranda told them, "No. There is no time."

Richard added, "We're going. Miles is gone. Charles and Adam, who died in 1813, just passed through."

Kate caught a flash of the afterworld's fog swirling around a tall, golden archway and felt Sebastian see it too. A man in mid-eighteenth-century clothing stepped into its hazy interior and vanished.

"We and Edmund are different," Richard said.

Miranda added, "Different rules, but we haven't long. Oh, my dear ones, we love you so. Have a long life together. Be happy."

Sebastian's father appeared beside Richard and Miranda. Kate gaped. She could see and hear him? Because she was touching Sebastian?

Reginald said, "Sebastian, dear boy, you're a credit to us all. I'm so proud of you. Kate, I couldn't have chosen better for my son, and…"

He vanished.

"Until we meet again," Richard said. His eyes widened. "Oh…"

His *goodbye* and Miranda's faded like whispers on the wind as the pair vanished.

Their disappearance hit like a punch to the heart.

Kate gasped. Tears welled in her eyes and spilled down her cheeks. Sebastian caught her in a tight embrace, and his eyes were suspiciously bright.

"We still have each other and the family," he said into her hair. "It's only… I love you, Kate Mainwaring."

"I understand, and I love you too." She pressed her face into his shoulder, and he said nothing about the tears soaking his shirt.

They stood together for long minutes, mourning those who were, at long last, truly gone. Their publicity campaign had started only a few weeks ago, surely not time to change very many minds. Producing the proof of the king's innocence must've been enough to satisfy the curse.

Finally, Sebastian raised his head. "We still have plenty to do, and they would want us to carry on. Especially with the Merlin Club."

"Yes. We have a war to help win."

EPILOGUE

London
May 8, 1945

Victory in Europe Day, the papers were calling this. VE Day. At last.

Smashed into the jubilant throng on the Mall between the Victoria Monument and Buckingham Palace, Kate and Sebastian grinned at each other. "Still can't believe it," he shouted, tightening his arm around her shoulders. In this happy, jostling crowd, they could easily become separated.

He wore his uniform with the star and crown of a lieutenant colonel on his epaulets. Kate had her arm around his waist. Loving their closeness, she also tightened her hold. "We did our part. I'm so proud."

"Bloody well ought to be." He caught her chin for a long, exuberant kiss. Others around them were also kissing. People climbed the monument, a huge pillar topped by a golden statue of the famously not amused Queen Victoria.

At the other end of the Mall, cheering crowds jammed Trafalgar Square. They splashed in the fountains, climbed on the statues and the National Gallery steps, and happily kissed strangers in uniform. Cars with uniformed and civilian men and women crammed inside and clinging to the running boards honked their horns as they tooled down Charing Cross Road and Whitehall.

It was complete, joyous chaos that gave the lie to the myth of the stoic British temperament.

A roar went up from the crowd on the Mall. Everyone looked to the palace balcony. The king and queen emerged with their two daughters, King George and Princess Elizabeth in their uniforms. The heiress to the throne had joined the Auxiliary Territorial Service, training as a driver and a mechanic. The nation loved her all the more for it. Behind them came a beaming Winston Churchill.

The king and queen had won the hearts of the East End by touring it on foot during the days of the Blitz, talking to people and consoling them in the rubble of their bombed-out homes. They'd even stayed in London in solidarity instead of retreating to one of the Crown's distant properties.

The five on the balcony waved, and the crowd waved back in an enthusiastic outpouring of shared delight. The cheering went on and on until, at last, the royal family and the prime minister went inside.

Almost immediately, a chant of "We want the king!" began.

Sebastian shook his head. "I've had enough. Ready to go?"

"Absolutely."

They made their way into Green Park, which was less crowded. Hand in hand, they walked uphill toward Piccadilly. The sounds of more cheering lay ahead, mixed with the honking of car horns. A red double-decker bus drove along the street, its open upper deck visible above the hedges along the park's edge. It too was jammed with laughing, celebrating Londoners. Someone had found a trombone and was blasting out "God Save the King" while his fellow passengers enthusiastically sang along at the tops of their lungs.

"You know," Sebastian said, "with my injured leg, I would've been wretched standing in that mob, and never mind walking home to Charles Street from the palace."

He had learned to manipulate the prosthesis magically. That skill allowed him to mount and guide a horse and to move almost as easily as he ever had.

Kate bumped him with her shoulder. "It worked out. So much did."

Yet she couldn't help wishing, maybe hoping, their ghostly kin could see this. Could know they won.

Sebastian squeezed her hand. "I miss them too."

He looked up at the trees overhead and the bright blue sky beyond. "Our son, should we have one, will be the first Hawkstowe heir born in more than 450 years without the shadow of the curse hanging over him. I hope they know. We couldn't have done this without their help."

"No, and I learned so much from them. They gave me lessons and friendship and another tie to my birth mother. When I hear Vera Lynn's recording of 'We'll Meet Again,' I think of them. And of James and Harry and Eve and all the others we've lost."

They walked on up the hill. Eve's grief over Harry's death had congealed into cold, hard rage. Early in 1941, she'd volunteered for Special Operations Executive. She'd parachuted into occupied France that April and played merry hell with the Nazis. Her Gifts had enabled her to last more than twice the six-week average survival time of SOE agents in France. When the SS came for her, as she'd known they eventually would, she'd had a surprise ready. The Merlin Club preparations before their raid on Sea Lion had inspired her to conceal black powder in the linings of her suitcase, radio case, and handbag. When she magically detonated them, the magic-amplified explosions had taken out the entire squad and the captain commanding them. And, of course, Eve herself.

Sebastian's brother James also would never come back to his family. His ship, the *HMS Hermes*, had been sunk by Japanese aircraft off Ceylon in April 1942. His body had never been recovered, so a stone marker in All Saints' Church at Hawkstowe honored him. Time had blunted Sebastian's grief, but a muted, silvery thread of it was woven through his happiness today, mourning for the brother who'd helped bring this about but hadn't lived to see it.

There had been so many losses with more sure to come in the Pacific, where the war still raged. But today was for celebrating the victory and being glad for those who survived.

Dwight had been shot down over France in 1944, but thanks to the French Resistance, he'd made it back to Britain and into the sky again. He'd also earned the Distinguished Flying Cross. Meanwhile, the US government had reversed its ban on service in foreign forces, so his citizenship was safe. He could go home.

Glenn survived D-Day as a combat engineer, acquiring a silver star and a purple heart in the process. He was somewhere in Germany, helping with the mopping up.

"We said we would wait until the war ended to start our family," Kate reminded her husband. "Our war is over. What do you think?"

He grinned at her, and the shade of grief in their bond winked out. "I think that's a perfect way to celebrate."

They kissed each other again, standing locked in each other's arms for several minutes.

When they resumed their walk, Sebastian said, "Our future eldest son and all of his sons will owe you a great debt. Your skill with words did much to lift the curse."

Kate shrugged. "Thanks, but Dr. Barton and the Fellowship of the White Boar trumpeted out the word and defended Dr. Faversham's authentication of the confession."

"Yes, they did. I couldn't have made it through the ward at Otterden Abbey without you, though, and the words they 'trumpeted,' as you put it, were yours. At the right time and in the right way, making people see King Richard as man and not a Shakespearean caricature, you laid out his case. You even made Edmund's dilemma sympathetic." He smiled at her. "No king ever had a more adept champion."

His praise no longer surprised her. He was always generous. But it still gave her a warm, happy lift.

"I was glad to do my part. For all of them and for us." She drew a deep breath of the light spring air. As he had done, she looked up at the green leaves and the sky. When she looked back at him, he was smiling, his eyes warm with love.

"The future is bright again," Kate said, returning his smile.

"It is. I can't wait to see where it takes us."

The End

ABOUT THE HISTORY

After the Dunkirk evacuation in the summer of 1940, Winston Churchill famously pointed out that wars were not won by evacuations. He was right, of course, but Dunkirk and the subsequent Battle of Britain are gripping, dramatic, and triumphant stories. The outcome of each was far from certain and could easily have gone the other way. If Britain falls to Nazi Germany, where is the launching pad for D-Day? High stakes are a writer's dream, and I've always loved reading about this period. It seemed like an obvious choice as the setting for the final book in the trilogy.

While the Royal Navy and the famous Little Ships (some with naval ratings and crews aboard but many crewed only by civilians) successfully returned almost 340,000 British and French soldiers to Britain, many didn't make it back. Some were killed by bombing and strafing of the beaches and the English Channel and by U-boats hunting the returning boats and ships. Many of those who held the perimeter around the beach open, providing an escape route for their comrades, didn't make it out. Each night, the perimeter contracted, allowing some of the units along it to escape to the beach. But other French and British units had to stay, to keep the corridor open for the last ones leaving. Those men had no choice but to surrender when the Germans arrived.

The Coldstream Guards and the Sherwood Foresters, who're mentioned in chapter one, were among those who held the perimeter for a time and then made for the beach and rescue. The North Yorkshire

Fusiliers, however, are a unit I invented so I could have one that went exactly where I needed them to be.

One intriguing detail I used came from the book *Forgotten Voices of Dunkirk*, an Imperial War Museum publication by Joshua Levine. One of the veterans he interviewed reported that the usually rough English Channel was calm during the days of the evacuation, and no one could explain why. I love finding little bits like that and incorporating them—like the phosphorescent trail the ships generated in their wakes.

On the heels of Dunkirk, the outnumbered and outgunned pilots of Fighter Command struggled to hold off the Luftwaffe while British industry cranked out more planes and the Royal Air Force (RAF) trained more pilots in the desperate hope of catching up to their enemy's assets. Those efforts paid off in August and September 1940, enabling the RAF to thwart the Luftwaffe's plan to cripple them by destroying their airfields.

Like Kate's brother Dwight, a few Americans defied their government and risked their citizenship to join the RAF. Though Dwight is imaginary, these men's efforts were not.

The King's Champion focuses more on the RAF than on the Royal Navy because the story is set mostly on land, but the navy also played a heroic role in the defense of their island and in the Dunkirk evacuation. We also shouldn't forget the role of Radio Direction Finding (RDF), which later became known by the American term, radar, in showing Britain's defenders where to meet their attackers.

A U-boat did sink the *Arandora Star* off the coast of Ireland, much as the *Lusitania* had been sunk during the Great War. The *Arandora Star* sinking led to heavy losses of Italian internees, German prisoners of war, and the ship's crew.

The Officers' Sunday Club was the brainchild of the Dowager Marchioness Townshend of Raynham, who appears briefly in the book. The other women Kate meets at the club are entirely imaginary, so far as I'm aware. The organization started at the Dorchester Hotel in April 1940 but became so popular that it outgrew its space there. It relocated to Grosvenor House that autumn. The "In and Out" actually was the nickname for the Naval and Military Club, which has since moved from Piccadilly to St. James's Square.

Also real is the controversy surrounding Richard III and his nephews, who're known as the Princes in the Tower. I've been interested in their disappearance since a college classmate gave me a copy of Josephine Tey's

The Daughter of Time. In the years since, I've read widely about Richard III's life and the legal situation involving his nephews—who were ultimately not princes because their father, Edward IV, had contracted marriage with another woman who was still living when he bigamously married their mother. The same Act of Parliament that declared the latter marriage bigamous and Edward IV's children bastards also recognized Edward's brother Richard, then Duke of Gloucester, as his lawful heir. Yet thanks to Shakespeare's play *Richard III* and the Tudors, King Richard is widely believed to have schemed all along to take the crown and to have murdered his brother's sons in furtherance of that aim.

No one knows what ultimately became of the two boys. If you've read the rest of this trilogy, you know bones discovered at the Tower of London in 1674 were supposedly theirs, but there are a number of [MG1] problems with that conclusion. Over the years, I've come to believe those two youths survived their uncle Richard.

I chose to structure this story around the idea that the boys had been murdered, however, because that worked as a story choice. I made the Duke of Buckingham the guilty party because he turned his coat in the fall of 1483, apparently trying to take the crown for himself. To do that, he would've needed to eliminate anyone with a colorable title to it who stood in his way. Richard III, in contrast, had the crown and so didn't need to murder his bastardized nephews, and there is no contemporaneous evidence that he did.

The Tower was not only a prison but a royal residence. If a king's two sons had mysteriously vanished overnight, there would've been people to attest to it when Henry VII came to power. Yet no one did. On the other hand, if they simply packed up and rode out, as royal and noble households often did, no one would've thought twice about it. There also would've been no advantage to Henry in spreading word of that.

Others who consider Richard III an unlikely murderer are members of the Richard III Society. This organization grew out of the Fellowship of the White Boar, the group mentioned in *The King's Champion*. The late Dr. Saxon Barton, who meets with Kate, really was a founder of the fellowship. He was also a physician who was awarded the OBE.

Modern historians differ in their opinions. Some subscribe to the Shakespearean theory of Richard III as the ultimate villain while others are saying, "Now, wait a minute." The disagreements are part of the fun of studying and discussing the king's life.

One of King Richard's staunchest modern defenders was the late Dr.

John Ashdown-Hill, OBE, FSA, FRHS. He was also a Fellow of the Society of Geneticists and a member of the Richard III Society and the Centre Européen d'Etudes Bourguignonnes. Ashdown-Hill wrote numerous historical studies of the Wars of the Roses. The Society of Antiquaries, which appears in *The Steel Rose* and *The King's Champion*, crossed my horizon because I read his books.

For more information, check out *The Mystery of the Princes* by Audrey Williamson and *The Survival of the Princes in the Tower* by Matthew Lewis. You can also visit the websites of the various Richard III Society branches around the world. My personal take is set forth in "Me and Richard III," an essay on my website, www.nancynorthcott.com.

Thanks again for reading!

AUTHOR'S NOTE

Thank you for reading *The King's Champion*. I hope you enjoyed it. If you've also read the first two books in the trilogy, *The Herald of Day* and *The Steel Rose*, you've been part of the Mainwarings' long quest to lift their family curse. Thank you for taking the journey with my characters and me. If you're inclined to leave a review on a vendor site, I would appreciate it.

While the story of the Mainwaring quest ends here, I didn't want to let go entirely of these characters and this world. Miranda and Richard, in particular, have lived in my head so long that it's almost like they have a condo there. So, Falstaff Books and I have launched a new series, all novellas, called *The Merlin Club*. The club makes its first appearance in *The Steel Rose*, the book that gave me the idea for the new series. The first book, *The Merlin Club*, is now available with others coming soon.

If you would like to receive periodic updates on what's coming, you can sign up for my newsletter on my homepage, www.NancyNorthcott.com. Newsletters come out every month or two, and subscribers get an alert when there's a sale or other special deal.

Thanks again for reading!

ACKNOWLEDGMENTS

Each book of this trilogy has led me down at least one research rabbit hole, some of them ultimately productive, some of them not useful but intriguing, and a few complete wastes of time. The friends to whom this book is dedicated have been with me for most or all of this journey. They've answered questions about past and present life in Britain, put me in touch with people who could answer questions they couldn't, recommended research avenues, helped me arrange research trips, and sometimes accompanied me on those trips.

On top of all that, they've sat around numerous lunch or dinner tables or in pubs for a pint or a glass of wine and listened to me blather on about my most recent research and the imaginary people I've entwined with real or imagined events in British history. As I said in the dedication, this is a better book and a better trilogy for their contributions.

Steve Hunnisett of <u>Blitzwalkers</u>, a company offering guided tours of wartime London, untangled a couple of military questions I'd pursued into one of those rabbit holes. Steve posts terrific photos of WWII London on his Twitter page, where he's <u>@Blitzwalker</u>.

Dr. Greg Wickliff helped me figure out what cameras Kate would use and steered me to information about them.

Air Marshal Sir Richard Knighton answered various RAF questions.

Dr. Darin Kennedy helped me with research about amputation in the 1940s and let me bounce ideas about Sebastian's condition off him to be sure what I did was plausible.

Bob Beard explained British Army numerical unit designations to me. I ultimately decided not to use them because I figured casual readers would be baffled, as I was, and thus possibly distracted by them, but I'm grateful to Bob for explaining.

Sid Barrett told me many years ago about American pilots who volunteered for the RAF despite knowing they could lose their citizenship for doing so. That nugget of information stuck in my head, and it naturally fit in this book. So Dwight Shaw owes his existence to Sid.

Even though Rifleman Moore of YouTube doesn't know me from Adam's housecat, as my mom would've said, videos on his channel provided a wealth of information I needed on British uniforms and particularly about bandages of the era.

Any factual errors are my responsibility and likely occurred because I failed to ask the correct questions of the people who so graciously consulted with me.

Jeanne Adams, Donna MacMeans, and Cassondra Murray helped me plot the arc of the trilogy and fine-tune points of each book, including this one.

Jeanne Adams, Amy Herring, Anna Sugden, and Debra Yutko generously read rough drafts of *The King's Champion* and gave me invaluable feedback.

My editor at Falstaff Books, Lucy Blue, offered insights and advice that made this book and its siblings in the trilogy much better than they were when they hit her inbox.

My agent, Beth Miller, has supported me in all my writing endeavors, and I'm deeply grateful for her advice and support.

Last but never least, my husband and son, Mark and Gavin, have never wavered in encouraging me to follow my dreams. They've tinkered with their schedules to make it easier for me to go on research trips and have writing time. I couldn't have done this without them.

ABOUT THE AUTHOR

Nancy Northcott's childhood ambition was to grow up and become Wonder Woman. Around fourth grade, she realized it was too late to acquire Amazon genes, but she still loved comic books, science fiction, fantasy, history, and romance.

Nancy earned her undergraduate degree in history and particularly enjoyed a summer spent studying Tudor and Stuart England at the University of Oxford. She has given presentations on the Wars of the Roses and *Richard III* to university classes studying Shakespeare's play about that king. In addition, she has taught college courses on science fiction, fantasy, and society.

The Boar King's Honor historical fantasy trilogy combines Nancy's love of history and magic with her interest in Richard III. She also writes traditional romantic suspense, romantic spy adventures, and two other speculative fiction series: the *Light Mage Wars* paranormal romances and, with Jeanne Adams, the *Outcast Station* space mystery series.

You can connect with Nancy via her website, www.NancyNorthcott.com or on social media:

Twitter: https://twitter.com/NancyNorthcott

Facebook: https://facebook.com/nancynorthcottauthor

Bookbub: https://www.bookbub.com/authors/nancy-northcott

Goodreads: https://www.goodreads.com/author/show/3468806.Nancy_Northcott

Pinterest: http://www.pinterest.com/nancynorthcott/

facebook.com/nancynorthcottauthor

x.com/NancyNorthcott

goodreads.com/Nancy_Northcott

pinterest.com/nancynorthcott

FALSTAFF BOOKS

Want to know what's new & coming soon from
Falstaff Books?

Join our Newsletter List
& Get this Free Ebook Sampler
with work from:
John G. Hartness
A.G. Carpenter
Bobby Nash
Emily Lavin Leverett
Jaym Gates
Darin Kennedy
Natania Barron
Edmund R. Schubert
& More!

http://www.subscribepage.com/q0j0p3